MADLANDS

to Bill + Greg with [fond] wishes, Jeff Oct 31 1993

J. Allen Kirsch

Waubesa Press
P.O. Box 192
Oregon, WI 53575

© Copyright 1993 by J. Allen Kirsch

Cover illustration by Mark Fearing

Back cover photo by Robert Giard

Published by Waubesa Press of Oregon, WI

Color separations by Port to Print of Madison, WI

Printed by BookCrafters of Chelsea, MI

First Edition

ISBN 1-878569-18-X

For Alda, Ken and Rick

Early 1985

1

There were no jetways. The job candidate deplaned and had a one-word thought: boondocks. The blustery March wind lashed her face and nipped at her ankles. Briefcase in hand, she burrowed herself in her lightweight coat, and another word came to mind: arctic. She surveyed the landscape; beyond the runways, a flat, snow-covered expanse. A third word suggested itself: tundra.

She stepped inside the airport into a long, narrow corridor. At its mouth, a small crowd awaited. She put on her job-aspirant smile, continued down the tunnel and reached the miniature main terminal. The work ''boondocks'' reasserted itself.

Hopefully, she surveyed the horizon of faces. Her smile frozen into place, she hung at the edge of the crowd, hoping for someone to claim her. No one did. She headed toward the baggage-claim area and stood by the motionless conveyor belt. On the other side she laid eyes on a small, handwritten sign and, squinting, deciphered her name scrawled on it: Cicely Pankhurst. She rounded the conveyor belt and, as the man holding it appeared asleep, tapped the placard with her index finger. It dropped to reveal a silver-haired head and a face with startled eyes.

''Miss Pinkhurst?'' he questioned, taken aback, and gave a feeble chuckle. "I'm Sumner Isaacson."

After the harrowing delayed flights, she felt relieved to be in someone's care. Sumner Isaacson was the Chair of the Department of Museum Studies. "Cissy Pankhurst. Pleased to meet you."

Their eyes locked and his followed hers to the placard, which indeed read "Pinkhurst."

"Pankhurst, did you say? My apologies. Our secretary..."

"Everyone calls me 'Cissy.'"

"I see." His tone verged on disapproval. Why did so many people think of "sissified" instead of "Spacek?" "I'm sorry. I must have dozed off. You were originally due in at 2:25."

"I know." He almost made her feel as if she should apologize. "My flight out of LAX left on time and was fine until. . ." She trailed off, noticing that she had but half the chair's attention. The other half scrutinized not the conveyor belt, now grinding into motion, but her face: blue eyes hidden behind glasses and features between round and angular, topped by ash blond hair. She forced her eyes to meet his, interrupting his appraisal. By his tentative smile, she judged she'd passed the first test.

At a loss for words, she turned to face the conveyor belt and saw her blue Samsonite make the journey toward her. "There's my bag."

"Then let's get out of here. We're late enough."

She hoisted it off the conveyor belt and, to her surprise, Isaacson snatched it from her in a pseudo-gallant gesture. He trudged out and she followed.

Twenty minutes later Isaacson deposited and checked her in at the Mad City Motor Lodge on the edge of the University of Wisconsin campus. In spite of her lateness, she still had almost two hours before the departmental cocktail party in her "honor." She'd simply be put on display and under more scrutiny.

Her bag unpacked, she showered and emerged feeling remarkably fresh. She lounged in her robe, steeling herself mentally for the evening. In the last two months, she'd had on-campus interviews at the University of Kansas, Ohio State and an embarrassingly inconsequential college she thought she'd have the pleasure of turning down. But any "pleasure" involved in rejections had been reserved for employers.

Leaving her high-buttoned grey suit for tomorrow's lecture, she put on a red silk dress. She toyed with the idea of unfastening her hair for tonight's semi-social occasion but opted against it. Her tight academic bun would off-set her being blond and blue-eyed, not to mention Californian. She knew from experience that in academia sexism came with the territory.

The cocktail took place at Isaacson's west-side residence, where Cissy was greeted by a tall, bony woman who wore streaked blond hair sprayed into immobility, a cavernous beehive atop her head.

"Cis'ly Pinkhurst, my wife Vonda." The chair's introduction reeked of coolness and alcohol. She hadn't smelled it on him in the car and didn't bother to correct his rendering of her name.

With a hand as glacial as her facade of a smile, Vonda Isaacson brushed Cissy's, then took her coat and drink order. Both Isaacson and his wife deserted her, leaving her again unclaimed, this time in the foyer. Vonda returned a minute later and handed her her drink, which she eyed suspiciously, fearing "gin" had been heard with "tonic." She rarely drank and no intention to tonight, when she had to be at her sharpest.

Before she could sample it, Isaacson reappeared and led her to the living room, where he made a flurry of faculty introductions, shunting her rapid-fire from one to the next, before she could remember the faces to go with the names she'd memorized from the university catalogue. At the end of the living room —elegant powder-blue furnishings on a white carpet— Isaacson presented her to Vance Rickover, whose vaunted scholarly reputation she knew. Issacson deserted them to refill his own drink.

''So, you're Pankhurst. Good to meet you,'' he bellowed, and thrust his hand at her, mauling hers at length.

A pea-green blazer and polyester slacks of a similar but conflicting hue hung loosely over his lanky frame. Cissy tried not to stare at his face, perhaps mangled in a car crash or simply sporting a case of acne masquerading as smallpox scars.

''I do conservation techniques,'' he announced, finally letting go.

Cissy guarded her crushed hand behind her back. "Of course, I know." She knew more or less. "I'm in pre-Columbian artifacts, with emphasis on the Mayan.''

A condescending smile settled into the asymmetrical contours of his face, as though he contemplated a novice grasping for a respectable specialty. Cissy's glance went to his hair, a mousy brown, greasy and stringy, then down to her drink. She dove in, gulped gin and choked.

''There, there.'' Rickover slapped her back, almost propelling her forward. "Are you all right? Not used to the hard stuff, huh? You'll learn. I've done some work on things Mexican myself." He traced a thin smile. "B.A. at Cornell, M.A. and Ph.D. at Yale.''

If it had sharpened his mind, The Ivy League had failed to improve his manners or apparel.

Following his cue, Cissy spat out her own degrees, a less impressive mouthful: "I did my B.A. at Cal State-San Bernardino and my M.A. and Ph.D. at UCI. University of California at Irvine."

''I thought you hadn't finished your doctorate.'' Rickover guzzled whisky and lapped his face clean with his tongue.

''Oh, I haven't,'' she quickly clarified. "I defend my dissertation the first week in May." She pretended to sip her drink and gazed about the room, wishing she could be part of another conversation.

Cissy guessed his age close to her own —thirty-one— as Rickover rubbed his semi-chin, as though in scholarly rumination. "I take it you've at least been publishing."

"I'm afraid not quite yet." Her dossier should have told him that. She forced a smile, bearing up under the interrogation.

"You will be soon, of course."

"Yes, I trust so." Her face glimmered with a mixture of hope and professional confidence.

"Where?"

She feared she had correctly heard the monosyllabic inquiry, but asked, "Pardon me?"

"Where do you intend to publish?"

She scoured her mind and mentioned the name of the professional journals that landed on her tongue.

"Hmmm. Quite a task you've set out for yourself." He sampled his index finger, then drew on his drink. "At Yale we had to publish. What about Irvine? I'd say California went downhill with the sixties, wouldn't you?"

"I think Irvine compares favorably," she said, omitting with what, but determined not to let him trap her. She tipped her glass to her lips and attempted to reel in an ice cube. "I've rather liked the program there."

"You have?" Rickover's face strained with incredulity. "I didn't know anyone was supposed to *like* graduate school. It's not supposed to be an amusement park. I got out at twenty-six. Was tenured here last year at thirty-one."

Cissy acknowledged his prowess and gazed about the room, wishing someone would rescue her. Here she was: Danielle being devoured in the lion's den, the others merrily oblivious to the carnage.

"Well, what do you think you can teach?"

Gladdened by the easier question, she responded, "Any introductory course, I'd think. And in advanced areas, anything archaeologically related."

Rickover sidled up to her and released alcoholic breath in her face, as though about to let her in on a big secret. It would help to have the support of the department's top scholar. "What about a course in Collections Management?"

She pondered before answering. Maybe this was what they needed, though they hadn't said so. Maybe her hiring hinged on this. She'd once taken a class in the field. "I think I could handle a course like that."

"Spreading yourself rather thin, wouldn't you say?" He cut her off before she could qualify her words. She doused an incendiary look at him and shot a longing gaze at the other faculty.

"Listen, I've got to go. But you can bet your high heels," he said, taking in her shoes and laughing at his remark, "that I'll be at your lecture tomorrow. 'Mayan Artifacts in Mexican Museums,' right? I'll read up on it tonight. I know you'll be disappointed if no one has any challenging questions."

He drained his glass, ice and all, and garbled a curt farewell. Before she could respond, he strode away.

She studied the remaining faculty. Again unclaimed, she tried to decide who might be safe to approach. After Rickover, the personnel could only improve. Before she could move, a blond-haired man and young black woman headed purposefully toward her.

"Evan Schultz, belatedly to your rescue."

"I'm Ginger Carter and I see you've just been 'ricked over.'"

2

C issy emerged drained from her lecture and Sumner Isaacson swept her off to lunch with a duo of lesser Fine Arts deans. Mentally fatigued, she answered perfunctory questions about herself and her field. She had to store up her intellectual forces for one final battle, with *the* dean.

Isaacson directed her to the top floor of the Fine Arts Building and she entered Dean Phipps' office. Apparently he hadn't even bothered to attend her lecture this morning. After a few minutes, a secretary ushered her inside and there stood the short, squat sixtyish woman who'd been in the back row at her lecture. Hadn't she just entered the office of Dean David Phipps?

"Miss Pankhurst, I'm so glad to have the pleasure, finally. I had to miss last night's cocktail party and had an appointment immediately after your lecture today and couldn't even introduce myself."

"My pleasure too. You can call me Cissy." Her head did an involuntary turn to the open door, where the nameplate read "Dean Davidine Phipps." Indeed, with "David Dean Phipps," she'd heard right, but hadn't quite gotten it.

The dean seemed to divine her confusion. "Our father wanted sons but got daughters. So we were named Davidine and Ralphetta." She shut the door and added, "You can call me anything but Dean Phipps."

As Cissy regularly did in awkward academic circumstances, she'd probably call her nothing.

"Nice view, isn't it? Please sit down."

Cissy's head turned to the window, which overlooked the campus and, behind it, a large lake covered by a sheet of ice.

"I enjoyed your lecture. I'd never heard the topic addressed before and you handled it in exemplary fashion." The dean was also a full professor in the Department of Museum Studies.

"Thank you." The lecture should have gone well; it was the fourth time she'd presented it. "I was just a little shaken by the end..."

The dean said the words Cissy didn't dare to say: "By Professor Rickover's prickly, pompous questions? I didn't have lunch with you today for several reasons, one of them being that we can talk more freely now." The dean's voice lilted, effusive, evocative of Julia Child's. "Vance Rickover knows a startling amount about the field, but he doesn't represent the department. His opinions — and questions — are strictly his own."

This was heartening to hear. Cissy had to contain an urge to repeat what Rickover had said after her talk: "Maybe I'll see you again _at a conference or an exhibit._" She'd been torn between belting him or thanking him for his brutal candor.

"As you know, this is a one-year appointment as Lecturer." Cissy knew well, her dreams of snagging a tenure-track job for next year having evaporated. "But..." Dean Phipps bestowed a conspiratorial wink on her. "We intend that the person hired this year be rehired next year when the job turns tenure-track, provided that she... or he perform satisfactorily. An added inducement to come to the cold for nineteen-five. But living here is rather inexpensive."

It was the first time Cissy had heard the meager salary. She didn't add that, with her desperation, she needed no extra inducement to come.

Showing more than the bare traces of humanity Cissy had seen among the rest of the ruling hierarchy, the dean asked her about California, grad school and Mexico, all comfortable topics.

"And," she concluded, "as for myself, let me say that I hope we'll see you in the fall."

The unexpected comment buoyed her. In the course of a mere half hour, her pessimism had fled.

She had a free hour before Isaacson would pick her up to go to the airport. Before meeting the dean, she would have chosen to hibernate. Now, as she stepped outside, the cold seemed less cold and the sun seemed to augur the possibility of success.

A UW map told her she was on Library Mall, where vendors abounded. Students crisscrossed the adjacent quadrangle. She gazed in the opposite direction, up State Street toward the imposing Capitol, and realized that the "Mad City" T-shirts for sale were emblazoned with Wisconsin's, not the nation's Capitol. She felt, at the moment, mentally vacant.

Nearby a crowd had assembled before an elevated concrete podium.

A woman dressed in Carry Nation garb flung her arms about and ranted at those below.

"'Ye shall not worship false gods,'" she shrieked. "But I know you students. You worship your beer! You worship your drugs! Your rock and roll!" After a rhetorical pause, she leaned forward, wagging a menacing forefinger. "And you worship your genitals!"

The students guffawed and heckled; a blind student's dog joined in by barking. Could this be part of a street theatre group? Or an exam for an degree in theatre?

A young man with curly black hair ascended the dais and addressed the woman. "You wouldn't know Jesus if he sat on your face!" he yelled. The crowd hooted, roared.

"They're quite good," Cissy remarked to a young woman next to her.

"Good??" Pie-eyed, she regarded Cissy. "Where are *you* from? They're for *real!*"

"You heathen!" the evangelist counterattacked. "A true Christian would never touch his genitals or talk about them in public!" She turned her back, hands uplifted in prayer.

"This woman preaches hate! Give her her way and she'll deny us our sexuality, abortions..."

Upon hearing "abortions," the evangelist whirled around, flailing the air with her arms, then stopped to shake a spastic finger. "You boys who pay for your girlfriends' abortions are murderers in the eyes of the Lord!"

The young man leaped into the crowd. "Stop giving this woman your attention!" he exhorted. "Don't let her spread her hate! Can't you amuse yourselves in better ways than this?"

"Yeah, we could be masturbating."

"She'd outlaw that too if she could, so go do it while you can!" Suddenly he stood in front of Cissy. She scampered away.

At the other end of the mall, leafleters and petitioners stood near the vendors, ignoring the spectacle.

"Fight the raise in the drinking age!"

"Support divestiture! Strike down apartheid!"

"Show your support for the Sandinistas!" A man with electrified hair met her eyes. He stood behind a table of literature, decals and buttons. Cissy stopped to look and learned that Wisconsin was the sister state of Nicaragua. Among other revolutionary paraphernalia, he was selling bumper stickers that read "Friends of Wiscaragua."

"What's Wiscaragua?"

"It's a combination of Wis-consin and Ni-caragua. A sort of symbolic union."

"Oh. I'm a little slow right now." He wore a button that read "Join Wiscaragua. Irv Barmejian."

"That's OK. Nice day, huh?"

"If you say. I'm visiting from California."

"It may have hit forty today. A minor heat wave. Our weather's very theatrical. Maybe you'd like some literature to take back to Reaganland."

Cissy ignored the slur to her state, but felt glad to talk to someone outside of academia. "If I'm lucky, I'll be moving here. I just had a job interview on campus."

"Hope you get it. This is the 'Berkeley of the Midwest,' or the 'Third Coast,' you know."

She was only vaguely aware. "Oh, I'm not from Berkeley." She was not about to admit she was from Orange County. "I do like it up there, though."

"If you like Berkeley, you'll like Madison. I have a friend who graduated from there, Ph.D. in chemistry. He started cooking up 'LSD for the people' and gave it away. Then the Mafia ran him out and he moved to the next most radical place in the country: Madison."

"It looks radical." Cissy took in her surroundings, as if her they could confirm her remark. "I'll buy a button," she offered on an impulse. She paid a dollar for it and thanked him.

"My pleasure, uh..."

"Cissy," she said belatedly, attributing his manner to some sort of hippie or Midwestern friendliness.

She walked down State Street to her motel and purchased a local newspaper from a machine in the lobby, as Jeb, her partner of five years, had instructed her. It was a routine gesture, not necessarily connoting hope of relocation.

"It's over an hour until your flight and the airport is less than 15 minutes away," Isaacson said when he drove up. He loaded her suitcase into the back of his station wagon. "Perhaps you'd like a campus tour. I'm afraid you haven't seen much of it."

Although mentally prepared to leave, Cissy agreed and propped back up her cheery professional front.

The car backtracked past Memorial Union and wound its way up a hill. He pointed out the undergraduate library, perched on the lakeshore. They rounded a hairpin curve; he pointed out a woods of larch pines on one side. The beauty of the campus overtook her. Exit tundra.

"Bascom Hill, back there. Wisconsin's coeds hike up it every day and must have the strongest calf muscles in the country."

Before she could figure out what to make of this remark, Isaacson spouted a slew of building names, ending with "The Tower of Babel." Apparently, it was the foreign language building that loomed high above them.

They passed a dorm and he pulled over. "A scenic overlook of Lake Mendota," he recited from a sign.

The car's engine purred. Cissy murmured approval and took in the natural beauty of the view.

"It was at this very spot, twenty-six years ago, that I was offered my job here at Wisconsin," he reminisced.

"Really?" Cissy feigned polite interest.

"And I've made it my practice during my tenure as Chair to offer jobs to others at this same spot."

Her pulse quickened and she felt her heart leap. Could this be the prelude to an on-the-spot job offer? Indeed, she might be the last or the only candidate flown in for an interview. She remembered the dean's hopeful remark. Perhaps she'd called him, they'd powwowed and agreed to hire her before she got a better offer.

She forced herself to tame her smile and directed her gaze back and forth from the lake to Isaacson, whose expression seemed to radiate fond memories.

His eyes pierced hers. Had her big moment arrived? Isaacson's lips parted, then rounded, preparatory to speech: "Well, Cis'ly..." First name: good indication, even if he'd slipped in the furtive L. Her eyes fastened on his. She strained to conceal her excitement. "Seen enough?"

She went expressionless and he sped away.

Her plane rose over the lakes —Mendota and Monona? Outside, a narrow isthmus of concrete crowned by the Capitol separated the two murky, vaguely bluish masses.

Adieu, Madison. Mad City, indeed.

The plane gained altitude and the lakes vanished, as had her hopes, after Isaacson's mean trick. Only farms and peaceful rolling hills lay below. She let her eyes fall shut, wanting only to sleep, forget and wake up in Jeb's arms.

3

The music and the reigning mode of dress quickly told Irv Barmejian that it was Punk Night at the Cardinal Bar. A generation gapped between him and the clientele. He wended his way through the main bar, stole a futile look in the disco for his housemate Juan, and, feeling out of place, hunkered up to the bar. He ordered a Point beer.

When a stool vacated, he took it, yawned and began to relax. He'd volunteered to spend the afternoon on Library Mall at Juan's "Wiscaragua" table. Afterwards he'd gone to his King Street law office, then headed to his near-east-side house for dinner, and finally to a City Council meeting to speak against an ordinance prohibiting chicken raising within the city limits. From the City-County Building, he'd walked six short blocks to the Cardinal.

He sipped his politically correct Point until he caught the attention of the bartender, who paraded in high punk attire, and ordered another. If Juan didn't show up before he finished it, he'd head home.

As Irv waved away his change, he saw her. Seated around the corner among the punk revelers, she seemed oddly alone. Her blank gaze met his but showed no discernible sign that she'd just made eye contact with another human being. Irv put it down to immaturity or drugs.

Thinking he'd glimpsed Juan, he jerked his glance to the door. False alarm. He went back to his beer, but caught her again, pouty or sullen, in his peripheral vision. This time his gaze fixed on her in spite of himself. Her jet black hair lay in two asymmetrical halves, one limp, the other jutting out. Her forehead was high, her nose round and lips thick. Closer scrutiny revealed the upper lip painted black and the lower one a deep purple. He threw back some more beer. A look sideways showed that she was now smiling at him. A look downward showed a more staggering revelation: Irv had a full-fledged erection.

Feminist men weren't supposed to get erections in public. And Irv was not only a feminist man, but a celibate one. Of his twenty years in Madison, he'd spent four in Law School, five in a commune, two in a childless marriage, and the last nine taking time off from romantic and sexual liaisons. Unable to vacate his spot, he ordered a third beer and snuggled up to the bar. The more he wished the swelling away, the more it persisted. He inched his vision back to the bar stool: empty. His gaze roved about the bar until he saw she'd planted herself right beside him. She said "Hi."

"Oh, hi there." He aimed to affect nonchalance.

"Shy." It was unclear if she intended a statement or a question.

"Uh, no. Just distracted." His faded bluejeans pulled at the crotch. In spite of his condition, he continued the interchange. "I'm Irv."

"Pep," she responded.

"Your name's Pep?"

She mumbled something unintelligible and he asked her again: "Schwepps? You want a Schwepps?"

She threw him an exasperated look and spelled it one letter at a time.

"I see. Dyspepsia. But you go by 'Pep?'" Nervous, he faked laughter, not meaning to poke fun at her name. The conversation halted. He took a drink and peeked discreetly at his lap, then opted for an easier line of talk: "You from Madison?"

"Nope."

He ran his fingers through his unkempt beard, scratched his bald spot and felt obliged to continue the game. "From where, then?"

"Nyork."

Smoke billowed around him; the music went up a notch. "I'm from New York too. Born in New Jersey, actually, but grew up in the City."

She made no response to this, but he invited her to sit. "How long have you been in Madison?"

"Week."

Her legs dangled from the stool and one grazed his. A ripple of desire shot through him. He panicked and gave a discreet shake of his body, hoping to loosen his clothing. "You're just passing through here?"

"Yep."

"Where are you headed?" His sophomoric interrogation made him feel foolish.

"West." She paused, then added, "Bay."

It took him a second to figure it out. "Ah. The Bay Area."

As if he were hopelessly slow, she rolled her eyes, naturally dark, the skin around them artificially darkened.

He saw her empty glass and asked, "Drink?"

"Coke."

He ordered a Point and a Coke, shoved bills at the harried bartender and felt her make knee contact with his thigh. His inflammation strained against his Levi's with renewed vigor. He angled his body away but turned his head toward her and let his eyes rove down her body to a pair of ample breasts, inviting melons that protruded above her folded arms.

He stopped himself. What was he doing? Forty-two years old, finally in control of his life, and celibate for almost a decade, he was salivating like a schoolboy, ogling a child of barely legal age. And feminist men shouldn't think of women's breasts as "melons."

She smacked her lips, luscious and tempting despite the coloration. Two interlocking safety pins hung from her left earlobe. "Dance?"

"D-dance?" he stuttered. "You want to dance? Sorry, I could never dance to this. Not my style. Haven't danced since the sixties, early seventies. The Doors, Jethro Tull, the Jefferson Airplane. You know. "

"Old," she said, not specifying what.

"Look, I've got to go." He covered himself with the lined Levi jacket on which he'd been sitting.

"Now?" She looked forlorn.

"Yes, now," he snapped. "You see, I can't dance, I can't do anything, because I've got a..."

"Hard," she said, before he could spit out "problem."

"What?" he asked, though feared he'd heard right.

"Hard."

He peered down. The jacket had slid off his lap onto the floor. "So you saw."

"See." Her black and purple lips formed a seductive oval.

Irv sighed and reached down to retrieve his jacket. "I've really got to go." He stood up, tied the jacket around his waist and clarified, "I'm celibate."

"Priest?"

He began to lose his embarrassment and a smile overtook his face. "No."

"Gay?"

"No." More emphatic, but still smiling.

"Why?"

"Look, I'm sorry. It's complicated. I have to leave and that's that."

"Me?" She slipped into a woebegone, but alluring pout.

Irv felt a slight pity — and more than slight lust — welling up inside him.

"Please?"

He remained frozen in thought and cursed Juan, whose appearance would have precluded this scenario. He observed Pep: Her shorn eyebrows had been painted on attractively. A seraphic calm, which hid any hope she might hold, had replaced her pouts and smirks. She heaved a tiny sigh. More cleavage tumbled out above a low-cut black satin blouse, dotted with pink stars. Ploy or accident? All Irv knew was that she was an enigma and that he felt himself still throbbing against his Levi's. His indecision began to mushroom, his resolve to melt. Maybe all she needed or wanted was a paternal talking-to. And if that was the case, he couldn't deny her that.

"Cute." She traced a smile and shrugged curvaceous shoulders.

"Who?"

"You."

"I thought you thought I was an old gay priest."

"Sgo?" Her deep voice came out brittle.

Irv deciphered the monosyllable, but said nothing. He had no good reason for continued celibacy; he'd gotten his head together long ago. Had he become afraid of sex? Then he told himself that this had nothing to do with sex.

He stood up and, her look hopeful yet defiant, Pep rose too. She scooped up a coat from the floor and put it on. Alternately she seemed a waif, a seducer. Her eyes pleaded with him. He let out a low, inaudible whistle.

"All right, come on."

He'd take her somewhere nearby for coffee. Maybe — no, likely — she needed help or guidance of some sort.

Punks packed the path to the door. He realized he probably could have dropped his Levi's and walked out unnoticed some time ago

August 1985

4

Cissy scraped up thirty-two cents for the last toll booth around Chicago. "This is all I can find."

"I'll do a Phi Slamma Jamma." All six feet and seven inches of Jeb was scrunched into their Fiat.

Cissy creased her brow in a question.

"You know, babe. A slam dunk. Like in basketball." Jeb fisted the coins and hurled them into the automatic toll collector. It gurgled, hesitated then flashed a "thank you."

"It let us through!" she exclaimed, as the Fiat, weighed down by a U-Haul, chugged along the Northwest Tollway.

It was August 14. Cissy had been hired in April, defended her dissertation in May, and Jeb had resigned his job as a high school phys ed teacher in June.

To stave off poverty, he'd taken a post as Recreation Director at an elementary school summer program, and they hadn't been able to leave California until August 10. They'd spent the last several hours creeping around Chicago, waylaid by rush-hour traffic and road construction. Momentarily, a small, tasteful sign welcomed them to the Badger State.

"Maybe we can count badgers until we get to Madison."

Jeb ignored her attempt at humor. "How far do we have to go?"

"There's a big sign up ahead." She read it with her rudimentary Spanish: "'INFORMACION PARA OBREROS EN LA PROXIMA PARADA.' I think it has to do with migrant workers."

"Migrant workers? Are you sure this is Wisconsin? In California the signs are at least bilingual. How will we survive here in the Northeast?"

"Midwest, Jeb." He'd never been east of Nevada.

"I can't even tell a badger from a dairy cow!"

"You'll learn. Look up ahead: Madison: forty-four miles."

Within an hour they pulled into the Mad City Motor Lodge, where Cissy, a creature of habit, had made reservations. They walked onto the balcony outside their room, overlooking State Street. The sky was dark, the air humid. A student hauled a mattress on his back; another carried what looked like stereo speakers in pillow cases. A bicyclist zoomed by with a toaster oven and coffeemaker in the baskets. Moving day," Jeb said. The thought made Cissy shudder. Tomorrow they had to begin — if not finish — their own search for suitable housing.

In the morning, Cissy called University Houses. They could have signed a lease by mail, but Jeb had nixed the idea, insisting on seeing the premises first. But now, before they could spurn the faculty complex, the manager vetoed them by phone, vowing that university regulations prohibited rental to unmarried couples. In the classifieds they found and called three west-side addresses, the area of town most faculty had recommended. Cissy took to the third apartment. It was the upper floor of a fifties-style California bungalow. The rent was $450, seventy-five over their set maximum. The landlady offered to lower it by five dollars. Jeb hustled Cissy down the stairs and out to the car. "I had to, babe. You were getting that wimpy look on your face and I could tell you were going to take it."

The Fiat loped into motion, jolting them. "Where are we going?" Her voice came out tiny and fragile.

"Remember, I don't have a job, you barely do, and that makes us poor. We'd better check out the east side." Cissy let out a whimper. "You said that guy Schultz from your department recommended it. It can't be that bad. We're out in the real world now, and since we can't afford this half of it..."

"I don't like being poor."

"I don't like being homeless."

They passed through the downtown and drove along Lake Monona until reaching the base of Williamson Street, which resembled a lapsed factory district. Doubtfully, they proceeded down it and passed an artists' collective, an abandoned "women's exchange" bakery, gas stations, bars and a food co-op. Private homes occupied the gaps in between. Six blocks down, Jeb parked the Fiat.

They got out and Cissy felt herself wilt in the humidity. A rock promptly landed at Jeb's feet. Up the block they saw a mother admonish her child and shrug her shoulders at them. Cissy was disposed to believe they'd entered alien territory. They hurried away.

"Look here, Jeb!" A fractured two-story house loomed in front of them. "For Sale or Rent" signs dotted its windows. Rent was $250.

"You never know." He led Cissy to a side window coated with dust. Inside they saw a gaping hole that rended the floor, where a kitchen sink lay. Behind the house, beer cans and a bra littered a caved-in porch. They wandered off.

"Beep, beep! Passing on the left!" came a shrill voice, jarring them. Jeb pulled Cissy near him as a helmeted woman passed, bicycling groceries down the sidewalk.

They crossed Williamson Street, headed toward the lake and reached a large park surrounded by tall trees and attractive older houses. Rental signs were nonexistent. The sun conspired with the humidity to suck away their energy. "How about a breather?" Jeb pointed to a shady area, where they flung themselves down. A racially mixed group of children break-danced on a mat spread on a basketball court. An artist wearing a beret painted at an easel, while a woman in a granny gown observed him. In front of them, a dog dug in a sandbox. Cissy's eyelids felt heavy; she let them close.

"You should be ashamed of yourselves!"

They sat up with a start. Across the street a woman stood on her porch and waved a menacing fist at them and the dog, which apparently had desecrated the sandbox. "Can't you people read? The sign says 'No Dogs in the Park'! Kids play in that sandbox!" She stormed back inside.

"Jeb, my nerves are shot. First the rock, now this. We're not wanted here. And nothing's for rent."

They took a different route back, via Ingersoll Street to Williamson. "Hey! A 'For Rent' sign!" Jeb pointed at a house at the intersection.

The two-story house sat well off Williamson, which it faced. A hand-lettered sign was tacked to the downstairs front porch, where two sofas, a washing machine and a small stove rested. A vegetable garden doubled as the front yard. They inched up a sidewalk that bisected the garden: corn and tomatoes on one side, stalks of miniature green cabbages on the other. The sign read: "Downstairs Flat for Rent. It Reasonable, You Responsible."

Suddenly a figure shot up in the middle of the garden. Breasts revealed the sex. She wore shocking pink pants and a black top and carried a small load of tomatoes.

"Is, uh, this place still for rent?" Jeb inquired.

Silent, the figure gawked at them. Cissy wondered if they'd caught her stealing tomatoes, but she made no effort to move, let alone to flee.

Cissy dug a fingernail into Jeb's upper arm. "Let's go. I've had it."

Clearly, they should go back to their motel, back to the west side tomorrow, or forge a marriage license to take to University Houses.

The tomato-gatherer slowly rounded her mouth and let out a blood-curdling scream: "Juaaan!"

A head popped out from under a sheet on one of the porch sofas. The tomato-gatherer vanished around the side of the house with her harvest.

"Is the downstairs still for rent?" Jeb asked.

"Oh. You caught me sacked out." The napper sat up and rubbed his eyes. "Yeah, it still is." He stood up, let the sheet drop to the ground, and with it, his pants.

A flasher. Cissy turned away. Jeb chuckled and tugged on her hand. She hesitantly realigned her eyes with the porch.

The man's pants, faded beltless bluejeans with holes in the knees, revealed a half-foot of white underwear. Short, with crew-cut black hair and a moustache, he wore no shirt, but an open vest with a button reading "US OUT OF NICARAGUA OR WISCONSIN OUT OF US." A book titled *How to Overthrow the Government* dangled from one hand. He pulled his pants back up to his waist.

"Come on inside and take a look, if you want. By the way, I'm Juan."

"So we heard," Cissy muttered as Jeb introduced them.

In spite of the Spanish name and Latin looks, he spoke without foreign accent. He went off and returned with an antique skeleton key that he maneuvered into the lock. "Any questions, just ask."

When Cissy looked behind her, he had disappeared.

In the living room the floor sloped, creating an unintentionally sunken effect. Doubtful, they edged over groaning floorboards to a dining area around the corner. A spacious kitchen jutted off it; windows outed on the backyard. From the kitchen, a hall led to a bathroom, then to a large corner bedroom. Under a stairway squatted a second bedroom, whose window faced a house a few feet away. In between, morning glories trailed upward.

Cissy tried to imagine living there. "Big enough for a small study." She indicated the second bedroom.

"Yeah. And when you're done studying, you can go tobogganing in the living room."

A back door led to a cement stoop bordered by hollyhocks on each side. In the backyard stood a tool shed and grew an array of unidentifiable greenery.

"Nice yard space," Jeb said.

"Except for the sunken living room, the inside's not bad either." Cissy opened the patched screen door into the kitchen. "Let's at least find out the rent."

It was three hundred dollars. "There's storage space, a washer and dryer when they're functioning, and negotiable garden space, if you're into it," Juan explained from the porch sofa. "Besides all that, you get Irv: landperson, lawyer and tenants' rights advocate. Those are probably his footsteps coming down the stairs."

A fortyish man with unruly black hair and a long beard sauntered onto the porch and greeted them. He wore white painter's pants and a pockmarked T-shirt. Behind him the tomato-gatherer stared at them unabashedly, as if contemplating interplanetary visitors.

Cissy first thought of the Addams Family; then a more recent memory dawned on her: "You sold me a Nicaragua button when I was here last spring!"

"That's likely." Irv beat down a sprig of hair.

"I was here on a job interview. You said I might want to take some propaganda back to California. Only you said 'Reaganland.'"

"Oh, yeah. I remember. So you got the job. Congratulations!"

"And now we've got to get an apartment here." She brushed back her hair, tied in a red kerchief.

"This is Dyspepsia." Irv presented the tomato-gatherer and stepped aside to reveal her.

"Pep," she said, a large tomato placed in between her cleavage.

A stocky young man wandered onto the porch. "This is Gil. Gil Kreuzer."

Unlike the others, Gil could pass for normal, an all-American boy. Blond, he could be either a bronzed, if slightly stout California surfer, or a typical Wisconsin farmboy, tanned from working in the fields.

"So if you're up a creek for housing, this place is cheap, as rents go. Lots of space and a fifteen-minute bus ride from campus." As Irv finished, Pep swatted his head.

"Bug," she stated.

Irv seemed unfazed. "A mosquito."

"The Wisconsin state bird." Gil spoke for the first time, puffing out his chest, covered by a T-shirt. Sure enough, around a drawing of a mammoth insect, it read: "Mosquito: Wisconsin State Bird."

Irv returned to business: "There's a wood-burning stove in both flats, which keeps heating bills down in the winter. A cord or so of wood will do you for the whole season."

Sweat-propelled, Cissy's glasses slid down her nose; she pushed them back up. "This *is* a nice place," she ventured, and shifted her gaze to Jeb, half-expecting a reprimand. None came. "And we *will* be on a tight budget."

"Security deposit is just a hundred dollars."

"Can't beat that." Jeb sounded interested. "We'll talk it over and get back to you real soon."

Irv spoke for the group: "We'll all be here. Upstairs."

Cissy wondered where they all slept. Before they walked away, she saw a hint of an answer: Juan had placed his arm around the all-American boy.

They discussed all the way to the car. The house was a little dilapidated, the upstairs neighbors a motley, odd bunch. But it was late in the apartment-hunting season, the location good and the price better. The $57-per-night motel would be denting their scant funds. They went back to look once more.

"You can move in on the spot for the first month's rent," Irv offered. "Give me the security deposit later, if you're in a bind. You both look trustworthy."

Cissy deemed it providential that she'd met back up with Irv. She had to keep their budget in mind, they couldn't afford the west side, and what else could they do? She eyed Jeb. They nodded at each other uneasily.

"Looks like we'll take it," he announced.

"You've made a good choice." Irv excused himself to get a lease. On the porch the all-American boy lit a small marijuana pipe. "Have a hit?" He held out the pipe, neighborly.

"No thanks," Cissy said.

"Don't wanna seal the deal with a toke?" Gil seemed shocked by this social faux pas. "OK, have it your way."

Juan lay back on the sofa and caressed Gil's shoulder. Gil made a point of removing the hand. Resolutely unoccupied, Pep stared at her and Jeb. After a second, she took the tomato from her cleavage and bit into it. Juice and seeds dribbled down her chin and onto her overexposed breasts. "Bite?" She extended the half-eaten tomato.

Cissy again rejected the hospitality, but saw Jeb looking on intrigued. She knew his interest lay not in the tomato and jerked him toward her.

Irv reappeared with the lease. "Read it over, ask any questions, sign on the line and it's yours for a year."

"We've already heard you're a great landlord."

"Landperson." Irv smiled and inserted his hand into his beard as if to dredge up a paperclip or pen.

Gil took a break from making slurping noises into the pipe: "He's not into being anyone's 'lord.'"

Irv produced a pen from his pocket and Cissy read and signed the lease. They handed over cash and Irv scribbled a receipt. In the morning they'd return with their scant U-Haul possessions.

"By the way," Jeb asked, "is there a garbage strike in this city or what? The downtown curbs are piled high with trash and old furniture."

"It's the students movin' every August," answered Gil. They throw away what they don't want and take off."

"You can go scavenging with me if you need furniture," Juan volunteered. "You can make some great finds."

They needed furniture, but Cissy hadn't imagined culling it from the curbs. "You never know. But thanks."

On their way back to the Fiat, she impulsively pulled Jeb down to her mouth. They kissed while walking, barely avoiding collision with a telephone pole papered with "US Out of Central America" signs.

"Williamson Street," he said. "Our new home."

Cissy detected an odd note to his voice. "Our new home," she repeated, camouflaging her own doubts.

5

A week later, Cissy and Jeb sat down to dinner as guests in the kitchen of their upstairs neighbors. Juan lowered a Brussels sprouts and turnip casserole flambé onto the table.

"Brussels sprouts are a staple here when Juan's the chef," Irv said, and dug in, as Cissy watched his beard narrowly escape entrapment in the entrée.

"It looks... delicious." Cissy, a lapsed vegetarian, bravely made a stab into this new variety of vegetarian cuisine. From her first bite, she failed to see that the flambé had added anything, except smoke to the room.

Gil and Pep both viewed the main course with undisguised contempt. Gil said, "Welcome to Juan's House of Arson."

"-Ick." Dyspepsia attacked a clump of casserole, disinterring a scorched turnip. She studied it with distrust, popped it into her mouth, grimaced and swallowed.

"Pep didn't say 'Ick,'" Gil said in purported defense of her. "She was just adding on to 'Juan's House of Arson.' As in 'Arsen-ic.'"

Juan paid no heed to the gastronomical commentary and twirled a Brussels sprout on a fork for all to see. "Anticarcinogens."

Having survived the first mouthful, Cissy swallowed her second. "These are the little cabbages growing on the stalks in the garden, right?"

Juan spoke with his mouth full. "Last year's harvest."

"It used to be 'A carrot a day keeps the cancer away,' but now he eats a Brussels sprout for every cigarette he smokes," explained Gil. "You should see him put 'em down on Saturday night to catch up for the week."

"Barf." Dyspepsia stuck her finger in her mouth. The conversation lagged; the labor of unearthing the main course —and apparently the only one— commanded everyone's full attention.

Cissy weathered her third bite and decided to break the silence. "What do you do, Pep?" The name gave her the odd feeling of calling a dog.

Pep grunted something resembling "ho."

"Pardon?" Cissy couldn't have heard what she thought she did.

"Dig," Pep specified, toneless.

"I'm afraid I don't dig you," she said unsteadily.

"Plant."

"Oh." Cissy put it together: hoe, dig, plant. "You garden."

"She gardens half the space in front," Juan clarified, emptying his first plate. "If you call raising white flies 'gardening.'"

"Thank God only half of it's Brussels sprouts." Using his fork as a gardening tool, Gil aimed at a blackened turnip and impaled it.

Cissy dropped this line of conversation, a seeming bone of contention, and Jeb picked up the dialogue: "Question for anybody here. I went down to the corner supermarket yesterday, then someone told me it wasn't 'politically correct' to shop there."

"See? I'm not the only one who goes to Fascist Foods!" Gil burst out.

"What's this 'politically correct' stuff?" Jeb pursued.

"You know, from the sixties." Juan said "sixties" as if that explained it all.

Irv, the obvious guru of the tribe, cleared his windpipe of culinary obstruction and elaborated: "When the antiwar and counterculture movement realized it couldn't really change politics in Washington, people turned the lifestyles they had evolved political. You know, the personal is the political."

Cissy knew, but not much. Everyone sat with their knives and forks aloft. She guessed it was not so much out of politeness as taking advantage of a reason not to eat.

"This coincided with the rise of the environmental movement. You walk, bike or bus instead of drive; burn wood for heating; cut down on energy use. Raise your own food and boycott the big guys."

"That was the sixties," Jeb said. "What about today?"

"Alive and well in Madison." Irv leaned into his casserole. "Especially on the near-east side."

Except for the Watts Riots and occasional trips to San Francisco and Berkeley, Cissy had pretty much missed out on the sixties, at least firsthand. "So Jeb and I are the only politically incorrect ones here?"

"Nope," announced Pep, maneuvering uneaten food around on her plate.

"No one ever admits to being PC." Gil seemed to imply that someone present should.

"If I have to be labeled, I prefer anarchist." Irv's beard mingled with the thick sauce masking the vegetables. Cissy remembered the vanity plate of

Irv's pickup truck: "ANARKY."

"I take on cases other lawyers wouldn't touch: defense of a hairstylist for serving her clients drinks from a next-door bar; paternity suits against neutered pets; kids' right to go to school with rings in their nose."

At this mention, Pep ascended to a previously unseen level of interest in the conversation. She beamed at Irv and Cissy noticed two tiny holes in her nose.

"I see," Cissy said, perhaps beginning to. She drank from a glass of tepid water to dislodge a hunk of turnip from in between her teeth.

"I'm a YUD." Juan took another helping of casserole. "Young Urban Dropout."

Gil pushed away his half-consumed plate. "Don't let him fool you. He's the most politically correct here."

"I have a Ph.D. in sociology and drive a cab. The quintessence of YUD. And not politically correct."

"Me, I'm VIP." Gil said, immodest.

"Very Incorrect, Politically." Juan's clarification dripped with disdain. "And proud of it."

Gil lit a cigarette, puffed, then spoke: "Juan heads, no, Juan *is* the Wiscaragua Society. Your involvement with the Sandinista cause makes you PC, like it or not."

Cissy remembered the Wiscaragua decal next to the "Nuclear-Free Zone" on the downstairs door. She watched Pep mold her remaining food into human form and stick toothpicks in it.

"Juan's one-quarter Nicaraguan." Gil raised a glass of homemade beer that she and Jeb had turned down.

"He lies. I was born in Cuba. Half-Cuban and half- French Canadian. That accounts for my surname: Bellefleur."

Gil ashed his cigarette onto the leftover food and Cissy saw that this topic too had reached exhaustion. "Gil, What do you do?"

Drugs," he answered, straight-faced, as Pep let out a whoop and stabbed her human casserole in the vicinity of the heart. She held up her plate, exhibiting it for all.

"Here, have mine too." Gil ground his cigarette butt into the sauce and shoved the ashed-over food toward Pep. "Actually, I'm about a seventh-year senior, except I've still got a little ways to go."

This was Cissy's first contact with a UW student. "What's your major?"

"Pharmacy," he deadpanned.

"He's serious," Juan said, as if reading her face.

Cissy's gaze roved around the table: Jeb valiantly helped himself to more of the charred entrée; Irv applied a napkin to his beard; Pep erected a castle from the dregs of Gil's plate; Juan finished another helping, pointedly oblivious to her creation.

"Teachin' anything easy?" Gil asked, as her eyes completed the circle and met his.

"I'll be giving an Introduction to Museums course and an advanced class on Archaeology and the Museum." She picked up her water glass and added, noncommittal, "I'm not sure how easy they'll be."

"You mean you're teachin' that big lecture class with all the museum tours and slide shows?"

"The Introductory class? I suppose that's what you mean."

"Need to up my GPA. Been thinkin' of takin' that one for years."

"Oh, really?"

"That course's got a rep for bein' a real snap. Piece of cake. One of the biggest in the university."

Cissy's eyes widened in distress as she tried to gauge his seriousness. She hadn't worked on the course all summer only to find this out now.

Juan's fork tines hit his plate, making the only noise at the table.

"No shit." Gil broke the silence.

"You are serious, aren't you?"

"Gonna be lots of pissed-off students if they sign up for a Mickey Mouse course that doesn't turn out that way." He shook his head gravely.

"This is very interesting," Cissy said, shaken.

"Regular student riots," Gil affirmed. Pep made a round of machine-gun noises, then smiled innocently.

"I'll have to find out what I can about this."

"Better find out quick so you can ease up before it's too late."

Juan extended the casserole dish. "Seconds, anyone else?"

Fall Semester

6

C issy approached her new academic home, the Fine Arts Building, commonly known as FAB. A thunderclap struck above. She looked up and contemplated FAB with a shudder.

Each floor seemed to be a separate compound. Pillars abounded between floors; several turrets rose eerily from the upper levels. Doors seemed to lead nowhere; windows were few and most, minuscule. She imagined entrapped graduate students behind them clambering to escape. FAB only lacked a moat and a drawbridge.

When she'd been there last week, the fifth floor, home to Museum Studies, had resembled a mausoleum. Last week she'd found no one, except Wilhelmina Wiggins, the departmental secretary, and Sumner Isaacson, whom she'd questioned about the dubious reputation of the Intro course. Resigned in the face of her dredging up this skeleton from the departmental closet, he admitted that her predecessor had had loose attendance standards, and even looser grading one s, with true-and-false exams skewed toward double-digit IQs. He'd admonished her to tighten up the standards.

Today, the first day of classes, the floor was faintly abuzz with activity. Cissy went down a long hall and around the corner from the departmental office to her own. A nameplate reading "Cicely F. Pankhurst" had been affixed to the door. The office held a large desk, two chairs, a filing cabinet and bookshelves. A long narrow slot posed as a window, which looked out onto a slab of concrete, where rain streamed silently down. She nuzzled up to the glass and tried to get a better view. There wasn't any.

Her watch read 8:36 when knuckles rapping on the door jolted her out of her contemplation. She spun around as Vance Rickover thrust himself into her office. Like the first time they'd met, he sported polyester and needed a haircut.

"I swore we'd never hire you, Pankhurst. But we did and now you're here. Welcome aboard. Frankly, I don't know if a woman can handle the Intro class. Four hundred of the little buggers. Students, that is. A hard lot to control. You'll have to whip them into shape.

"The going will be rough, but the tough will survive." He extended his fist and aimed a good-natured punch at her shoulder, stopping a fraction of an inch short. "Just wanted to see if you'd flinch. Maybe you're hardier than I thought."

Rickover fractured a smile, accompanied by a baritone guffaw and a lewd sort of wink. "I'm sure we'll meet up again during the week's maneuvers. Chin up, Pankhurst!" He marched off.

Dazed, she sat down and pondered the strange encounter. At least someone had welcomed her, if indeed on his own brutally candid terms, an apparent constant.

A few minutes later she looked up to see the department's young black Assistant Professor standing in the door. Like Rickover, Ginger Carter appeared to be Cissy's age. She wore matching red heels and dress, short hair and heavy makeup.

"Good to see you again." Ginger slipped into the office, closed the door and took the chair next to her desk. "Rule number one around here: Never say anything on the fifth floor except in a whisper and behind closed doors. Are you all right? You look like you've just seen a ghost." She brought her fist to her chin, imitating *Le Penseur.* "Correction." She sat back up. "You look like you've just seen Rickover. Am I right, Cis?"

"Right you are." She suspected that Ginger was the all-knowing, all-seeing gossip that academic departments inevitably had.

"I'll bet he came by to give you his 'rough-seas and welcome-aboard-ship' talk, like he did when I came here last year."

The accuracy flabbergasted Cissy. "You certainly know the department." Trusting that Ginger would confide in her, she asked, "What's with that man?"

"Well…" Ginger crossed her legs and poised herself as if to spill some juicy tidbits. "I'm sure he told you, if you didn't already know, that he does conservation techniques." Ginger tittered and rolled her mascaraed eyes, savoring something yet unmentioned. "But do you know what his true conservation specialty is?"

"No."

"Scat." Ginger erupted into brief hysterics, then composed herself. "His aim in life is to be the world expert on scat-conservation techniques. Fitting, no?"

"Indeed." Cissy found herself caught up in Ginger's laughter. "When he came in here this morning, I'd swear he made a pass at me, or at least a suggestive wink as he went out the door."

"So you got 'ricked-over' again." Ginger seemed unconcerned or at least used to such behavior. "I don't think he'd really harm a woman. It's mostly his version of what he thinks is bravado. His most vicious weapon sure isn't below his belt. Listen, do you want to know the real dirt on him?" She perched expectantly on the edge of her chair.

"Sure." Cissy tried to subdue her enthusiasm for the "dirt."

Ginger needed no prodding to relay it: "About two years ago he went to one of his scat-exhibition conferences at Michigan and met a grad student writing her dissertation there. A month or two later, he married her. Then... No one knows exactly what happened. Word has it that he locked her in his attic to finish her dissertation, and she's never been seen or heard of since!"

Cissy's mouth gaped. Could this actually be true?

"I swear to God, it's true, Cis. I figure either she's escaped and divorced him or she's still in there writing. And Rickover isn't talking."

As if finished with her day's ration of gossip, Ginger stood up. Cissy saw that her tight-fitting dress left little to the imagination.

"I wouldn't want to scare you off before you start, Cis. This department needs you." Ginger peered at her watch, coiled around her wrist by a red plastic band. "Time for me to go work on tenure. I don't teach today. Just came in to get my mail."

With a flourish, she glided out the door before Cissy could mumble good-bye. Her eyes swept over her own watchface: 9:00. In less than an hour her first class would begin.

The 10:45 bell marked the end of Cissy's first class in Introduction to Museums. It left her with a minute's remarks to condense into a few seconds.

Before she got a few words out, students began to rustle papers, slam notebooks shut and bolt for the door. A partied-out coed awoke and recovered the sandal which had dangled from her lacquered toenail until falling to the floor with a thud.

Cissy gave up, gathered her papers and descended from the podium.

"Isn't this class supposed to be Art Therapy 101?"

"When are we going to see the museums?"

"Missed the assignment." Cissy recognized the sandal-dropper.

"Must've dozed off."

"The answers to all these questions are in your syllabus. And, no, this isn't Art Therapy 101."

"Is there an opening in this course?"

"Hey, man, I might be droppin'," said an edgy voice. It belonged to one of a trio of fraternity brothers, judging by their Greek-lettered shirts.

"Me too," chimed in a second brother. "If we gotta take all these exams." He brandished the syllabus accusingly.

"Three exams are standard, I'm told."

She walked brusquely away, found the stairs before locating the elevator, and took them. The hike to the fifth floor would do her untoned muscles good. She still hadn't established a regular jogging routine in Madison.

Arriving at the fifth floor out of breath, she went to her office and collapsed onto her swivel chair. After collecting herself, she decided to decipher the class list.

Official enrollment hovered at two below the 400 maximum. Painstakingly she counted the occupied squares in the four-part seating chart she'd passed around, subtracted from the total enrollment and came up with twenty-nine absences. Checking the seating chart against the official class roster, she found that not all those who attended had officially registered. No wonder her predecessor had had loose attendance standards.

Her eyes fell on the name "Kreuzer, Gilbert P." Out of curiosity she scanned the seating chart for his name: absent. She shook her head hopelessly at the nine-page class roster. At least the Intro course, with its heavy workload, counted for two preparations.

"What's this!? Rough seas already, Pankhurst?"

Cissy's gaze jerked up. Rickover stood at the door. He shook his head gravely at her, then strode away before she could erase her imbecilic look. If she was going to look like an idiot, she preferred to do it in private. She went to close the door.

Before she could sit back down, a knock came. She stifled an exasperated groan and whipped it open.

"Excuse me. Are you Mrs. Pankhurst?"

In the door frame hulked a large form. A second glance revealed it to be female. Cissy threw a sharp glance at the nameplate on her door, then at the student.

"I'm sorry. I read the name. I, uh, you see, I just wasn't sure who, uh, you were," the student stammered.

Cissy softened. "How can I help you?"

"I'm in your Introduction to Museums class," the student sniffled. She wore overalls and carried a large, neon-orange backpack.

"Come in and sit down."

The young woman crashed onto a chair. After several false starts and more sniffles, she managed to go on: "I'm Lou Lautermilk." The voice had a rich, sweet quality to it, the face was lightly freckled, and the short brown hair looked unceremoniously chopped off.

Cissy scanned the roster and found the name.

"I wasn't in class today. You see, my great-grandmother died, the funeral was yesterday, and I missed the only bus from Ladysmith to Eau Claire because of the funeral. So I didn't get to Madison until this morning. By the time the bus arrived and I got to my dorm and left my things, I'd missed class. I was wondering if I could get the assignment?"

"Certainly." Cissy noted a chord of panic in the student's voice and handed her a syllabus. "Official attendance policy permits only three absences." She pointed to this information on the syllabus, which contained the department's harsh numerical grading scale. Isaacson's eyes had shone with Machiavellian glee when he'd pointed out that the lowest A was a ninety-six.

A look of gravity filled the student's face; she nodded contritely. "I won't miss again." She spat out a "thank you" and lurched awkwardly toward the door. From the hall she flashed Cissy a look of appreciation, heaved the backpack onto her shoulders and ambled away.

Cissy found herself smiling. The obviously new student was more nervous than she, the new teacher. She sized Lou Lautermilk up as a typical Wisconsin farm girl, although she'd never met one. Then again, she'd thought Gil Kreuzer a Wisconsin farm boy and had been wrong.

She decided to escape the confines of FAB, eat lunch and walk it off with a long stroll. Farm girl or not, Lou Lautermilk had served to remind her of the peril of obesity.

7

Lou Lautermilk's pre-dawn breakfast left her famished by noon. Her stomach growled as she endured the wait in the long cafeteria line. When her turn came to enter the food arena, a cafeteria worker locked the turnstile until the crowd inside trickled out.

Finally gaining entrance, Lou made herself a submarine sandwich, then took two entrées and three side dishes. The cashier punched in $12.39 on her dining hall card. Lou did quick mental calculations: At this rate her cards would be spent by mid-semester and she'd have to buy more. She'd have to monitor her expenses closely.

After lunch she took the elevator to her fifth-floor dorm room. Perhaps this time she'd meet her roommate. University Housing had notified her of her name and address and she'd promptly sent off a friendly letter to Beth Yarmolinsky of Skokie, Illinois, but received no reply. Last week, when Lou had come to register — before unexpectedly heading back home for the funeral — Beth hadn't been there.

She unlocked the door to her room and Beth's possessions came into view. Lou's jaw fell as she took in her roommate's belongings littering the floor, lower bunk bed, desk and dresser: a clock radio, computer, stereo, television, coffeemaker, microwave oven and small refrigerator. A number of bottles stood beside the coffeemaker. She moved up close to read the labels: tequila, vodka, gin, vermouth, sherry and Triple Sec. The only personal stamp Lou had put on the room was a crocheted framed plaque that read "Dorm Sweet Dorm."

Wanting to lie down on her lower bunk, she began to pile appliances on the floor. Her mother had prophesied that her out-of-state roommate was probably "some rich girl," and, by appearances, had been right.

Suddenly Lou reversed her piling and heaped the appliances back on the bed. She didn't want to be caught unaware, tampering with Beth's things. She felt strange, having revealed herself to Beth but getting no answer. In her mind, beautiful went together with rich; Lou was neither. It would be better to go for a walk and burst in on her later.

Two blocks away Lou landed at the bottom of State Street and headed up it. She swallowed up atmosphere: bars, curious and kinky shops, street musicians. In Ladysmith, street musicians would probably be arrested, not applauded.

She caught a whiff of something novel in the air. When she'd commuted from Ladysmith to UW-Eau Claire, she'd found it sophisticated and exciting. But it couldn't compare to Madison, the biggest city she'd ever visited, after Minneapolis, years ago.

To her left, a large plate-glass window faced the sidewalk. Behind it sat a row of guys with beer bottles. Each held a card with a hand-scrawled number: four, three, three, four, two. Lou stopped, inquisitive. "Forty-three thousand three hundred forty-two," she mused. It seemed to be the university enrollment.

She looked back again. The faces now focused on long-haired blonde coed who wiggled past in bluejean cutoffs, a revealing halter top and reflector sunglasses. New numbers popped up: nine, ten, nine, ten, nine.

Lou turned red — then a shade green — as the rating system dawned on her. She simmered up State Street. Perhaps the overalls didn't become her. Nor did they befit the late summer heat of southern Wisconsin.

She shook off the encounter and again took stock of her surroundings: Bicycles zoomed down State Street at fearful speeds; others plugged laboriously up the slope, delaying buses and taxis. Bicyclists called to passersby, taxis honked horns, buses spewed exhaust and aloof pedestrians breezed by her on the sidewalk.

A bearded man veered toward her. "Got any spare change, ma'am?"

Lou broke out in a nervous sweat, instinctively thrust her hand in her pocket and redoubled her pace. As a child she'd received warnings about accepting money from strangers; she'd never gotten any about giving it to them.

She neared the upper end of State Street, where a group of preteens smoked cigarettes. Next to them a huddle of dark men spoke in a foreign tongue — French, Swahili, Spanish? Indeed, Madison was cosmopolitan.

She stopped to admire the Capitol, ruling over the downtown. A bag lady jostled her, growling something about blocking the sidewalk.

Lou headed back to campus on the opposite side of State Street. A young man with hair like wheel spokes skateboarded past her. Two bemetalled girls clanked down the street in front of her, sporting green and purple hair.

Madison: the Big City, Capital City, and, her parents had warned, Sin City. She had to agree that the potential for sin seemed to lurk here. Uneasy and sizzling in the heat, she skedaddled back to the relative safety of her dorm room.

"Hey! You must be Lucille!"

Lou did a double take. She scanned it at eye-level and saw no one.

"Up here, kid!"

Lou followed the voice to the upper bunk, where a tiny figure — surely a dwarf or midget— waved at her.

"You must b-be B-Beth."

"Right-o! Hey, mind changin' bunks with me, Lucille? You at least stand half a chance of gettin' up here without riskin' your life."

"Sure." She could hardly deny a midget such a request.

Beth Yarmolinsky took a flying athletic leap off the bed, exhibiting formidable agility. She landed on her haunches and stood up next to Lou.

"Four-foot nine, eyes of wine," she said.

No midget, just short, Lou saw. Upon hearing "wine," she glanced at the liquor bottles, then back at her roommate's eyes, half expecting to see them bloodshot. They were indeed an unusual deep purple.

"Steve says I have Manischevitz eyes."

Lou didn't quite understand.

"Steve's my Dad. Oh, by the way, thanks for the letter." Beth produced it out of her bluejeans pocket. "Me and Nick were in Europe most of the summer. Nick, that's my mom, Nicole. I just got the letter when we got back to Chicago this weekend, then I found out school starts today! Ain't that the pits?"

"Yeah, the pits," Lou muttered, uncertain.

"I thought it didn't start till after Labor Day. So I missed Registration Week, which I hear is a drag anyway. So Nick and me loaded my stuff and drove up early this morning."

"I had to get up early this morning too. My great-grandmother's funeral was yesterday..."

"Damn! I think I forgot my VCR!"

Lou gave a faint nod of sympathy.

"Dorm deprivation." Beth gave a percussive snap of her fingers. "Tried to get Nick to buy me a condo here, but no go." She lunged for a pack of Marlboro Lights. "I smoke, so I hope you don't mind." Before Lou could answer, she lit one. "Signed up for four classes this morning. French Women Writers, Psych 101 and Geology. All sciences suck if you ask me. For a foreign language, I figured I'd do Spanish, since it's easy, you know. But it was closed, so I walked around the language building and saw this sign sayin' 'Fill Your Language Requirement with Telugu.' They speak Telugu in India!" Beth seemed to marvel at this, as if no languages were spoken there. "So what're you takin', Lucille?"

"Just call me Lou." She tried to collect herself in the face of her roommate's verbosity. "I'm taking..."

"Shit! No ashtrays." Beth stubbed the cigarette butt out on the tile floor. "Don't worry, kid, I'll clean this pit up for us later."

Lou eyed her watch. Her class would start soon. "I'm taking Introduction to Museums," she began, precise.

"Museums!" Beth howled. "You mean they give you credit for lookin' at museums! I oughta take that. I must be a regular expert by now. Nick dragged me to every damn museum in Europe this summer. So I sucked up lotsa culture. Hey, Lou, if you want a drink, hard stuff's on the dresser, beer and wine in the fridge."

"Thanks, but I have to leave for class in a few minutes. You asked what I was taking..."

"Oh, yeah."

"I'm also taking German 204, which I have right now, and two advanced psychology classes."

"No shit! How'd you swing that for a freshman?" Beth's head ducked in, then out of the refrigerator. She clenched a bottle of wine in her fist.

"I'm a transfer student. A junior."

"A junior? No shit?"

Lou wondered if she'd even read her letter.

Beth spilled wine into a tall glass. "Me, I'm a freshman. Couldn't decide where to go to school. Nick and Steve wanted the Ivy League. But I was lucky to get in anywhere. Wisconsin's always been on the Top Ten Party School List, the Cool School survey an' all that, but then they went and upped the drinking age." Beth paused, dragged on a new cigarette and drank. "But then I found out I made the cutoff date by two weeks, so here I am! Are you *really* goin' to class now?"

Lou inched toward the door. "I don't think I should miss the first day."

"You think it's important the first day?" The notion seemed to appall Beth. "I thought I'd go *one* day this week."

Lou shrugged her shoulders at this dubious notion of responsibility.

"Well, kid. I'm gonna take a nap." Beth surveyed the disarray of her belongings. "By the way, I don't mind if you don't smoke, but you do drink, don'tcha?"

"Well, yes." Lou opened the door. Since turning eighteen, two years ago, she'd drunk beer. Exactly twice. And less than a bottle each time.

"Great! We'll get along super!" Beth slapped her palms together, her cigarette dangling from the corner of her mouth. "Later, kiddo!"

"I'll see you later, Beth." Overwhelmed, Lou mustered a modicum of cheer in her face, shut the door and lumbered down the hall.

8

Aftter lunch, Juan headed for the Memorial Union Terrace. The afternoon boded lazy, the temperature a perfect seventy. The Terrace was ideal for wiling away time, seeing old friends and watching supple student bodies.

Several hundred others also thought so. Finding a seat was never easy. Even gale-force winds off Mendota didn't daunt the regulars of the Terrace. Students, non-students and vagrants alike populated it during the five-month period of habitable weather —eating, drinking, studying and socializing at the hundred or so outdoor tables between the Union and the lake. Without doubt, it was the most popular summer spot on campus. The reason was simple: The Terrace sold beer.

Searching out an unoccupied table, Juan strolled through the crowd. Students threw Frisbees on a second-floor balcony. Salsa music blared from a boom box hidden among the yellow, red and green tables and chairs. African graduate students drank beer and gestured animatedly, resorting to sign language to combat the salsa. An Asian wore earmuffs to read. Retired and perennial students smoked pot and consumed *The New York Times.* Undergraduates swilled beer by the pitcher, brought in their own flasks and let dogs roam below a sign that prohibited alcohol not bought on the premises, and pets.

Behind all of this, the Union's ivy-clad walls served as a faint reminder of academia.

Juan had driven cab until dawn, gone home and slept until ten. Gil had stumbled out of bed, threatened to go to class — he'd missed the first day — and told Juan he could be found on the Terrace by afternoon.

Juan had spent the time before lunch working on SPELL, the Society for the Preservation of the English Language and Lexicon, of which he was founder and president. He sent letters to notify businesses of misspellings in their advertising, a free service he provided for the benefit of his adopted language. After spotting a potential offender last night, he'd checked the apostrophe-free telephone book this morning and called the establishment whose sign read "Glady's." Gladys, not Glady, answered, confirming his suspicion. The sad fate of the apostrophe in the eighties...

He'd then tended his Brussels sprouts, while Dyspepsia contemplated the undersides of tomato leaves across the sidewalk. She was likely picking off white flies and squashing them. Or eating them, he'd thought mischievously.

Gil was nowhere to be seen on the Terrace. At one edge Juan located a free table, bathed in sun. A pile of newspapers and plastic dishes and cups confronted him. He tossed the latter in a trash can and began to peruse a newspaper. A duck that had waddled over from the lake took to sudden flight inches from his head. Juan felt like drinking a beer, but legal age wasn't the only criterion for buying one on the Terrace. Either a valid university ID or a Union membership was necessary. With luck, he'd run into someone he knew who could buy him a bottle.

"Juan-Boy!" He jumped at the familiar voice calling his name and turned around to see Roz Goldwomyn. "Roz! How're you doing?" He got up to kiss her on both cheeks. She gave him an unexpectedly hefty slap on the back.

"Down here taking a break from the big D?"

"You know perfectly well that I defended my dissertation in 1980," he said coolly.

Roz remained belligerent: "Then what're you doing down here?"

"The same as you, who, if memory serves me, dropped out of grad school in 1976." Which meant she couldn't buy him a beer either.

"Very funny. I'm joining you." She sat down and the table wobbled. "What good did finishing do you anyway?"

"It wouldn't be Madison if cabbies didn't have their doctorates."

Juan and Roz went back a long way. She'd once been Irv's lover, when they all lived in Amelia's commune. Like many former students, she'd chosen to make Madison her stomping grounds and had stomped more than most. She'd become the first woman in Dane County legally to get rid of the family patronymic, changing Goldmann to Goldwomyn. She soon after copped her first arrest by donning a cow's head, labeling her body as different quarters of meat and mooing her way on to the stage of the Miss University of Wisconsin Pageant, which soon went defunct.

"Cigarette?" Juan pulled out his pack of ultra-lights. Roz made a face and pulled out own Camel non-filters.

He pointed to the penny loafers sticking out below her white anklets. "What are you wearing in them these days?"

"Take a guess." Roz regularly inserted coins from downtrodden countries with leftist governments into the penny slots.

"Let's see, Edna." Juan used the name stitched above the pocket on her yellow bowling shirt. "Vietnam is passé. Nicaragua should be the number-one contender. El Salvador could figure in too. Even Grenada could slip in. And Cuba's never out of the picture. There."

"There, what?" She blew smoke in his face and spat on the ground. "You just named half a dozen. Now pick two."

Juan drew on his cigarette and deliberated. "OK. Nicaragua and El Salvador."

"You cheated."

"How? I'd have to get down there and smell your feet to read what's in those tiny slots. And that's one olfactory pleasure on which I'll pass today."

She ground her left loafer into his knee, exposed by a hole in his bluejeans.

"Hey, I just guessed luckily. Loosen up."

An odor of marijuana floated through the air. Roz perked up and sniffed.

"I wish I could get a beer." Juan yawned and scoured the Terrace for Gil. "There's got to be someone here I know who can get it for me."

"Forget it. Your generation's old, gone and raising their own teenagers."

"Speak for yourself." Behind Roz's crew cut, Juan saw his new neighbor wandering in confusion. "Cissy!"

"What a name to call your gay brothers!" Roz chain-smoked a Camel, lighting it with the butt of the first, and looked idly over her shoulder.

Briefcase in hand, Cissy walked up to the table, disconcerted. "Hi, Juan. I'm supposed to meet a colleague from my department here. But I had no idea this place was so big. I don't know how I'll ever find her."

"Pity." Roz puffed smoke.

"Roz," Juan said firmly, "this is Cissy Pankhurst. Cissy, Roz Goldwomyn. Cissy's our new downstairs neighbor. Would you like to sit?"

"Thank you." Cissy sat down and smoothed her dress.

"Roz works at the Co-op. Maybe you've seen her there, Cissy. She also works at Womynspace, the women's center on campus."

The two women regarded each other with suspicion, making no attempt at direct conversation.

"Cissy's just come here from California to teach in Museum Studies."

"Oh. Academia," Roz grunted, puffing away, and put her feet up on the table. "So what do you think of Madison? Must be different for you."

Seeing Roz scowl at Cissy's attire or appearance, Juan doubted that she was making completely polite conversation. He also saw Cissy focus on Roz's underarm hair where she had cut the sleeves off her bowling shirt.

"We like it fine, so far," Cissy answered.

"Oh, so you're plural," Roz said. "How interesting."

Juan lit another ultra-light and sucked in hard.

"Museum Studies, huh?" Roz went on. "Used to be an all-right department when they had 'Red' Ned Raitt for chair back in the sixties. Since he died, I'm sure it's been on a downhill slide. Ned was a regular CP card carrier."

Juan saw Cissy's eyes round in a question, and he clarified "Communist Party" for her. He decided to steer the conversation to safer territory: "How are your classes and students?"

"Besides Gil, who hasn't been there yet..."

Juan bolted up from his slouching position. "Do you mean he missed today too?"

"I'm afraid so, but they seem to they skip like crazy in the Intro class. But in my advanced class it's heartening to see so much interest. I have several girls who are majors and want to apply to graduate school."

Juan tightened, saw Roz stiffen. Their smoke immobilized in the air. Cissy looked on perplexed, her mouth slightly open. A misthrown Frisbee landed squarely on the middle of their table, which teetered.

Juan tossed it back as Roz said, "Oh, I didn't know the university was teaching preteens these days."

"Excuse me?" Cissy squeaked, smiling and attentive.

"You mean 'women,' not 'girls,' Cissy," Juan said.

"But some of them barely look sixteen."

"Women," said Roz, hard-boiled.

A long ash detached from Juan's cigarette. "You see, in Madison one ceases being a girl by the time she menstruates, if not right after kindergarten."

Cissy's face reflected more uneasiness than comprehension. She looked across the Terrace and, with obvious relief, exclaimed, "Oh, there's Ginger! My colleague. I've got to go. Nice seeing you, Juan. And nice meeting you,

Rose." She scurried away, briefcase in hand.

"Poor Cissy." Juan muttered.

"Poor, my ass." Roz extinguished her Camel on the metal table top. "I knew the university was going down the tubes. Hiring a California Yuppette like her!" As Roz spoke, Juan saw Cissy and her friend disappear into the Union. "Yuppette and Buppette. At least she's well-paired."

"Don't be racist, Roz." She glared at the accusation and Juan went right on: "And I take it you're using the diminutive in its derisive rather than affectionate connotation."

"Don't give me your grammatical mumbo jumbo. And, while we're on the subject, Mr. Grammar Smart-Ass, you don't say, 'I've guessed luckily.' You say, 'I've guessed lucky.' You talk like you hopped off the boat yesterday, not back in '52."

"I was born in '53 and, as you so tastefully put it, 'hopped off the boat' in '60. With your mouth and grammar, you're hardly one to talk, Roz. If anything, I've overlearned the language, as opposed to you natives, who abuse it."

"Eat horseshit, Juan." Roz set her jaw and gnawed on her upper lip. "I still can't believe it. The YUDs rent to the YUPs!"

"Come on, Roz. Just because Cissy dresses nicely and has long blond hair..."

"And acts like she's just graduated from a sorority."

Juan refrained from comment on Roz's own social polish. He inspected the Terrace and wondered what Gil had done with himself this afternoon. Not to mention this morning.

"So how are you and Erva Mae doing these days?" He knew that anyone living with Erva Mae couldn't be doing too well.

Roz soured. "It's complicated, Juan-Boy."

He let himself smirk. "Isn't love always?"

Roz brightened, which usually meant she had bad news. "You forgot to have Cissy get you a beer."

The sun dropped down behind the Union. Wind from the lake propelled a paper plate toward their table.

"Time to leave anyway." He stood up and stretched. His pants fell, exposing his midriff.

"Middle-age spread on its way," Roz quipped. Juan saw her fist coming playfully at his stomach and tightened his abdominals.

"Go ahead, try."

"Fifteen years since I laid a hand on a man."

"No reason to start now." He pulled his T-shirt back down, hiked up his sagging pants and tucked the shirt in.

"That's right, Juan-Boy. You're too old to be exposing yourself. Face it."

"And you'll always be two years older, Roz. I don't forget."

"Better move on, old man. I see Erva Mae and the separatists coming."

Juan looked to his left and saw Roz's lover, clutching a clipboard and leading a a group of women. Erva Mae planted herself boldly in a passage among the tables and shot accusing looks at those who occupied them.

"For once, I'll follow your advice. *Ciao,* Roz."

"Later, Juan-Boy."

He hurried away and, behind him, heard Roz bellow, "Hey! Over here! I got us a table away from any men!"

9

When Cissy began to spend her days at the university, Jeb was left home alone to construct a life for himself. For starters, he had applied as a substitute teacher for the Madison Metropolitan School District. He hadn't expected calls the first week and none had come yet.

"Just wait, babe." It was the third call-less day; he knew Cissy worried for him. "The weather will get bad, right? Then the kids will get sick. The teachers will get sick from the kids or *of* the kids. Then the calls will come pouring in. Anyway, there's never such a thing as an unemployed substitute teacher on Fridays."

Cissy gave him a kiss and went off to walk, if not jog, to work.

It was still warm and humid. Jeb spent his days outside, rehabilitating scavenged furniture, and made the front porch his workshop. For entertainment, he'd shoot baskets in nearby Orton Park with truant adolescents, watch his favorite soap operas and talk with the upstairs neighbors.

None of them seemed to have normal or regular jobs, giving him a feeling of solidarity in unemployment: Juan drove cab nights and spent days at home, often sleeping; Irv came and went all day long, giving no illusion of prolonged work; Gil and Pep not only had no job to report to, but Jeb had yet to see them once abandon the premises.

After Cissy left, he went outside, bought a newspaper down the street and sat down to read it on the porch. By midmorning Gil wandered outside and sat on the opposite end of the remaining porch sofa, the other now in their living room. Gil's red eyes bespoke a morning bowl of marijuana to go with his coffee.

"No classes again this morning, huh?"

"Nothin' happens the first week, man."

Jeb got up and attacked a mass of planks to be fashioned into a bookcase for Cissy.

"I oughta know. Been at it seven years."

"Rough life." Jeb swung a hammer, narrowly missing his thumb.

"All you gotta do is go once the first week to keep from gettin' disenrolled.''

"And you haven't made your move yet, right?" Cissy had told him, not without irritation, that Gil had skipped her first two classes. "Tomorrow, huh?"

"Never know. Think I'll go back to bed for awhile."

Friday dawned cloudy and cooler. The Madison Metropolitan School District failed to call. Gil failed to appear on the porch.

Jeb spent the morning finishing two bookcases. Although he was economizing, employment would have to come soon. Cissy's first paycheck wouldn't arrive until October 1.

After lunch, he stayed inside to watch *All My Children.* It began to drizzle outside. He turned the volume up to combat blaring rock music from upstairs, a sign that Juan had gotten up and Gil was still there. His gaze roved from the TV screen to the window screen. On the other side of it, Pep faced the garden. Jeb moved to a chair near the window. He was close enough to count the hair follicles on the back of her shaven neck.

All week long she'd titillated him. As she stood in the garden, her breasts would mingle invitingly with harvested tomatoes, just like he'd seen her the very first time. Bent over in the garden, she offered another view, equally inviting. His mind strayed from the soap opera. He flicked off the set and strode manfully outside.

In spite of his presence, Pep remained motionless and mute, staring straight ahead. Jeb felt himself tremble a little.

"Whatcha watchin'?" His voice came out soprano, suitable for the Vienna Boys' Choir.

Pep turned an incurious gaze on him, gestured at the patently obvious. "Rain."

Jeb planted his feet firmly on the porch's cement floor. "Yeah, it's raining all right. What else is new?"

"Growth." She pointed to her half of the garden.

"Yep. When it rains, things grow." He tapped his sneakered foot, drummed his fingers into the denim of his jeans.

"Weeds."

"Cissy and I had a garden once in California."

Pep stared blankly in front of her.

Perhaps he should say or do something bold. Brazenness had paid off before. When, at twenty-one, he'd been racked with lust for his Fine Arts Teaching Assistant, he'd finally asked her if she'd like to get together outside of class.

Cissy's face had registered pleasant surprise. Then she'd hesitated. "But university regulations prohibit student-teacher dating."

To which he had responded, "But do they prohibit student-teacher fucking?"

Cissy later claimed that he'd quaked perceptibly as he said it and that she wouldn't have given in two weeks later, had he not apologized for his language and had she not thought him her own age, twenty-six. Since then they'd been monogamous.

Or at least he had. He didn't know for a fact that Cissy hadn't. Of course the notion was ludicrous, but... All he'd need would be a quick roll in the hay with Dyspepsia to put her out of his mind.

Irv was seeing a client, Juan upstairs, and Gil professionally stoned. And Cissy wouldn't arrive home for two hours. This was his first real chance to connect with her, verbally. Then, after the verbal... He ventured speech again: "Just the two of us here." An appropriate baritone this time.

Enigmatic, Pep regarded him.

"You and me holding down the fort," he said, to say something.

Her gaze fluttered past his own. "No," she stated.

No, what? No, they weren't alone? No, nothing would ever happen between them?

Jeb wiped his chin with a finger and realized he was drooling. Barefoot, she still sat motionless. Today she'd color-coordinated her clothes with her lips: Black shorts clung to her thighs; a dark purple top displayed less than usual. "So who else is here besides you and me?"

"Plants." Once more, she gestured at the obvious.

He gave a mechanical nod; his mouth hung open. "Now I'm on your wavelength. *The Secret Life of Plants* and all that, right?"

Her eyes remained transfixed in front of her. Jeb ground the right toe of his sneaker into the cement. Hope fading, he shifted his weight to the opposite toe.

Pep stood up, took several steps forward, and held out a cupped hand. "Stopped."

Jeb saw that she referred to the rain, then looked down at his shoes: His big toe protruded through the fabric of his left sneaker. When he looked up, she had darted into her half of the garden. Between rows of corn, she flashed him a wide, disconcerting smile.

He bent over and edged his toe back inside his sneaker. Before retreating inside, he let his eyes meander once more in her direction. She crouched next to a leafless tomato plant, denuded by blight, and chomped on one of the fruits of her harvest. He watched her watching him.

He turned his head, then refocused on her, but saw an airborne tomato headed his way. Athletic, he jumped and caught it in cupped hands. The force of the catch exploded it. Pep roared.

So games it would be. He flung away the remains and went in to wash himself off. Inside he still heard her peals of laughter.

10

Irv left his law office on his bicycle. Pedaling past his house, he caught a glimpse of Pep under a tomato plant in the garden. He threw her a kiss, which she returned. It was as if she'd been crouched there waiting for him to pass. One of the many tiny miracles of their unexpected relationship.

He still wondered how long it would last. At five months, it had already surpassed his wildest expectations. To his own astonishment, he had become acclimated to her and the relationship. One thing he knew for sure: The end he'd put to his celibacy would be permanent.

A block past the house, he chained his bicycle to a telephone pole. He went into Ho Chi Minh's, the ever-popular neighborhood bar and restaurant.

A sport jacket thrown on over his T-shirt for the day's consultations, he ordered a Point and sat at a table. Nearly empty, Ho Chi Minh's was having its midafternoon lull.

Seth Reubenstein had chosen the locale for their meeting. Always flexible, Irv would have met him on a Madison Metro bus if Seth had willed it. The time to meet Seth came and went. Irv downed the beer and wondered how long he'd have to wait.

Fifteen minutes late, he sauntered in, wearing a suit and ponytail, gave Irv a sixties handclasp and made excuses. His pants flared. Irv smelled what seemed like a combination of incense and patchouli oil.

"Business or pleasure first?" Irv asked. The two of them went back to the sixties; their meeting would include some social catching-up.

"Business. As soon as I go to the bathroom and get a beer."

Irv arched his eyebrows. "Watch where you get your beer, Seth."

Seth regarded him, puzzled, then faked laughter and walked off.

Seth was the defendant against his west-side neighbor in civil court. Claiming an allergy to his front-yard prairie, she was suing for medical bills, lost income and mental anguish. As opposed to neighboring Sun Prairie, which had made national news by outlawing prairies in its limits, Madison permitted prairies as lawns when a detailed land management plan was submitted to the city and approved.

Irv was one of few who knew that Seth not only idolized the prairie; years ago he and his wife Sunshine had conceived their daughter Wisconsiana on a patch of it just west of Madison.

Seth returned with a beer and Irv whipped out the statute protecting endangered native Wisconsin prairie plants. Seth read it over, pensively scratching the scraggly hairs he sported in the guise of a beard.

Irv scratched his own, a reflex action. "You've brought me the list of all plants growing in your yard, I take it."

"All native to Wisconsin. As well as to Minnesota, Nebraska, Iowa..."

Irv interrupted the geographical litany. "Doesn't matter as long as the city approved your plan."

"I did my homework this time."

Irv knew from experience that bringing Seth down to specifics was not easy. He would wax on, elevating goldenrod to eucharistic heights, extolling the grace, curvaceous form and subtlety of the purple cone flower, and end up painting a verbal portrait of swaying prairie grasses that could rival Willa Cather's best. All without being able to tell you exactly what was growing in his own front lawn.

Irv finished perusing Seth's list and other documents. "It looks like we're all prepared."

"Buy you a beer?" Seth offered. Irv nodded, having sat through their business with an empty glass.

Seth returned with the beers and launched into familiar complaints about his job. Although Seth didn't admit it, Irv knew that he was plagued by doubts of having "sold out." The same had happened when he'd "sold out" many years ago by moving to the west side, though he'd gotten over it. Personally, Irv thought that any company that would tolerate ponytails on men couldn't be all bad.

Seth exhausted the topic, then asked, "Should I ask how your celibacy is going?"

"You should, because it isn't." Irv fingered his bald spot, distressingly large. "I'm a changed man since I met Pep."

Seth's brow corrugated gravely. "I hope not too changed. How did you meet, uh... her or him?"

Irv relished Seth's uncertainty. "It's a her, don't worry."

"Thank God. I thought you'd said 'Pepe' there for a minute."

Irv saw a little too much relief on Seth's part.

"I thought it could be another of your phases, Irv. You know: poverty, chastity, homosexuality."

Irv mildly resented Seth's characterizing his life by "phases," but let it pass.

"So how'd you meet her?" Seth's tone anticipated high romance, unbridled lust or both.

Irv related their meeting, omitting a select detail or two. "Now we've been together for five months."

"Good to let those juices flow, isn't it?"

Irv said nothing. Seth's own juices, evidently stimulated by his tale, seemed to be flowing a little too much.

"Consy's seventeen now." Seth beamed.

"How's she doing?"

"Top of her class." Seth radiated pride. "You remember how we almost pulled her out of school after the Reagan incident."

"Refresh my memory." As he spoke, Irv saw Seth begin to roll himself a suspicious cigarette. "Seth, Ho Chi's is liberal, but not that liberal."

"Tobacco, Irv." Seth sealed the cigarette with his lips. "You remember, don't you? When they announced the Reagan assassination attempt at school, Consy jumped up and applauded. They threatened to put her on detention and called me and Sunny in for a parent-teacher-principal conference. An issue of free speech —or free applause— if I'd ever heard one."

Irv had forgotten the story and was surprised that Seth, with his litigious bent, had never taken the school to court.

"By the way, Consy's going to pick me up here after school. We'll give you a lift."

"I brought my bike. It's not far." Irv drained the last of his Point.

"It's pouring. You can't ride in a downpour."

A minute later, they stood under Ho Chi Minh's awning, as rain splattered the streets, curbs and their tennis shoes.

"See. We'll take you."

A battered station wagon soon pulled up and stopped. "Pile in."

Inside Seth reintroduced Irv to his daughter, strikingly mature. Rain cascaded down the windshield. The car reeked of marijuana and incense. Irv half-expected to see an altar on the dashboard. When he looked up again, he did.

Wisconsiana passed a roach to her father. Irv remembered how Seth and Sunny had given their daughter marijuana to calm her when she was a child.

Seth turned to Irv in the back seat. "Don't worry. She stopped toking for ten years. But she's responsible now and chose to take it up on her own."

Irv abstained from the roach as well as from making comment on her driving under the influence. The car slowed to a stop in front of the house. He'd go back for his bike when the rain stopped.

"Thanks, man." Seth repossessed Irv's hand in a farewell clasp. "It was groovy."

Irv hadn't heard the word since he'd last seen Seth.

"Groovy seein' you, Irv," parroted Wisconsiana.

"See you in court." Irv saw her wince as he said it and suppressed a smile. He wouldn't be surprised if Seth would be asking him some day to act as his daughter's lawyer for a DUI case. He got out of the station wagon and made a dash for the house.

On the porch, he shook the rain off, then bounded inside.

"Boo!"

As he went in, Pep jumped him, grabbed him by the neck and kissed him. Irv succumbed to the kiss, felt a surge of passion and closed his eyes. Opening them a few seconds later, he had the eerie realization that Pep was barely older than Wisconsiana.

11

Roz ended her four-hour shift at the information desk at Womynspace and bicycled to the flat she shared with Erva Mae Voelp on East Wilson Street. Erva Mae would be home early tonight; they had a volleyball game and a potluck to attend.

She dumped her possessions in the kitchen, wandered into the living room and lit a Camel. Erva Mae had proclaimed the whole flat non-smoking territory. Arguing that cigarettes were a laxative for her, Roz had gotten her to relent on the bathroom.

Cigarette in hand, she strolled into the bathroom and closed the door. She stood at the sink, idly tapping ashes in the vicinity of the drain.

She stubbed out her cigarette in the sink, doused it under a stream of cold water and threw it in the waste basket. She removed her clothes, turned on the water and stepped into the bathtub. Adjusting the temperature, she stood under the harshest jet of the shower's faint spray and let it trickle down on her. Head tilted back, she closed her eyes. The water refreshed and invigorated her. Reflexively, she reached down to turn off the water after two minutes, but stopped herself. She'd endured Erva Mae's mandate of energy-saving showers long enough. Today she'd savor the hot water until it ran out. Erva Mae had long ago discovered political correctness, which still dominated her existence and all who dealt with her.

In her senior year at Madison, Erva Mae had come out and Roz met her soon after. Together they'd spray-painted the university sidewalks with the slogan "Pro-Lifers Eat Caviar," chained themselves to the door of a local adult book store and "sat in" to block the entrance to an anti-lesbian film. The last two events had netted them both newspaper and television publicity as well as arrest records.

Roz doubted she'd ever know the whole truth about Erva Mae's past, but she too had her own secret: Her lesbianism had never been more than a political statement. Now, almost fifteen years later, the few who had known this had either moved away, ceased to believe it or simply forgotten.

Erva Mae would be home soon. The water in the shower soon became lukewarm, then cool, and Roz turned it off. She rubbed herself dry with a scratchy threadbare towel. She lit another cigarette, watched the smoke ricochet lazily off the vanity mirror and stared into it.

After a final puff, she tossed the butt away, dressed and wandered into the kitchen to prepare tabbouleh for tonight's potluck. She had already put the bulgur to soak and had gotten onions, fresh mint and parsley from the Co-op.

Moments later Erva Mae bulldozed into the flat, leaving Roz behind in a whirlwind. The bedroom door slammed. Roz heard the thud of a backpack crashing to the floor, then a sound resembling a desk hitting the wall.

Their relationship had been stormy for the last ten days. If the current storm was related, Roz didn't know.

Erva Mae was sufficiently chemically pure to be a card-carrying Mormon: Cigarettes, alcohol, non-herbal teas, coffee, marijuana, aspirin and antiperspirants were on her off-limits list. But Roz knew that she had to have some sort of addiction somewhere deep down. She'd first discovered it in the form of herbal lip balm, which came in lime, cherry, orange and other sundry flavors. Erva Mae had often complained of Roz's cigarette kisses, so Roz lost no time in bringing up the offending balm.

"Erv, honey. With that lip balm of yours it's like kissing a banana."

"Banana breath!" Erva Mae gasped. "There's nothing on my breath! In any case my lip balm this month is not banana." She trotted out her algae toothpaste and read to Roz what it did to keep one's mouth clean and fresh.

"Lemon lips, then. There's something I taste on you."

Erva Mae bought a spiraling number of personal items in trendy, organic or herbal varieties. Soap, one of the most popular, disappeared with startling rapidity in Erva Mae's antispetic hands.

Last week Roz had picked up a particular whiff on Erva Mae's body. She was leaving no place — but no place — unscrubbed.

Roz broke off in the middle of the act. "Erv, we've got to talk."

"Huh?" Erva Mae moaned, her pleasure interrupted, and sat up on the bed.

"Erv," she began tenderly. "I know you go to great pains to keep your body clean."

"Good Goddess! Did I miss something?"

"No, no," Roz soothed.

"Then what?"

"I think you just go a little overboard on washing yourself sometimes. Especially with things scented."

"What!?" Erva Mae squawked, her dander up.

"Don't tell me that you didn't scrub yourself inside and out with cinnamon-scented soap tonight. I just got a strong whiff of it down there."

"Oh! I declare!" Erva Mae shrieked, her feminism never having eradicated a few vestiges of the would-be Southern belle with Kentucky roots. "I most certainly did not! How could you say such a thing!?" Teary-eyed, she fled from the bedroom. They hadn't been together in the same bed since.

After the current storm of desk-throwing came a calm. A few minutes later Erva Mae graced the kitchen. Any trace of expression that might account for the bedroom incident had been erased, and she put on her best manners. "What are we taking to the potluck, Roz?"

"At the moment, soaked bulgur. Whatever else depends on you."

"Oh." Erva Mae's best manners began to evaporate.

"So, what gives?" Her hands under an icy stream of tap water, Roz nodded toward the bedroom.

"What do you think Roxanne did?" Erva Mae demanded. Roxanne was Director of Womynspace, Erva Mae's boss and Roz's ex-lover.

Roz dried her hands on a kitchen towel. "Goddamned if I know, but I'd believe anything dastardly."

"Roz, don't you know that profanity promotes violence against women?" Erva Mae's hands landed on her ample hips. "If you find it absolutely necessary to swear, at least use the female form."

Roz feigned oblivion to the sermonette, but tried it out to herself: Goddessdamned? Damn it, Goddess?

"Nope. The female form doesn't work. So what did Roxanne do, Erv? Here, start chopping onions."

Erva Mae sat on a stool at their chopping block table and Roz dropped the onions under her nose.

Always resenting others' orders, Erva Mae brushed the onions aside and stomped off ceremoniously. She opened the refrigerator door, pretending inspection of its goods.

"Everything we need's on the table."

Erva Mae flashed a look of spite, gave the refrigerator door a muscular push and sulked her way back to the table. She repositioned herself on the rickety stool; Roz pushed the onions back at her.

"Here, chop. Tell me what Roxanne did and you'll feel better."

"I will not. Feel better, I mean."

Erva Mae began to mutilate the onions, grooving the chopping block with a fierce glee, then blurted out, "She put Isak Dinesen back on the shelf after I'd taken her off! I know what's feminist and what's not."

Roz chuckled to herself. Upon transferring to the University of Wisconsin, Erva Mae had found more fertile territory for minorities and opted to exploit her rightful place in the minority of women. She'd earned her B.A. and M.A. in Women's Studies, and was now Assistant Director of Womynspace. Never mind that Roxanne had a Ph.D. in Literature.

"And I thought she appreciated my removing offensive works from the shelves!" Erva Mae wavered between a sob and a snarl, then let the snarl win out. "Isak Dinesen was no feminist. Just read *Out of Africa!* Not only was she male-centered, not only was she not a vegetarian, but she hunted and killed animals too!"

"Erv. Feminism and vegetarianism never used to go together. Matter of fact, still don't. Look at me, for example."

Erva Mae regarded her balefully.

Roz spoke as she chopped parsley: "Can't you just call it 'womanist' literature and let it pass?"

"That's the issue. Would you put Barbara Cartland on the shelf and call it 'womanist?' Of course not. Some people just won't listen to reason." She glowered into the onions.

"There, parsley all done! I'll do the mint, you can garnish it with tomato, and then one dish is finished!"

"One dish?? We only have to take one dish per couple." Erva Mae frowned, betraying uncertainty.

"Yes, but how do you define 'couple?'"

Erva Mae spouted the definition: "Any two women-identified women who constitute the prime source of emotional support for each other."

Roz wiped her brow, exaggerating relief. "'Emotional.' Then I guess we still qualify."

Erva Mae threw her an accusatory look. Roz ignored it, then noticed Erva Mae wiping away tears. She'd gone too far, said the wrong thing.

"Th-these onions!" Erva Mae sputtered. "I can't take it any longer! I've got to go wipe my eyes this very minute."

Roz offered her a paper towel.

"No, thanks, Roz. I'll go to the bathroom and be right back."

Roz finished chopping the mint alone.

"Roz, darling?" From the bathroom, Erva Mae's voice rang out, sweet as pecan pie. The tone meant one thing only: trouble.

"Yeah?"

"Roz, I have to get this onion stench off my body right this instant and feel a powerful urge to take a shower. Can you finish the onions for me?"

Roz surveyed the large unchopped portion, then remembered the shower and the unreplenished hot water.

"Sure, I'll chop. But good luck with the shower!"

"What do you mean, Roz?" Erva Mae screeched back, distrusting.

"You'll see!"

She lowered the knife to the onions and squinted, their fumes on ocular attack.

12

Beth yawned over her Telugu text in the smoking room of Helen C. White, the undergraduate library. Her four-hour evening study period had eroded to three, then to two, and tonight, to one.

She got up and gathered her possessions. In the smoking room — technically a study room — couples not only smoked, but chatted, drank, popped bubble gum and necked, sprawled out on the floor below "Quiet" signs dotting the walls. She passed through the main lobby, where others hollered and squealed on the way out, severing the bonds of academic servitude for another weekend. Only the diligent populated the library on Fridays; for most, the weekend had begun on Thursday.

An early fall wind brought a chill to her arms as Beth made her way down North Park Street toward her dorm. To her right rose Bascom Hill, to her left lay Library Mall. The clock on the mall signaled 8:45.

No matter how late she returned from the library, she found Lou studying in the dorm room. True, Lou provided a good example. Too good. She would study blithely until midnight or later, as if pulling an all-nighter in the room were her divine right. Then she would stumble out of bed, waking her, by six the next morning. Beth preferred to sleep until noon, though she'd had to make slight modifications to accommodate her classes.

The first time Beth had laid eyes on Lou she knew they came from different worlds. When Lou had been learning her ABCs, the ABCs that Beth knew best were Aruba, Bonaire and Curaçao.

Beth put the key into the lock of her room and opened it tentatively. The crack in the door revealed a slice of Lou's nose immersed in a book. Beth breezed in; her roommate's position didn't change. She began to speak, but Lou's index finger shushed her. Beth bit her tongue, stuck a cigarette in her mouth and lit it with a two-inch Zippo lighter flame. After a half-minute, Lou's book fell to the desk, exposing her haggard face.

"Hittin' the books hard and heavy, I see." Beth expelled a cloud of smoke and tossed her own slender tome on the lower bunk.

"I have 400 pages of Psych to read for Monday, plus a quiz in German on the passive voice." Lou swallowed a yawn. "I don't know why I'm so tired tonight."

Beth pointed at Lou's neon-orange backpack on her desk chair. "If I shlepped around forty pounds of books all day long, I'd be tired too. How about a drink to pick you up?"

Lou regarded her as if she'd suggested ritual double-suicide.

Beth shrugged her shoulders, went to the mini-refrigerator and poured herself a tall tumbler of Burgundy.

"Oh, Beth. I put a small carton of milk in there. If you don't mind. Sometimes I get thirsty at night."

"Yeah, me too, kiddo." It was about time Lou smartened up and took advantage of some of the conveniences. She tipped her glass and knocked back a long, healthy slug.

"I'm going to have a couple friends come over tomorrow night. A little party. You're welcome to join us, if you want."

"Thanks, kiddo. We'll see." Beth sucked in deep on her Marlboro Light and blew smoke out of her nostrils. "Gotta find something to do in this dump of a town. 'Cool School,' my ass." Beth saw Lou wince and pick her book back up. "Speakin' of which..." Beth finished off her wine in a gulp. "I'm outta here, kid. Don't go blind readin'." She squashed her cigarette out, let the door fall shut and set out to prowl the corridor. Though she'd had little success her first weekends, tonight she could surely find something better to do than to drink alone while her roommate hid behind the spine of a book.

On Saturday evening, Helen C. White was a tomb and Beth felt like one of the dead. She needed noise and sleep in order to study and lacked both. The only noise in the library was a Walkman turned up loud at the neighboring desk. As for sleep, she'd slept until three in the afternoon, but tonight had arrived so tired that she'd gone in the wrong door and run into a giant portrait of the purple-clad Helen C. White herself. Reading the description, she learned that she had been a famous English prof at UW, and was now deceased.

Later, in the women's john, where she had taken her volume of George Sand, the toilet flushes and running tap water soothed her, saving her from the eerie silence of the smoking room. She read five pages behind a closed stall door, then tired of the position. She reread the graffiti on the wall and understood the joke for the first time: "Why did Helen C. White always wear purple? Because she looked like hell in white."

She returned to he smoking room and surveyed the clientele. If on Friday nights only the diligent populated the library, Saturday nights only the masochists, nerds and genuine weirdos showed up. Bored and with no plans for the evening, she decided to leave.

Last night she'd found a group of girls down the hall going out "to do

State Street." Beth joined them and quickly learned that "doing State Street" meant drinking in as many of its many bars as possible. Which set well with her. After five bars came closing time and a trip to a fraternity house, where an older brother of one of the girls lived. Her companions all proved boy-crazy, the boys reciprocated, and Beth sat alone in a corner and drank herself into a stupor. Hungover, she awoke at seven in the fraternity living room and stumbled home, where she'd returned to bed to sleep more of it off.

She made a quick, brisk walk to her dorm. Outside her room she heard conversation behind the door and remembered Lou's party. Her spirits resurrected.

"Hi, Beth." Lou played hostess. "This is Amy and this is Heidi. That's Beth, my roommate."

The two greeted her in unison, almost in harmony.

Now she remembered: She'd heard Lou talk of her friends — Amy Lautzenheiser, Heidi Kitchenheiser, or whatever — from her home town. The Milkmaids, she'd dubbed them without seeing them. She looked down at the floor where they sat, almost expecting to see to see a gallon of milk.

A twelve-pack of Pepsi Light rested next to them. Rotund, Amy approached Lou in bulk. Heidi could pass as thin, but only next to the other two. The three of them were attaching patches together — needle, thread and thimbles in their hands. What was this? A sewing circle? A quilting bee?

"A Pepsi Light?" offered Amy.

"Uh, no thanks."

"We've got chips and Bucky Badger Bean Dip too," Lou chirped, indicating the dip in a red and white container from the university dairy.

"Thanks. I'll pass for now."

"We're making a giant Risk board, four feet square," Lou explained. "When we're finished, Heidi's going to paint it."

"Nice," Beth managed.

"Want to join us?" Lou's eyes blazed bright and hopeful.

"Don't think so, kids. I flunked Home Ec."

Amy appeared horrified. "How do you flunk Home Ec?"

"Oh, skip class, burn holes in tea towels, sabotage cookies, you know."

Seeing their expressions, Beth concluded they didn't.

Lou's forehead furrowed. "How do you 'sabotage' cookies?"

"Easy enough." Beth pulled up a chair to the circle. "You make them with marijuana butter. The teacher had been flunkin' me all year and I'd been counterfeitin' my grades. Just takes one stroke to turn an F into an A, you know. So I figured before Nick got too suspicious, I'd get her fired."

The story produced only baffled looks. Beth went on: "So she had to evaluate everyone's cookies, our final project. So I slipped one of mine in everywhere I could and she must've eaten several of 'em, had to be stoned all day. But instead of her gettin' fired, I got suspended from school, grounded by Nick and Steve and had to retake the course."

"Quite a story, Beth." While Amy spoke, Lou and Heidi smiled politely; no one laughed. With her luck, Lou's friends were probably studying to be Home Ec teachers.

"Such a place you've got here." Heidi gestured at the makeshift wall unit of appliances. "They didn't used to allow all this when I lived in a dorm."

"Feel free to use anything," Beth jumped in, aware that most of it still wasn't allowed and hoping that Lou didn't know or care. "There's the TV, we could make popcorn, there's beer and wine in the fridge." Beth went to the closet, stood on her desk chair and pulled out a bottle from an upper closet shelf. "And Russian vodka, if anyone'd like a taste."

"Thanks but no thanks," said Heidi. "Diet."

"Diet," echoed Amy. "Besides, I hardly ever drink."

Beth expected Lou to echo "diet." She was the one who needed it the most.

"If I'm not alert, I'll miss a stitch," Lou said.

"A little music, anyone?" Beth began to imitate a dance.

"If you want, Beth." Lou looked up while stitching. "Don't let us stop you."

"Whatever you guys want," Beth said and sat back on her bed while the three stitched in silence. Her alcoholic Friday night had hardly been enjoyable. A booze-free Saturday night could prove no worse. She watched the three Milkmaids sew.

And this was a "Top Ten Party School?" Maybe she hadn't met the right people so far. No, not "maybe." Definitely.

"Oops! My needle came unthreaded!" cooed Heidi. "Come on, Beth. Give it a try. You couldn't be any worse than me."

Though thoroughly out of her element, Beth had nothing else to do. "OK. Wanna bet?" She grinned with mischief and saw Lou eye her warily.

13

The crisp, early October air invigorated Cissy more than the forceless spray of water that passed for a shower at home. It was Friday morning; she waited at the bus stop a block from home. She looked down: Dew dotted the ground.

The bus named "Burr Oaks" arrived. The first time she'd heard it, she'd understood "Baroques" bus. Since then, she'd seen enough baroque people in Madison to fill more than one. Perhaps one of them could point out a burr oak to her.

She stepped on the bus and less than twenty minutes later reached

FAB. Its fifth-floor hall was dimly lit by cracks of sunlight streaming from under the closed doors of those whose privilege conferred them a better view than hers. The dark halls once again reminded her of a giant mausoleum. She pictured professors' doors, with nameplates reading "Published," "Perished," or "Published but Perished." Wilhelmina's distant pecking of typewriter keys was the only sign of life on the floor. Cissy had fifty minutes in which to review her notes accompanying slides on the architecture of North American museums.

The quiet, though lending to concentration, was baffling. How could a university of 44,000 students appear so abandoned, its halls so spectral, on a class day? True, the only faculty member she ever saw at this hour was Vance Rickover, who taught at the hour widely held as ungodly: 7:45. His office hour followed until 9:30 and, accurate as clockwork, at 9:31 he would show up at her door. His presence always signaled the ten-minute warning before she had to leave to go teach.

On schedule, Rickover appeared, in a maroon shirt and red plaid pants, an affront to the university's official colors. "Pankhurst! What time is it?"

"Why, 9:31, as usual."

"Oh, you have the sixth sense too! We're two of a kind, Pankhurst, I swear! You just told me it was 9:31 without even looking at your watch. Amazing."

"But..." Cissy began to protest. She and Rickover were not two of any kind.

"You're right, Pankhurst. It's 9:31, not 9:32." Rickover pushed his watchface up to his own. "Well, now it's 9:32, not 9:33, but it was 9:31 when I came in. You'll confirm that, won't you?"

"Well, yes, but I don't see..."

"The point is, the FAB clocks are all one minute fast. My recruits think they're arriving at 7:44 and they are, but the clocks register 7:45. So my recruits are late, I have to stop to take attendance, and we lose class time. It's a disgrace, Pankhurst. A major university like this whose clocks can't even give you the correct time of day!"

"Maybe you could..."

"I've talked to Sumner and Davidine about this. If I don't get results, I'll go all the way to the Chancellor!" He balled up his fist, threatening punches at the air. "Rest assured that I'll do what it takes, Pankhurst. No one else here has inner clocks like you and I, but simply believe what the university and its timepieces tell them." He shook his head gravely. "I sometimes fear we're sailors on a sinking ship here."

Cissy's lips curled into a smile at the inevitable military metaphor.

"Just about time to go drill your battalion, isn't it? So I'll be off. We wouldn't want you to be late." Rickover gave a semi-salute and backed out the door.

Cissy had fallen to daydreaming, picturing a high-seas battle among waterlogged universities and departments, when a bang startled her out of her reverie.

A shooting in the main office? A boiler blast from the bowels of FAB? She heard it again, tentatively identified it as a clash of cymbals.

Cymbals? Had the marching band stormed the halls of FAB? Or were students engaged in some sort of demonstration against classes on Friday?

Langdon Street, home of fraternity and sorority row, buzzed early for a Friday morning. After the weekend's Thursday night kickoff, scooting out of bed before eleven marked a true rarity.

Homecoming Weekend. By 9:15, Langdon Street's fraternities and sororities had nonetheless revved up for this morning's Homecoming Queen and King announcements.

Partied-out from the night before, Betsy Johns, the sandal-dropper of Introduction to Museums, waited anxiously in front of the Union. Her roommate, already a member of the Homecoming Court, stood a chance of being Queen.

As the Greeks readied themselves next to the Union to announce their royalty, Betsy saw members of the Boom Box Band converge on Library Mall for their selection of the Boom Bosom Queen. Uniformed band members synchronized their boom boxes to the appropriate wavelength, where a local radio station was playing their selected tunes. Other members, armed with cymbals, clanged away, making it hard for Betsy to hear.

Local media soon deserted the official festivities to film the Boom Boxers. As soon as her roommate lost, Betsy wandered away. Five balloon-bosomed band members mounted the concrete podium, as their drum major announced the runners-up. Class-bound students stopped, filling the mall. Betsy looked back at the Greeks' pageant, whose observers, like she, had trickled over to check out the hubbub, leaving the official ceremony with a skeletal crowd.

As the Boom Buxom Queen was announced, a Holstein cow shuffled down a plank from a nearby truck and was led up to carry away the winner. Cow and Queen led the Boom Box Parade up State Street, as band members marched behind with their tuned-in frequencies. Out belted "Old MacDonald Had A Farm," to which they sang along, substituting sorority names for animal noises. The collective ire of the Greeks spiraled, Betsy's too.

The phalanx of Boom Boxers weaved up State Street. A few Greeks threatened to go at them with rocks. Others, she saw in the distance, entered a bar and came out with pitchers of beer, dyed red for Homecoming, with which to douse the unofficial Queen.

Waylaid from going to class, Betsy observed the dousing. Since she was out of bed and too hungover to think of drinking more, she decided to check out Museums, in spite of her "Never on Fridays" motto.

At 9:55 — or was it 9:54? — the bell rang, signaling the start of Cissy's class. Could there be something to what Rickover had said? There had to be over 100 absences.

"It's Homecoming!" a student announced cheerfully from the front row. "That's why no one's here."

Cissy shook her head, bewildered. "I thought the alumni came home, not the students went away."

Five minutes into her slide talk, ten latecomers had straggled in, each banging the door, each bang heightening her annoyance. At the eleventh bang, Cissy recognized the sandal-dropper, who deposited herself in a front-row seat. Within ten minutes Cissy heard snores, then the plunk of a sandal to the floor.

After class, Betsy Johns ambled out aloofly. Cissy considered calling her aside. Perhaps she had nighttime insomnia or daytime narcolepsy. Cissy vowed to talk to her the next time it happened.

It was 11:00 and her office hour. Within two minutes, a knock came at her door. Her colleague Evan Schultz popped inside and Cissy felt herself brighten. She'd been hoping to get to know him better, away from Ginger. If ubiquity existed, it had crystallized in her.

"Hi, Evan." She tried not to sound overly eager.

He took a few steps inside. "How's it going?"

Outside her open door, she heard a rat-a-tat-tat of high heels gouging the floor. Ginger appeared panting in the doorway and gasped, "Cissy! Did you hear the news?"

Ginger whisked inside and fell into position on the chair next to her desk: perched on the edge, legs crossed, elbow on knees. Evan, as if expecting this histrionic arrival, flanked her, a boyish, indulgent grin on his handsomely chiseled face.

"The only news I've heard is that the clocks are all off by a minute."

Evan swatted a lock of hair off his forehead. "Sounds like you've been talking to Rickover."

Ginger solemnly closed the door, then squealed, "Your job announcement is coming out today!"

A beat passed before it clicked in Cissy's mind; then her adrenalin began to flow. Ginger referred to the tenure-track job that would replace Cissy's lectureship. A job for which, she'd been told, she was the logical choice, provided she "perform satisfactorily."

"They've announced it rather early. I guess this means I'll have to get my updated *vita* together."

Ginger shook her head ominously. "That's not all you're going to have to get together."

Cissy kept up an optimistic front. "Why's that?"

"You obviously haven't seen the advertisement." Evan maintained his smile.

"Why, no." Cissy poured herself a cup of spearmint tea. "I didn't know it had been made public. Tea, anyone?" No one took her up on her offer.

"It hasn't," Ginger said.

"How do you know then?"

Ginger turned to Evan. "Evidently we have to teach Cis a few tricks."

Evan explained: "You talk to Wilhelmina, position yourself behind the typewriter and read what she's typed or the copy she's typing from." A hunk of hair fell over his left eye. "Everyone does it. Either Wilhelmina doesn't realize or doesn't mind..."

"Oh, the things you can learn that way!" Ginger jumped in. "Hirings, firings, salaries of new faculty, you name it." She writhed in her chair, savoring stolen tidbits. "Last year I found out they were getting rid of John Gitlitz, the guy you replaced, even before he did."

Cissy's eyes turned to saucers. "You did?"

Evan pushed back his hair, uncovering a blue eye. "It's been going on ever since Wilhelmina's been here."

"But back to the job announcement." Gravity laced Ginger's voice. "You might want to put a little shot of whiskey into that tea, Cis."

"To the point, Ginger," Evan said dryly.

"Right." Ginger smoothed her dress, checked her makeup in her compact mirror, then raised it and studied her hair, as though preparing to go center-stage and announce an Oscar winner, not a job description in Cissy's office. "Listen to this. It's a tenure-track Assistant Professorship all right, but listen to this.''

"We're listening, Ging." Evan winked at Cissy over Ginger's head.

Ginger stood up, only lacking a microphone, and got to the point: "They want three years of full-time teaching experience and substantial publications." This announced, she sat back down.

Cissy's smile melted; her heart skipped a beat. She'd never considered the possibility that she might be effectively written out of the pool of applicants.

Ginger took over, a battle plan drawn up. "So, one: You're going to publish your ass off, girl."

"Girl!" Cissy snorted, without explaining. So some Madisonians did say it...

"Two: How much teaching experience do you have?"

"I was a full-time lecturer two years ago in graduate school. Plus this year, that makes two."

"Keep going."

"I'm afraid that's it."

"How about publications?" Evan's blue eyes rained charm.

"I've got one article almost finished. Actually it's been accepted for publication, though I haven't submitted it yet."

"Accepted for publication, but not submitted yet! Ev, I think she's the one who needs to teach us old dogs some new tricks!"

"Oh, it's nothing like that," Cissy interrupted. "You see, my major professor at Irvine is chair of the editorial board for *The Southwest Review of Archaeology* and he knows my paper."

Ginger batted her eyes suggestively. "You want to send him some of our papers? We can all use a friendly editorial connection."

"They always overwrite these job ads," said Evan, as Cissy's gaze darted from him to Ginger, who centered a pendant above her cleavage. "'Substantial' publications means two, with the intention to produce three. As for three years of teaching experience, they'll take what they can get." He threw back his golden mane of hair. Cissy thought he might neigh instead of laugh and suspected that he was purposely softening bad news.

Pendant in place, Ginger perked up. "Cis, why don't you go have a little chat with Wilhelmina? It'll take her the whole morning to type the job description."

All three snickered. Wilhelmina's typing speed was one of several standing departmental jokes.

Their laughter was cut short by an abrupt rapping on the door. Cissy and Evan froze. Ginger fell out of position, elbow slipping off her knee and flailing the air. Evan opened the door as they all assumed a studied casualness.

"I heard voices." It was Wilhelmina, clad in a sack dress that could pass for a tent. "I thought maybe someone would like to finish off this pot of coffee."

Rendered paranoid by contagion, Cissy let out a barely perceptible sigh of relief.

"No, thank you," all three protested.

"I swear, you people are already buzzed up on coffee or *something*," she drawled, then ambled away.

Ginger discreetly shut the door. "She knows," she said with a fatalistic air.

"Knows what?" chorused Cissy and Evan.

"Knows that we read over her shoulder and are telling Cissy and that we'd better be more quiet if we don't want someone to suspect something."

Evan's voice fell to a hush. "That's brilliant, Ging. But let's get going. How's Cissy supposed to find time to publish with her friends pestering her?"

Evan punctuated his remark with another wink at Cissy while Ginger examined a long manicured fingernail.

"Well, Cis." Ginger snapped out of her contemplation. "What do you say you write two articles this month, apply for the job, and we'll see you in November?"

After Evan guided Ginger out, Cissy let herself moan. Her job had barely begun and she had to think about next year already.

She wandered down to the main office, closed for lunch. She opened her mailbox from the outside and pulled out a memo.

Sumner had authored it: "As Chair, I have requested Professor Rickover to visit one of your classes and write an official evaluation of your teaching for this semester. The two of you should decide on a mutually agreeable date some time before the end of October."

Now Cissy groaned. The month had started off with a bang and showed no sign of easing up. To get her work done, perhaps she should start sleeping in her office and tell Jeb she'd see him in November.

14

Juan pulled his cab into the company lot at 10:00 p.m. and walked home, chain-smoking, since a city ordinance prohibited smoking in cabs. He'd failed to quit with aversive therapy, rapid-smoking, hypnotism, Smokenders, The American Cancer Society, the Wisconsin Lung Association and Nicorette gum. All that remained to try was acupuncture. The thought made him shudder. He'd tried smoking dried celery flakes, horehound, borage and comfrey as tobacco substitutes. All this netted him was nausea and a near arrest by a policeman inexperienced in drugs.

He fantasized about a relaxed, romantic night with Gil. Tonight marked their seventeenth anniversary. In months.

As he neared the top of the stairs, an avalanche of music hit him. He followed it to the bedroom, where it assaulted him full-force. If Irv and Pep were sleeping, it had to be with industrial-strength earplugs. Gil lay splayed at an angle on the bed. Juan turned Nina Hagen off and heard a raucous snore.

His eyes scanned the room. A bong rested beside the bed, a hash pipe on the nightstand. Around the pipe lay a Quaalude, two Darvons, three 10-milligram Valiums, a half-dozen Codeine pills, a handful of speed and caffeine tablets, plus several roaches.

God only knew which of them he'd taken. Knowing Gil, Juan guessed he'd taken them all. Only brownie crumbs were missing.

He laboriously rolled Gil over and lifted the skin above his eyes: beet-red, but free of contact lenses. Breathing and pulse were normal, heartbeat too. Gil half-opened his eyes, then passed back out.

Juan went to the kitchen to take vitamins and Brussels sprouts. He returned, removed his clothes and slid into an unoccupied slice of bed. As if to acknowledge his arrival, Gil farted.

Happy anniversary.

At 5:20 he got up to the alarm and the thrumming of rain. Juan shook Gil to ask if he should reset the alarm for his class. He remained inert; Juan set the alarm anyway.

Today, like many others, he drove split shifts, morning and evening. After four years, he still lacked seniority to get regular daytime shifts. PC Cab's overqualified and steadfast workers seemed uninterested in more upwardly mobile positions, content to be employed by Madison's only politically correct and collectively owned cab company.

He smoked a cigarette in the rain before spending four hours maneuvering around the rain-slick streets and inclines of Madison. When he returned home, it was midmorning, and a gentle drizzle still fell.

In the kitchen he found Gil and Dyspepsia playing an animated game of Scrabble with Alpha-Bits from a cereal box. Gil wore only pants and slippers. Dyspepsia's outfit looked as if she'd slept in it; perhaps wrinkles formed part of her ensemble. A smoldering bowl of marijuana rested at their side.

"Hi," he greeted.

Deep in concentration, Gil and Pep kept their attention on the game. Pep placed an A and P below a Z and applauded herself wildly. Gil contorted his face. Juan hung by the kitchen table as the two studied their letters. "Heavy night last night."

"Huh?"

"You must have had a heavy night. You were passed out cold when I got home."

"Oh, yeah."

"It was our seventeenth..."

"Whoever wins, gets to eat every one on the board," Gil interrupted, signaling the letters.

"...anniversary." Juan raised his voice: "Maybe I should sit on the board if you win."

Dyspepsia roared, catching the remark. Gil continued to study his letters and added onto the P in "zap" to make "pot." "Speaking of which. . ." He thrust the pipe at Juan.

"I think there are already enough stoned people here. Don't you have Cissy's class this morning?"

Pep looked at the kitchen clock. "Had."

"Do you ever intend to go?"

She answered again: "Nope."

"Do you give a damn if you flunk?" Juan stared her down, daring her to answer this time. Gil was sufficiently irresponsible on his own, without an accomplice. He shrugged his shoulders and said at length, "I'm gonna study at home. Weather's too nasty to go out. Maybe later I'll invite Cissy up for a bowl and see what I missed."

"I hope you mean of Alpha-Bits," Juan said, and left the room, the living room floor creaking under the heels of his boots.

Juan napped until three. Gil and Dyspepsia had apparently vacated the premises. Sun had replaced the rain. He put on a sweater, heated up coffee and took it to the porch to drink.

The air was warm for early October. He moved the wicker chair to catch the sun's rays, setting it down next to the Brussels sprout patch. His glance strayed over to Pep's half of the garden and he did a double take: Her tomato plants had been pulled up, her half of the garden cleared except for several withering stalks of corn.

He observed his Brussels sprouts close up. The bottoms of the stalks sported healthy, fat little cabbages that diminished in size as they went up the stalk. The outer leaves of the fatter ones had begun to unfurl, turning pale. It was the perfect time for his first small harvest.

His coffee mug drained, he fetched a basket and began to snap off sprouts from the bottom of the three dozen plants. His basket half-full, he carried the harvest upstairs to freeze before it lost more nutrients than inevitable. Clad in leatherette pants and a black blouse, Pep stood at the kitchen sink. Her arms were submerged to the elbows, green tomatoes aswirl in the water.

"Green tomato relish?" he asked, amiable.

She threw her head over her shoulder. "Pklz."

Juan's eyes landed on a recipe on the counter for green tomato pickles.

"Do you want some help?" he offered, to speed up the process and get to the sink quicker.

She answered without turning around. "Nope."

"Have it your way." Juan fumbled in his pocket for an ultra-light, smoked it and fumed. She'd probably timed her work to conflict with his. "If you could cede the sink as soon as possible, my Brussels sprouts and I would appreciate it. When you're finished, of course."

"Seed?" she squawked, throwing him a cursory glower.

"Cede. C-E-D-E. Use it in your next Scrabble game. It's English for 'to give up.' Not that you speak the language."

Pep snorted. Juan inhaled down to the filter, stubbed it out and began to prune damaged leaves from the sprouts. When he finished all he could do, he went to read the afternoon newspaper.

Twenty minutes later, she was still there. Dyspeptic Dyspepsia, who intruded on his garden space, his kitchen space and, now, even the mail.

Juan gnashed his teeth and let a hiss escape, drowned out by gurgling water on the stove. He observed his nemesis: Her clothing and hair highlighted the cadaverous hue, apparently natural, of her skin. Only her sun-browned feet softened the severity of the black-and-white contrast. He noticed a letter protruding from the back pocket of her pants. "So that's what you've been waiting for."

She circled around, eyeing him boldly. "What?"

"The letter."

She snarled in response.

"It must be important, since you've hurried every day to get the mail, which is almost never for you."

"Yep," she agreed smugly, and turned away.

Juan smelled a strong odor of brown sugar. She must have chosen a recipe for sweet tomato pickles. The sweetness permeated the kitchen, combating the aggressive stench of the vinegar. Or of her feet.

"What's on the stove, anyway?"

Dyspepsia glared, stomped to the stove and tried without success to hoist the pot. Juan walked over and peered in. "What are you doing? Boiling your pickling solution? Anyone knows you don't have to boil it."

"Huh?"

Juan repeated.

"Fuck!" Pep aimed stiletto eyes at him and marched off.

Annoyed, he turned off the flame under the burner and heard her slam Irv's bedroom door. Then came another rumbling of doors. About to urge her to return, he saw Irv and Seth Reubenstein appear in the living room.

"We won!" Irv announced, his tousled black hair almost standing on end.

"Congratulations! Rube, How are you?" Juan greeted. "I haven't seen you in ages."

Nor had Seth changed in ages. He entwined his hand in Juan's. He still wore his POW bracelet from the early seventies; it seemed a miracle the copper hadn't permanently colored his wrist green.

"Now that I've won, I'm gonna file a harassment suit against her," Seth proclaimed.

"You've always been a feisty son of a bitch, Rube," Juan joked.

"A little victory celebration, Juan." Irv went to the refrigerator and surveyed the beer supply. "Homemade or Point, Seth?"

"Either's fine."

Irv clenched a bottle and a canning jar in his fists and let Seth choose. He went for the bottle. "Where's Pep?" Irv asked.

"She just stormed into the bedroom. When I told her she didn't need to boil the pickling solution, she deserted her would-be pickles."

"Let me go check on her."

Juan knew that the last thing Irv wanted was for Seth to witness a scene. Unable to load his Brussels sprouts into the occupied sink, he grabbed a beer and sat down, glad enough to occupy Seth.

"So now you're going to sue her, huh?"

"Keeps Irv in business, you know."

And he'd gladly do without yours, Juan thought, knowing that Irv considered Seth a mild pain in the ass. He heard escalating voices coming from Irv's bedroom. Dyspepsia screamed Juan's name. A shiver crept up his spine.

"Good to get that anger out," Seth quipped, and they heard Dyspepsia yell, "Done!"

"Done with what, I wonder," Seth thought aloud.

"Done with the garden, I suppose," Juan said unconvincingly, pondering what she really did mean. Done with Madison, done with Irv or done with Juan himself?

Such speculations raised his spirits. He smiled thinly, perversely pleased.

15

At dusk Roz and Erva Mae bicycled home from the organizational meeting for the Fall Female Festival, the feminist version of Halloween. Always prepared for any contingency, they were about as bicyclically well-equipped as any two women could be: lights, mirrors, chains, reflectors, helmets, gloves, water bottles and anti-rape whistles. Roz's bike had a horn; Erva Mae found a verbal beep more effective, at least for pedestrians. For self-defense, she also kept a vial of Mace in her pocket, and a miniature nightstick and a wire hairbrush in her backpack.

As they were cycling toward Monona Bay, a car door up ahead opened into their path.

In the lead, Erva Mae swerved. "Pigfucker!"

Whizzing by behind her, Roz saw the astonished door-opener and tried to pretend she wasn't with Erva Mae.

"That'll teach 'im!" Erva Mae boomed when Roz caught up.

"I thought you said profanity promoted anti-woman violence," Roz panted.

"At times you have to give men a dose of their own patriarchal crap," Erva Mae retorted, slowing to a stop where the causeway bisected Lake Monona and its bay.

"Bullshit," Roz muttered, as they waited for the light to change.

"There you go, using male expletives again."

"Then you should have said 'Sowfucker,'" Roz countered.

Erva Mae sneered in response.

Roz knew they both should have kept their damned mouths shut, a task at which neither excelled. "Let's devote our attention to the road."

They biked onto John Nolen Drive and breezed past choppy Lake Monona, wind almost buffeting them. Erva Mae beep-beeped her way down the bicycle path, clogged by unwary pedestrians. John Nolen ended, Willy Street began, and several blocks down they cut over to East Wilson, where railroad tracks went down the middle of the street.

They hadn't been bedmates for a month, dating precisely from the night of the cinnamon-scented soap episode. Erva Mae had suggested a month of healthy polygamy for both. Women, after all, weren't supposed to own each other. When Erva Mae's quest for meaningful polygamy proved less than fruitful, she announced her readiness to resume monogamy. Roz answered that she preferred continued abstention, and they'd left it at that. Erva Mae had given her a month more "to come to her senses." Roz knew that they urgently needed to talk.

"How about a pot of chamomile?" Erva Mae offered in a peacemaking mood when they'd reached home.

Roz heard the word "pot" and thought only of one thing.

"Roz, did you hear?" Erva Mae persisted, cheery.

"Yeah, I did."

"You seem a little lethargic." Erva Mae put water on to boil. "Since lately we've dedicated fewer energies to each other, I'd think you'd have more time for women's causes."

Roz perked up. It was rare that Erva Mae referred, even obliquely, to the change in their relationship, as if by keeping quiet, she could pretend nothing had happened. Disposed for conversation, Roz slid onto a kitchen stool.

"Well, I went to the meeting tonight, didn't I? That should count for something. Not that the Fall Female Festival is exactly a 'cause.'"

"A harassment-free post-equinoctial celebration certainly is a cause," Erva Mae stated. "And I still say it should be called the 'All-Female Festival,' not the 'Fall Female Festival.' Everyone knows it's fall, but we have to emphasize that it's an all-women event."

"Except for male preschoolers," Roz added, playful. Then, serious: "We could just call it a Halloween party and stop arguing about it."

Erva Mae went to get tea cups and set them on the table. "Of course child care is a basic right."

"Since we're going to be costumed, a man could always sneak in," Roz continued, frustrated but mischievous.

Watching for her pot to boil, Erva Mae distorted her face at this ugly possibility.

"Unless we institute a chromosome check at the door," Roz went on.

Erva Mae lifted the teakettle off its flame and grimaced. "I wish the Latinas would listen to reason about the music. Can you imagine? Ronnie Gilbert, Holly Near, Jasmine and Sweet Honey, mixed with salsa! I know it's a pluricultural event and I respect their right to their own cultural representation, but still... Don't they know that salsa, being a dominant cultural force, is a product of the patriarchy?"

"Evidently they don't see it that way. Besides, salsa is very in these days. What do you want, the Beer Barrel Polka?"

Erva Mae frowned; an idea seemed to click in her mind: "There is such a thing as 'progressive' salsa."

"In Madison and on WORT. It sounds like a misnomer to me."

"There must be women's salsa bands somewhere."

"I know of one."

Erva Mae looked up from watching the tea steep. "You do?"

"Yeah. The All Señorita Salsa Band. Led by Kay Pasa."

"Tell me more," Erva Mae enthused, obviously missing the pun.

"They're a drag band."

"A what?" Pouring the tea, Erva Mae almost scalded herself.

"Guys in drag. Led by K-A-Y Pasa. Get it?"

"Men parodying women!" Erva Mae shrieked, outrage bubbling. "Some separatist you are, Roz!"

"You forget. I haven't been a separatist for several years." Roz tested the tea temperature with a fingertip.

"I think I'm beginning to have doubts about a household with one separatist and one halfhearted one."

"There's no 'halfhearted' about it. I'm not a separatist and that's that.

I only don't invite my male friends here because of you. The least I can do is keep to the terms of our agreement."

"I suppose," Erva Mae huffed, and sat down with her tea.

"Listen, Erv. It's a nice night out and there won't be many more of them. Why don't we sit outside?"

"Sure," Erva Mae agreed, her eyes getting dreamy.

"And I can smoke a joint on the steps. We really need to talk about our relationship and a joint is just what I need for thinking and talking."

"Mother, Daughter and Holy Ghostess!" In dismay she knuckled the chopping block table. "You mean to say you can't even talk without having your substances!" Chamomile tea splashed onto her saucer.

"Our compromise includes nothing that prohibits smoking marijuana outside."

Erva Mae mulled this over. "If you have to have your substances, Roz, I can't stop you. But I'm not going to share your air. If we can't talk in here... ''

"What I have to say is heavy, Erv. The least I need is a cigarette, which you won't let me have in the house." Roz stared at the pyramids and palm trees on her pack of Camels.

"I've no doubt that your lesbian-feminist soul is pure, at least somewhere deep down inside. But if you can't refrain from substance abuse for a few minutes of conversation..."

"Fuck off," Roz mumbled, certain that Erva Mae, caught up in her tirade, didn't hear.

"You'll have to excuse me. I'm going to go read a report on comparable worth. And let me add that smoking reduces yours." Erva Mae trotted off with her tea.

Roz made a last stab at compromise. "You can join me outside later if you want."

"After you've stunk up the atmosphere?" Erva Mae's voice sliced the air. "No, thank you."

Roz was about to say, "It's a beautiful starry night out," but stopped herself. For a woman supposedly in touch with nature, Erva Mae certainly failed to appreciate some of its basic beauties.

In the cupboard Roz found her stash. She'd disguised it in a supermarket-chain jar of oregano, knowing that Erva Mae would thus boycott its use. Checking her pockets for rolling papers, she took the "oregano" outside. The constellations seemed to reach down to her. She tried to see how many she could recognize and found the two Dippers. Unsuccessfully she scoured the sky for Cassiopeia.

As she sat down on the crumbling stoop steps, a piece of cracked concrete gave way. Roz watched the pieces tumble down the steps to the ground. Soon there would be little left to sit on.

16

In her office Cissy stared at the last sentence she'd typed. She glanced at the three-by-five index card at her side where she had copied her three reminder rules for writing: "1) Avoid the verb 'to be' whenever possible; 2) Avoid passive constructions whenever possible; 3) Avoid adverb abuse." Her most recent sentence had been dismantled, reassembled, disemboweled, reworked, then pared down to conciseness.

Wishing she had a computer, she sat in front of the Selectric typewiter and stared out her slot of window at the grey concrete. She had truthfully claimed on her dossier, turned in yesterday with her job application, that the current article was accepted for publication. It simply wasn't finished. She now had to put in it final form in case the Search Committee asked to see it.

Arms akimbo, she put her concluding statement through the same torture. A tad prosaic, perhaps, but it flowed well enough. She yanked the paper out from under the platen.

"Finish your oeuvre?" came a voice through the crack in the door.

Ginger stepped in, ensnarled in a mass of scarlet: dress, shoes, pendant, nail polish and lipstick. Only a matching pillbox hat was lacking.

"Pardon?"

"Your scholarly oeuvre," Ginger repeated.

"I don't know if it qualifies as an oeuvre, but it's finished." Stealthily Cissy licked off a speck of liquid correction fluid from her thumb.

"Oeuvre or not, quantity's what counts most." Ginger lowered herself into the chair as she spoke. "I've hardly seen you this month."

"You were the one who said I should lock myself away and reappear in November." Cissy smiled, mentally fatigued.

"Welcome to academia. You're in the classroom nine hours a week but work ninety."

She took in this sad truth, regarded Ginger and glowed modestly. "I finished my 390 Intro exams. That deserves a medal."

"Medal? Honey, that deserves tenure. I thought they gave you a grader to do that."

"They did. But I had to double-check the exams, figure out the letter grades, record them and deal with complaints from the 360 students who didn't get As in what used to be a 'Mickey Mouse' course."

"So Mickey turned into Mighty, that's all."

"But the students think that Mickey turned into Minnie, who should be a pushover. You couldn't have gotten into my office last week with all the students encamped outside to complain, bully and cower me into submission.

Between complaints I had to get my dossier together and finish this article."
Even talking about it made her feel tired.

"Thank God I don't have to apply for jobs. At least not until next
year. If and when they don't renew my contract." Ginger examined her ring,
a recent acquisition, she'd told Cissy, from her fiancé Melvin.

"And then I had to prepare for my teaching observation by Rickover
last week."

Ginger stopped counting the carats in her diamond. "How mean was
he?"

Cissy directed a poisonous thought at him. "He said I 'passed,' whatever that means."

"Sounds good, for Rickover." Ginger leaned back and jangled her jew-
elry.

"Late afternoon girl talk?"

Cissy jumped in her chair as Davidine Phipps peered through the crack
in the door. Ginger had violated her own cardinal rule by leaving it open. Was
"girl talk" a euphemism for "gossip?" Had Davidine Phipps heard them bad-
mouthing Rickover?

"Come in, Dean Phipps," Cissy sputtered, immediately remembering
that she didn't like the title.

If Ginger was a study in scarlet and black, the Dean was a study in
grey and white: grey tweed suit, grey shoes and greying hair. "My, we're here
awfully late today, aren't we? Since I'm up in the dean's office so much, I
hardly get to fraternize with my own department. Or, in this case, I suppose
I should say 'sororize.'"

Cissy and Ginger smiled dutifully. Ginger acted the paragon of hu-
mility, seemed ready to bow before royalty.

Davidine threw a look behind her into the empty halls. "As usual, the
men have gone home. No one can say we women don't hold up our half of
the department."

"Indeed they can't," said Ginger, right on cue, and batted her eyelashes, almost flirtatious.

"In the old days, the department seemed to be one nice, big, happy
family," Davidine reminisced. "Nowadays, I wonder." She seemed to ponder
an unsavory thought. "I take it, Cissy, that your job application came in by the
deadline. I haven't seen any of them yet, but assume Sumner's burrowed them
all away somewhere in his office."

"I delivered it personally yesterday morning."

"Just making sure. I thought I'd say hello. I'm off now to a meeting."

Ginger's effusive good-bye drowned out Cissy's; the Dean strode purposefully out of the office.

After a moment, Ginger closed the door silently. "Meeting," she scoffed. "At this hour of the day, all she's going to meet is a brandy and seven."

Cissy thought the comment spiteful and was inclined to doubt its veracity.

"I wonder, what did this little visit mean?" Ginger sat back, as if ready to indulge in seamy conjecture.

"Did it *mean* something?"

"Around here, everything means something," Ginger asserted. "Or maybe she's just looking out for your welfare. It's rare around here, but it does happen. It's time to go myself. See you, Cis."

Ginger waltzed away. Cissy inserted her completed article in a folder, inserted the folder in her briefcase and slammed her door shut, homeward bound.

On the bus home she noticed the trees' change from multicolored lusciousness a month ago to their current leaflessness. The drop in temperatures had barely registered. Oblivious to the world, she might have well spent October as a cloistered nun.

Jeb had returned from a day of substituting when Cissy arrived home. She thought he looked particularly sexy today, his thick brown hair sweeping down just above his collar. She'd been so wrapped up in her work that she'd put her sex life on hold. Tonight she hoped to rectify it.

"For you, babe." Jeb kissed her and extended a piece of mail. "From your department. Looks pretty official."

"I wonder what..."

Jeb arched one eyebrow, then the other. "Maybe they gave you the job for next year."

What could be so official they'd mail it to her at home? She attacked the envelope and saw a photocopy of her teaching evaluation. Rickover had mailed it to her himself, an apparent favor. Perhaps the man wasn't all bad. She began to read it, as Jeb observed, arms crossed over his chest.

Dear Professor Isaacson:

On Friday, October 11, 1985, I observed Lecturer Cicely F. Pankhurst's class, Introduction to Museums 101, at 9:55 a.m. Pankhurst's class was, overall, successful.

Let me, however, make the following suggestions for improvement:

1) Pankhurst should insist on a stricter attendance policy in regard to tardiness. She permitted twelve students (by my count) to enter the classroom thereby creating minor commotions during the first ten minutes of instruction. (Three of these tardy arrivals

could have been prevented, had the FAB building
followed my suggestion to set its clocks accurately.)

2) Pankhurst has to watch her spoken English.
Nervousness may have accounted for some, but perhaps
not all of her errors in grammar. (Errors common to
the masses, but not to academicians.)

3) Pankhurst could use some elocution lessons,
perhaps. Her lecturing voice does not carry well.
I, as did several rows of students, had difficulty
hearing her at times.

4) Something needs to be done to prevent students
from falling asleep. (A faculty cattle prod,
perhaps?) While Pankhurst did show enthusiasm for
her subject, she failed to snag at least three, whom
I caught dozing.

I recommend that Pankhurst be reobserved Spring Semester,
to see how she is progressing with these difficulties. The class, however, was
quite passable for a beginner.

Sincerely,
Vance R. Rickover
Associate Professor

Cissy's face pinkened, reddened, then purpled. A vein throbbed in her neck.

"What's wrong, babe?"

"I can't believe this! Rickover says my class was successful, then all he does is list my faults! Here, take a look!" She shoved the letter at Jeb, who began to read.

"Maybe it's not that bad, babe. He says you're good at both the beginning and the end."

"Which make up exactly two percent of the letter!" Cissy stormed to the dining room table and swatted at it.

Jeb puckered his face. "OK, let's say it *is* that bad."

"Don't be patronizing, Jeb."

"Don't jump on me, babe. I'm just trying to help."

"I'm sorry. This is just so... incredible! Why do I even want a tenure-track job in this department?" She flung her hands upward.

"I presume because no one else may hire you." Jeb ran his eyes over the letter again.

"The question was rhetorical." She reclaimed the letter and waved it in the air. "The nerve! To criticize my English! I've never seen anything so mean-minded and petty!"

"Welcome to academia."

It seemed the second time she'd heard the remark today. She sent the letter soaring to the table.

"Go ahead. Swear, babe!"

"I don't know how to swear."

"All you need is motivation. Your department supplies that."

"Rickover, you..!"

"Say it, babe. You'll feel better. Externalize that stress." Jeb reached out to touch her. He nicked her elbow and she shied away.

Cissy pounced on the letter and wadded it into a ball. She hoisted her arm and threw it with force across the kitchen. It sailed through the open bathroom door.

"Take that, Rickover!"

She wandered into the bathroom, Jeb on her heels. The letter had landed in the toilet bowl.

"Strong arm you got," he said over her shoulder. "Now flush it."

Her lower lip jutted out, childlike. "I can't. I might need it some day." She reached down and with her thumb and forefinger extracted the sopping letter from the bowl.

Jeb shook his head. "Learn to swear, babe. It's easier in the long run."

She wrinkled her nose in response, took the dripping letter to the kitchen counter and flattened it out.

17

Lou's German class took a Friday evening cultural outing to the Essen Haus, where they ate German food, drank German beer and spoke not a word of German that wasn't on the menu. Lou drank one stein of beer and felt pleasantly high when she got back to the dorm.

"Lou, kiddo! You're out late tonight! It's 9:15."

"Hi, Beth." Lou began to explain her "lateness" and her trip to the Essen Haus, but saw that her roommate wasn't listening. Beth paced, a burning Marlboro Light affixed to her fingers.

"Beth. Your cigarette."

"Oh." Distracted, she pried it loose.

Lou hung up her coat and noticed an empty wine bottle in the waste basket. "Beth, what's wrong?"

Her tone was uncharacteristically grave: "We gotta talk, kid."

"About what?"

"Are you fortified?"

"Well, like I started to say, I had a nice heavy German dinner. Just like home. Well, almost."

"I meant drink, not food."

"I had a stein of beer."

"Hey!" Beth let out a low whistle. "And the kid's still standing." She stood back as if to admire this feat. "Whaddya say we hit the bars? Have a couple belts and talk about it there?"

Hit the bars. Have a couple belts. Beth made it almost sound dangerous.

Lou had nothing else planned and no particular academic pressure. Heidi and Amy had left town for the weekend. Going out with Beth tonight might stave off a bout of homesickness. Besides, wasn't it time she got to know her roommate a little better? "Sure, I'll go."

"Great!"

They headed through the cool fall night to a State Street bar. Judging by the number of Greek letters adorning shirts and jackets, they had entered a frat hangout. They sat at the bar; Beth ordered a glass of Burgundy and Lou decided on a beer.

"Next round let's both order somethin' with a little more pizzazz." Beth pulled out money to pay. "On me." She nestled into the red plastic of the stool and tasted her wine. "I got good news and bad news, kiddo. Good news is Nick sent me next month's allowance after I notarized my six-week grades for her. She could hardly believe 'em. Me neither, for that matter."

Beth had been elated. After she discounted the F in Telugu, which she'd promptly dropped, her GPA had zoomed up to a 3.00. Lou herself had been pleased with her own 3.50. Beth only had to hide from her mother the fact that, having dropped Telugu, she'd fallen below the twelve-credit minimum for a full-time student and had thus lost her student health insurance.

Lou inspected her beer and wondered how much she could drink before getting drunk. "What's the bad news, Beth?"

"Let's wait till the next round for that, kiddo."

The beer went down easily. Lou pondered what Beth's dilemma could be. Her usual concerns were money, grades and alcohol. Right now she had all three.

"Ready for another?" Beth tipped her glass and swilled her remaining wine.

"Sure." Lou could handle one more. She was actually starting to like beer for the first time.

"I'll order for us."

Lou heard Beth ask for two Long Island Iced Teas and her spirits deflated.

"Iced tea? I thought you meant alcohol."

"I did. Just wait. You'll like it."

Lou tried in vain to see what the bartender concocted. He set the drinks in front of them and Beth again insisted on paying. Was she trying to indebt her to her? Or was this simple goodwill and generosity? She sipped at the tall drink. "Gee, this goes down smoothly."

Beth's lips curled devilishly. "Damned right it does."

"What's in it?"

"What's not?"

Lou began to feel oddly carefree. Though the drink didn't even taste of alcohol, it gave her a boost. "So what's the bad news?" She felt ready to handle anything: flunked exams, parental hassles, boyfriend problems, even pregnancy.

Beth bolstered herself with a long swallow, lit a cigarette and put on a somber face. "Either we shape up or it's Streets City, kiddo."

"What??" The words didn't make an ounce of sense to Lou. She squinted up her eyes at her roommate.

"Dorm room inspection," Beth went on. "We flunked."

"Dorm inspection. We flunked," Lou repeated dumbly.

"Right-o, kid. Either we clean up our act or we're out on the streets by next week." Beth knocked back a liberal swig of her drink.

Lou fixed on Beth's use of personal pronouns and let the information filter into her mind; it took longer than usual. A bit of righteous indignation came out: "I didn't know anything about any dorm inspection."

"My fault, kiddo. I took the notice out of your mailbox. Sorry."

"You what?"

"Ripped it off from your mailbox." Beth raised her voice in defense. "I'm sorry, all right? I didn't get suspended from high school three times for nothin', you know."

Lou remembered the tales of the sabotaged cookies and grade forging. "So why'd we flunk?" Beth sent her a sheepish look and Lou realized she knew the answer. "OK. It's more like what isn't wrong with our room, right?"

"You catch on quick, kiddo. Microwave..."

"Coffeemaker..."

"Etcetera."

"Uh-huh."

"Right. And one week to correct the infractions." Beth downed the rest of her drink. "Let's have another, kid. We gotta work our way out of this."

You mean drink our way out of this, Lou thought dubiously. But her room, in violation, grew into an ugly abscess. She had no desire to return right now to the illegal premises. The House Fellow might come by and reprimand both of them. Lou found herself drinking up and agreeing with Beth.

"Two Bionic Beavers," Beth ordered.

"Beaverwhats?" Lou bellowed. Laughter sprouted up behind her. About to look back, she instead turned toward Beth, who covered her head with her arms on the edge of the bar. Had she missed something?

This time she saw the bartender pour: beer, one shot of vodka, one of whiskey, two of cherry brandy. Beth sat back up with money in hand. They toasted and drank. Though stiffer than the last drink, the Bionic Beaver glided right down. This time she tasted the alcohol and didn't even dislike it.

Streets City. A vision of the bag lady she'd seen on the Square galloped through her mind. "So what are you going to do?"

"I been tryin' to think." Beth stared off in the distance at a collage of sorority sisters, then back at Lou. "Simple. We dump the goods."

"Dump the goods." Lou pictured the dumpsters behind their dorm.

"Yeah. I was thinkin' of the Milkmaids."

"What?"

"Somebody who has an apartment. Somebody we could loan the stuff to. Like your friends from Ladyslipper."

"Ladysmith. You mean Amy and Heidi?"

"Yeah, the Milkmaids. Loan 'em the stuff for a couple weeks, then after we pass the inspection and the heat's off, we take it back."

Lou passed over the "Milkmaids" remark and tried to concentrate, her mind fuzzy. "Loaning the stuff out sounds all right, but I'm not so sure about taking it back so soon."

"We'll worry about that when the time comes. We gotta dump the stuff first." Beth's tone turned adamant: "Though I'm not givin' up the coffeemaker. I'll hide it in the closet when we're not usin' it. All they care about is us usin' electricity. Cheapskate bastards. An unplugged coffeemaker in the closet's not illegal."

Lou eyed Beth; her vision blurred. "I thought we were going to loan the stuff out, not cram it in the closet."

"D'ya think Amy and Heidi'll take the stuff?"

"We can ask."

"Great! Let's call now."

"We can't. They're in Milwaukee this weekend."

"Shit." Beth tried to light a cigarette, which fell out of her mouth, unlit. She began to retrieve it from the floor, but instead pulled another from her pack. "At least we got time before it's streets."

"Streets," Lou echoed dully. In a bout of lucidity, she added, "Yeah, it's good we have a whole week."

Beth knotted up her face. "One more detail, kid. *Had* a week. We got the notice on Monday. So now we only got three days."

Lou slowly processed this additional bad news, but, sufficiently drunk, it didn't faze her.

"Gottagotodajohn," Beth slurred, then staggered away.

Lou heard the bartender announce "last call." She looked at her watch. After a second, the hands stopped rotating: 12:45. He repeated the announcement as Beth returned.

"Last call? Let's do a quick shot, Lou!"

Hit the bars, have a few *belts*, now, do *shots*.

Numb, she heard Beth order two cinnamon schnapps before she could protest. The bartender observed the two of them doubtfully, but served up the shots with the warning, "You'll have to drink up quick, ladies." Beth shoved money at him before Lou could even approximate the location of her wallet.

"Aargh!" Lou groaned, the whiff of cinnamon under her nose. Half of her Bionic Beaver remained untouched. "You drink mine, Beth."

Beth downed her own shot and started in on Lou's.

"Time to go, folks," boomed a voice. "If you don't like it, go to Milwaukee, where they're still open a couple hours."

Beth finished Lou's schnapps as they were herded out with the crowd. They stumbled abreast down State Street, like two typically intoxicated freshmen their first weekend on campus.

Lou's head began to spin, her stomach to churn. The sensation was not pleasant.

Four blocks later they tumbled into the dorm elevator, their motor skills visibly impaired. As they reached the fifth floor, Lou began to feel queasy and clutched her stomach. In the hall, they seemed to stand at their door for an eternity while Beth fumbled for the key. Inside Lou collapsed on the lower bunk.

Beth landed next to her. "Gettin' under the blanket or goin' upstairs, kiddo?"

It took Lou a few seconds to understand. She stared at the bottom of the upper mattress, hopelessly distant. "Can't make it."

"That's OK, roomie. I'll go upstairs tonight."

"Gooood," Lou muttered drowsily.

Several minutes later she woke up in the dark and realized Beth had moved. She herself must have passed out. She was still clothed and lay on top Beth's blanket. "Beth," she moaned, "I think I'm going to be sick." She heard a grunt in response. As if Beth could help, she repeated her words.

This time Beth anwered: "Close your eyes, rub your tummy, think good thoughts, and it'll go away."

Instead it started to come right up.

18

Roz sighed as she looked at the weekly calendar of events at Womynspace, where she worked part-time at the information and reception desk. She looked from the calendar to the glass-enclosed lobby, which revealed a chunk of dull, grey sky outside. It matched her mood.

Womynspace housed a library and held concerts and films. It held support groups for older lesbians, young lesbians, alcoholics, incest survivors and women with eating disorders. It provided services to rape victims and battered women and referred them to shelters. It did midwife and medical referrals and gave workshops on sexual harassment, home birth and pornography. It also held non-credit classes in herstory, astrology, Wicca, tarot, herbology, massage and healing. It offered every service imaginable except the one Roz needed: a support group for straight women coming out.

She picked up her work schedule for the next two weeks and saw that it conflicted with her job at the Co-op. "Hmph." Doubts entered her mind.

Erva Mae, as her immediate superior, made up the schedule. Was it an accident or a sign of their deteriorating relationship? Roz feared she knew the answer. So much for an egalitarian feminist workplace.

Among the papers littering her desk, she picked up a journal of feminist poetry and skimmed it absentmindedly. Venomous reflections on Erva Mae worked themselves into the verse. She read on, absent-mindedly fingering her "Solidarity" button in Polish script. The phone rang.

"Womynspace," she answered, as brightly as her radical politics permitted. It was a wrong number.

Seconds later, the phone jangled again. "Womynspace," she said, less brightly, to a caller who canceled an abortion counseling.

Hmmmm. Pregnancy, Roz mused, and the topic took a personal turn: Do my own maternal desires have anything to do with moving away from lesbianism? Do I merely want a child or truly want a man?

Restless, she pulled the local weekly, *Isthmus*, out from under a heap of papers. She blew her nose and saw that smidgens of grime were sprouting under her fingernails. As she held the newspaper, the bits of dirt magnified themselves accusingly. Forcing herself not to focus on them, she speed-read reviews of a Meg Christian concert and a Lina Wertmuller film, then flipped to the advice column, "Ursula Understands." Would Ursula understand her dilemma? She dismissed the notion and kept turning pages. The *Isthmus* personals soon stared up at her.

She read a few with interest. Casually picking up a pencil, she drew the biological symbol for female, followed by a Star of David. She crossed these out, replacing them with SF ISO SM.

Could SM be confused with S & M? She tried again, this time writing the words out: "Straight female in search of straight male." Then she inserted "feminist" between "straight" and "male."

Roz despaired at the question: Where were all the gentle, caring, feminist men?

She despaired even more at the answer: Sleeping with each other.

She told herself that this was nonsense, or so she hoped, and wrote on: "Age, race, religion unimportant. Radical politics..." She debated between "necessary" or "preferred." With some misgiving, she chose the latter. Good so far. Now what would she want him for?

"Must be gentle, caring and want committed relationship."

"There," she beamed. The bogus ad didn't look half-bad.

"Adrienne Rich at work, I see." Roxanne surprised her from behind, peering over her shoulder. Roz slapped her hand down on the would-be ad.

"I didn't know you wrote poetry, Roz," said Roxanne, friendlier than usual.

"Actually, I don't." Roz tried to stay cool. "I was just doodling. Scribbling, you know." She kept her hand securely on top the paper.

"I know," Roxanne patronized. "We all scribble and scribbling our innermost thoughts can be embarrassing when others see them. But if no one else sees them, they can't become literature. Literature doesn't exist without the reader, Roz."

Roz grunted in cursory acknowledgment. And if literature didn't exist, you'd have no teaching job.

Roxanne stuck her hand out. Roz shrank back, firmly concealing the personal.

"Come on, let's see." She placed her hand on top of Roz's. Roxanne was a lover of literary criticism, especially when giving it. "I promise not to be harsh."

Roxanne's hand bore down on hers. Did she think that her status as Roz's ex-lover gave her special privileges or what? "No. I'm sorry, Rox," she said curtly.

Slowly Roxanne removed her hand. "You really should come and read at the Womyn's Poetry Group, Roz. Everyone listens and participates by offering criticism for bettering your work while encouraging feminist expression."

Roz feigned agreement: "Yeah, sure. But my work's not at all polished. I'm certain it's quite different from what the women in the group are doing."

"All the more reason to attend, Roz. Variety is the spice of literature." Roxanne's eyelids fluttered; her eyes spangled.

Was it love of literature or ill-hidden lust she saw in her eyes? Had Erva Mae been blabbing to Roxanne, who was now trying to move in and get her back? She couldn't have chosen a worse moment, Roz concluded smugly.

"No one can ever discover your genius if you hide it."

"I'll take my fame à la Emily Dickinson. Posthumous."

"Seriously, Roz. If you ever want to show it to anyone, I'll..."

"Sure thing, Rox. You'll be the first."

Doubt saturated Roxanne's face. "I'm serious, Rosamond."

Roz bristled at hearing her full name. No one ever called her that except her mother, Roxanne and Erva Mae, and all three knew she hated it.

"Any time you have a piece ready, I'll be glad to read it for you," Roxanne gushed. "Why, all the years we spent together and I never even knew you'd been struck by the muse!"

Just like you never knew I'd rather have been with a man than with you, Roz thought. She asked herself if she really knew this back then, or for that matter, was even sure of it now.

Roxanne shrugged her shoulders, flapped her hand in a cutesy wave and strolled away, her tight slacks revealing every last bump and crease in her figure. You'd think the patriarchy still dictated her wardrobe, Roz scoffed to herself.

She waited until she heard Roxanne's office door close, then let up the pressure on her hand, its knuckles turned white. There lay the ad, pristine, but destined for an early death.

A violet trampled in its youth, she mused poetically, an impish smirk on her face. She squeezed the ad in her fist and reached her arm out over the waste basket. It hovered there for a moment. Then she flattened the crumpled paper back out, folded it in a square and inserted it furtively in her pocket.

19

When Cissy opened the door, Juan was holding out a flyer with an outline of Wisconsin linked to some vague geographic entity. "How'd you and Jeb like to go to a neighborhood Nicaraguan freedom movement with us?"

Were there Nicaraguans to free in the neighborhood? Cissy processed Juan's question again to be sure she'd understood correctly, then asked, "What does the neighborhood have to do with Nicaragua?"

Juan pointed to the decals on the outside door glass.

"Oh, how stupid of me. Wiscaragua. Wisconsin and Nicaragua, sister states." She'd also seen phone poles plastered with posters advertising concerts, poetry readings and coffees, all to benefit Nicaragua. Correction: the Sandinistas.

"It's tomorrow night at Ho Chi Minh's at 8:00."

"I'll ask Jeb. I don't think we have anything planned." Understatement.

Juan told Cissy and Jeb the "Ho Chi Minh Story" before they went out.

Named after the North Vietnamese leader as a protest when the City Council failed to rename a downtown street in his honor, Ho Chi's had always thrived. As other establishments born of revolutionary impulse languished and failed, Ho Chi's acknowledged that the sixties had ended and adapted to the eighties. As much as co-owners Ron and Emily Skinner-Rosenblatt had once hated the word, they had become *capitalists*. Not only had they turned their business into a success, but Ron had begun to brew and market his own beer, Mad City Suds, made from the absolute purest ingredients and, therefore, the most politically correct beer on earth.

They compensated for being capitalists by hosting numerous political benefits and served a variety of healthy vegetarian dishes. As interest in their "Marxist Reading Room" waned, the corner it had occupied now housed a pool table. In a rack on the wall, a copy of *Socialist Workers News* served as a reminder of the corner's original function. The owners had, however, drawn the line at video games. It was bad enough that many of today's kids thought Ho Chi Minh was a famous Kung Fu fighter.

Cissy and Jeb arrived with Juan and Gil and met Irv and Pep there. Irv was drinking a beer and Pep sipping an indeterminate concoction through a straw. A waitperson came; Jeb and Cissy ordered natural-flavored sarsaparillas, and Juan, a Mad City Suds. Glassy-eyed, Gil passed on ordering. Cissy imagined he'd probably taken sufficient drugs at home; he'd even had the temerity to come down and offer her a pipeful of marijuana one day when he'd skipped class.

She surveyed the patrons. Two or three long-bearded men in their fifties or sixties were treated as local gurus. Younger men wore earrings, ponytails and torn bluejeans. Bikers, punks and gays all wore leather, each, apparently, for their own reasons. Women's attire was laid-back and eclectic. The politically correct wore their politics on their vests, berets and backpacks. If the fire marshall imposed a limit on the number of political buttons as well as patrons, Ho Chi Minh's would be in gross violation. Juan adjusted the "Wiscaragua" button on his vest.

Emerging from his drug haze, Gil said, "Like I told you guys, Juan's PC. Don't let him fool you."

Cissy saw Juan put his arm around Gil, who wiggled his way out of its grasp. "This isn't a gay bar."

"But this place is liberated."

A tattooed biker with a beer gut lumbered past them.

"If this is liberation, I'll pass." Gil got up and wobbled away.

The drinks arrived and Irv insisted on paying. Pep snuggled up to him.

"Glad you two came out to get to know the neighborhood," Juan said to them.

Cissy wasn't sure she liked what she was getting to know. But she had to admit she was getting an education. She read aloud a sign from the wall: "We do not serve alcohol to intoxicated individuals."

"Yeah, but it doesn't say anything about intoxicated groups," Juan quipped. Gil reappeared with a creamy concoction in hand and sat down.

She noticed a commotion on the opposite side of the bar. Through the mingling throng she could see, but not read a large banner.

A head appeared above the crowd and the jukebox wound to a halt in mid-song. Mild protests went up.

"Sisters and brothers of Willy Street," began a voice that corresponded to the head. "I'm Rip Wilcox. Thank you for joining us here tonight in the struggle against US militarism, imperialism, racism and environmental rape. Ho Chi's has kindly given us ten minutes of time tonight to ask you to help the downtrodden in our sister state, Nicaragua." Cheers went up for Ron, Emily and the bar.

"The time has come for a daring deed. Ho Chi Minh's is about to be the site of a giant step. Tonight we kick off our 'US Out of Nicaragua or Wisconsin Out of US' campaign!" A banner crayoned in red and black was unsheathed and hoisted, proudly proclaiming the threat. More applause rumbled through the bar. Gil flashed a button that read "US Out of North America!"

Rip introduced various neighborhood residents who had gone to Nicaragua for their own fact-finding missions on the status of women, native peoples, gays, Jews, health care and forests under the Sandinistas. "...and finally, I know he's out there somewhere, Juan Bellefleur, of the Wiscaragua Society."

Juan half-stood up, gave a token nod at the crowd. "Who hasn't been to Nicaragua," he said, then sat back down. "Which probably makes me a minority in this bar tonight," he added privately.

"We're calling ourselves 'Friends of Wiscaragua,'" Rip went on. "Right now we're only in Madison, but soon we hope to be all over the state!"

"Good luck in Green Bay!" shouted Gil.

Laughter went up around the bar. "Tonight we'll be passing around petitions. We urge you to sign. We want to send a clear message to the Raygun that Wisconsin will not support his intervention in Nicaragua and that we're prepared to take a drastic measure —secession from the US— if necessary!"

The revved-up crowd hooted cheers.

"We need your financial backing too. We'll be passing around a hat."
Now the crowd cheered less.

"U-S-Out-Of-Ni-ca-ra-gua!" Rip began to chant and motivated the
crowd to follow. After a half-dozen repetitions, he switched to: "We-are-all-
Ni-ca-ra-guans!"

Swallowed up in the atmosphere, Cissy found herself joining in along
with Juan and Irv. Gil sat bored, drugged and smoking; Jeb, baffled; and Pep,
mute. Tonight she wore her nose ring.

The chant continued and Rip switched into Spanish, coaching the
crowd on *"Todos somos sandinistas."* Cissy deciphered it: "We are all
Sandinistas."

"I'm no Sandinista," Gil announced to the table. On cue, Juan glared
at him. The petition came around and Irv led off the signing. Cissy craned her
neck as it reached Pep, wondering if she'd mark it with an X.

When the crowd had barely mastered the Spanish, Rip again switched
the chant, this time to "We all want to nix the Ray-gun!"

Evidently more popular and easier, it caught on quickly, but some
sectors soon changed it to "We all want to nuke the Ray-gun!"

"No!" others hollered. "We don't want to nuke anybody!"

A shouting match followed on whether to "nix" or "nuke" "the Ray-
gun." Buttons on vests indicated a large number of anti-nukers, who didn't
want to nuke anyone, even their worst enemy.

Cissy signed the petition and saw that Pep had scrawled something
illegible. Pep inserted a straw in her nose ring and alternately grunted monosyllables: "Nuke." "Nix." Gil dozed off midway through his drink. Cissy felt a
little silly among the crowd, but enjoyed the atmosphere, so alien to the stuffi-
ness of so many academic social functions.

She saw someone motion to Rip that his ten minutes were up. Rip
paid no heed, as though it were petty to cut the crowd off amid such spirit. A
minute later, a bartender ducked under the bar and plugged the jukebox back
in, while the diehards tried to outshout it.

The hat arrived at their table. Cissy watched Irv put in a bill too large
to have Washington or Lincoln on it. Juan dropped in a Washington and she
followed suit, noticing that Pep had pierced a napkin with the straw she had
slid through her nose ring. More than anything, she resembled a mobile.

Proud of her donation, Cissy wondered if she would ever come to
feel like part of Madison or this neighborhood. Was this what was meant by
"community?" She looked doubtfully at the "community" at her table. Juan
placed his arm gently around Gil, who stirred, then began to breathe the deep

breaths of drug-induced sleep. Pep aimed her facial mobile at Irv and guided the napkin into his beard. "Crumbs," she said. Sure enough, several tumbled out of the beard onto the straw-powered napkin.

The political part of the evening over, they finished their drinks and roused Gil while Pep detached her mobile.

Outside Jeb encircled Cissy's waist with his arm. A glance behind her revealed Gil staggering down the sidewalk as Juan steadied him. They crossed Ingersoll Street and headed up to the house, Jeb and Cissy in the lead.

"That's strange." she heard Juan's voice from behind. "I thought we left the porch light on."

"Jeb!" Cissy screamed. "Someone's on the porch!"

Everyone stopped in their tracks. Gil teetered.

"Oh, that's just Menominee John," Juan said.

Pep let out a war whoop. Irv cast her a tempered scowl. Repentant, she smiled cherubically.

"He spends summers in Madison, usually sleeping on the streets, then goes back up to the reservation in winters," Irv explained. "Sometimes when he's drunk, which is frequent, he crashes here on the porch sofa."

"I see," Cissy said, not wanting to pass judgment.

"He's usually back up north by now. If you'd rather he not sleep here..."

"Oh, no." Cissy didn't want to appear ungenerous. "At least he's not outside our bedroom window."

"Sorry we forgot to tell you about him." Irv now wore a Wiscaragua button in his beard, Pep's work. "He's harmless or we wouldn't let him stay here."

Drunken groans came from the sofa. Gil seconded the groan. Still on his feet, he began to snore.

"If he ever bothers you, let us know." Irv led the way past him.

Cissy followed, Jeb shielding her. She hadn't even known that Wisconsin had Indian reservations.

After saying good-night, she and Jeb watched as Juan pushed Gil and Irv dragged Pep up the rickety stairs.

"If sobriety's a factor in getting to bed, perhaps we should make it easier and all switch apartments," she said to Jeb after closing the door.

20

For the first time since she'd received her teaching evaluation, Rickover planted himself in Cissy's door frame at 9:31 Monday morning. "Hello, Pankhurst. Good to see you, more or less."

What kind of greeting was this? More or less good to see you?

As if prompted by her quizzical gaze, he explained: "It's not that it's not good to see you, but I can only more or less see you today." He took off his glasses and poked a finger through where a lens should have fit. "Last night I fell asleep on the wrong side of the bed and laid my glasses on a chair on top of a pile of shirts to go to the laundry. I got up this morning, sat on the shirts and heard a crunch."

"Uh-huh." Cissy began to picture this scenario, but judged it too gross for the imagination. Rickover rocked back and forth, his wrinkled shirt attesting to part of the story. His shoes appeared to be coated by cobwebs; his pants bore red ink smears.

"Pankhurst." He cleared his throat as a prelude to speech. "I trust you didn't get your feelings hurt by my evaluation."

"Well..." Cissy searched for an answer. He might have chosen a more appropriate expression than something like "get your little feelings hurt."

"We can all stand to shape up a bit before we become entrenched in embarrassing bad habits."

Cissy felt her temperature rise. Was he referring to her use of English? What other "embarrassing bad habits" did she have?

"Evaluation is simply a practice maneuver before the battles. As we all know, the seas can get quite rough, the big battles notwithstanding. So don't jump ship yet. Choppy seas and rocky ships abound. Later, Pankhurst."

He jerked his head good-bye and went awkwardly out the door.

Yale, she snorted, half-doubting his credentials. He sounded more like a product of the Naval Academy, but didn't look like one. At least there they learned to shine their shoes and dress snappy.

Strange types filled the museum field as well as academia. Combine the two and you got the super-strange: Rickover. Every Museum Studies Department had one.

But, as Jeb had asked her, why did she even want to stay here? Idly, she began to enumerate the reasons on the back of an envelope:

1) Convenient, since already here.
2) Easiest job to get, since they know me here?
3) Madison not really boondocks; many jobs in worse places.
4) Madison relatively cheap to live in.
5) Few other possibilities.

Thinking of her dwindling bank balance, she went back to number four and parenthetically added "cheap salary too."

Her department probably typified the majority: Almost everyone hated almost everyone else. She added another reason to her list:

6) In-fighting and incompatibility pervasive; here no worse than most.

Later that morning she still fumed over Rickover's evaluation and the "embarrassing bad habits" comment. The report was patently unfair. Since all senior faculty were privy to it, might they not consider it an unofficial part of her job application? It certainly wouldn't enhance it. Indeed she shouldn't sit back and take this, but rather stand up and act. Isaacson had office hours between eleven and twelve. It would be the perfect time to air her concern and get his perspective on the matter. She worked up her gumption and headed for the main office.

She knocked and heard Isaacson's bored voice say, "Come in." She straightened her shoulders, exhaled and entered.

"Cis'ly. What can I do for you?" His tone invited her to state her business promptly.

"It's about my fall teaching observation by Professor Rickover."

She waited for a response or acknowledgment, but got none. Shakily, she went on: "He wrote that my class as a whole was good, but mentions so many negative details, that the report ends up sounding… unflattering. I was concerned…"

Isaacson observed her inscrutably. Then, as if resigned to her presence, he motioned her to sit.

"I don't know if you've seen it," she continued, then, fumbling for words, repeated herself. "I was concerned…" She wanted to add "in light of the job I'm applying for here," but didn't.

"If it was done by Professor Rickover, I'm certain he turned it in, probably within an hour, if he didn't take his portable and type it right out during your class. Let me have Wilhelmina go get it out of your file."

He called the outer office by phone, and, getting no answer, stood up and went out. Several minutes later, he returned, the evaluation in hand. He raised his glasses up on his nose and read, evidently for the first time. Finishing, he stifled a chuckle. Cissy wondered if she was supposed to join in on the fun.

He lowered his gaze on her. His private joke over, his demeanor now turned stern. Cissy suddenly longed for breezy informalities, wished she hadn't broached the subject. "These comments are meant to help you." Isaacson's tone stopped just short of exasperation, as if having to explain the obvious. "Professor Rickover meant well, I can assure you."

If he did, he had a particular problem expressing it. Cissy groped for words. "I mean, uh, the report sounded rather contradictory."

"Of course, we'll observe you again next semester and have someone else do the report." Isaacson stroked his temples and scanned the evaluation again. "He does say the class was successful."

She directed an unconscious glance out the picture window. When she looked back, his eyes met her at breast-level. He raised them to hers, as if caught off guard. "It's just that some of the criticisms seem rather petty," she blurted out, nervous, and broke eye contact with him, focusing on the shelves of books lining the walls.

"Perhaps, yes. But you're just starting out and it's natural you want to do well and are concerned."

Yes, about the tenure-track job. Instead she specified, "The late arrivals, for example. It's hardly within my power to control the tardiness of almost 400 students."

Isaacson gave a mysterious chuckle. "Of course you're right. We wouldn't want you to lock out the latecomers, now would we?" He smiled widely, without the chuckle. Perhaps it was she who was supposed to chuckle at this rare specimen of department Chair humor. "Really, Cis'ly. You should relax and enjoy your teaching experience."

Enjoy, she snapped to herself. Isaacson was evidently exempt from the joys of returning 390 undergraduate exams, more than half of which were lower than Bs. She brushed her hair back and again noticed his eyes on her. "I hope you understand why I was worried."

"We all need outside opinions to make ourselves aware of things only others can notice."

The first person plural. How clever of him to include himself among those who might have shortcomings. She wondered when was the last time one of his classes had been observed.

"Look at it this way, Cis'ly. Your class was probably so good that Professor Rickover had to look for minuscule details. None of us are allowed to be perfect the first time around, you know."

"Thank you for your time," she said mechanically, and stood up, considering this last remark. Decidedly upbeat or perhaps patronizing? She supposed Isaacson imagined that now, the second or thirty-second time around, he was perfection incarnate.

He smiled, fatherly. His dapper silver-grey suit matched his temples. She suddenly felt a little guilty for her unkind thoughts.

"Is there anything else I can do for you?" The tone had turned gentle.

Now that she'd stood up to go, had he gotten chatty? Did he want her to stay? He continued to cast an approving glance on her. She felt both heartened and uncomfortable.

"No, thank you," she managed. Not wanting to appear curt, she hesitated, then mustered her best grateful smile before leaving.

The encounter left her confused. Perhaps the man was a decent human being; maybe she should take less stock of Ginger's appraisal of the faculty. As she walked back down the hall, the door to the women's room opened in her path. Wilhelmina shuffled out. "Professor Pankhurst."

"Mrs. Wiggins."

"Do call me Wilhelmina, dear. Are you by any chance coming from the ogre's office?"

Rickover's was in the opposite direction. "I suppose I am."

Wilhelmina shook her head. "Back to the lion's den for me. In any case, it's almost lunch hour, so I can escape again." She plodded back to the main office.

Wilhelmina spoke as if she were Sumner's prisoner. Ginger would have her believe Rickover actually kept his wife captive. Sumner was patronizing; Rickover, insulting. Ginger exaggerated, and Rutledge and Rothschild, perhaps smartly, avoided them all. Only Evan didn't seem to have odd or obnoxious quirks.

Davidine's words rang in her ears: "The department used to be one big, happy family."

Yes, definitely, used to be. She found it hard to imagine, even back then.

21

For Juan, cab-driving, drinking and Halloween didn't mix.

Begun in the era of the toga-party craze, the university-sponsored Halloween bash —with beer, bands and costume judging— had swelled in attendance from 10,000 to over 50,000 in a few years. In a "good" year, enthusiastic crowd estimates reached 100,000; students flocked to the bacchanalia from Minneapolis to Milwaukee, Chicago to Sheboygan and Duluth to Dubuque.

Partygoers reveled in the principal arenas, State Street and Library Mall. The few politically correct who ventured out were subject to beer spilled on their Birkenstocks, cigarettes singeing their beards and hands jostling their persons or tugging on the cords of their drawstring Indian pants.

Although some women now held their own harassment-free Halloween, Roz and Erva Mae still rounded up "concerned citizens" of either sex to brave State Street and document the depravity. The offenses were detailed in a report to the City Council in hopes of canceling the following year's debauchery —so far without success. Roz always persuaded Juan to record "moving violations." He dutifully agreed, though his own Halloween hassles generally fell outside of her sphere of interest.

His usual six-to-ten shift would go until two tonight. Everyone at home had left for State Street: Gil to terrorize it with his fraternity brothers; Irv and Dyspepsia to blend right in with their normal attire; and Jeb and Cissy to observe from a safe distance, if any niche in central Madison was safe.

Juan fetched his first party passenger, Sherlock Holmes, complete with pipe, chair and ottoman. Depositing Sherlock in an alley close to the action, he saw his second worst fear realized: The "portable" furniture stuck in the back seat. He turned off the motor, put on emergency flashers and called PC's maintenance. A light rain streaked the windshield.

He observed a slice of the festivities and in the mirror watched Sherlock gnawing on his unlit pipe. Trying to make out costumes in the distance, Juan saw a group of toga-clad young men enter the alley right in front of him and turn it into a sprawling pissoir. He knew the problem well, having transported many a reveler with bursting bladder: Forty thousand guzzled beer, while the portable johns could be counted on two hands.

Maintenance arrived and extricated Sherlock's living room from the cab, as the winners of the costume judging were announced in the distance. Too late to compete, Sherlock snarled, paid what the meter read and left no tip.

Juan backed out of the alley, barely avoiding collision with a group costume: a walking Madison Metro bus. He swore, backed into University Avenue and did a double take. Amid the walking six-packs, flashers and tampons, three bouffants bobbed above one body: the Supremes.

He next picked up Gandhi and five Hindu followers who had carried their guru on a litter, which he warily placed in the cab's trunk. Four rain-drenched admirers piled into the back seat, Gandhi and one of the entourage into the front. The cab hit a pothole, jolting them, and he saw his worst fear realized: vomiting.

Juan had his trusty vomit-cleaning kit on hand. He pulled up to a curb and two of the followers assisted him in the cleanup, while Gandhi continued to vomit, safe from the confines of the cab, on the steps of a nearby bar. At their destination, the young men apologized and among themselves managed to cough up a fifty-five-cent tip.

The dispatcher next sent Juan to Womynspace. Women who preferred to ride free with the Women's Transit Authority were notoriously small tippers. By now he no longer cared about tips; he only hoped that the he was included in the freeedom from harassment of the Fall Female Festival.

The Festival moved into full swing by 9:30. Roz saw Erva Mae scowl as a salsa tune came on. "How about a swirl across the floor?" She clicked her heels like a flamenco dancer, sidling up to Erva Mae.

"You know how I react to this music, Roz." Dressed as Carry Nation, Erva Mae wielded a hatchet.

"Don't be monolingualist," Roz teased. Not that anyone recognized her costume, she was dressed as Emma Goldman, with whom she'd always felt a political, if not genealogical kinship. "Concentrate on the rhythm and not the words."

"Roz!" Erva Mae raised her hatchet and her hackles. "I'm as in favor of linguistic pluralism as the next woman, as you well know. It's a question of patriarchal culture, nothing more." Her lecture finished, she softened her tone: "It's nice, though, to see so many women being women-identified for the evening." She pointed at all the same-sex dancers.

"I don't see as they have much of a choice. Nor do I see any straight women dancing with lesbians."

"You always have things sexual on your mind, Roz." Erva Mae chided, caressing her hatchet blade. "I'm talking about powerful woman-energy, and you're here with your mind on sex! Some people…" Erva Mae shook her head, then tipped it back and swallowed a swig of all-natural cider.

"Listen, Erv. Tell me every dyke in here isn't watching with an eagle eye to see who's dancing with who."

"I'm not." In her hatchet-free hand, Erva Mae strangled her paper cup, almost empty.

"Why don't we join all this positive woman-energy on the dance floor?" Roz figured that dancing would be a simple affirmation of some sort of coupledom. She gripped Erva Mae by the arm. Her remaining cider slopped onto the floor.

"Roz! Someone could slip in this!" She scurried off and seconds later returned with a rag to wipe up. The salsa melody wound to an end and a sextet of female voices replaced it: Sweet Honey in the Rock.

"Still dance with me?" Roz asked uncertainly, her eye on the hatchet.

Erva Mae surveyed the room and agreed halfheartedly. She tied the hatchet to a string around her waist and let it dangle in a large pocket of her skirt.

Roz led her to the dance floor. The month that Erva Mae had given Roz "to come to her senses" was almost up. Would she return to Erva Mae's bed, their bed? Doubtful. Broaden her definition of "couple" and pretend nothing had happened? Possible, but dangerous. Declare them no longer a twosome? She'd like to, but so far she'd lacked the nerve to do anything, except ask Erva Mae to dance. She only knew that tonight she wanted to hang on to something, to hold someone.

They finished the dance. As they abandoned the floor, Roxanne glided up to them and batted her eyes. As Cinderella dressed for the ball, she had even glittered her eyelashes.

Roz should have little trouble finding someone to hold tonight. If anything, she'd have to fend off Roxanne, whose brazenness had never before stopped her from horning in on couples.

"I'd say we've pulled it off quite nicely tonight, wouldn't you? Maybe you could write some occasional verse for the evening, Roz," Roxanne jested.

Roz sloughed off the comment, as Roxanne explained to Erva Mae: "Do you mean Roz has never told you she's a bard? I caught her writing poetry at the reception desk not ten days ago."

She bristled at the memory and Erva Mae shot her a curious look.

"Let's go for more cider," Roxanne suggested to her.

"Sure, let's. But I think I'll go for the drugs." Erva Mae and Roxanne glared, not getting or caring to get the joke. To avoid a sermon on marijuana or nicotine, she specified, "Caffeine. Coffee."

To her surprise, the two of them skipped off without her. Their body language seemed quite chummy for a Director and Assistant often at each other's throats.

"Lizzie Borden and Cinderella's wicked stepsister," Roz said to herself, alone at the edge of the dance floor. Rox and Erva Mae filtered through the fairy princesses, replicas of Susan B. Anthony and whiskered faces of cats undistinguishable from mice. A convenient way to hide real moustaches, Roz mused spitefully.

She saw the two of them fill their cups in the distance. Instead of returning, they hung at the other side of the room, chatting amicably. Or gossiping about her? Suddenly ill at ease, she wanted to disappear, then remembered the child-care room. They always needed help there. She headed off, passing on the coffee.

Rox and Erv, whispering in each other's ears, didn't notice her. A flickering light dawned on Roz. They couldn't be..? No, they must be discussing business. She went down the stairs and tried to remember if Emma Goldman had ever had any children.

22

The shouting, drinking and general antics where Lou and her date sat in the student section of Camp Randall Stadium baffled and distracted her. The stands resembled one large party, to which the football game seemed almost secondary. It provided an afternoon of exercise for players as well as fans. If cheering and jumping up and down for three hours didn't suffice, the fans could always rip out the bleachers. Rusty informed her that, in the past, some had.

It was Lou's first UW football game and Rusty her first date this fall. They'd met in German class and studied together. When he asked her out to a football game, she wavered. She wanted to see a game, had to gauge her study time and realized he might try to get amorous if she accepted. Finally she said yes and figured she'd take her chances, still viewing him more as a pal than a romance.

Next to them, Lou recognized the sandal-dropper of Intro to Museums, who sat with her date and consumed small bottles of liquor hidden in her purse. "How do those cheerleaders keep warm?" she asked her date. "All that jumping and yelling helps, but they can't even drink down there. Thank God I didn't make the squad." She tipped a mini-bottle of Korbel to her mouth.

Lou turned her attention back to the game. She didn't need anything or anyone to keep her warm; her extra pounds at least were good for something.

She looked down to the field. The third quarter ended as Ohio State kicked a field goal and took a seventeen-point lead. The game looked bleak for the Badgers, but most fans didn't seem to care. Lou was holding out for a fourth-quarter comeback.

Clouds blocked the sun and a chill wind whipped down into the stadium. Rusty edged closer to Lou and put his arm around her, as he had, like clockwork, at the beginning of every quarter. Each successive time he'd pulled her closer, extended his hand farther. Each time, she'd slowly worked her way out of his grasp.

This time Rusty's hand got all the way around her neck and lay above her left breast.

She recoiled. "Rusty."

He withdrew his hand. "How about a beer?"

"Thanks, but I don't think so." She wasn't about to facilitate a situation where Rusty could take advantage of her.

Sudden shouts went up behind them. "Body pass! Body pass!"

Lou glanced behind her and, startled, saw a body passing horizontally over the rows of spectators. Cheers and yelling intensified as the body neared their row. Instinctively she ducked, as those around her handed the body down, but she got a whiff of alcoholic breath as it passed. At the bottom of the row stood two policemen ready to intercept the passee when she arrived at the bottom of the section.

"Fourth-degree sexual assault," she heard someone say to her left.

"I did that once," the sandal-dropper said to her right.

So much for football. The true sports in the student section seemed to be drinking and sex. The game might as well be over. Lou hoped Rusty's romantic intentions were, too. She moved a few inches away to be sure he got the message. If Harold Steuerabend, also from her German class, had asked her out, things might be different.

Jeb had always been a football fan, not to mention basketball, baseball, soccer, golf and tennis fan. After two months in Madison, he decided to go a Big

Ten game, played practically in his own backyard, rather than to watch college games on TV. He acquired two tickets through a newspaper ad.

Who to take along? Cissy had no interest, nor time. Maybe one of his upstairs neighbors would be interested — if any of them ever indulged in anything so normal and American as football. He went upstairs, found them all at home, and announced a general invitation for any one person.

Juan and Irv looked at him as if he'd asked them to go to the moon. Gil simply regarded him with glazed eyes. Pep stared at him intently, as if visually undressing him. Or so he let himself imagine.

Irv fondled his beard. "Soccer's my sport. Less violent, more Third World."

"But what it lacks in violence, the fans make up for by rioting and trampling each other to death," Juan countered. "Go to a game in Latin America and you'll see."

Gil perked up. "Sounds like the football games right here. I already have tickets myself. But if you wanna get rid of them, I could sell them for you, maybe even at a profit."

"At most, I'll have just one to sell."

Gil shook his head. "Nobody usually buys just one."

"Cissy's not interested, so I was just looking for someone to invite," he repeated, ready to give up.

"Me," Pep piped up.

Jeb looked at Pep, Pep looked at Irv, Irv looked at Jeb. It was decided: Pep would go.

Early in the fourth, the Badgers scored, leaving them down by eleven. Deigning to notice, the crowd screamed as the football soared over the goal posts, the extra point pulling them within ten. Then again, Jeb noticed, the crowd screamed at anything, whether the Badgers were even on the field or not. The game had passed in a flash. It seemed no more than a half hour ago that the Badgers had first scored. Pep had remained silent through most of the game as Jeb explained its basics and nuances.

They sat nestled together, thighs and legs touching, warming each other in the chilly afternoon. Before he even made his first move, Pep put her arm around his waist. Now her hand inched up in between his sweater and his undershirt. Encouraged, he put his own hand under her black sweatshirt: She wore nothing underneath. This compensated for her overdressed exterior: Whenever she moved, she rivaled the percussion section of the marching band with her crosses, chains and other metallic adornments.

Her hand worked its way vertically up Jeb's side, her multiple bracelets clanging in an off-key concert. Cissy flashed through Jeb's mind; at least he could truthfully claim Pep was the aggressor. Her fingers went up his undershirt. They approached his nipple, caressed it and squeezed. Jeb's whole body electrified; he closed his eyes. He had never known that his nipple could be an erogenous zone and, apparently, neither had Cissy.

When he opened his eyes, time had run out. The Badgers lost, 27-17. He had always been a fan who never missed a play. Where had the game gone?

Those fans who hadn't been ejected for rowdiness, alcohol, fighting or body passing remained for the "fifth quarter." The band strutted onto the field, playing various songs, punctuated by a cheer to the Budweiser tune: "When you've said Wisconsin, you've said it all!" The fifth-quarter fans joined the cheer, an evident favorite. The performance over, they began to stream out.

Jeb and Pep remained entwined and unmoving. He wished they had somewhere else to go besides home.

Gil was always welcome at Chi Omicron Beta fraternity. Although he was no longer an active in the house, he was its most reliable drug supplier, and could always be counted on to take out the brothers' younger sisters who came to town. This often provided an additional release to satisfy his megasexual nature.

Today's date was eighteen-year-old Amy Arnesen, sister of his fraternity brother Buck, who had arranged football tickets. During the game, Gil had plied her with brandy. Now, back at the COB House, tap beer flowed freely.

"Hey, Bernie! Can Amy use your room to lie down?" Gil brandished a stein brimming with foam; Amy had been sent to the bathroom to throw up.

Bernie Clarkson came over to Gil, his own stein in one hand, his girlfriend hanging on his shoulder. She had been taken advantage of by nearly a dozen brothers, including Gil. She shot him an inebriated smile and Clarkson steadied her. "Dirk's in the room, isn't he?"

Gil had already verified the roommate's absence. "No, he's out walking the dog."

Bernie rested his girlfriend on the bar and beckoned Gil over to a corner to talk. "If she's just going to lie down, Amy can do that in her brother's room, can't she?"

"Loosen up, Clarkson. Let her use your room."

"You mean let the two of you use my room."

"Right. Somebody's gotta be there to help her if she tosses her cookies. I mean, uh, I don't think she'll do it in your room, but she's gotta have a place to lie down." Gil tipped back his stein and noisily inhaled beer.

Bernie drank, lapped foam off his moustache. "I thought she went to the john to throw up."

"C'mon, Clark-o," Gil cajoled.

"I can't have you laying Arnesen's little sister in my room. What if he finds out?"

"That's why she can't go lie down in his room. He'll get suspicious, even if nothing happens. Since she's feeling sick, we probably won't do anything anyway." Gil sucked down the rest of his beer.

"Don't bullshit me. I know you, Kreuzer."

"Just a sec." Gil walked back to the bar, where Bernie's girlfriend teetered, and shot her a lusty wink. He had a pledge refill his stein and went back to resume negotiations with Bernie.

"Arnesen knows I'm not taking his sister out just for my health. Besides, I'm doing him the favor. I gotta get something out of the deal besides football tickets. Might as well give Amy a little thrill."

"I'm sure it's little, Kreuzer."

"Fuck off, Clarkson, and give me the key."

Looking green in the face, Amy strayed back into the social room. Gil gestured to her to wait a minute and hoped that, if she had to vomit, she'd already done it.

"Listen, Clarkson. Remember the dope I said I'd sell you for fifty? I'll give it to you for forty."

"Thirty-five."

"Thirty-seven fifty, you bastard. Here comes Amy. Gimme the key."

"OK. Thirty-seven fifty," Clarkson grumbled and handed Gil the key.

Dirk came through the door with the house dog, Spike, renowned for his studded leather collar and for extinguishing lighter flames with his mouth.

Clarkson stated the obvious: "You gotta get Dirk's OK too. And if he gives it, you can only have the room for an hour."

"Shit, Clarkson, you got all night to get laid. I don't."

"One hour," Clarkson stated, firm. "Besides, Arnesen'll be back soon."

"OK," Gil agreed, realizing he'd better pull this off before Amy's brother returned. "But you talk to Dirk. If he doesn't say yes, your dope deal's off."

"Kreuzer, you son of a bitch." Clarkson went to prop his girlfriend back up on the bar, then to intercept his roommate.

Amy walked up to Gil, essayed a sickly smile and belched.

Gil put his arm around her. "I'll get you a place to lie down."

"Great," Amy whispered, melting into his thick, manly arms.

Clarkson returned. "One hour. And you deliver the goods tomorrow."

"If I can," Gil sneered, and guided Amy toward the upstairs rooms.

23

C issy's gradebook resembled a sea of blood. Each red checkmark indicated an absence in her Intro class. Today's totaled 49 and it wasn't even
a Friday.

"I hoped not to have to bring this up again." She cleared her throat,
nervous when she had to reprimand a class. "This is not a typical course and
attendance counts. When you miss slides or a tour, you can't copy someone
else's notes to get what you've missed. Attendance is irreplaceable and absences are inexcusable, except by a doctor. More than three unexcused absences may cause a penalty in your grade." The class let out a collective whine.
"I'm sorry, but that's official department policy. There are forty-nine absences
this morning, for example."

"You should be telling those forty-nine, not us."

"There are legitimate excuses besides a doctor's."

"Yes, I know," Cissy admitted. Students bombarded her with unofficial excuses: divorcing parents, sick pets, jammed door locks; depressed room-
mates, fraternity pledge kidnappings, religious conversions. But she didn't
really want to know why they were absent; all she needed was a head count.
"I know some of you haven't missed a class. But I can't imagine there are legitimate excuses for this morning's forty-nine absences."

"Forty-eight," announced the sandal-dropper, smirking, as she sailed
in through the open door. A surly look on her face, Betsy Johns plopped herself down in the middle of the front row, the popular aisle and back-row seats
already taken. The students regularly distanced themselves from Cissy, as if
she had some plague.

Angered, but not quite losing control, she realized she had to say
something else: "There's another matter that applies to some of you. I'm
talking about tardiness. It's quite distracting." A new logic occurred to her:
"Sometimes I may forget to strike the absences from my gradebook. So arriving late may cause you to be marked absent, you see."

Betsy Johns stood up. "So I'm late again. Shoot me." She fell back
into her seat, as the class giggled.

Cissy gave up and began the day's lecture. After class, she spent the
bulk of her office hour dealing with students who had overslept. She considered putting a sign on the door: "If you don't have time for my class, my office hours don't have time for you." This, however, would reflect badly on
her availability and professionalism. Instead, she decided to end her office hour
fifteen minutes early for lunch. She hadn't packed one; she'd have to go out.

"Are you sure you want to go out?" She heard a voice from the hall as she was putting on her coat.

She turned around, saw Sumner and panicked. Just her luck to run into him when she was skipping out early on an office hour.

"There's a nine-degree windchill factor outside," he said with sinister satisfaction, and went his way.

Relieved, Cissy glanced at her coat, a winter one only by California standards. Fall had ended abruptly; snowflakes had been sighted. She'd soon have to get a Wisconsin winter coat.

"Hurrying home?" said a voice behind her as she stood waiting for the elevator. "Two inches of snow predicted," Wilhelmina chirped, joyful.

Cissy had noticed the phenomenon lately: Unpleasant weather turned the most laconic Wisconsinite talkative.

She strolled earnestly into the cold. A speaker held a crowd's attention from the base of the elevated clock on Library Mall. She stopped to button her coat up as the speaker continued: "...some of you already have children. Many of the rest of you will. If you want your children to have a future on this planet..."

She felt a tap on her shoulder and turned around to see Evan. "What do you think of the nine-degree windchill factor?" she greeted.

"Pardon me?"

"Everyone's been telling me there's a nine-degree windchill factor. Maybe even two inches of snow."

"Oh." Evidently unimpressed, Evan smiled anyway. His thick blond hair tumbled out onto his forehead from under his hooded parka. "I don't notice it until it's about twenty below."

"You must be from a polar-bear climate," Cissy said, focusing on his handsome Nordic features.

"Minnesota, originally. Makes Madison look tame. It looks like you're not quite dressed for this."

She looked down again at her thin coat. "I suppose not."

"Are you passing through or here for the rally?" Evan rubbed together his gloveless hands.

"I was passing through."

"California's been quite active in the Movement. The anti-nuclear movement," he clarified. "Madison is too. Largest nuke-free city in the country."

"Really?" So not only was her house a nuclear-free zone, but the whole city?

Evan scooted up his sleeve to see his watch. "Five minutes before the die-in," he said with incongruous zest.

"Excuse me?"

"A symbolic die-in."

Cissy began to get the idea. Sit-in, die-in.

"When the emergency warning sirens they test once a month go off at noon, everyone falls dead on the spot. Just like in nuclear war. Then we all lie dead for five minutes."

"It's a good turnout for this weather." Cissy observed the crowd, better potected than she was. She supposed that her own exposed legs could be taken for a case of stupidity or hardiness.

"Afterwards there'll be a march to the Federal Building, protests, chainings to the door, arrests."

"You don't get arrested, do you?"

"Not always. The department doesn't much like it, but they tolerate it as long as I'm not in jail when I have to teach. Anne and I take turns getting arrested, so there's always one of us to take care of the kids. Want to join us?"

Cissy imagined herself locked up with the criminally handsome Evan and calling home: "Jeb, I'm in jail for the weekend. So watch football to your heart's content."

"The die-in, not the rest of it," he specified.

"You need bodies for the die-in, don't you?" Her own question surprised her.

"Corpses." A wry grin overtook his face. "But you can't die very well with a dress on."

"I can't?" she said, bent on proving her climatic endurance.

"You'll freeze."

The cold pierced her legs. "No I won't."

"Then die on my coat." Evan whipped it off in a grand gesture.

"Now you'll freeze."

"This is balmy for me."

"Right," she acknowledged, shivering.

"It's almost time. Get ready."

The sirens went off and some two hundred bodies slumped to the ground. Cissy fell into a sort of prone crouch on top of Evan's parka, thick and soft, and tried not to wiggle around too much. Gusts raced off Lake Mendota, lowering the windchill factor by the second.

Feeling slightly ridiculous, she craned her neck to get a glimpse of Evan. Eyes closed, he lay completely immobile, convincing.

Catcalls roused her out of her contemplation. "Just lay there while the Russians nuke us, you dumb sons of bitches." Evan hadn't told her about this. Embarrassed, she closed her eyes, wishing she weren't there.

"This country has to protect itself."

"Stupid socialists and commies!"

"Lay off 'em!" Someone came to the defense of the dead.

"No, let's go lay *on* 'em!" Scattered laughter.

"Let 'em freeze their asses off!"

"Hey, man! They're peace-loving. That's better than you!"

"Let the assholes lay down and die. Who's dumb enough to die before their time?"

Isolated guffaws went up. Cissy opened her eyes to see one of the dead resurrect and answer: "That's the point!"

Some of the onlookers applauded and began to insult the heckler.

It was the first time she'd heard from Madison's right wing. Could any of her students be in the surrounding crowd? She dreaded what they'd think if they saw her get up off the ground. More important, she wondered how many more minutes it took before frostbite set in. She began a furtive massage of her legs. Probably no one could see; she'd died-in in the middle of the protesters.

When the die-in ended, the dead revived quickly, some dancing a clumsy jig to warm their limbs. Cissy looked for the hecklers, half-expecting more insults, but they had dispersed, not about to confront the protesters on equal footing.

"Here." She held out Evan's coat and thanked him.

He seemed unfazed by the cold. "Thank you. Every corpse helps."

Cissy's teeth chattered. "Will you d-d-die-in all winter like this?"

"A few of us will. Want to go for some tea?"

"How about tea and lunch?"

"Sure." Evan grinned his boyish grin. "You're chilled to the bone. Put my parka back on."

"You need it."

"No, I insist."

Cissy complied. At least there was one gentleman in the department. One who didn't leer, stare or wink obscenely at her. And who was already taken. As was she, she reminded herself.

24

"Well, Roz, you've had time to think, haven't you?" Erva Mae sat down on a chair next to her and crossed her legs at the ankles. Her toe brushed Roz's foot.

Roz tensed upon hearing the unavoidable question. The time Erva Mae had allotted her to "come to her senses" had more than expired. "Yes, I've thought." She marked the book she was reading and prepared for the fallout. "And?"

Roz heard so much hope in the one word that it hurt. "It's not you, Erv."

"Have you noticed?" Erva Mae tossed her hair and modeled her torso for Roz. "I've cut out everything. Even the scented soaps. It's taken you to make me into a totally natural woman."

Although she'd phased out the scents, Erva Mae still reeked of vitamins. From the smell, Roz guessed that she'd added garlic pills to her repertoire, and not the odorless variety. "It's not that, Erv. The problem's me."

"Oh." Roz saw Erva Mae's face sour. "Roz, get some therapy, why don't you? I can tell you're having a separatist crisis. Or the two of us could go on a retreat and experience a wonderful dyke weekend in the country. What do you say?"

"I work the information desk. I know these things."

"I know you know, Roz. But sometimes we forget that these services are meant for us too, not just for others."

"The problem's me, not us." She glued an uneasy facsimile of a smile to her lips. An impulse to tell Erva Mae the whole truth overcame her, but she doubted she would believe it. "The problem's in my head."

"I'm sorry, Roz." Erva Mae's tone shifted from understanding to long-suffering. "For you."

"I'm sorry, too. For you and for us. That's just the way it is."

Roz reached over to give her a hug. Erva Mae shrank away and shrieked, "'The way it is!' But not the way it had, or has to be. I've certainly done my share."

"I suppose you have," Roz said soberly, watching Erva Mae clench and unclench her fists.

"'Suppose??'" Erva Mae's face went apopletic.

Roz sensed danger. "Don't let's quibble over semantics."

"Suppose??" Erva Mae stood up. "I've bent over backwards, Roz. What I haven't done to save this relationship!" She threw her arms up histrionically. Roz couldn't tell if she was going to gnash or weep. "Oh! My first primary relationship over! I... I..." Then, one last stab, holding out hope: "Are you sure you know what you're saying, Roz?"

She nodded grimly.

With a dramatic flair, Erva Mae left the living room and slammed the bedroom door. Seconds later, the familiar thud of furniture being thrown against the wall resounded through the flat. In between thuds, Erva Mae spewed invective, which, if Roz heard correctly, wasn't in the female form.

Destroy the walls, so pollute the atmosphere. Roz lit up a Camel.

Smoke assailed her eyes, as though bent on wrenching tears from her. She was determined not to let them come.

A day passed. Roz had to take that first step, to tell someone, "I'm straight." She likened it to support-group sharing: "Hi, my name is Roz and I'm a compulsive overeater."

Who to tell? Definitely not a lesbian. Lesbians would see it as forsaking the Movement, joining the Enemy, abandoning the Cause. A straight woman? Better, but doubtful. A straight man? Out of the question. A gay man? Gay men generally didn't understand lesbians.

But, wait.... She was no longer a lesbian, or about not to be. Gay men and straight women often got along notoriously well. The answer became obvious: Juan, who'd always accepted her, no matter what.

She called and he answered. Could he come over one afternoon this week, if possible today, to talk? He said he could be there in forty-five minutes. They'd have several hours before Erva Mae returned from Womynspace.

Roz needed something to relax her. The oregano jar beckoned, but marijuana could jumble her thoughts. A beer or two might loosen her up just enough. She ran around the corner to the liquor store —the Co-op didn't sell beer— and bought a six-pack.

"Light up, if you want. I've banished the chem-free zone for the afternoon," she said to Juan, sprawled on the thin rug on the living room floor.

"Sorry, Roz, I didn't bring a joint."

"I meant cigarette."

"Oh." They both lit up their respective brands. She handed him one of two beers she'd brought from the kitchen.

Juan regarded the can with curiosity. "Beer, not dope. A 'male drink,' as Erva Mae would say. This must be heavy." They flipped open the beer can tops.

"I'd guess that you and Erva Mae are having problems." Juan sat up straight and set his beer can to one side, ashtray to the other. "But you're always having problems. You wouldn't have called me over here just for a regular spat."

"Right, Juan." Roz sucked her filterless cigarette almost down to the end. She stuck a finger in her mouth, dislodging pieces of loose tobacco.

Coming out as a lesbian should have been harder, should have prepared her for this. But that had been a spur-of-the-moment act on the revolutionary bandwagon, and she merely a small part of the band. This was different.

"Do you want me to guess?" Juan asked.

Whether he was joking or not she didn't know, but a light tone of atmosphere might help. "Guess away."

"Let's see… You and Erva Mae are going to have a baby and want me to be the godfather." Juan paused, then slapped his cheek, mock-chiding. "Nope. It couldn't be that. Erva Mae would only permit godmothers."

''Goddessmothers, Juan."

He swatted his cheek again.

"We're not having a kid, Juan. We're not even having a relationship."

"You're not?" He glanced into the study, where Roz now slept, the bed visible. "You don't seem particularly upset. Then again, most people wouldn't be if they were getting rid of Erva Mae." A playful smile tugged at his unshaven face. "I never saw what you saw in her anyway, not that it was my place to ask or criticize."

"After Roxanne, I was looking for one thing: fidelity."

"Not to be disdained."

"Right. Up for guessing again?" If his guesses got more outrageous, he just might stumble onto it.

After a brief pause, he spoke: "You've decided to become a separatist again and are going to banish me from your life after today's ritual good-bye."

"Right, Juan. But I'll say Kaddish for you. It's been real." Roz reflected back eerily on her first coming out. When she'd told her mother she was a lesbian, she'd threatened to sit shiva. "Sorry, Juan-Boy. That was a bad joke."

"That's OK. I'll try again." Juan ground out his ultra-light. "Erva Mae is bisexual and you want a feminist man for a ménage à trois. Sorry, Roz. Count me out."

She shook her head no.

"OK, I'll try once more. Your mother's dying and you've decided to make the gesture and get married to please her. A marriage of convenience. On paper only." He sipped his beer, almost untouched. "Sure, I could do that for a friend. But one rule, Roz: Just in case you have bisexual fantasies, I don't. So we're not going to screw. If you want kids, you'd better adopt."

He'd come closer than he knew. The hour of truth had arrived. Roz took a giant gulp of beer and swallowed. "Juan, Erva Mae isn't bisexual. I'm not bisexual." Her throat felt like sandpaper, despite the lubrication. She cleared it and hoped the words would come out. "I'm straight, Juan."

"Funny, Roz. If you're straight, I'm Alice in Dairyland."

"Welcome to Dairyland, Alice."

"What??"

"You said it, I didn't. I'm straight. Period."

The blood drained out of his face. "You wouldn't bullshit me about something like this, would you?"

"No, Juan. Straight. S-T-R-A-I-T."

"I can spell, Roz, as opposed to you. This isn't some humorless lesbian joke, is it?"

"It's no joke and I'm no lesbian. And, Erva Mae notwithstanding, lesbians do have a sense of humor."

Juan's paleness went a shade whiter. "So you're really leaving the Church? Leaving the Fold?"

At least he hadn't said "joining the Enemy" or "abandoning the Cause." "Right, Juan. My lesbianism was only a political statement."

He looked truly aghast; his beer and cigarette consumption went into high gear. "You mean you want to screw a man?"

"You don't have to put it so crudely."

"You're certain this isn't another sign of the times? Everybody came out in the seventies, but just because the eighties are harder, you don't have to go back in the closet."

"I'm coming out of my closet. Nothing to do with politics or the times."

"Roz Goldwomyn goes straight! You're not changing your name back?"

"I think I can be straight and still be Goldwomyn. After all, I'm not changing my sex and I'm still a feminist. I know that for some unenlightened men 'feminist' equals 'lesbian,' but..."

"You're straight! You're straight!" Juan rocked on the rug, his elbow almost upending the beer. "Oh, wait till this gets out!"

"It's *not* going to get out, Juan. I didn't call you over here to have you write it up for the neighborhoood newsletter."

Disappointment filled his face. "Do you mean I can't tell anyone? Not even Irv? Not Gil?"

"Especially not an ex of mine like Irv. I suppose, though, it would be unfair to demand you keep it a secret from Gil." Roz picked up her empty beer can, set it back down. "Do you swear on your left ball to keep the secret, the whole secret, and nothing but the secret?"

"You can bet your boobs I will, if it's important to you."

Roz looked down at her chest and smiled wanly. "Not much to bet on, is there?"

Juan shrugged his shoulders. "Some men don't care if they're not big."

"Yeah," Roz grunted. "Just like some gay men don't care for big dicks. One-tenth of one percent."

"Don't exaggerate, Roz. I thought we were all beyond hang-ups about shape and size of our body and its parts. Don't worry. Everything will work out. This must be terribly hard for you."

Grateful, Roz wobbled across the floor on her knees to hug him. At least he didn't shrink away. She nuzzled her face into his shoulder.

25

I t was exactly one week before Thanksgiving. Although classes continued until the day before the holiday, some students had already taken off for an extended vacation. Beth told Lou that the three-day week would be a "non-week" and assured her that no one would go to classes.

"How about a Screaming Orgasm to top off the night?" Beth suggested.

Lou went rigid. She didn't hear what she'd just heard, did she? She remembered when she was eleven and a male cousin pulled down his pants in front of her in the barn. She'd fled in panic. Her urge to flee now was only slightly less.

"It's easy to make." Beth contemplated her closet liquor cache. "Vodka, Kahlúa, Irish Cream — preferably Baileys — and Frangelico. I'm makin' myself one."

Lou should have known. Bionic Beavers, why not Screaming Orgasms? She watched as Beth pulled out various exotic bottles.

Beth surveyed the quantities in the bottles. "Goddamned maids. Probably took a few nips themselves. And I'm sure they were the ones who ratted on us about the room."

Lou discounted the theory, but said nothing. Everyone had a room inspection. At least she and Beth had passed their second one. Amy and Heidi had taken the microwave and larger illegal appliances; Beth had concealed the rest deep in the closet.

"How about it, kiddo? I'll make the drinks if you go down to the ice machine, now that the Milkmaids got my fridge and we got no ice."

Lou debated the offer. She only had two classes tomorrow. One drink couldn't hurt. She'd never had a real orgasm, so she might as well try this one. She took the elevator to the basement ice machine. Since the night of the Bionic Beavers, she and Beth hadn't socialized much. Lou herself had hardly touched a drop, and Beth had taken to frequent weekend disappearances.

She returned with the ice, which Beth dropped into the drinks. Smooth but potent, the Screaming Orgasm knocked Lou out. She lumbered up to her bunk, while Beth, having already "topped" off the evening, was now "capping" it with another drink. Horizontal and almost dizzy, Lou watched as Beth announced the ingredients she was pouring into a large shot glass: Amaretto, Frangelico and Kahlúa. If she flunked out of school, she could always become a bartender, Lou thought hazily. With childlike glee, Beth lit a match to the concoction, which flamed briefly. Lou drifted off to sleep.

A wailing siren went off. Lou bolted upright in bed, realizing that she'd been dreaming. She'd been running out of the barn, engulfed in flames, and shouting "Screaming Orgasm!" as her mother looked on sternly from the farmhouse porch. The siren was not a fire engine, but Beth's alarm.

"Beth, your alarm."

That Beth's alarm was going off before hers meant bad news. Lou must have forgotten to set her own or not heard it. She covered her head with a pillow until the siren subsided.

She climbed shakily down from her bunk. Her head swam. When her feet touched ground, the swimming continued. Groggy, she focused on Beth's clock. Her Museums class would begin in less than an hour. The siren still reverberated in her head. "Gee, I have a headache."

"Hangover," Beth muttered from under the covers.

"Headache."

Beth popped her head out from under the sheets. "If you got what I got, it's a hangover." She slinked back down and concealed her head with a pillow.

Lou went to take a long shower. When she stepped out of the stall, more awake, her head still throbbed. OK, a hangover. Back in her room, she saw it was 9:30. The shower must have taken twenty minutes, not ten. She lacked time to eat breakfast and felt like going nowhere except back to bed.

Beth sat up in hers, her head propped on a pillow. "Hey, skip class, Lou. You deserve it. You never missed this Museums class before, right? Do yourself a favor. Jump back in the sack."

"I only missed it once before. The first day of the semester, when I arrived here late from Ladysmith because of my great-grandmother's funeral..."

"All right, already! You had a good excuse then and you got one now."

"We are allowed three absences," Lou remembered. "And I don't feel too well."

"You got a hangover. You're sick. Sickness makes an excusable absence."

Lou considered this questionable logic.

"But next time take aspirins at night. You might feel better in the morning. Get yourself a couple from my bottle and give me a handful while you're at it."

After several tries and various indentations in her thumb, Lou popped the plastic top off. Grainy tablets tumbled onto her palm. She separated two for herself, gave four to Beth and trudged down the hall to the water fountain.

When she came back, Beth had vacated the bed. "Take 'em with this." She extended a glass. "It's warm, though."

Lou sniffed it. "Tomato juice?"

"Right. With vodka. Ever heard of a Bloody Mary?"

"Alcohol? In the morning?"

"Sure, kiddo. It picks you right up."

Lou's head still ached. Fifteen minutes till class.

"It's Friday. The weekend before a major holiday. You can't live your life a slave to classes." Beth swallowed the aspirins with her drink. Lou had no other class until midafternoon. She watched as Beth made a second Bloody Mary, which she handed her. "Goes down easy. You'll feel better."

Lou figured she couldn't feel worse. Twelve minutes till class. She couldn't possibly attend in her current state. "OK, I won't go."

"That's the spirit, kiddo."

Lou took a sip. After several more, she began to feel better, but... this was degenerate. Here she stood: not even ten in the morning, a weekday no less, and drinking alcohol. To "recuperate" from last night's alcohol. Decadence. Precisely what her parents had feared, though alcohol hadn't been the focus...

"Remember what that city did to your cousin Will," Mildred Lautermilk had warned. "He went to live with some weird bunch of hippies, then got hooked up with some crazy foreign girl who turned out to have a husband." Adultery, miscegenation and the Charles Manson family seemed to jockey for position in her mind.

"Madison is far," Ed Lautermilk said, gentler. "You could apply to the University of Minnesota too, Lou. It's lots closer."

Five hours away geographically, Madison, downstate capital and den of iniquity, was five light-years away politically and socially. Madison's unsavory reputation had even reached Ladysmith and still lingered in the eighties.

"Then there's that movie, *At Home and War*," Mildred reminded.

"*The War at Home*, Mom," Lou corrected.

"We all saw it, right here in this very living room. Riots. Anti-Americanism." Saving the worst for last, her mother spat out, "Communism! And all down in Madison!"

Her parents had exhausted their basic repertoire of anti-Madison arguments: distance, communism and decadence. But Lou had held her ground and gone off...

She swallowed more of the warm Bloody Mary. She didn't even taste the vodka, but, as Beth had said, the drink gave her a boost. Intro to Museums was now beginning. Guiltily, she took another sip.

Beth downed her drink and licked her lips clean. "College. Ain't it the life?"

Gone were Lou's six a.m. risings, though she usually managed by seven. Monday of the "non-week" she showered, then had a leisurely breakfast while reviewing her Museums notes. Back in her room, she stuffed notebooks and books into her backpack and put on her coat. Beth stirred in her sleep. Lou hoisted the pack onto her shoulders. "Up, Beth."

"I dropped Telugu."

"Yes, more than a month ago. It's your bus that leaves in two hours."

"Oh, yeah. Thanks, kid. Have a good vacation. Gobble up some turkey for me."

Lou wondered why Beth had even stayed in Madison for the weekend. Again, she'd suspiciously disappeared after Friday morning. She'd glimpsed her down the hall in the dorm, but unless Beth had tiptoed in and out during her sleep, she hadn't spent either night in the room.

The quick walk in the cold exhilarated Lou. As she entered the lecture hall by the rear door, a blank piece of paper was thrust at her. It had space for a name and blanks to answer five questions. She took a seat in the front row, hoping she could somehow compensate for what she'd missed Friday. Nervous whispers buzzed all around her. The bell rang and the professor ascended the podium. A faint, uneasy laughter went up from the class.

"This, as you may guess, is a pop quiz."

The uneasy laughter turned to murmured obscenities.

"I'll know who are present from the quizzes turned in. For writing your name on the paper , in other words, for being here, you get at least a D minus. To receive a higher grade, here are five questions on Friday's slide presentation, which 142 of you missed." Cicely Pankhurst paused; another short chorus of whines followed.

"Better a D than an F," thought Lou, peeved at herself. A latecomer took the seat beside her. She recognized the sandal-dropper, who had traded in her sandals for furry boots.

The professor read the first question. The sandal-dropper began whispering to Lou and held up her blank paper, in need of an answer.

"I missed Friday," Lou whispered, and exposed her own blank paper.

"No whispering or roving eyes, please." Cicely Pankhurst's voice came out sharp. "Now, number two."

Lou cringed with embarrassment, unsure if the warning was directed at her or the class at large.

Beth lay in bed until after ten. Her 11:30 bus to Chicago would leave from Memorial Union, a few minutes' walk away. She'd just have time to shower, drink some coffee and pack. Her hand groped for her Marlboro Lights. She lit one and plodded down the hall to the drinking fountain. Furtively she filled the empty coffee carafe, checking for the presence of the maids. Back in her room she got out the hidden coffeemaker and prepared the coffee, which would be ready when she finished showering.

She slipped into the bathroom right before the maids closed it down for cleaning. As if by ten everyone had gotten up... Often, because of the maids' cleaning schedule, she had to shlep over to the one at the other end of the fifth floor. This morning she'd enjoy thwarting their efforts with a nice, long shower.

She fantasized about her week's vacation in the Miami Beach weather with her grandparents and Nick. She turned the hot water off, dried herself and stepped into her slippers and robe.

The cleaning crew banged around and bantered with each other as they cleaned the toilets around the corner. Still not quite awake, Beth wandered over to a sink to put in her contact lenses. She took the right one from its case, washed it in solution, rinsed the solution off and swished it around in water in the basin. Someone had already plugged it with a stopper.

Suddenly she could no longer feel the lens on her fingertip. She peered down at the water. It emitted a foul smell and had a strange color. "What the fuck is this?"

A cleaning woman came around the corner from the toilet stalls, her look inquisitive, a mop in one hand, the other on her hip.

"What's this shit in the sink?"

"It's Keen Kleen," the maid informed her. "Acid to wash away the lime accumulation."

"Acid??" Beth blurted. "This acid just ate my contact lens right off my finger!"

"No doubt," said the maid coolly. "Must've dissolved it away."

Beth's anger soared at the maid's offhand tone. "Why can't you people wait till everyone's finished in the morning? These lenses cost $250!"

"Look, I'm sorry your contact lens got eaten up. But if you kids would pay attention to what you're doing... A Sunday night, and half of you are out getting drunk, stagger in here and vomit all over, then stumble in hungover the middle of the next day."

"I just expect to use the goddamned sink and not find it full of acid. I ought to sue you for this! My Dad's a lawyer..."

"Look, kid. I don't care what your Dad is. All you kids do is come here and tear the place up."

"Who the hell are you to be yellin' at me? You destroy my lens an' then try an' blame it on me!"

Two other cleaning women, having heard the commotion, now hovered behind their comrade, witnessing the scene.

"What your Dad ought to do is wash out your foul mouth with a good dose of Keen Kleen! They send you rich brats here and all you do is rip up your sheets and make rags and ropes out of them, set pizza-box and beer-can traps to fall on us when we open your doors to change the linen! You turn your rooms into brothels with red lights, or fast-food joints with microwaves and coffeemakers. Only thing you girls don't do is piss in the bubblers."

Bubblers? It took Beth a second to remember the Wisconsinism for water fountain.

"She's right," seconded a maid wielding a toilet bowl brush. "You oughta see the room down the hall. Appliances galore, booze bottles all over the place, cigarette butts in the ice buckets. You kids got no respect for anything!"

So Beth was right. The maids *had* ratted on her. She began to sizzle. "You goddamned bitches! I'll sue the whole fuckin' lot of you! My Dad'll sue this whole fuckin' university!"

With a sweep of her arm, she landed her remaining possessions in her toiletry case, flung a damp towel over her shoulder and stormed out. "Bitches!" she screamed as the door slowly fell closed. "I'll teach you a lesson!"

She stomped down the hall. She'd have to go to the other bathroom to put in her remaining lens. And get the hell off campus before the maids reported her to the House Fellow. A dorm memo had warned students against abusing the cleaning crew by beer-can traps and other pranks. The warning probably applied to verbal abuse too.

In any case, she didn't give a damn. The maids deserved it. She'd call her father and have him draw up a threatening, legal-looking bill for the lens. That would teach them. Or maybe at least scare them into not reporting her.

26

The November temperatures lowered and lowered. Jeb anticipated his first real snow; instead he got true Midwestern cold. *Upper* Midwestern cold.

Since October he and Cissy had used the woodstove for heat. Just as she'd been caretaker of the garden, Pep made herself caretaker of the wood. The upstairs pile was perfectly, even aesthetically stacked: six logs sideways, four crossways, six more sideways, crevice-free. Each row neatly accommodated the next like pieces of a jigsaw puzzle. Plastic draped the whole pile, bricks bolted down the bottom and small logs the top.

The day before Thanksgiving no call came for Jeb to teach. When Cissy left for work, he stepped outside to get wood: Their pile had been reworked to match the upstairs one. He caught sight of Pep at the corner of the house, watching him admire the stack. "Thanks, Pep!"

Her eyes hooked into his. She traced a smile, which quickly faded, then disappeared around the corner.

Since the football game, Pep had seemed ever-present: bundled up on the porch sofa; bringing in wood; making mysterious trips up and down the stairs and around the outside of the house. When Jeb saw her, she'd give a nervous, enigmatic grin, as if caught *flagrante delicto*. What *delicto*? If lust was a crime, they were probably both criminals.

The mercury reached a high of twenty-two by early afternoon, discounting the windchill factor. As California lived by tides, Wisconsin lived by windchill. At least Jeb had eased into it: Arriving in August was simply culture shock; arrival in late November would be culture jolt.

It was time to throw more logs on the fire. Each new stoking made the fire roar, but the air, indisposed to round corners, remained coolish. Jeb put on his coat and decided to haul in enough for the rest of the day. Outside he heard a noise around the corner of the house, something akin to trash cans blowing in the wind.

"Jeb!"

He turned and saw Pep, coatless, dashing toward him. He did a double take. One of her two bouncing halves of asymmetrical hair was gone, shaven. She was half-bald.

"What happened, Pep?"

She touched the hairless side of her head.

"This?"

"Yeah, that," he said, unsure whether or not to make light of the new coiffure.

The answer came out garbled, vowels swallowed: "Mrng."

"You did it this morning?" He loaded logs into his arms.

She shook her head in an emphatic yes, then, displaying frustration, an equally emphatic no. She repeated "mrng."

He was in no mood for figuring out puzzles in this temperature. But the message seemed important: half-shaven head, sad face (but still with a vestigial seductive pout) and "mrng." Not unusual, she wore black.

Black. The answer hit him: "You're in mourning?"

"Yep." The pout turned from seductive to sad.

"For what? For who?"

She pointed to herself and Jeb, then pulled the corners of her lips down. "Us." Then she pointed to herself and the upstairs flat. "Us."

Wind battered Jeb's face. "For you and me? And for you and Irv?"

A hangdog, almost guilty expression came over her. "Yep."

Before he could ask why, she stepped up and encircled him and the wood in her arms. Her breasts nestled themselves between the logs. Jeb wished he were a log.

Exerting pressure on the nape of his neck, Pep pulled his head down and planted a quick dry kiss on his lips. "Bye."

He steadied his toppling load of logs and watched as she fled around the corner of the house. Her half-head of hair tilted back and forth, strands fluttering in the wind. Perplexed, he stood immobile for a second, his glance fixed on the corner, as if expecting her to reappear. He took the logs inside and realized that both her upper and lower lips were painted black.

Irv spent the late afternoon in his office with Seth, trying to talk him out of a countersuit against his neighbor. Not a true diehard about bicycling, he had taken the bus, standard procedure in temperatures below twenty. When Seth offered him a ride home, he accepted and, in a holiday spirit, invited him in for a beer.

As they entered the flat, deafening music battered the walls, belting out from Juan and Gil's room. Which meant that Gil or Pep was home and Juan wasn't. He ushered Seth through the living room and into the less embattled kitchen, where the aroma of Pep's cooking wafted. He peered into the oven and saw a casserole — brown rice, green peppers and tomatoes. The smell of curry hung in the air. He went to the refrigerator and pulled out beers. Juan had stocked it with Mad City Suds.

"So am I going to meet Pep or have you hidden her away?" Seth seemed just short of drooling in anticipation.

"Let me go find her."

He went to his bedroom. An envelope with his name was inserted in the crack of the door. Removing it, he pushed the door open and had a premonition that he needn't even look for Pep's scant possessions. He closed the door, sat on the bed and began to read.

Irv,
dear:

Me?
Here?
No.
Done.

Loan.
Split.
Bus.
Bay.
Band.

Love?
Yes.

Stay?
Could.
Should?
Doubt.

You?
Hurt?
Me?
Hurt?
No.
Sad.

Learned?
Yes.
Loved?
Yes.
Grew?
Yes.

More?
Here?
No.
Can't

So...
Leave.
Must.
Change.
Grow.
More.

Thanks,
Gil.
Thanks,
Juan.

Meal?
Stove.
Eat.
Please.

Irv,
Thanks.
Thanks.
Thanks.

Love,
Much,
Pep.

He shoved the letter back in the envelope, breathed deeply and wiped his face with the tip of his beard. The whole episode in Madison had been a lark, a fluke, hadn't it? They'd simply filled a temporary void in each other's lives.

But as sure as Pep had filled a void, she left a larger one.

He realized that his feelings for her had turned as paternalistic as amorous, had known that it couldn't continue forever. At least she dared to make the break. He wasn't sure if he would have.

The blasting music ended. Irv soon heard Gil offering Seth a bowl of marijuana. The talking ceased as they toked, then resumed, as Seth plied Gil with questions about Irv and Pep, then answered them himself: "Must've had a little tiff, those two. Nothing like patching it up in bed. I'm in no hurry."

Just what Irv feared. Though he was a man of the sixties who had learned to express his feelings, he couldn't go out there now.

27

E rva Mae came home from work later and later. One night, after eight inches of snow had fallen, Roz saw her unloading her bicycle from the trunk of Roxanne's car. Everything began to click. She remembered their chumminess the night of the Fall Female Festival.

It took Erva Mae several minutes to dispose of her bike before she breezed in, snow-covered to the knees. "Waiting up for me?" Her tone aimed for nonchalance.

"Hardly. You're dripping all over the floor," Roz said. "I just heard all the banging around outside and came to see…"

"To see what?" Defensiveness overtook Erva Mae's nonchalance. "That Roxanne gave me a ride home? We happened to have a late meeting."

Roz's words came out in spite of herself: "I don't remember any meeting scheduled."

"Of course it wasn't a *board* meeting. Just a *tête-à-tête* between Rox and me."

"More like *tit-à-tit*," Roz said under her breath as Erva Mae brushed off snow. "Whatever you say."

"Believe what you will." Erva Mae stepped primly out of her coat and smoothed her snow-strewn hair. "In any case, I don't know that it should matter, should it?"

"No," Roz said curtly. Of course it shouldn't matter. But she had to admit that it did. She found herself surveying Erva Mae's appearance, as if for lipstick smudges or alien strands of hair.

"Good. Now, if you'll excuse me, I'm tired."

Erva Mae ensconced herself in the bedroom. Roz went into the bathrooom to smoke and think, and sat on the toilet lid.

The evidence presented itself starkly. She had to admit she was jealous. It was ridiculous, but true.

Erva Mae wasn't wasting any time, so why should she? Roz had always been a go-getter. Though the thing to go get had never been a man. Even in her distant heterosexual past, she'd never had to go out looking.

The question of how to go straight in near-east-side Madison still gnawed at her. She'd told one person. Big deal. And Juan probably didn't know a single straight man, besides Irv, in the whole city.

Hadn't she, like so many others, chosen to stay in Madison because of its radical politics, counterculture and freedom?

Freedom to be gay, freedom to be straight.

No, she couldn't let near-east-side Madison warp or stifle her newfound priorities. She refused to vegetate or feel sorry for herself while Erva Mae was out merrily cavorting with Roxanne.

The following day, a Thursday, the *Isthmus* delivery person dropped off a large stack of newspapers during Roz's shift at the Co-op. She remembered the personals and snatched a copy during a free moment, barely containing an impulse to flip to them. She rang up purchases, the copy behind her burning a hole in the counter.

When she got home, the flat was empty. She went to her bedroom and devoured the column. It contained an assortment of ads from straight women, who called themselves intelligent, attractive, caring, sensitive, romantic and spiritual.

Most sought partners for intellectual chat, candlelight dinners, moderate wine-sipping, smoke-free evenings in front of fireplaces or watching sunsets.

"Yuppies," she scoffed.

Advertise was precisely what she, in her unique situation, needed to do. She snatched an envelope out of the waste basket and began to scribble on the back of it:

"Dope-smoking ex-dyke trying to go straight..?"

"Plain-looking woman with no time for bullshit or pseudo-intellectual claptrap..?"

"If you have an aversion to cigarettes, alcohol, marijuana or feminists, don't read on..?"

In earnest she got up and looked for the original ad she'd written. She'd had it hidden in her jacket pocket for some weeks, then transferred it to her desk drawer, where she'd stowed it with important papers in an envelope marked "Personal." She pulled it out and read: "Straight female in search of straight feminist male. Age, race, religion unimportant. Radical politics preferred. Must be gentle, caring and want committed relationship."

She began to rewrite: "Me: '60s person, into politics. You too, preferably."

She fought off lingering doubts that the personals were sleazy. Maybe once they had been, or limited to the lonely and forlorn but no longer. Right? After all, respectable west-side yuppies were using them.

There was only one way to be sure. She could simply study the responses that trickled in and proceed from there. If she never contacted any of the respondents, no one would ever know that the ad was hers.

Mildly astonished at herself, she filled in her final copy on the *Isthmus* classified form, counted the spaces per line and reached for her checkbook. Once she committed her pen to the check, the decision would be made. She would run the ad for two weeks. One might not be enough; three might make her seem desperate.

Before she lost her nerve, she shrugged on her coat and headed for the mailbox, a block and a half away.

Snowflakes were falling. A car pulled up: Roxanne was again dropping off Erva Mae and her bike. Roz blushed, as if caught red-handed. She got hold of herself, sent them both a perky smile and went her way. Snow getting inside her boots, she turned around and hollered at Erva Mae: "Your turn to shovel! It's almost knee-deep."

28

It took Cissy twenty minutes just to pass back the twelve-week exams to her remaining 350 Intro students, leaving insufficient time to go over the whole test. After class a horde of students surrounded her. Some looked at her menacingly; others seemed ready to weep.

"When can I talk to you?"

"This class used to be easy!"

"Number forty-nine was ambiguous."

"This department's grading scale sucks!"

"This is the first C I've ever gotten! I'll never get into Law School!"

Cissy used her best professorial persuasion: "Can some of this possibly wait until Wednesday when we've finished going over the exam? By then everything will be clearer. My office hour that day would be the best time to see me. If there's something that absolutely can't wait…"

The group sighed, muttered profanities and threw her looks of dismay and disgust.

At least she'd had the presence of mind not to say, "But C is an average grade." Maybe it used to be, and it was on this exam, but today's students saw it as tantamount to failure.

Back upstairs, she closed her door for a few minutes' peace before her office hour. Within moments, a quick rap of knuckles was followed by Ginger, who stepped in urgently, shut the door and scrutinized the office as though Cissy had Rickover hidden under the desk.

"Hi, Cis." She flopped onto the chair and smoothed her pantyhose. "I just wanted to be sure it's safe."

Cissy knew better than to ask, "Safe from what?" Ginger evidently had a hotter-than-usual tidbit today.

She began without any prompting. "I just discovered a piece of information, or lack thereof, that I'm afraid you ought to know."

Afraid. So it was bad news. Cissy leaned uneasily over her desk and heard a loud bang.

"Probably just the Executive Committee blowing its top," Ginger joked. "Or maybe Rickover's students shot him when he assigned two more papers by next week."

"You mean mutinied and set him adrift." Cissy smiled at her own metaphor.

Ginger took a second to catch on, eyed Cissy absentmindedly, then went back to her news: "I don't know what you might know that I don't know about this."

Cissy didn't think she knew anything about anything this morning, except that she had 300 out of 350 students dissatisfied with their exam grades. Ginger's comment about Rickover, she realized, wasn't so funny. Her Intro students probably wouldn't mind stringing her up right now.

"Evidently, you don't know what I'm talking about." Ginger seemed almost pleased. "Have you had any good news recently that you'd like to share?"

Good news? Cissy racked her brain: Jeb hadn't insisted on sex for three whole days; Rickover hadn't come by this morning. "No, no good news," she said, certain she smelled smoke.

Ginger's tone became ominous: "That's what I was afraid of." She stopped, sniffed. "Smoke? What's this? Maybe they're threatening to burn

Rickover at the stake."

"That's not funny." Cissy got up.

Ginger beat her out the door. "Smoke coming out of the air ducts."

Not surprisingly, the fire alarm sounded, a long, earsplitting buzz. "This doesn't seem like a drill."

"Let's get out, but get your coat. This is Wisconsin in December."

Cissy did as told. A minute later the two of them coincided by the stairwell. They eased themselves into the droves of students stampeding down the stairs.

Cissy saw smoke billowing above them. "What do you think it is?"

"An art project blew up on the sixth floor," Ginger replied flatly, as if this were already common knowledge.

By the third floor the smoke had lessened, but they duly kept going, as the alarm continued to sound. They reached the first floor and went out into the snow amid whoops of student merriment.

"As I was saying..," Ginger began, and looked over her shoulder for eavesdroppers. Cissy followed her gaze and saw Rutledge and Rothschild, safely out of earshot.

"I was in Sumner's office this morning, asking him about my teaching schedule for next year." Ginger seemed oblivious to the sirens of the fire engines that drove up and the fire fighters who stormed FAB. "He had to go out to the main office to get an old timetable and I saw a paper on his desk. I tilted my head discreetly..." Ginger did an imitation of the tilt, evidently adept at reading from awkward angles. "And saw a list of names and universities. I began to read, upside down, of course. You can't be too obvious. The heading read 'NMA Interviews.' I read down, or rather, up the list of names and didn't see yours."

"Oh."

Ginger's voice turned bright: "But maybe they're not interviewing you since you're right here, they know you and they don't need to."

"That's possible," Cissy admitted, trying to stave off feelings of dejection. Perhaps it was just a list of candidates who had to be called long-distance.

"I was hoping maybe it was just a list of candidates to call long-distance, but, no, these were definite, scheduled interviews."

Cissy had wondered why she'd heard no news. It was already the first week in December and the selection process underway. The National Museum Association Convention, site of the interviews, always met between Christmas and New Year's. This year it would be in Los Angeles, where she and Jeb would head as soon as the semester ended.

But she had another reason for going to the convention: She had applied for three other jobs, and George Washington University had called her to set up an interview. She had immediately decided that, lest she imperil her chances here, she wasn't going to tell this bit of news to anyone. Especially not to Ginger.

"Don't take it too badly. I'm sure they're still considering you."

Cissy saw the fire fighters come back out. "But it would be nice if they'd let me know something."

"I thought you'd want to know. Sorry to dampen your day."

A snowflake fell on Cissy's nose. "It's already damp enough."

"Don't be pessimistic. Things just might turn out fine." Ginger flicked snowflakes off of her coat while others melted into her hair. "It looks like the faculty are heading in. The students sure aren't going back to class."

They went inside and crammed into an elevator. Ginger signaled to Cissy, who turned her head discreetly and saw Sumner in the back. They remained silent for the ride up, the elevator spewing out passengers at every floor.

"Thanks for telling me, Ginger," she said after they'd exited and Sumner had vanished around the corner.

"Hang in there, Cis." Ginger patted her shoulder and glided away, leaving a wake of perfume.

Cissy peered down the hall for the presence of students waiting outside her office. Espying a potential one, she dodged into the restroom. Inside, she went into a stall to pull herself together. She began to feel sorry for herself and blew her nose loudly into a wad of toilet paper. Tears started to dribble down her cheeks. She dried her eyes and stepped out of the stall. At the same time, the toilet next to her flushed and Davidine appeared from behind the door. "Smoke in your eyes? So you stayed in too?"

"Pardon me?"

"Your eyes were tearing, were they not?" asked the dean, giving her no chance to answer. "I'm sorry, it's none of my business. I just assumed you stayed inside like I did. I realized this wasn't a drill when I smelled smoke. But I figured it would go away, so I locked myself in for a moment's peace and privacy, which are not easy to find around here."

"I know what you mean."

Combless, Davidine patted her hair in front of a mirror. "Are you going to the convention, Cissy?"

"Yes, I'm giving a paper." She controlled an urge to ask about the department's job interviews.

"I'll see you there," Davidine beamed. "Not that I won't before. You'll be at the department's Christmas party, won't you? Take care of yourself." She breezed out the door, the scent of smoke — not from the explosion —

hanging behind her.

Another stall door opened and out came Wilhelmina.

"Indeed, Professor Pankhurst, if you haven't learned it, learn it quick. There's little peace and less privacy around here."

Cissy could only gawk in amazement at Wilhelmina's presence.

"I won't tell anyone you were crying. And I won't tell why either."

29

Afterter a D on the pop quiz and a B on the exam in Museums, Lou decided that it was time to buckle down. But when Beth proposed they "do the town" Friday night, she felt ready to relax.

"As long as I'm in bed by midnight, no matter what."

"You got legs, don'tcha? Whaddya say we leave here by nine?"

"OK. That way I can study a little more first."

When she returned from the library, she found Beth with Robin Hatchman, who lived down the hall.

"Robin's goin' with us, kid."

Lou tried to mask her disappointment. "Great." She sensed that Robin was equally disappointed. They walked to a bar on Frances Street, off State. It was the last weekend before the end of classes and students packed the premises. The three of them squeezed into a booth for two, Lou on one side, Robin and Beth on the other. The aisles were jammed, music blaring, conversation strained. Lou looked up: A stereo speaker thundered right above them. "Should we move?" she screamed across the table.

"Louvre?" Beth screamed back. "Get museums off your mind, kid. Loosen up."

"Move," Lou repeated, her lips meeting to form an obvious M.

"Move?" Beth hollered back. "Where?"

"Yeah, where?" Robin butted in.

Lou looked around, embarrassed. She'd meant to another bar. Here they were lucky even to be seated. "Forget it."

"Whatcha havin'?" Robin shouted at her.

"Oh, a beer."

Robin held out her hand for money. Lou forked over a dollar and some change, noticing that Beth gave her neither an order nor money.

"Well, kiddo, this is it." Beth rubbed her hands together.

"Which is which?" Lou yelled back. "I can't hear you!"

"Kid, you're a *meshuggeneh* sometimes."

"Meshuggawhat?"

"Crazy woman. It's Yiddish."

"Yiddish? I can't even understand you in English in here."

Lou gave up on further communication and Robin returned with drinks. She set a beer down in front of Lou and identical mixed drinks, orange topped off by a crown of red, for Beth and herself.

"What are you drinking?"

Beth answered and Lou repeated what she'd heard: "Wee little sunshine?"

Beth and Robin erupted into laughter. Lou felt foolish and wasn't about to ask again, but the two of them screamed back at her, loud and clear: "Tequila Sunrise."

Tequila. That much Lou understood. What turned tequila into a "sunrise" she didn't know or care.

Beth and Robin seemed to enjoy some secret complicity, which, along with the noise, stymied conversation. The evening was proving a failure. Lou felt like leaving right now, but decided to finish her beer. At least she'd get home early and be fresh for studying tomorrow.

The rest of the weekend Beth remained moody and distant when not gone. Lou knew something was wrong and wondered if she'd done it. Whatever it was.

She knew she was the cause of another case of bad interpersonal vibrations: Rusty was angry that she'd "broken up" with him. Not that there had been much to break: one simple date to a football game. In German class she had been directing long, inviting glances at Harold Steuerabend. Harold, hot of body but slow of mind, finally smartened up, seeing that the best student in the class wanted to help him. He moved next to Lou, who began explanations before, after and even during class, while Rusty directed them stares of unabated contempt.

Sunday night after dinner Lou went down the fifth-floor hall to the restroom before leaving for the library. Coming out, she swung the door open and almost collided with Robin.

"Lou, good to see you." Robin's tone belied her words.

Lou tried to cover up her intuitive dislike. "Yeah, hi, Robin."

"I suppose you and Beth are off somewhere tonight." Robin smiled without warmth.

"No. Beth's gone. Probably studying." Personally, Lou doubted this.

"Why don't you close the door?" Robin pointed at it, held open by Lou's palm. "Some people might like a little privacy."

Irked by Robin's tone, words and everything about her, she let the restroom door fall shut. Her glance neutral but appraising, she regarded Robin. Like Beth, Robin was short, but unlike her, thick-boned, almost muscular.

Her hair was as thick and as short as her body.

"All I can say is the two of you certainly seem to be keeping each other busy lately." Robin crossed her arms, challenging her to deny it.

Lou shot her a look of incomprehension.

"You and Beth," she specified. Lou wrinkled up her face in a question. "All right, Lou. Play dumb if you want. But I'm not blind. Lots of people around here have their eyes open."

"I have no idea wht you're talking about."

"Like I said, play dumb if you want, but you're not fooling me."

Lou felt tension creep into her body, her muscles and vocal chords tightening. Her voice came out a pinched soprano: "We go out drinking once in a while. What of it?" She felt suddenly protective of Beth. Why was she having to defend her like this? "If Beth wants to do things with anyone else, she's certainly free to."

"I would hope she is." Robin's words cut like a knife.

Lou moved away from the restroom to let someone enter. "Since Thanksgiving vacation we haven't even gone out together, except the one time with you."

Robin's eyes turned defiant. "My ass, you haven't."

"I have no idea what you mean, Robin. Beth does whatever she wants."

"And obviously has."

"I'm not her keeper and you're not either. Beth can fend for herself, it seems to me." Lou didn't want to continue this strange interchange.

"Keep away from her. She's trouble for you, Lou. You'll find out some day," Robin said enigmatically. "Now, if you'll excuse me…" She brushed by Lou to go into the restroom.

"Good-bye, Robin."

Robin threw her a parting sneer and vanished behind the swinging door.

"And good riddance," Lou added.

30

Her nose in a book of feminist crossword puzzles, Roz chewed on a pencil stub, removed it from her mouth and, as if flicking ashes, tapped it on the reception desk.

Eight across: "Suffragette Pankhurst." Why did the name ring a bell? She remembered that Pankhurst lived at the turn of the century, was British and had a name like "Evelyne" or "Isabelle." But neither of these fit.

She got up and went to the kitchenette to fill her coffee mug. On her return she penciled in seven down, cluing her that the fifth letter of "Suffragette Pankhurst" was an L, followed by an I, as she already knew. She tried "Amelia" and lip-synched an obscenity when it failed to fit. She then cursed B. Cecsarini, author of *All-Feminist Clues Crosswords*, who, besides including dumb clues like this one, didn't even know proper feminist language, or she would have put "suffragist" instead of "suffragette." For all Roz knew, B. Cecsarini was a man masquerading as a woman or some right-wing scholar calling herself a feminist. But at least these crosswords spared her the likes of "River in Iceland" and "Watusi for goose."

While her job paid little enough, it also demanded fairly little. The non-smoking regulation was the main drawback, although the board of directors, with Erva Mae dissenting, had finally capitulated and created a smoking room in the rear of the building. But it did Roz little good at the front. She flicked more imaginary ashes with her pencil.

Giving up on "Suffragette Pankhurst," she concentrated on thirteen across: "Egyptian goddess of motherhood and fertility." Lucky to know who Athena was, she despaired over any item mythological. She stared thirteen across into a blur, then stared the entire puzzle into blankness. Her eyes rounded into white hollows. Thirteen across loomed in her mind like King Kong poised to destroy Manhattan. She removed the pencil from her mouth; she had chewed off a hunk of eraser. She spit rubber into the waste basket.

Egyptian fertility goddesses. Test-tube babies, in-vitro fertilization, alternative insemination. Meg in *The Big Chill.* Twins born here, fertility drugs causing quadruplets there, baby-making everywhere: cousins, couples and friends, both straight and lesbian. The continuation of the race, the family line and the now- butchered family name, according to her mother. General baby bombardment everywhere. And Roz with her biological clock hurtling away.

She put the phone on hold, took out the "Back in 5 Minutes" sign and dashed to the rear of the building and the privacy of the smoking room. She sat down in the cubicle — the size of a handicapped toilet stall — and rolled herself into a ball. Her only legacy to the world would be the Roz Goldwomyn Memorial Smoking Room. On that note, she lit a Camel.

Hearing the door to one of the directorial offices open, she stiffened. Although she'd held back tears, the last thing she wanted was to give Roxanne or Erva Mae the satisfaction of thinking she was upset over the breakup. She sucked in smoke, held it in and heard the steps come closer. When they turned the corner and headed away, she exhaled.

Shaken by the close call, she stubbed the cigarette out and went to the restroom. She examined her eyes for redness and, seeing none, returned to her desk, where she answered call after call. Finally free for a moment, she stealthily dialed *Isthmus'* number. "Any responses for Box 980?" she asked in a hoarse whisper.

"Just a moment, sir."

After a minute, the bouncy voice came back. "Over a dozen. Do you want to pick them up?"

"Sure," Roz grunted in her best deep voice and hung up.

She delved back into the crossword and waited for the clock to tick off the final minutes of her shift. Two "down" items helped her solve Pankhurst as "Emmeline" and the fertility goddess as "Isis."

Already bundled up, she walked out as soon as her replacement arrived, still wondering why the name Pankhurst sounded familiar. She gave up and tried to remember if she'd included "possible child" in her ad.

Roz went into her room, locked the door and lit a cigarette in anticipation. Her heart pounding, she tried to gauge the envelopes' contents with her fingers as she counted them: fifteen in all.

First came an Episcopal priest. Did Episcopal priests marry or was this to be on the sly? She started a pile marked "dubious." A young male stripper, in search of an "older woman of wide sexual experience", described himself as "technically a virgin." Roz disqualified herself for his defloration and tossed the letter toward the trash.

She pondered a sincere-sounding letter from a librarian. "Fag," she concluded, never having met a straight male librarian. Never mind that she'd only known two. Probable trash can.

The next letter revealed a man "between jobs, but eager to produce Aryan offspring with the right lady."

"*Goyishe* pig." Roz balled the letter into a tiny wad and bounced it off the window into the waste basket.

Next came a Senegalese graduate student, who had left behind a wife and five children. He offered stud services for up to a year and a half, depending on when he completed his dissertation. If Roz truly wanted a child, without having to endure the father, wasn't this a possibility?

No, that was lesbian thinking. Roz wanted the man as well as the kid. Exit Mr. Senegal.

A farmer who understood "feminist" as equal division of labor, promised lifelong financial security in exchange for egg-gathering, hog-slopping, cow-milking, and "three round meals a day" for him and his three children. All at a mere ten miles from Madison.

Hadn't she once wanted to rusticate? Yes, but in a dope-moking commune with antiwar activists, not in a labor camp with a trio of someone else's brats. Trash.

A chemical engineer with a word-processed letter. Automatic trash.

A prison guard sought to participate in a "dominant/submissive lifestyle." Roz wondered what exactly he meant and read on: He was gentle, caring, humble, modest, worshiped superior women and wanted to be dominated. Kinky, but out.

A Christian gentleman sought... Definite trash.

Curious, she pulled it back out. It was worse than she'd imagined: "Christian gentleman seeks wife with whom to raise children and willing to join in the struggle against abortion, pornography and homosexuality." Roz lit another cigarette and made a bonfire of the Christian, as the *goyim* had done to the Jews. She retrieved the Aryan from the trash can and added him to the flames.

She read through the rest and ended up with a grand total of two she might answer: one from a widowed lumberjack and former draft-evader, the other from a bicycle repair person, both in her age range. She was glad to have run the ad for a second week.

She heard Erva Mae slam her way through the kitchen. "Good Goddess! What's burning!? Roz, are you here?"

Roz scooped the letters out of the trash and hid them in her desk drawer, mixing the good with the bad. The smoke still hanging in the room, she lit a stick of incense to mask it before Erva Mae overreacted and called the Fire Department.

"Just meditating," Roz said, emerging from her room and shutting the door quickly behind her. "Is the incense too strong?"

"Don't bullshit me, Roz. I know you've been abusing substances in there."

"Only cigarettes. And I think you mean 'heifershit.'"

31

The weekend was Gil's last orgy of drugs, sex and sleep before final exams, after which he'd spend two weeks with his parents, where only one of his three passions would be possible.

Saturday was a university-designated "study day": no classes, no finals for anyone. A few unfortunates had to begin exams Sunday morning; Gil considered himself only slightly less unlucky: His Museums final was at 7:45 a.m. on Monday.

He awoke with Juan at two Sunday afternoon. After a brief respite for breakfast, he renewed his drug-taking for one final bout before the time to study arrived; he and his fraternity brothers had agreed to begin at eight. Gil and Juan went back to bed at five. Their nap turned into foreplay, and foreplay turned into the inevitable, leaving little time for sleep.

Gil got up and began to pack, throwing his notes, a bag of pills, a pair of underwear and a toothbrush into his backpack.

"Toothbrush? Underwear?" Juan blinked and yawned from bed. A sheet covered him to the waist.

Gil sensed the surprise and hurt in his voice. "I don't know what time we'll be finished. Did you wanna come pick me up at midnight?"

"I would. You know that." Juan twirled the end of his moustache.

"But then, what about morning?" Gil put on a holey T-shirt and red long underwear. "I'd have to get up at six and take a bus in. You can't take me since you're driving cab, right?"

"Right."

Gil pulled on thermal socks, bluejeans, the knee holes exposing the red underneath. "If you want to have me closer, maybe I should go down and sleep with Cissy. It'd probably do me more good anyway."

"Sexist."

"It was a joke," he said, unable to admit he was quite democratic about whom he went to bed with.

"I'll give you a ride now in Irv's pickup. Otherwise you'll be late."

Large, looming snowbanks lined the well-plowed roads. The heads of the parking meters peeked out above the white. Juan pulled up to the COB house just after eight. Gil jumped out before Juan could kiss him good-night, although no one could possibly see from the house.

The three of them were ready to begin studying by nine. A fourth brother, Dirk, had dropped the class. They'd worked out a schedule for one of them to attend each day so that they'd have all the notes among them. By ten they'd assembled their joint notes and still were missing four lectures.

"Maybe Dirk can help," Gil suggested. "Didn't he give you his notes, Clark-o?"

"Hell, he skipped most of the classes he was supposed to attend before he dropped."

"But he didn't drop till the twelfth week, did he?"

"I would've dropped too, but I needed the credits to keep my financial aid," Clarkson complained. "Why'd Dirk have to drop? He was gettin' a C in the course."

"He dropped," said Arnesen, "because he needed a B and Pankhurst wouldn't promise him one."

"Dirk, that asshole."

"Pankhurst, that bitch."

"Clarkson, you were supposed to attend class on November 30. That's one of the days we're missing."

"I overslept. You were supposed to wake me up."

"I was building igloos for the Eskimo Fest that Friday," said Arnesen, House Social Chairman. "And don't tell me you overslept. You were fucking your brains out with Melissa."

Clarkson sneered, but didn't deny it.

Gil could have added that most of the house had also fucked their brains out with Melissa.

"Goddamnit, how will I ever get into law school?" Arnesen whined. "My old man promised me a car if I pulled a 3.75 this semester. I gotta get an A in this class, or at least an AB." "Half-grades" took the place of pluses and minuses.

"Look Arnesen. According to my schedule, you were supposed to go to class on November 21, which we're missing."

"That was the day she gave the pop quiz."

"Yeah, but five questions couldn't have taken the whole period. She must've lectured," Clarkson argued. "So cough up the notes, Arnie."

"Let's get started," Gil said during a break in the recriminations. "We can see if Dirk maybe has any of the notes we need."

"Yeah, I need a break," said Clarkson.

"Fuck you and fuck a break. We haven't even started." Frustrated, Gil lit a cigarette. Clarkson lit one off his.

Arnesen went off to search for Dirk. He returned with a scant notebook of undated notes. After perusing them, they determined that he had attended for the last time on November 2, a day the rest had missed.

"So Dirk is good for something after all."

Arnesen snickered. "More than we can say for you, Clarkson."

Gil played role model: "Let's get moving. The exam is gonna be comprehensive..."

"She wouldn't ask about those museum tours, would she?" asked Arnesen.

"Hope not. I never went." Clarkson wiped his brow.

"That's why you're gettin' a D so far." Laughing, Arnesen elbowed his fraternity brother.

Gil banged the table for order; cigarettes jumped in the large plastic ashtray. If we don't start now, we're all gonna get a D."

"Why don't we quiz each other?" said Clarkson.

"Waste of time."

"What about the three classes we all missed?"

"Screw it. We got too much to study as it is."

Arnesen leaned toward Gil. "Kreuzer, you got any speed?"

"Sorry. Maybe a caffeine tablet or two. That's about all."

"Kreuzer, you're good for nothing." Clarkson shook his head.

Arnesen jumped on the accusatory bandwagon: "Yeah, Kreuzer, you're worthless."

"I get you guys drugs, I take your little sister out, Arnesen…"

"And laid her too," Clarkson added.

Arnesen threw Gil an aggressive, macho stare.

"Don't get bent out of shape, Arnesen. She was sick. She had to lie down. We didn't do a thing."

Arnesen gave another threatening gaze, then turned on Clarkson. "You're the one who gave him your room. If I found out they did anything…"

"Fuck off, Arnesen. Kreuzer, let's go over to your place and get some speed. I know you got some at home."

"I'm tellin' you I don't." Gil wouldn't take them over if he did.

"I'm gonna take my own notes and go study," said Arnesen.

"You can't do that!"

"Wouldn't be too brotherly of you," Gil said. "Let's get down to business."

"Yeah, let's start," Clarkson seconded.

"Right." Gil got out his plastic bag of pills, a peacekeeping, if not altruistic gesture. "I got No-Doze and caffeine tablets. Let's pop the pills and begin, for God's sake."

The brothers assented and downed their pills with Coke.

They finished at 2:30. Gil, who had hoped to sleep in the living room, found it occupied by two brothers beginning an all-nighter. Clarkson alerted him to an empty bunk uptairs, whose regular occupant had shacked up with his girl-friend for finals week.

At 7:30 Gil awoke to Arnesen shaking his shoulder.

"Time to go. Me and Clarkson are leaving."

Gil rolled over, realized the exam began in fifteen minutes and scooted out of bed.

At 7:36 he was out the front door. If he'd had time to shower, his hair would have frozen and cracked in the cold. It was a day when zippers stuck to lips and wire-rimmed glasses hurt faces. Even his forehead smarted from the cold. Nearing campus, he decided to stop for coffee at the old Rennebohm's drugstore. It was 7:42.

Standing in line at the checkout, he recognized Betsy Johns, whom he knew slightly from fraternity/sorority mixers, and known by all for her sandal-dropping and other antics in Museums class. She stood in front of him, trying to come up with enough money for two candy bars. Slowly she counted out nickels, dimes and pennies.

"Shit," she said to the clerk. "I forgot to go to the money machine. I'll have to write a check."

Gil groaned audibly, the hot Styrofoam coffee cup about to scorch his hand. "Need some change?"

"No thanks. That's OK."

He watched as she dug in the depths of her purse for a checkbook. She flipped through it for a blank check, then dove into her purse for a pen. Laboriously, she wrote out the check in round, fat letters. Gil saw the seconds tick off on his digital watch. "I'll have to see two forms of ID," stated the clerk.

Betsy retrieved a thick Velcro wallet from inside her purse, then slipped her student ID and driver's license out of their plastic wallet casings. The clerk searched for expiration dates and copied down numbers. Gil drummed his fingers on the counter, tapped his foot impatiently. Snow melted from his boots.

"We're gonna be late."

Betsy turned around and checked her watch. "It's 7:48. So we are. Won't be the first time."

"Know anything about the exam?"

"Only that it includes the slides and museum tours."

"Shit," Gil said as he paid the clerk. He'd missed two slide shows and had only taken one of the four tours.

"That's what I say," said Betsy. In no apparent hurry, she waited for him. "I don't have too many notes for this course." She stopped to unwrap her breakfast, oblivious to the pedestrians whose path she blocked on the sidewalk. "I just don't know what happened."

"Yeah," Gil agreed. He watched his digital watch change minutes. "Now we're six minutes late. It's 7:51."

"Hey, what the fuck?" High-spirited, Betsy chomped away, devouring energy. "I don't know enough to write for two hours anyway."

32

Lou survived her first three finals; only German remained. Tonight she was going to review with Harold Steuerabend. Not that the review would help her much, but being with Harold would compensate. She had a solid A in the course and needed only a few hours of study alone tomorrow.

After dinner she returned to the room to find Beth in front of her computer. Behind her the coffeemaker gurgled. Lou warily eyed the contraband.

"Don't worry, kid. They won't bust us during finals week. How'd Museums go?"

"It went. Though Mrs. Pankhurst really has an eye for detail. You'd think…"

Beth cut her off: "I gotta finish this paper by noon tomorrow. Then I gotta take Geology right after. History on Wednesday. Then I'm outta here. What about you?"

"Since I finish tomorrow, I'll probably leave Wednesday or Thursday."

"Oh, stay till Thursday, kiddo. We'll do it up big Wednesday night."

Beth's computer hummed in front of her. Lou had yet to see her touch the keyboard. "Well, that would give me time to Christmas shop in Madison."

"Great. I really gotta get this paper done." Beth switched off the computer and blew a cloud of smoke. "Didn't have to type all semester. And now this. I can't type for shit."

"This is for French Women Writers? What's it on?"

"Colette."

Lou's tone turned suspect. "But you do have it all written?"

"Hell, no. I'm composin' it right here right now." Beth squashed her cigarette out and Lou knew she wasn't kidding. The coffeemaker stopped dripping and Beth went over to it.

"Harold's coming over in a bit to study German. But don't worry, we'll go somewhere else."

Beth sipped her coffee. "Too hot. I'll be right back."

Lou removed her Museums material from her backpack, then separated her German text and notebook, and a pounding came at the door. Had Beth locked herself out?

"Hi." Harold stood in front of her. He was smaller than Lou, in height as well as weight, and had a head of dark brown curls. "I'm a little early."

"Oh, that's OK." Anything Harold said or did was all right with her. She ushered him in.

Harold glanced around the room. "Nice stuff." Beth had brought back all her possessions earlier in the month. "You guys have the coffee concession for finals week?" Lou brimmed with laughter, too loudly, she was sure. "Nice computer too."

"It'd be nicer if she knew how to use it."

Harold laughed back, relaxing her, then observed the computer close up. Lou's eyes fell on the clutter of books around it. Harold's followed hers before she could pretend she hadn't seen them.

"Hey, what's this? *Homosexualities and French Literature? Lesbian Images? Lesbianism and You?*" Harold's smile dissolved, replaced by curiosity, which faded fast in favor of distaste. "Your roommate a lez or something?"

Lou's relaxation was short-lived. She didn't know whether to pretend he was joking, rebuke him or whisk him out of the room. The awkward conversation she'd had with Robin raised its ugly head, making her unsure of everything. Harold's bugged eyes required an answer.

"Oh, it's background material for a paper she's writing. French Women Writers."

Relieved, Harold eagerly accepted the explanation. "Funky paper."

"We have to go somewhere else to study." Lou lunged for her coat and gloves. "Beth's writing her paper in here tonight."

"No problem."

As they headed toward the door, Beth opened it in their faces.

"Hi, Beth." Lou aimed for casualness, but blanched. "This is Harold. Harold, Beth."

Beth regarded the two of them oddly, as if they'd just sniffed her intimate apparel and had the guilt stamped on their faces. Lou hurried him out the door. Not that he needed prodding.

When she returned around eleven, Beth was unplugging her computer. "Oh, you finished your paper?"

"No. I'm takin' this thing to Robin's room an' we're gonna pull an all-nighter. That way you can sleep, kid."

Lou lay in bed wondering about Beth and Robin. Harold's question nagged at her. The conversation with Robin, which before simply baffled her, now upset her. Although she felt exhausted, her mind whirred with doubts.

She woke up at 7:30 when Beth tiptoed into the room. When she came back from breakfast, Beth had set her computer back up and perched in front of it, spastically attacking the keyboard with her index fingers. "Do you want a little help? I've got some time, since my German exam's not until 2:30 and I don't need to cram that much."

"Really, kiddo? You'd help me out? I'm beat. Robin and I didn't get to sleep till six this morning."

"Sure. I mean it."

Beth had ended up writing in longhand. She gave Lou a crash course on the keyboard functions, then tumbled onto the lower bunk. Lou began to type and slowly absorbed the content, which left no doubt: The paper read like a catalogue of lesbian references in three Colette novels. Why had she chosen this topic if she wasn't..? And why had she spent the night with Robin? Beth's words echoed in her head: "Robin and I didn't get to sleep till six this morning."

But why should she imagine the worst? Wasn't it all innocent, weren't there two bunks, hadn't Beth only gone to study there so that Lou could sleep?

And if one of them was really a... lesbian, certainly it was the tomboyish Robin and not Beth. Right? Maybe Lou should say something to Beth about the company she kept. On second thought, perhaps not. Right now she had a paper to type and vowed to finish it. Beth never could.

When she had arrived at the conclusion, distressingly similar to the introduction, Beth woke up, rubbed her eyes and asked the time.

"It's 11:45." Lou went back to typing and three sentences later proclaimed, "Finished!"

"Finished? No shit? I'll get it in on time if the printer works!" Beth hopped out of bed. "Lou, kid, you're a real *mensch!* I could hug ya!"

What was this sudden hugging desire? And what was a *mensch?* Beth put her arms around Lou's neck. She tightened, ever so slightly, then began to choke.

"Oops, kid, didn't mean to strangle ya." Beth rested her hand on Lou's shoulder. Lou managed not to flinch.

"Since it's done, why don't you go turn it in right now, while it's still on time?" Lou said, her tone one part acid, one part urgency.

"Right, kiddo." She pressed several keys. "See? The printer's startin' to print it. Then I gotta find out if I can get an incomplete in Geology. Otherwise I better forget that exam."

Lou sailed through her German exam, didn't see Beth the rest of the day and the following day went Christmas shopping. She ended up making her purchases from University Bookstore: Bucky Badger T-shirts and sweatshirts for her nieces and nephews (more appropriate than the "Fuck 'em Bucky" T-shirts she'd seen on the mall), a set of University of Wisconsin drinking glasses for her mother. Without finding a gift for her father, she took the presents back to the dorm. Beth would be finished with her exam; they could start celebrating any time, without Robin, she hoped.

In the room Lou found no trace of Beth. She took off her coat and unloaded the presents. Then she saw a note on the desk:

Lou, kiddo:

Flunked geology, got by in history. Nick called this morning, telling me to get myself home, since we fly to Miami tomorrow, then Jamaica on Friday. Where the hell were you this morning? I'm taking the 12:30 bus to Chicago. Sorry about our celebration. I bought this bottle for you. Sorry I'm not here to help you drink it. Thanks a heap for the typing. Merry Christmas. Love ya,

Beth

It was 12:20 and Lou had missed the daily bus to Eau Claire. She felt betrayed, and considered running to the Union to say good-bye or scolding Beth for ruining their celebration.

She fixed her glance on Beth's gift, an Israeli liqueur called "Sabra." Packaged along with it came two long-stemmed glasses. She felt like tearing the package open and beginning to gulp, but restrained herself. It might make a nice present for her father. She hoped he wouldn't associate Israel with Communism or something worse. She doubted he knew what a *kibbutz* was anyway and doubted he would approve if he did.

33

T he Department of Museum Studies had scheduled its Christmas party Saturday night. Cissy had little desire to attend, but knew she should show up for the sake of propriety. Although students had finished finals that day, that didn't mean professors had.

"Go to this one by yourself, babe. I'll drive you out there, drive you back. I've never met a single one of them and prefer to keep it that way."

True: After what he'd heard about them, he could hardly be blamed for not wanting to meet them. But... "Be a sport, Jeb. We'll just stay a little while. It might even be fun."

"Just like a hernia operation 'might be' fun. *You* go. And make it worth your time. Show them they're making a big mistake if they don't hire you for next year."

"They're not even interested in me, Jeb."

"Your interview will probably be at the party. They want to see if you can get loose with the old boys and fit into the network."

"Hardly. Don't make me endure this alone. It's probably the only departmental social affair of the year."

Jeb grumbled, grunted and eventually gave in.

Monday morning Cissy sat recording final exam grades. She had to deliver the course grades to FAB by 4:30, since she and Jeb had a flight to Los Angeles the following morning.

She'd put 250 questions on the comprehensive final. Multiplied by 350 students, that made 87,500 answers. While her grader had done the computerized answer sheets of 200 questions, the non-computerized half-hundred had fallen to her. A mere 17,200 handwritten responses discounting blank spaces, the latter not negligible.

"If there's any way students can flunk a final, they will," she bemoaned, repeating what the grader had told her when he'd delivered the exams.

"Sounds like a Rickoverism to me," Jeb snorted.

"Please, not Rickover again. You promised." Since Saturday night, Jeb had ranted, raved and changed his tune, swearing never to let her go to a departmental function alone.

The party had begun innocuously enough. Everyone had been there but Rickover: Evan and Anne, stoned and giggly; Ginger and her fiancé Melvin, who, by his third eggnog, announced the price of Ginger's engagement ring; Sumner drunk and Vonda drunker, enshrouded in gold and varicose purple.

Round two: Ginger deserted Melvin and went off "shmoozing for tenure," as she called it, with R & R, her nicknames for Rutledge and Rothschild. Davidine's sister Ralphetta accosted Jeb for a lengthy interrogation. Anne and Evan disappeared for round of marijuana with their hostess, Amelia Raitt, widow of an ex-Chair. Vonda dashed off to the bathroom, where vomiting sounds ensued. Cissy caught Sumner glaring at her across the room; he then screwed his face into a painfully artificial smile. She took refuge with Davidine and Wilhelmina until Vonda deoccupied the bathroom. Fortunately she'd sprayed it with Lysol.

Round three: Cissy emerged from the bathroom. A hullaballoo attended another arrival and she ran into Rickover and his bourbon breath. "Sailing high too, Pankhurst?" He patted her on the rear.

She saw Jeb looking on. He marched over and planted himself next to her. "There's someone Cissy would like you to meet," he said to Rickover, who paled. Uneasily, Cissy introduced them. Jeb held his hand out, obliging Rickover to take it, shook it lengthily and said, "This is the proper way to occupy your hands."

"Maybe the hour of the exam was bad." Jeb read off another low score, corresponding to a D.

"Maybe the day was bad." Cissy stretched her arms and yawned. "Mondays are never good."

"Maybe the exam was bad."

She looked up from sipping her apple mint tea. "This isn't the time to joke with an academic."

"Just don't get academented on me, babe. That's what Evan called it. Academentia, right?" His brown eyes enlivened; a mischievous smile fluttered on his lips. "And I know just the remedy to prevent it."

"I have to figure final grades first."

"C'mon, babe. We haven't done it on a Monday morning in months." His tone was a cross between a tease and a whine.

"Tomorrow. To celebrate the end of the semester."

Jeb's eyes rounded. "On the plane? Kinky."

Cissy rolled her eyes hopelessly. "Let's at least finish the grades first."

"You'll be too tired to make love later. I know you."

"Go stoke the fire if you're not going to read me more grades." Still in her robe and nightgown, Cissy doubled up her arms in the ample sleeves.

"Put on some clothes and maybe you'll warm up." Jeb took two logs lying next to the stove. "Or better yet, take them off and I'll warm you up."

Cissy threw a rubber eraser at him and searched for a name in the gradebook.

The fire stoked, he came back to the table. "Give me the exams." He sat down wearily and began to read scores. "Lorna Snowden. 205."

Cissy consulted her scale. "C."

"Betsy Johns. 191."

"D."

"Gil Kreuzer. 201."

"C."

"Better watch it, babe. We wouldn't want student riots. Not to mention poor relations with the neighbors." He made a wry, mischievous face. "Bernard Clarkson. 149."

"F," Cissy stated. "Half of them are going to flunk the course."

"Hey, babe. Just think. It's over tomorrow. We'll be on the plane, headed for smog paradise."

Cissy looked out the window and saw snowflakes swirling down. "If we finish and if they don't close the airport."

"What? That couldn't happen, could it?"

"According to Irv, it can."

Jeb panicked. "No. It couldn't. It wouldn't."

"You were the one who wanted to see snow. If the airport's closed, it's only a day's drive to the North Pole. We could celebrate Christmas there."

"OK, you win. We'll hurry up and forget making love. For the moment." He read off the next exam: "Lucille Lautermilk. What a name! 236. If that's not an A..."

Cissy's eyes focused on the scale. "I can't believe it! It's a high AB. The students are right. The department's grading scale s..."

"Go ahead. Say it, babe."

"Stinks."

"Wrong word."

"You know what I mean. It, uh, sucks." Cissy turned up her nose in triumph at him. "There."

"You're learning, babe. That way you'll survive."

"But will the students?" White swirled behind the glazed window. "Will we?"

Jeb echoed her exact thought: "Not if we don't hurry up and blow this Arctic wasteland. Next score, babe..."

When Cissy left her final grades at FAB, she passed by closed doors decorated with yellow grade sheets posted for students' benefit. She couldn't resist looking at Rickover's. His second-year class read: "D, C, D, D, F, F, BC, C, C, D, F." At the bottom he had scrawled his signature and added "Merry Christmas."

Semester Break

34

The Willy St. flat was becoming claustrophobic. Juan tried to look out the window, but the ice-clad windowpanes rendered him legally blind to the outside world, reduced to the likes of an Antarctic ice mass. It was two days after Christmas; Gil had been gone for a week.

He left to meet his friend Eric Levi, who had suggested the Bull Dog, a local gay bar. On his way he detoured in Irv's pickup past two closed automatic tellers, then went to Library Mall for a third try. He parked without plugging the meter and walked briskly toward the outdoor machine. He watched as the potential user in front of him persisted doggedly, trying to insert her card. Juan swore as the machine succumbed, apparently to hypothermia, flashed its "closed" sign and shut its door to the cold.

The outdoor mall was nearly deserted. As he walked back to the truck, a tiny woman dwarfed by her furry parka closed up shop where she peddled copies of her book, *Wisconsin Winter Wonderland.* A trio of Asian students hurriedly entered Memorial Library. Juan passed the Catholic Center, on whose steps a small flock of streetpeople puffed on cigarettes as if they provided sustenance. Always preferring to feed the panhandlers over the parking meters, he pressed a quarter into a man's hand and dashed back to the truck: no parking ticket.

The Bull Dog was dark, abetted by the 4:30 sunset. A high-tech jukebox blared from one end of the room. Juan sat at the other end of the U-shaped bar. A bartender served him a vodka and tonic. He paid and left a quarter tip, his billfold now empty and a nickel in his pocket. As he lit up an ultra-light, he felt a tap on the shoulder and turned to face Eric. Beneath thick bushy eyebrows and shaggy dark hair, his lively green eyes pierced Juan's.

"Hey, Juan. See that guy over there? I told him last week I was twenty-seven and he believed me." Eric was, to Juan's memory, thirty-four, two years older than he himself.

"I take it you didn't meet him feeling up eggplants at the Co-op. They are, I believe, out of season."

Eric smiled suggestively. "Right. But safe sex is never out of season."

"So go for him, if you want. I know you haven't become a conceptual homosexual over AIDS. You're still negative, right?" Eric, hypochondriac *par excellence* before AIDS had ever appeared, had had the antibody test the first week it was available and every three months since then.

"Right. I did go for him, then he told me he was twenty-three and not interested in 'older men.' What the hell, he has a small dick anyway."

"I thought you didn't get far enough to tell."

"You don't have to get 'far' to tell. Just look at his build. That body has 'small dick' written all over it."

"Whatever you say," Juan said, resolutely skeptical.

Juan had known Eric since his draft-counseling days, his own part in the antiwar effort, when he'd explained how to gain conscientious-objector status to some and urged others to claim homosexuality. When Eric had come to the counseling center and announced his own, Juan befriended him and came painlessly out of the closet. After recommending so much deviance to others, he'd figured it was time to start practicing it.

After a few minutes of conversation about the bar, the weather and the neighborhood, Eric asked what he always asked:

"So how's your safe sex life?"

"Monogamous," Juan answered as always. "Safer than safe."

"Not unless you've both been monogamous for seven years."

"Yeah, yeah, I know." Juan had heard Eric's spiel before, had read it in the gay press. He hadn't had the antibody test, nor had Gil. And nor were they practicing the safest sex.

"No motivation like a negative test to make sure you stay that way." Eric's expression wavered between smug and lewd. "You can be active. And safe." The bartender, having been flirting with the 23-year-old, finally brought Eric his beer.

"So how's your frat boy?"

"Gone to Green Bay for semester break. We just had our nineteenth anniversary."

Eric turned pensive and rubbed an eyebrow. "Nineteen months, huh? I think my longest affair in years has been nineteen days. Not that those years have been exempt of numerous carnal joys."

"To each his own."

"You know, lately you sound awfully possessive for a liberated, feminist man."

Eric's words jarred him. "Me? Possessive?" Then, recovering: "I didn't know that liberation and polygamy went together."

The sexual revolution," Eric said dryly. "Where were you in the sixties?"

"Counseling you, as I remember. And it was the seventies by then."

Eric's eyes turned to cruise again; Juan's followed: moustache, short dark hair, trim, bluejeaned, and T-shirted. A clone like a thousand others in Madison.

"What I meant was," Eric went on, "for someone liberated, you're awfully fixated on one person."

Juan squared his shoulders. "Oh, so that's passé? Even in an AIDS crisis?"

"All too common right now, I'm afraid." Eric let his vulnerability show.

Juan tried to make him bounce back: "All you mean is that lots of guys are afraid of sex these days and your sex-partner quotient is down."

Eric gave a faint smile, which withered. "No, really. I just think it's an outdated notion that one person can make you happy, fill all your emotional and sexual needs."

"I have other persons," Juan retorted. "At least in the emotional realm."

"Monogamy's unnatural. True happiness, I don't know if that exists. But sexual ecstasy, that's another matter."

Juan started to protest, but Eric cut him off: "C'mon. Are you truly happy, really in love with Gil?"

Was he truly in love? He thought so. Truly happy..? Less certain. He remembered his first love. It was the commune, 1972. Pepper Isaacson had moved out of his parents' house and into Amelia's commune. It was love at first sight for Juan and, shortly after, love reciprocated. Juan spent a year of happiness, ecstasy. Pepper was graduating and going off to get a Master's at Stanford. Juan awaited the invitation to accompany him. He could easily switch programs himself, get his degree out there. Money, if an obstacle, could be overcome. But the invitation never came.

"I'm satisfied," he hedged, swishing the vodka around his mouth, like mouthwash.

"I have a good orgasm and I'm satisfied too. For maybe six hours."

"I hope you have some of your orgasms by yourself."

Eric tipped his beer to his mouth, then set it down. He raised his voice over the jukebox, its volume cranked up. "But you're not happy. I can tell."

"Tell it to the whole bar, why don't you?" Juan said. "But OK, I'll agree with you: Monogamy's probably unnatural to most species, including us."

"The term's unnatural. Hard to spell, hard to achieve. I've never known a truly monogamous gay man. It's 'serial monogamy' at best. Monogamy with one partner, then two weeks later, monogamy with another... When did you last have sex with anyone besides Gil?"

Juan was proud to admit the truth: "More than nineteen months ago."

"Lesbians are the ones who specialize in 'serial monogamy,'" Eric continued. "Most gay men go through 'serial polygamy.'"

Juan heard the word "lesbian" and thought of Roz. Telling her secret to Eric, her coworker at the Co-op, would certainly put an end to this unwanted line of conversation. What could it hurt? Could Eric keep the secret? Doubtful. He'd probably start trying to set her up with every straight man who passed through the Co-op.

"Juan? You look off in space."

"Oh, yeah. Just thinking."

"About how you'd like to have sex tonight."

Juan flashed him a nasty look, but Eric remained undaunted: "Look, Gil's been gone for how long? A week, ten days? Do yourself a favor. Live it up a little. Safely, of course. How do you know he's being faithful to you?"

The remark struck a sore point. He'd once caught Gil, circumstantially, in an act of infidelity and had to admit it could happen again. He'd told him it would spell the end of their relationship if it did. "I know he is," he said, unsure.

Eric regarded him doubtfully.

"Don't you believe me?"

"I believe you've been faithful. But Gil, I can't say. Anyone can fool anyone. And I can't believe that you don't get a craving for something else from time to time."

Juan decided to be truthful. "Sure, once in a while." Then he added on, less truthful, "A great while."

"Just as long as you're not stifling it in the name of AIDS."

"I 'stifled' it, as you put it, long before AIDS, in the name of meaningful sex. It's called romance."

"Look, I have nothing against romance. I don't mind it myself when it happens."

"You have to make it happen. Don't be so cynical."

Eric looked away, as if shunning some painful truth, or perhaps cruising the last customer who'd entered the bar. He turned back to Juan and said, "I just hope you're having first-rate sex with Gil."

"Good enough," Juan clipped. When they had it, that was. When Gil wasn't stoned, otherwise drugged or passed out dead-drunk. "Besides, sex isn't everything."

"For a gay man, that remark puts you in a minority."

"I think I'll drink up and go." Juan sucked ice in his glass, the drink drained.

"It's Happy Hour. Stay for two. Never know what you'll find here."

Juan was tempted to say "disease," but didn't want Eric to start discussing safe sex again.

"There's lots of hot safe sex to be had. Politically correct, healthy sex."

"Fuck political correctness. I just want to be happy. And I don't do too badly."

"Hey, I didn't mean to say you did." Eric patted him on the shoulder. "Me, I just want to be satisfied."

Juan pulled on his jacket and rubbed the stubble on his chin. "Which takes much less work."

35

R oz rode her bike from Womynspace to the *Isthmus* office, where two more replies to her personal awaited.

From the Square she descended on her bike, braking carefully. Ten blocks later she rounded the corner onto East Wilson Street. Her bike skidded on ice, shooting toward the railroad tracks. She rode with the skid and finally pedaled herself out of it, coming to rest on the edge of a grey snowbank.

Winded, she pushed her bike the half-block home, brushed snow from it and hefted it up the stairs into the kitchen. She took off her coat and put on a sweater, turning the heat up from 55 to 60 degrees. In the kitchen, she sat down, the two letters in front of her, and gazed out the window: Sun sparkled on the snow drifts, which had risen to eye level. Erva Mae had left town, doubtless to play Southern belle to her parents, who knew nothing of her real life. New Year's Eve she would return to Madison to rendezvous with Roxanne.

Roz opened the first letter with a steak knife. It came from a divorced, retired policeman. Since his wife had left him, he had replaced her, apparently, with three German shepherds and said he wanted to meet a woman who liked dogs. He specified that his age, sixty-two, seemed just what she was looking for. She realized that he had misconstrued "'60s person" in her ad.

The second letter had a return address from the neighborhood. Roz pulled the letter out and went progressively paler as she read each line:

> *Dear Box 980:*
>
> *I'm a 41-year-old feminist and politically active SM and a remnant of the '60s and its counterculture on Madison's near-east side. I'm a lawyer with a touch of anarchy that saves me from stagnating in the '60s. Though, without doubt, they're still part of me.*
>
> *I've recently ended an eight-month relationship, which itself had ended some years of celibacy. During those years, I engaged in constant community activism in an attempt to fill my life. This activity alone —my mind was fired, the soul at times thirsty and the body occasionally rebellious— failed to fill the void. Prior to this, I had been married and, before that, involved in an intense relationship before my partner left me to explore feminism. Had I known then what I now...*
>
> *I, like you, am looking for a partner of my own generation and, offhand, I'd say from your ad we seem to share similar values.*
>
> *If you're game for a try, you can write or call me at the address or phone below.*
>
> *Sincerely,*
> *Irv Barmejian*

First came shock, then embarrassment. Roz scrambled for her Camels.

Some fifteen years ago she'd deserted Irv and his bed, leaving what seemed now a near-perfect relationship to combat the patriarchy and, as he'd remembered, "to explore feminism." She'd never expected to end up reading about *herself* in one of the responses.

Numb, she ashed her cigarette on her bluejeans and mindlessly brushed them off. She had a sharp memory of breaking off with Irv; it had been one of the most painful moments of her life.

"Someone in this society has to fight male privilege," she'd lectured him. "If you men are not going to give it up willingly, we women will have to remove ourselves from your sphere. We're not going to sit back and play second fiddle to your revolution or your phalluses."

Irv had regarded her stunned. "But, Roz, I thought we were equals in this relationship."

"I once thought we were too, but we're not. Inequality is built into the social infrastructure. Women need time alone. To share, to think, to organize." Roz had just spent a week without him, while he was tending to his dying uncle; she knew her timing was horrible. "In this past week I've discovered so many things. I have a lot more discovery to do."

"I can give you all the time alone you want."

"I'm afraid I'll need a lot. I don't see how I can have any relationship with a man while I'm going through this. It's not you personally. I hope we can remain friends."

They hadn't. Irv had been too hurt during the following year they both still lived at the commune. Then Amelia's "flower children" slowly disbanded and Irv had married. Roz knew that the marriage was short and had ended in divorce.

Over the years they'd brushed elbows at various neighborhood and political events, but had always kept a respectful distance, acknowledging each other politely. She'd been privy to some of his doings through Juan. In recent months she'd hardly even thought of Irv, living a mere two and a half blocks away, as a candidate for the man she now wanted in her life.

1970 hadn't been the right time for her and Irv. Or at least not for her. She remembered when one night they'd made love outside and he'd said he wanted to make an "antiwar baby." The thought had appalled her. She later cited that night as the beginning of her estrangement, a pivotal point in her own feminist consciousness-raising: the right to do with her body exactly as she pleased and not feel guilty for it. That night she had felt guilty. But had he had his way, she probably would have been pregnant. Had they married, today she'd probably be a single mother of multiple teenagers and in psychotherapy.

Were the waning days of 1985 a better time than 1970?

Roz reread his letter: simple, to the point, charming. She crushed the remains of her Camel in the ashtray.

Embarrassment for herself gave way to embarrassment for him. How would he feel knowing he had written to her? She reflected that maybe he'd been hesitant to write, just like she'd been hesitant to place the ad, his letter arriving in this last batch. What if she anwered and he never responded? Or worse, responded with a firm "thanks, but no thanks?" It was a distinct possibility. She began to falter. Would she even have the nerve to contact him?

But she knew that if she was going to respond to any of the letters, it would have to be to his.

Sitting at home alone, her only company the oregano jar and the radio tuned to WORT, Roz spent the worst hours of the year: New Year's Eve. She'd been invited to a lesbian party and tactlessly asked the guest list. It excluded Erva Mae and Roxanne, who would probably be kindling passion to bonfire force on the west side.

She'd toyed with the idea of going and announcing her heterosexuality at midnight, but ultimately opted against it. Now she watched the clock strike, alone. To celebrate, she struck a match, which she put to a joint, and made a resolution as she watched the smoke encircle her: She'd write to Irv by the weekend and banish possible consequences — or lack thereof — from her mind.

The next morning she put her resolution into effect. She brewed a pot of coffee from Nicaraguan beans, took out pen and paper and lay an unopened pack of Camels at her side. She pondered beginnings, middles and endings, then gave up. The perfect letter didn't exist. Spurred on by her resolution and unwilling to procrastinate, she finally dove in:

Dear Irv:

Are you shocked to know it was me? You might have guessed that a woman searching for a feminist man might well be from our neighborhood, quite possibly someone you knew. Not, of course, that you'd have ever guessed I'd be looking for a straight male. But this time I do know what I'm doing. If you'd known it was me, would you have answered?

Times have changed in many ways, changed me. I presume, from your letter, you've changed, too. 1970 was the wrong time for me, the wrong time for a man — not to mention a child — in my life. I never would have guessed that my woman-identified phase (Did I just write that euphemism?) would last 15 years, but when you start out, you never know how long it will last, right?

No one knows about the "new" me except one other person. (By the way, that person lives with you. He doesn't, however, know about my ad, your letter or this response.)

Thanks for the sweet and revealing letter, which far outshines the other replies I received. I'd respond to it first, even if I hadn't known you already.

Irv, if there's a chance you harbor no resentment for what happened back then, consider contacting me. If you can't, I understand. I can't say that I regret what I did then or what I've gone through since, but I'd be willing to risk exploring a new start, if you're willing to take a risk on the same, yet different person.

Yours,

Roz

She quickly skimmed the letter. The phrase "if there's a chance" made her seem insecure. And the truth was that she was. After all, how could she expect a man she'd summarily dumped to want her again? But she simply had to know Irv's answer before she could go on. Her own letter seemed not only imperfect, but insufficient. But she felt tentative and didn't want to say too much. Short and to the point seemed best.

She dashed off to mail it before losing her nerve. Outside she pulled her beret down over her forehead as far as it would go. As she breathed, her breath froze in the air.

At the mailbox, she stopped. After she mailed it, how long would she have to wait in suspense? Wouldn't it be easier just to walk up Willy Street to his house, wave his letter in front of him and say, "Guess who, Irv?"

Simpler it might be. Though she had the nerve to slip the letter into the mailbox, she didn't to go knocking on his door. Besides, she didn't want him to have heart failure. In any case, he'd get enough of a jolt when he opened the letter.

With her mittened hand, she swiped unsuccessfully at the ice glued to the mailbox lid, pried it open and dropped the letter in.

36

Irv spent the morning with Seth licking labels for his anti-military newsletter. After Seth left, he ate without appetite in the living room, stared at the unfinished labels, then at his unfinished readings on the bricks-and-planks bookshelves. He'd once justified his celibacy to a friend by saying that if he were involved in a relationship, how would he ever have time to read? Outside of his work, his reading time had been limited to the "three B's": the bathroom, the bed and the bus. Pep's arrival had eliminated the one where he'd done the most and, since her departure, he hadn't resumed the habit. Today might be a good time: a cold winter afternoon, a warm bed and a good book.

He went down to get the mail; the whoosh of frigid January air almost propelled him back up the stairs. Among several pieces of business mail and a half-dozen letters from charities, he saw a hand-addressed envelope with no return address. He remembered the personal he'd answered on a lark and his heart began to race.

Irv stared at the envelope for a second. The handwriting looked oddly familiar. He opened it up; his eyes flew to the signature at the bottom of the page. He speed-read the page in astonishment and fell into a chair.

Roz... He remembered the spring of 1970. They had had an eighteen-month relationship. One night, after the two of them had participated in one of Madison's most vociferous antiwar demonstrations, they made love outside by Lake Mendota. Irv experienced a sort of cosmic bliss that caused a desire to procreate. Roz, it turned out, didn't share the same urge and mumbled something about "responsibility."

When they returned to the house, he found an urgent message to call his uncle, who wheezed that "there was little time left."

Having been orphaned by a car crash, Irv was raised by his father's brother, the wealthiest member, though black sheep of the family. When not in boarding school, he'd enjoyed worldwide travel with his uncle, especially to South America. It was there that Irv gained his first social conscience. While impressed with Rio de Janeiro's steamy beaches, scenery and the ocean-front penthouses, he was more impressed by the poverty. His first run-in with his uncle was for giving away his spending money to the poor.

At age eighteen he was sent off to Brown University and Uncle Julius retired from international business. When he left his Manhattan penthouse, Irv's childhood home, and Irv came to remove some of his belongings, he found a chest of supposed family memorabilia. The ''memorabilia'' turned out to be two passports for his uncle, neither bearing his real name and both heavily stamped.

When his uncle's name later circulated in connection with an international smuggling ring, Irv was less than shocked.

Bachelor's degree in hand, he left the Ivy League for an ambience better suited to his social conscience: the brewing hotbed of radicalism at the University of Wisconsin, where he'd been accepted to Law School. He began to refuse his monthly checks, certainly the fruit of ill-gotten avuncular wealth. His already keen conscience mushroomed and he took a vow of poverty to make Saint Teresa envious. By his second year in Madison, he got a teaching assistantship in Economics to support himself, broke off all contact with his uncle and moved into the commune where he met Roz and Seth and, soon after, Juan.

Although his uncle's message distressed him, he was irked at the thought of missing some of the best protests of the decade. Nonetheless, he went off to Bar Harbor, where his uncle had retired.

"I've consolidated all my monies and put them in a trust for you," Julius promptly stated.

A model of political and social rectitude, Irv said he didn't want them.

"We're talking about some four million."

Irv had expected an estate one-quarter that size, maximum. He quickly came to see how he could put the money to use for progressive social causes, but still he was loath to accept funds that might have stemmed from anything from cocaine to slavery. He had to find out their origin.

Uncle Julius glared at his impudence for asking. "If you must know, largely emeralds. But you deserve this money more than you know. Of course you remember the endless supply of custom-made leather boots I bought you?"

Irv hadn't thought of the boots in years. He wondered how many other memories would be lost with his uncle's death.

Julius put on a benevolent, yet chiding smile. "Even now you don't catch on. There was always a part of you that was too trusting.

"The heels. Hollow and removable. You transported a fair portion of my wealth into this country."

Back in Madison a week later with his uncle's ashes and his newfound financial clout, he was ready to change the world with Roz at his side.

His return coincided with her emergence from a weeklong consciousness-raising session with other newly liberated women. That they'd managed to ignore the antiwar effort for seven whole days and instead talk about their self-actualization as women and control of their own bodies left Irv incredulous. Other men in the commune were equally dumbstruck, now denied the "free love" they'd taken for granted.

"In short, I can't make love with you any more," Roz expounded from her lotus position on the floor. "Don't take this wrong. It's not you. I can't do it with you or any other man."

"If this has anything to do with that untimely fatherly urge I got the night before I left..." Irv trailed off as Roz shook her head no. She'd cut her hair in his absence.

"The point is," she went on, "that someone's got to fight penis power in this society."

Her words first left him uncomprehending, then shattered. She contorted her face into a lame smile, hopeful but unconvincing. The Roz who had just spoken was not the one he knew.

"I hope we can remain friends," she said feebly, before locking herself in the communal bathroom.

And she'd seemed locked away in another, all-women world since then. When the commune disbanded, he found himself with Harriet, who possessed an unshared predilection for premarital chastity, but a shared one for children. On the rebound from Roz, he'd married her. After eight months of failed tries at conception, she went to her gynecologist, who assured her the fault lay not with her. Promptly, she divorced Irv, married the doctor and moved in with him in his Lake Monona mansion.

Irv leaned back into the chair, not quite knowing what to think. Would he have responded to the personal had he known it was from Roz? Did Roz really know what she was doing, even now? Had her sexual orientation done a flip-flop from one day to the next? Could she be bisexual?

He didn't have time to ponder the questions. Juan burst into the room. "You look like you just saw a ghost."

"I did, of sorts."

All seriousness, Juan planted himself next to Irv. "No, don't tell me. Pep's not coming back, is she?"

Irv remained stone-faced.

"You heard from Harriet."

What ever possessed Juan to think of her? "No. You see... I got this letter — just as surprising — from Roz."

Now Juan went pale. "Do you mean she's announcing it by mail!?"

"Announcing what?"

"I was prohibited from telling. But it looks like you just found out.

What's she doing? Having a coming out party? She's always been unpredictable."

"I'll say. But there's more to it than that."

"I'm all ears."

"Well, you see... I was feeeling a little lonely after Pep left, as you
know. Anyway, I saw this intriguing personal in *Isthmus* about six weeks ago..."

Spring Semester

37

Lou arrived in Madison Sunday night of Registration Week for Spring Semester — a whopping misnomer. The temperature had fallen to ten below zero.

Beth had vowed to return early in the week. By afternoon Monday afternoon Lou expected her to zoom through the door any minute. She pictured her roommate's vacation: yachting off the Virgin Islands, drinking exotic cocktails on white-sand beaches and mingling with the jet set at luxury hotels. Making smart conversation about deep-sea fishing as her plane soared romantically above the clouds, before its fluffy descent into Madison, where she'd stun the lily-white locals with her bronzed skin.

After keeping vigil until eleven, Lou went to bed and imagined a night flight that served caviar for breakfast as the aircraft landed in Madison, illuminated by Tuesday's sunrise. She'd awake, look down and see Beth sprawled atop her bunk dreaming tropical dreams.

But the lower bunk remained empty. Lou registered for her own classes. She didn't know whether to be worried or irked. Beth could at least have sent a postcard, she concluded huffily to the mirror, "irked" winning out for the moment. That evening Robin Hatchman invited her to go drinking. Maybe Robin deserved a second chance. Lou accepted, feeling that this was somehow a way to take revenge on her tardy roommate. She didn't know whether to be anxious or glad that Robin hadn't had any news of Beth either.

Thursday afternoon the phone rang. It was freshman registration day. After two rings, Lou pounced on it.

"Hi, kiddo. Thought I'd never find ya. How ya doin'? How was the vacation? How's Mad City?" Beth paused for breath, but not to hear Lou's answers. "Look, I just got in to Miami from Kingston. O'Hare is closed down and I don't want to risk flyin' through Detroit and gettin' stranded. Do you think you can pick up my registration forms for me today? That'll really help when I get into town tomorrow. Thanks a million, kid. See ya."

Lou trudged through the snow to the Stock Pavilion, home not only to livestock, but to political rallies, concerts and student registration forms.

"I'm sorry. You need a written form filled out by the person in question to pick up someone else's forms and register by proxy," a student worker informed her.

She walked the mile back to the dorm, defeated, yet energized by Beth's imminent arrival. Lou spent the evening content in the dorm, beginning to read one of the works in the 20th-Century Women's Autobiography class she'd signed up for. The phone, nearly silent all week, rang; perhaps Beth had arrived early.

"Hullo," she answered brightly.

"This isn't Beth, is it?" The voice, female, was a cross between urgent and rude.

"No, I'm afraid it isn't," Lou said less brightly. "I don't expect her until tomorrow."

"I see. I expected her back tonight." The connection sounded long-distance.

"Would you like to leave a message?"

"No message. I'll have to try again after tomorrow. Thank you." The caller abruptly hung up.

By Friday morning, the temperature had deigned to rise to zero. Beth arrived, looking indeed as if she'd changed her skin color. "This semester I'm gonna register on time. Wanna come along, kid?"

Within an hour of her arrival, Beth stormed the campus, accompanied by Lou. On Friday, registration day for latecomers and "special students," there were no lines to combat. Nor were there spaces in most courses. Beth took whatever was available.

"I'll change everything next week. At least this way, I'm in." She'd signed up for second-semester Norwegian, Advanced Calculus, Medieval English Lit, and an advanced sociology course on "Deviant Behavior."

"This 'deviant' stuff sounds interesting, but, I don't have the prerequisites for this class or any of 'em."

"Speaking of classes, what did you get last semester? I was worried."

"Not as worried as me. I got a 1.9 and probation. Gotta do better or they'll cut me off." She swept her palm horizontally across the throat.

"You've just got to get into some easy, I mean, decent classes this semester."

"You got that right. And the word is 'easy.'"

After dinner, Lou suggested they go out for drinks. Beth agreed, but dawdled. When they finally left, she saw Beth look longingly at the telephone.

"Beth!" Lou burst out, louder than necessary, she realized. "I'm sorry, but I forgot to tell you that a phone call came for you last night. I'm sure it was long-distance. No message, though."

Beth's expression first lit up, then turned dour. "Oh."

She said nothing more. Lou left it at that, having given the message. Or non-message.

At the Kampus Klub bar, unofficially dubbed the "University Extension," Lou listened to Beth's account of her vacation. Recounting it, she seemed more preoccupied than wistful.

"You wanna walk a tired woman home, partner?" Beth said after two glasses of wine. "Or I'll go and you can stay."

Lou had just warmed up to the evening and Beth's companionship, more than the drinking. "No, I'll go with you."

Over the weekend, Beth remained moody and distant. It was as though something had changed in their relationship. To Lou's eye, nothing had, though she noted the lengthy, long-distance phone calls Beth was getting. She realized they were private, guessed the caller was the one she'd talked to, but made a point of not asking.

Lou felt left out, if not lonely, and realized her repertoire of friends was indeed limited: Heidi, Amy, usually Beth and maybe Robin.

Robin? She must be desperate for even thinking of her. Last semester had also produced Rusty, then Harold, whom she doubted she'd see again, their German class over, her usefulness to him finished. She'd simply have to make more friends. After classes started, she trusted she'd have the chance.

38

Over the loudspeaker came the pilot's voice: "The current temperature in Madison is a crisp twenty-two below zero. Skies are clear, winds at twenty to twenty-five miles per hour from the northwest. The windchill factor is... No, on second thought, you don't want to know." The pilot laughed lowly as the plane began its descent into Madison.

Cissy watched as Jeb repositioned his legs in a futile attempt to fit them comfortably into the available space. He turned to her and spoke: "The guy's smart. He knows if he tells us the windchill factor, we'll refuse to get off the plane."

A flight attendant came briskly down the aisle to do a final check for unfastened seatbelts. "Excuse me," Jeb said to her. "Does this plane turn around and go somewhere warm?"

"I'm afraid not."

"We're stuck, babe."

"If only this airport had jetways..." Cissy's ears popped.

"Plans are in the works for remodeling."

"A lot of good it does us now."

"I'm not getting off this plane with a fifty-below windchill factor."

The plane touched down, jolting them slightly. Cissy's ears popped again. "At least I bought a winter coat. And long underwear." She barely heard her own voice.

"And had the good sense not to pack them away."

Had she heard right? "You *packed* yours, Jeb?"

"Why do you think I don't want to get off? That job at Mississippi is looking better and better, babe."

"I can't disagree." At the NMA Convention, The University of Mississippi had posted a last-minute job, for which Cissy had interviewed on the spot. Now, besides Wisconsin, she had two other possibilities.

They braved the weather, Jeb borrowing the plane's blankets for extra protection, and arrived inside chilled, but not frostbitten. PC Cab's Airport Limo took them home. They'd left the thermostat set at 45 degrees. It had gotten so cold that the furnace had come on.

Jeb stepped up to the window. "The wood pile's buried in an avalanche."

Cissy drew up beside him. "Try glacier." She tried to peer through the window, covered by kaleidoscopic ice patterns.

"Thank God I left some wood inside."

Jeb crouched down in front of the stove, beginning to build a fire. Within a minute Irv was at the door.

"Welcome back, but don't bother with the stove." He handed a stack of accumulated mail to Cissy. "These stoves are only efficient down to about twenty below." He pointed to the thermostat on the living room wall. "You might as well crank up the heat. I would've myself, but didn't know if the airports would be open and when you'd be back."

Cissy observed Irv. Under a down vest, he wore an open sweater, and under it, a T-shirt. She pointed at the icicles that formed off the bottom of the letters spelling "Minnesota" across his chest. "You're dressed appropriately."

"Just to remind us that there are places worse than here. By the way, leave the faucets dripping hot water tonight. Pipes can freeze at twenty-five below."

Cissy feigned a shiver and began perusing the stack of mail, looking for job-related letters. A quick check showed none.

"Nights like this I sometimes wonder why I've stayed here two decades," Irv mused.

"I couldn't take two days of this!" Jeb rubbed Cissy's palm between his.

"You have to keep me warm," she joked. Then, to Irv: "Is the furnace still efficient at this temperature?"

"I don't even know if *I'm* efficient," said Jeb, while Irv nodded in reassurance.

Cissy no longer had to feign a shiver. She put her coat back on. "How will I ever get to school in this weather?"

"Hell, the university will be closed, babe. We'll be snowbound for days. Just you and me and the new electric blanket."

"Don't count on it closing," Irv said. "It closes for weather maybe a half-day every ten years. And this doesn't qualify as the worst weather of the decade."

"Tell me more and I'll be on the first plane out of here tomorrow."

"What about your electric blanket fantasy?"

"You're the fantasy, babe, not it."

"I'll leave you two to your fantasies." Irv scurried out the door.

"Alone at last. I'll go plug in the blanket."

Twenty minutes later, Cissy crawled underneath. It was more than toasty. The blanket tingled her back as she lay on top Jeb, as he caressed her. The blanket gave the term "hot sex" a new meaning.

Cissy preferred not to know the temperature when she left for FAB the next morning. She wore her winter coat over a thick sweater, and slacks over thermal underwear. She'd stopped short of buying a face mask with holes for eyes and nostrils. Instead she wrapped a scarf around her face, just below eye level. A furry Russian hat topped off her ensemble. The sun was out, the bus prompt, her journey less excruciating than imagined.

Inside FAB she retrieved her mail to digest privately in her office. No job news meant bad news. Of course, any written news usually meant bad news. Employers didn't call you up to reject you.

Having found nothing of interest, she reached the bottom of the pile and encountered a note from Sumner, asking her to see him as soon as possible.

Perhaps the Search Committee had had time to meet, she was a final-ist, they wanted to schedule a lecture for her. She knew well that departments acted quickly after the convention, wanting to snap up the best candidates before they took jobs elsewhere. If Sumner's note wasn't about the job, she'd certainly ask him about it.

She wedged her way past students inside the main office, then up to Sumner's door.

"Come in, Cis'ly," he stated matter-of-factly, and adjusted his glasses. "I assume you received my note."

"Yes, I did." Cissy searched for a some hint of what was to come, but found none. Isaacson got up and closed the door, then lowered himself into his cushioned chair. "I trust your vacation was pleasant, if not the convention." Before she could respond, he went on, curtly: "It's this: your Anthropology in the Museum class. Only three students registered in the last two days. Since it's limited to juniors and seniors, who've already registered, I foresee no more enrollment. So it looks like we'll have to cancel it and let you do the Intro class again." He put on a smile, perhaps to soften the blow, perhaps devilish.

Cissy tightened, deflated, then tried to regain a modicum of presence. "All my preparation..."

"Well, yes. That's unfortunate." Isaacson furrowed his brow. "These things happen. As you know, the academic ball sometimes bounces in infelici-tous directions. Ten students is the normal class minimum. Dean Phipps of-ten lets us get away with eight, even six in a graduate course. But I don't think your class will even reach five." Then, aiming for cheer, or to pacify her: "At least the Intro class will be easier the second time around."

"I suppose so." But only if I have 300 fewer students, she thought.

"I trust you haven't left your course notes in California."

Cissy remained unsmiling. "No, I didn't."

A long, slow knock rattled the door, which then opened. "A ques-tion about enrollment in 229," Wilhelmina interrupted.

"If you'll excuse me, Cis'ly." Isaacson jumped up, attentive. Or, she imagined, glad to have an excuse to cut the conversation short.

"Certainly." She got up and headed back to her office, anger simmer-ing to a boil. She jerked open her door and let it bang shut. At her window, she vigorously traced the swirling pattern of ice. Then she remembered: She'd forgotten to ask about the job. She rapped the window pane, stinging her knuckles.

39

G il arrived at the Willy Street house and found it empty Friday morning. He put on a Lou Reed album, full-blast, and unpacked. When he finished, he took his bong from the closet, changed the water and filled the bowl. He sucked in deeply until the water bubbled and repeated the process until stoned. He turned off the light, lay down on the bed and let Lou Reed filter into his consciousness, obliterating all else.

His eyes shot open when he felt a hand touch his shoulder. Juan stood above him and bent down to kiss him. "Finally." His tone was good-natured. "When did you get in?" He walked over to turn down the volume while Gil forced himself into coherence.

"Oh, a little while ago." He feared a barrage of questions and hoped he could cover his tracks of the past week. His father had cut off his tuition money after viewing his grades: D's in Pharmacology II, Compounding and Dispensing, and Pharmacy Jurisprudence and Ethics. The BC in Cissy's course hadn't helped enough to pull him up to a 2.00. And, worst of all, the Academic Progress Committee of the School of Pharmacy had declared him ineligible for registration in the third professional year. His quick solution: He'd simply not register this semester, and appeal for permission to continue in the professional curriculum. In the past he'd often come up with his own spending money only by using tuition money for living expenses until he'd made sufficient drug sales, then registering and paying a late fee. Since Juan and Irv thought the fraternity supplied Gil with drugs and not vice versa, he'd had to operate from the frat house to make his connections. After five frenzied days he'd come up with enough marijuana and pills to keep the COB brothers stoned and himself in money for at least two months.

Juan stood back and viewed him approvingly. "How'd you get here?"

"Cab." He hoped against hope that the response would suffice.

"Who drove you? Anyone I know?"

Gil knew that Juan imagined he'd taken PC Cab. But he hadn't, lest he have to explain his whereabouts to one of Juan's friends, or worse, to Juan. He told the truth, or partial truth: "Oh, some guy. Thirty, brown hair."

"Let's see who that could be." Juan ran a finger through the cleft of his chin. Gil rubbed his eyes awake. "It could have been Sam or Quinn or... I suppose it doesn't matter." He sat on the bed and pulled off his boots. "So when did you get in?" Juan snuggled up horizontally to him. "I assume you didn't leave Green Bay at five in the morning to get here."

Gil had prepared for the question. He got up to flip the record, feeling safer answering from a distance. "I got a ride last night from one of the guys in the house." It was true that one of them had given him a ride: to go pick up two pounds. "It was easier to stay at the house than to come over here when I got into town after midnight." Again true: to get the dope, they'd left the city limits and got back into town after twelve. Gil surveyed Juan's expression for a reaction, assuring himself that his story was plausible.

"I suppose it was easier." Juan emphasized "suppose."

"You were driving last night anyway, right?"

"From two until right now." He yawned, then stretched. "So what's been happening? We haven't talked on the phone for a week."

"Bad news." Gil flopped on the bed next to him. Now ready to tell a raw truth, he hoped proximity would lend to commiseration. "I got turned down for registration for the third-year courses."

The bed creaked. He saw Juan's facial muscles tense. "That's outrageous. How could they?"

"Same old reason."

Still reclined on the bed, Juan patted Gil's knee, his head tilted back. "So are you going to register today? Or pay a late fee as usual?"

Gil wished the interrogation would end. He was stoned enough that it became a chore to answer without tripping himself up. "What's to register for? I'm not going to at all."

Juan looked up, his mouth ajar, eyes reverberating in their sockets. Gil knew that Juan feared that if he were not in school, he might not stay in Madison. The truth was that he had nowhere else he cared to go.

"So what are you going to do?" Juan rolled over on his side to face him.

"Oh, spend the semester here and make one last try for admission in the summer or fall. Wanna get high?"

"No, thanks, not right now." Juan slid out of his bluejeans, revealing grey thermal underwear with a seductive button fly. Sex leapt into Gil's mind. It never had far to leap.

"But don't you think that, if you registered for something this semester, your chances of getting back in the program would be better?"

His attempted deflection of the conversation having failed, Gil pondered this. "Maybe. But my old man said he'd wasted enough on me in tuition. I've got no choice, at least not this semester."

"I can't believe they won't let you continue. What did you end up with last semester?"

"A 1.4. That BC Cissy gave me didn't much help."

"I doubt that Cissy was the overriding factor in the whole picture."

Gil didn't want to get off to a bad start by arguing, by accusing Juan of having limited sympathy for his poor academic performance. He had one ploy left; it almost always worked. "Let's get into bed, why don't we?"

Juan took off his remaining clothes and scooted under the sheet and heavy Peruvian poncho that served as winter blanket. "It's my regular bedtime anyway."

Gil grinned with studied mischief. "But not sleep time."

40

I rv made an admirable stab at his fried egg at Willy Street's greasiest spoon. The underside of the egg propelled itself to the opposite edge of the plate before he cornered it, raised it to his mouth and let it slither down his throat. Roz cracked a smile and subdued her own egg.

When he'd glimpsed her at the Co-op last night, he feared her eyes had caught his. By this morning, the last of his indecision had melted. Feeling guilty for his procrastination, he called her right up.

"I had a premonition it might be you when the phone rang at eight. Not my most social hour of the day." Roz sat with her elbows stationed on each side of the plate. When she tried to move one, it stuck to the red-and-white checkered plastic tablecloth.

"Once I make up my mind, I act. I thought if you were free, I was free, and we might as well get together on the spot."

"Right. It left us no time to worry what it would be like. Not to mention time to wake up or get ready for those of us who aren't terminal insomniacs."

"It's simply five a.m. rising by choice." Irv remembered their preferred sleep schedules, which once overlapped by only three hours, and doubted they'd changed. He tried not to stare at Roz's Auschwitz haircut. She couldn't claim she'd needed time to comb her hair this morning.

"You know I saw you too last night." She trapped another hunk of egg, shoveled it into her mouth and spoke while chewing: "I figured if you didn't call today, you wouldn't call at all. I had to convince myself you weren't avoiding me. Of course, I thought you were."

"And last night I still was. But I concluded I might as well get up the nerve to do what I wanted to do promptly."

He saw Roz flinch as he conquered the last of his egg. "Don't get me wrong. I didn't invite you to breakfast to tell you I wasn't interested."

"My heterosexual ego's still very fragile." Roz parted her lips, revealing a row of slightly uneven teeth. "I'm glad you overcame your tendency toward indecision."

"You don't forget, do you?" Irv folded his paper napkin and brushed it across his mouth. "You knew it might well take me a week or two to make up my mind."

"There *are* times I'd like to forget." She pulled out a filterless Camel.

"For me too. For example... No, let's remember the good times. Dow Day..."

"I wasn't thinking of the Dow Chemical riots, but some of the more tender moments."

"I blotted out a lot from the interpersonal realm." Irv pushed away his plate. "My most clear memory is the night I returned with my uncle's ashes, and you..."

Roz exhaled smoke like a volcano. "Please, let's not relive that." Then, after a pause: "The difference then was that I was out for the Cause. Today I'm learning to look out first for myself."

"Ah, the eighties."

"But not without renouncing causes."

"A mere shift in emphasis. Now it's fifty-one percent for you and forty-nine for causes."

"Right." Roz seemed distracted, perhaps uneasy. "Sally! How about refilling these coffee cups?"

He watched as Sally slung a rag over her shoulder and slogged over to the opposite side of the restaurant. She had a singular talent for going deaf when her services were requested, as well as a hard veneer, developed during years of work at a now-defunct co-op restaurant. "I see some things in this world never change." Irv nodded toward Sally. "Then again, the fifty-one percent she used to give customers seems to have tapered off a little."

"You might too if you'd been through what she has."

Irv accepted this mild rebuke as they looked toward Sally, now involved in a powwow with the chief grill cook.

"Her station in table waiting has certainly gone downhill," Roz said, as Irv turned his eyes to a menu scotch-taped to the wall. His eyes kept roving; they both surveyed the grungy premises, politically correct only if there existed a correlation between dirt and politics.

Roz broke the silence, which had momentarily degenerated to contagious uneasiness: "Since we first knew Sally, she's been married twice, battered, has at least three kids, one of them in a juvenile detention facility. If it weren't for places like Womynspace... Think, Irv. That could be me today if we'd married fifteen years ago."

"Minus the battering, I trust."

Sally turned around and Roz held her coffee cup upside down. She made a "be-there-in-a-sec" gesture, pointed at the empty carafe on the coffeemaker and shuffled over to the jukebox.

Irv knew that social interaction with Roz tended toward the intense and he still felt tentative. He remembered her quick decisions: In 1970 it had taken her but a week to declare war on the patriarchy. Might she not decide just as quickly now that men weren't for her after all?

But this was negative stereotyping. Feminist men were not supposed to think women fickle. He knew that he still didn't understand Roz. And the obligation to understand her better was his. "I needed ten years to work things out after the sixties."

"Me, fifteen and still working on it." Roz twirled her empty coffee cup in her hand and demolished her cigarette butt with a squash of the thumb.

"At least the sixties happened early in our lives. Who knows how we'd react if they happened today?"

Roz scrunched up her face. "How would we have made it till now if they hadn't happened?"

"Coffee's drippin'!" Sally announced from the jukebox, alternately contemplating its titles and the coffeepot. Seconds later a woeful Crystal Gayle tune came on. To Irv it seemed appropriate to the premises. Or perhaps it merely summed up Sally's mental state.

Roz suddenly turned her face to the wall.

"Is something wrong?"

"Erva Mae just pedaled by. She doesn't know about, uh, my change."

"So she'll find out, won't she."

"I probably shouldn't make such a big deal out of it. It's like being gay and having people find out before you come out of the closet."

"I've never known you to be hampered by closets."

I haven't been." Her tone came out harsh. "It's just that I'm not ready to come bursting publicly out while living with Erva Mae and working at Womynspace."

"Our meeting *is* innocent. Two old friends getting together, nothing more." Irv hoped she'd buy this logic, but began to envision her dilemma.

"Old friends of opposite sexes don't get together in some cases."

"So she finds out you're not a separatist."

"She knows it damned well. But her seeing me with you is another matter. So Womynspace disowns me..." She gave a lame shrug of her shoulders.

"Lots of straight women work at Womynspace, no?"

"Yeah, but they're not the ones who are my bosses." Roz looked at her watch. "Speaking of which, I've got to be there at ten. Drink a cup of coffee for me."

"Right. Go catch your bus."

"I'm biking it," Roz said, as he contemplated a snowbank out the window.

Irv felt relieved at their parting, though it hadn't gone badly. He turned to face her, trusting that she agreed, that they could slip back into easy informality. "Shall I call you or you call me?"

"Whichever." Roz stood, put on her coat and pulled her beret down to her eyebrows. "I'll call."

"Sounds great to me. You always were the control freak."

Roz paused, perhaps registering this truth, made a face and pressed two one-dollar bills into his hand. He knew better than to refuse them. He squeezed her hand briefly and Roz walked away.

Fondling the bills, he walked up to the counter. "How much do I owe?"

"I thought you and Roz wanted coffee." Sally indicated the pot, now two-thirds full.

"Wanted. Past tense," Irv specified with a wide smile.

Sally stared at the numbers on the check, lowered her pencil and did laborious addition. "That'll be $4.02 for the two of you."

Irv handed her a five and one of Roz's ones. "All for you," he said.

He walked outside, wondering how to get downtown. Tire tracks corrugated the snow on the street. If he didn't have to go uphill to reach his office, he could cross-country ski to work. He decided to walk.

Outside he saw Roz pedaling bravely down Willy Street. At the first intersection sparrows lined the telephone wires above him. Their perch looked precarious, though wasn't.

It was his own with Roz that was.

41

"When they hired me here, I was interviewed at the NMA in December, on campus in January, and they offered me the job at the end of February." Ginger paused, either for emphasis, drama or to admire the sheen from her gold. "And if I hadn't told them I had seven other offers, they probably wouldn't have grabbed me up so 'quick.'"

Cissy swiveled in her chair. "Seven other offers?"

"Of course not, Cis. I only had two, one at a black school where they wanted me to create a museum with $20,000 capital, and at a salary even lower. The other was in North Dakota, where by hiring me they probably thought they'd fill their Affirmative Action quota for the whole state. But I put the pressure on here and it finally worked. So you do the same. You've got nothing to lose."

On her way out, Ginger opened the door and almost collided with a young man before her heels went gouging down the hall. Cissy vaguely recognized the student, burly and attractive.

"I'm Bernard Clarkson from your Intro class last semester." The hunk stepped partway inside and adopted an aggressive, masculine stance, exuding a sexual aura students were not supposed to exude. "I think I deserve more than a D for all the effort I made in your class last semester." His voice was steady, with smug superiority.

"Sit down, if you wish. Let's see," Cissy said coolly, well-prepared after three other grade complaints this semester. She'd refined her defensive techniques: Grades were based on numbers and facts, were neither disputable nor discussible, save for clerical errors.

Students who came to "discuss" their grade inflamed her. At least this one hadn't used the offending word. She opened her gradebook, guessing without looking what she'd find.

"Seventeen absences," she stated after counting red checkmarks. "And I probably missed some." Pointedly not looking at him, she turned to the exam grades. "C, D and F on your exams, plus an F on the pop quiz. You can see this averages out to a D, without even taking your absences into account." She scribbled the immutable evidence on a paper, keeping her physical distance and the gradebook from him.

"You wouldn't believe how many hours I put in studying for this course."

Cissy was tempted to agree: yes, probably about ten for the whole semester.

Defensive techniques to the forefront: Ignore unproven statements and stick only to the facts. "You know, you're actually much closer to an F than a C."

His masculine veneer rapidly vanished. "I'm going to lose my financial aid over this."

Empathize, console. But only momentarily. "If it's any consolation, I once received a D myself. In Botany."

"You did?" His tone brightened, then dissolved into a whine. "But I bet you didn't lose any financial aid over it."

Cissy detected the beginning of a sniffle. Don't be swayed by emotional ploys. Or, in this case, by the crumbling macho act of a young hunk. Stick to the evidence. Assert authority.

"If you lose your financial aid, I'm sorry. But please don't pull any guilt trips on me. In order for you to lose your aid, I'm sure you had to get other grades just as low."

"B-b-but..."

Cissy brandished the grade book. "Facts are facts. I'm sorry, but there's nothing I can do."

"You could do a guy a favor." Wounded, he tried to resurrect an appealing swagger. "You wouldn't believe the money I'm going to lose over this. It's no skin off your back to change a D to a C, is it?"

If this was his idea of suavity, he failed in that department too. Keep on deflecting sentiment. Reassert authority. Give advice. "In the future I suggest attending class more regularly to prevent these situations. Seek out your instructor, your TA or classmates for help. I never saw you in my office once last semester."

Bernard Clarkson had no comeback. He was at least smart enough to see he wouldn't get anywhere. Cissy stood up, hoping he'd do likewise. Reluctant and glaring, he did.

The next morning she again had a note to go see Sumner. The tenure track job? She doubted it. But this time, she'd at least remember to inquire. She had nothing to lose. Except, in the face of rejection, her self-esteem.

"How's life down in the trenches?" Rickover greeted her when she walked into the main office. She threw him a bewildered glance and he clarified: "The Intro course."

Before she could answer, Sumner's voice rang out from his inner office. "Cis'ly, is that you? Please come in."

Inside she observed the snowscape below, where sidewalks crisscrossed the quadrangle and met at a fountain, the winter metal covering of which resembled a large bluish-green breast.

"How are your classes going this time around?"

"Artifacts, quite well.'' The full name of the course was Materials and Techniques in Art and Archaeological Artifacts. ''I have thirteen students, mostly majors."

"Yes, to be expected. And your Intro class? Or 'the trenches,' as Vance puts it?"

Cissy aimed for something positive to say. "I have 340 students." For her it was positive; the fewer students, the better.

"So I've seen. Enrollment is down, isn't it?" He spoke with an optimism that would indicate the opposite, then sifted through a stack of papers. "Indeed, 341 on the official list. Usually we have no problem reaching 400. But enrollments are always down in the spring."

Cissy made a gesture of assent, hands clasped on her lap. Sumner cleared his throat. "I wanted to speak with you about grading, Cis'ly." Thumb under his chin, he tapped his forefinger to his face, ruminating. "Students change, times change, standards change," he began, philosophically, as if suddenly inspired.

Cissy retained a facade of polite cordiality, wondering where this would lead.

"Your predecessor converted the Intro class into one of the most popular on campus, by rarely giving a grade lower than B. Popularity is fine as long as you have standards. Gitlitz let them go, but you did a good job of raising them last semester."

The compliment was welcome. Cissy felt her facade turn mildly re-splendent.

"I've had several grade complaints about your course. That certainly never happened when Gitlitz taught it." Isaacson seemed to fondle some humorous memory. Then his face went blank, before turning almost severe. She felt a hairline crack in her facade.

"I questioned these students thoroughly." He squinted at a page, as though trying to decipher his own handwriting. "Here's one named Clarkson, who gave some sob story about losing his financial aid. The D seems totally justified. Another, who got a C, said that your course is one of those intended to 'flunk the people out of their university.' That's a new twist." As though amused, Isaacson wadded up this complaint and tossed it into the trash. "Here's another, from a boy named Johns..."

Cissy interrupted successfully: "A girl, I believe. Betsy Johns. The sandal-dropper. Never mind about that. She missed over twenty classes, and I lowered the grade, as per departmental policy."

"I'm not questioning your grades. Far be it from me..." Isaacson kneaded his chin with his forefingers. "When I hear complaints from students, I know that standards are being maintained. When I never hear a complaint about a particular teacher, I begin to wonder."

Cissy pondered this odd academic logic.

"The Introductory course is our departmental bread and butter." A slight ponderous tone crept into his voice. "It supports all our upper-level courses. Reputations about classes spread like raging fire here. I'd hate to see next fall's enrollment down again. I trust in your good sense."

Cissy was tongue-tied. He seemed to approve, yet disapprove of her grading. Did a veiled accusation lurk somewhere? Apparently he'd said all he had to say. She had to order her thoughts quickly. "I have an unrelated question," she blurted out. "If you have another minute."

As Isaacson grunted assent, she stalled, choosing the proper wording: "I wanted to inquire... about the tenure-track position here. I haven't heard anything..."

"I see." His voice went flat. "We'll be proceeding shortly. You'll know something soon, one way or the other. But I suggest you keep other avenues open."

The tone hardly invited her to pursue the matter. She felt embarrassed, anxious to get away, and stood up. Her facade fairly crumbled, she reconstructed it into a faint smile and left.

Wilhelmina rolled her eyes wearily toward Sumner's office, as if all the world's woes stemmed from there. "You got to watch out for yourself 'round here," she said. "Otherwise they'll swallow you up. But I know you're doing fine, Professor Pankhurst."

Perhaps she should begin reading over Wilhelmina's shoulder, as Ginger and Evan had suggested. She'd probably learn more that way than she ever would from Sumner, whose opinions proved either contradictory or indecipherable.

She headed back to her own office. The words "keep other avenues open" echoed in her head. Right now they were all too open, devoid of traffic. She needed security or at least encouragement. Today she might have to be satisfied with Wilhelmina's.

42

"In short, Violette Leduc's La Bâtarde is one of the most probing, penetrating, forthright accounts ever written by a woman, of a woman limited and dwarfed by her sex and sexuality."

Lou perked up at the mention of sex, as the professor's clinical voice paused. The professor spoke as if she had been talking about the price of hogs instead of the intimate life of a courageous woman. She continued: "Regarding the instances of intertextuality between Leduc's autobiography and her novels, please refer to your bibliographies."

A rustling of papers went up as Lou attempted to locate the page. She pulled it out, uninterested. By enrolling in Women's Autobiography, she wanted to hear about women's lives, not intertextuality, deconstructionism and grammatology. It hadn't taken long to realize that the professor, steeped and stolid in her scholarship, deemed that the less said about such earthy realities as sex and passion, the better. Besides the works themselves, the closest they'd come to dealing with the body was an article entitled "Cancer as Leitmotiv in Modern European Feminist Prose," required reading for all.

Lou's mind drifted back to class. Ennui incarnate, she looked at the page where the professor was surgically deconstructing Leduc. She might as well have been speaking Urdu to Lou, and, to judge by the faces of those around her, to the vast majority. The professor announced another page and paragraph and plunged her intellectual scalpel into the meat. Lou tried to follow. She thought she'd understood Leduc, but each successive word of the professor's left her as perplexed as a cannibalistic people listening to a lecture on the nuances of a French sauce. She swallowed a yawn and watched the clock creep forward.

"For next Friday..." The class rumbled at the hint of an assignment. "You people are going to deconstruct. I'm not going to say a single word. As a matter of fact, I'll be giving a paper at a conference in Boston. But my tape recorder will be here and you will all receive a participation grade for the day." The professor then recited a list of pages and assigned them collectively to groups of three students each. By the time she went around the room, only Lou and one other person remained. "The two of you should be able to tackle this on your own," the professor said to them, then dismissed the class and bustled out. The students lingered, looking with bewilderment at their co-horts in deconstructionism. At least Lou seemed to have company in her ignorance. Her partner turned to face her.

"Hi. I'm Verla McSurely," she bubbled. She was round-faced, with long blond hair, and wore imitation designer bluejeans and a white lace blouse. "This should be challenging. I'll look forward to doing it with you."

Taken aback by this unbridled spunk, Lou jarred herself out of her lassitude. "Well, it's just you and me, I guess. I'm Lou Lautermilk."

Verla's smile held on, radiating sweetness, if not unadulterated joy at the project.

"We have to do this for next Friday," Lou said. "So that gives us a whole week."

"Why don't we get together early next week?"

"Sure, I guess. It shouldn't take us too long, should it?"

"I wouldn't think so," Verla effervesced. "How about next Wednesday? Would that be good? How about seven?"

"The dining hall closes at 6:15, so that would give me time for dinner. Do you want to meet at the library, the Union, somewhere else?"

Verla's eyes peered into Lou's with an odd intensity; her lingering smile grew as wide as Lake Mendota. "I've got an idea. You could come to my house. It's much quieter than the library."

"The library can be a zoo."

"I was thinking..," Verla went on, her white teeth shining like squat, sun-bathed pillars. "I remember how bad cafeteria food is. So, if you'd like, you could have dinner at my house. It's no extra work, really. We could eat at six and be studying by seven."

"I wouldn't want to put you to any trouble. It's not really necessary."

"It's no trouble at all. Of course it's not necessary that we eat, or even get together at my house. It's only a suggestion, only if you'd like."

Under the circumstance, why should she refuse such an invitation? "Sure, I'll come. And in case we get stuck Wednesday night, there's still Thursday," she added, wanting to insure that the endeavor proved successful in the academic realm, if not in the social.

"Wonderful, Lou. I live near the Capitol, just a fifteen-minute walk from here. I can give you directions in class next week."

"That's great. Thanks."

Verla bade an effusive farewell and glided away, intent on some destination or purpose. Lou had noticed her in class, always well dressed and smiling courteously. She only hoped there were brains behind the smile.

She had set out to find new friends this semester and, with Verla, might make the first. Exhilarated, she hummed her way back to the dorm.

Astonished, Beth walked out of Dean Constance Romney's office. That there were deans to help students amazed her. That there were deans to help students find easy courses flabbergasted her. She had imagined only stern-faced deans who handed down reprimands for truancy or suspensions for low GPAs or cheating. After she had dumped her entire original schedule, she managed to get into modern American Lit and a History class, but needed two or three more. The dean had just found them for her, but it was Friday afternoon of the second week of classes, the last day to add courses. She'd have to hurry.

She stepped outside; she was half-way up, or down Bascom Hill, depending on perspective. The algae-green statue of Abraham Lincoln, whose eight-feet-high lap made a favorite sitting place for mind-altered students agile or determined enough to reach it, presided over the steep hill.

She looked up the hill, where she should go to register for the freshman Seminar on Nuclear Issues; then down, where she could enroll for Intro to Museums. It was also the same direction as her dorm, where she was expecting a call from Jamaica.

Undecided, she looked at her watch. She lacked time both to register and to return to her dorm for her call from Amber. She and Am had agreed on 4:00, three days a week, when Lou was in her autobiography class and they could have privacy.

Beth compromised, rationalizing that Math for Humanists — which Dean Romney said was hard to get into — must be closed. If she got into only two of the three suggested classes, she'd be content.

She hurried to the Social Science Building and claimed the next-to-the-last spot in Nuclear Issues. Backtracking down Bascom Hill, she quickened her pace in spite of the steep incline, confident that her surefootedness would lead her safely over hidden patches of ice under the snow, beaten down by the imprints of some 88,000 feet. As Bascom Hill abruptly bottomed out into North Park Street, she darted across it, beating the oncoming traffic. She entered the Fine Arts Building and on the fifth floor located the Department of Museum Studies office, where a secretary registered her, her movements as slow as her Southern accent. Beth fretted as she eyed the wall clock, hoped she was making the right move by following Dean Romney's advice on this course. She knew Lou hadn't found it all that easy.

Duly matriculated for her twelve credits, an acceptable if not heavy load, she dashed to the elevator with her registration forms and, impatient, instead took the stairs. She jogged partway back up Bascom Hill and turned them in. It was 4:20; Lou usually returned around 4:30.

On her way out, she saw a pay phone. The immediate area afforded privacy. She could call Amber from here with her mother's credit card. She pulled it out, dialed the number of the Windward Sloop in Kingston and a minute later was connected.

"Miss Amber Aragno, please," she said with the worldly air of one requesting to speak to a rising actress.

The phone rang in Amber's suite and Beth turned to the wall, savoring the memory of her delicious curves and sensual skin.

"Yes?" came the voice, sultry yet expectant.

"Am!" she said in hushed exclamation, as if about to swoon. She grabbed the wooden panel of the phone booth, as a tingle shot through her body.

"I thought I was going to miss you today. I called at four, but you were out." Amber's tone was flat, without sympathy.

"You didn't miss me after all," Beth replied with ardor, transplanted mentally into the arms of her newfound lover. "But, oh, I miss you." Her new schedule, Madison and the snow all melted from her mind.

"I've missed you too," Amber cooed over the wires, competing with a harsh static.

"I don't know how I'll stand it here without you." Beth leaned into the wall, caressing the bottom of the receiver with her free hand. "Right now I don't even wanna be in school."

"It's your choice. You know you can come be with me any time."

43

Teeth chattering from the cold, Juan stepped into Steep & Brew with Eric. They had just fallen out of the ranks of some fifty marchers heading up State Street, following the rally that culminated the "US Out of Nicaragua or Wisconsin Out of US" campaign. Since its kickoff last fall, some 1,100 signatures had been collected in support. The marchers now trooped to the Capitol to hand the signatures to the governor.

"We'll just have a quick coffee and you can join them in ten minutes," said Eric. He was hatless, wearing a leather jacket and seemingly oblivious to the cold.

"Sounds good." Juan still trembled under his T-shirt, two flannel shirts, down vest and pea coat. Outside, the tail end of the marchers passed by, shouting, "*El pueblo! Unido! Jamás será vencido!*" A few patrons inside peered out to see what was happening.

Eric stepped to the end of the service line. "What'd you think of the turnout?"

Juan huddled up next to him. "At seven degrees and an unmentionable windchill factor, what can you expect?" He had counted some seventy-five people at the rally, including news media and the organizers. He himself had been personally responsible for getting Gil, Irv, Roz and Eric to attend.

Eric's turn to order came. "One cup of Panamanian."

Juan went livid. "We go to a Nicaraguan rally and you come in here and order Panamanian!"

"It's today's special." Eric pointed at the chalkboard and counted out the exact change. "Seventy-nine cents."

"The Nicaraguan's only ninety-nine and much better," Juan argued, and proceeded to order it. "You throw politics out the window for twenty cents?"

"Yeah. Plus, who knows, it could be Contra coffee."

Juan paid the cashier and followed Eric to the back.

"You know, that's curious about Roz and Irv," Eric said.

Roz's secret still intact, Juan conjured up a reasonable facsimile of perplexity. "What's curious?"

"She seems different lately. I mean it's the same old Roz on the surface, but something's odd."

"I wouldn't know what."

"I don't know either. I watch her at the Co-op. She seems more attentive, more friendly."

"She's not unfriendly, if you really know her."

Juan warmed his hands over the steaming coffee.

"Then I see her with Irv today. Whatever it is, I don't know what to think." Eric brought his cup to his mouth, but put it back down. "Aren't you even going to take off your hat and scarf? You look like an Eskimo."

"Wrong ethnic background. And no, I'm not. I'm still cold."

"Isn't Gil keeping you warm these days?"

Juan was glad for the change of topic, but it was barely an improvement over Roz's newfound friendliness. "He came to the rally. I suppose I should consider that a special favor in view of his political nature, or lack thereof."

"Sounds decent of him to come."

"But he's not marching up State Street."

"Hey. Give him a break. Neither are we." Eric blew on his coffee, then sipped it.

"Yeah, but neither one of us disappeared with the cameraman from Channel 7."

"Maybe he was giving an exclusive interview."

"Try giving something else."

Eric waved his hand dismissively. "C'mon. How could he?"

Juan didn't want to imagine. He tested his own coffee.

"Listen. That's what monogamy causes: paranoia. Besides, I thought you told me he was a model of fidelity."

Juan remembered the conversation at the Bull Dog. "So I lied. He's been unfaithful once, that I know."

"Ah, the truth comes out."

Juan turned an incendiary glance on him. "Don't gloat."

"All right. But you're upset."

Juan took a healthy gulp of coffee. "I am not."

"Then why are veins throbbing in your neck and forehead?"

"Caffeine overdose?"

"Don't drink Nicaraguan. Too strong."

"You're right. Not about the Nicaraguan, but Gil. I am upset, though I hope over nothing. I know I don't own him."

"Say that like you mean it."

Juan mumbled the words.

"I don't think you believe that, but won't press the point."

"He probably got cold, went to the frat house to smoke a joint, and I'll see him at the Capitol shortly." Juan failed to convince himself; he slurped his remaining coffee.

"That sounds better." Eric raised his cup to his mouth, brought it down and wiped his moustache with his tongue.

"Coffee warm you up?" Juan extracted a mangled ultra-light from his pack, straightened and lit it.

"I froze my ass off at your rally."

"As far as freezing your ass off, you could put on some winter clothes, instead of going to a rally dressed like a sex symbol. At least wear a hat and some long underwear."

"Long underwear? Hell, I never wear any underwear. Don't look so puzzled. Underwear, you know, obscures things."

"You're hopeless."

"You never know when, where..."

"...you might bump into a randy cameraman from Channel 7." Juan's words came out before their reality stung him. Trying to mask his worry, he quickly went on: "Speaking of which, have you met anyone interesting lately?"

"Oh, so you want to hear what you're missing out on? Vicarious polygamy. You want me to talk dirty."

"I was asking in the romantic, not sexual realm. And in general, not for details."

"At least you didn't say 'sordid' details, you prude."

Juan stuck his spoon in his cup. "I'm finished. You too?"

Eric clanked a spoon in his empty cup.

Juan gathered up his gloves, the only clothing he'd removed. "Shall we go then? We could take a bus to the Capitol in time to see them give the petitions to the governor."

"I thought they rerouted the buses because of your march up State Street. We could take a bus to the Bull Dog instead."

"You have a one-track mind."

"No, two tracks. One is safe sex. Two is romance."

"How good not to hear you be cynical. But the two tend to travel on the same track."

"In your mind."

Shaking his head, Juan got up, Eric behind him, and threaded his way through the tables and down the corridor to the front. "So you're not coming to the Capitol with me?"

"Hey, I went to the rally, man. I support the Cause. Up to where it conflicts with my own priorities."

"OK. I hope you find Mr. Safe Sex of your dreams and that it turns into major romance."

"Hey, don't put your cigarette out! Blow some smoke in my mouth, will you?"

Since Eric had stopped smoking, he'd become a fan of secondhand smoke, inhaling all he could get. Juan obliged him, crushed the butt in his pocket ashtray, and they walked outside. At the top of State Street, he could see the end of the marchers. He patted Eric on the back. "So long. Have some sex for me."

"I knew you weren't getting enough. Just stop brooding about Gil and the cameraman, or better yet, find your own and have him take some hot photos of you."

Juan slapped him playfully and began his own brisk hike to the Capitol. The petitions wouldn't ultimately achieve anything. But at least it was something. As was Gil. But not exactly the something that he'd always dreamed of.

44

"Let's talk in the living room." Erva Mae wielded a knife, dissecting a hunk of goat's milk cheese. "You'll want to sit down for this, Roz."

"Yeah, I'll sit. But in the bathroom first. Gimme a minute."

Leaving Erva Mae to chop, Roz locked herself in the bathroom and purposely lingered. She lit a Camel and, moments later, heard Erva Mae muttering in a low voice, as if rehearsing a speech. If she spoke up a little,

they could have their conversation through the door, while Roz sat content-
edly on the toilet lid and smoked.

Erva Mae had left her a note that morning requesting a "house meeting." They hardly saw each other, passing at work and occasionally at home,
when Erva Mae came to get mail or clothes. Most nights she slept at Roxanne's.

Roz flushed her cigarette butt down the toilet and went into the living room. Erva Mae turned abruptly on her heels, facing her, and made a point
of offering a chair. As if I can't take it standing up, Roz thought. She stood
opposite her, two boxers ready to square off.

Erva Mae fixed a defiant gaze on her, though her tone was measured,
studied: "Roz, I know we can be civil about this. At least I should hope."

"Go ahead." Roz stepped back off the circular rug onto the wood floor.
The rubber of one sneaker screeched. Erva Mae frowned, as though Roz had
purposely interrupted her concentration. As if to regain the advantage, she
tugged at the bottom of her sweater, stretching the wool tightly, outlining her
breasts. The battle lines were drawn. Erva Mae hooked one thumb in the
pocket of her bluejeans and began: "I'm moving out, Roz. Roxanne has asked
me to move in with her."

More likely, you badgered her into it, thought Roz, who said nothing for a moment. Erva Mae poised herself, as though awaiting outrage or congratulations. Roz let several beats pass, then spoke: "I wouldn't tell you who
to live with."

"And I'm not asking you to," Erva Mae pounced. "Just because you
couldn't make it work with Rox doesn't mean I can't now."

Roz ignored this slight to her own coupling skills. The announcement,
not unexpected, relieved her.

"I know I'll have to get someone to sublet and I think I've found just
the right person."

Roz cringed at Erva Mae's idea of the "right person." For this she decided to sit down.

Still in the center of the rug, Erva Mae shifted her weight and faced
her. "It's Lorna Taney. She needs a place until summer, since she broke up
with Annette. They'd shared a room at the women's co-op and there were no
other rooms to move to. So they flipped a coin, Lorna lost and has to move
out." Erva Mae twisted a strand of tousled hair. "So what do you think?"

Roz leaned forward as Erva Mae strangled the ribbing of her sweater.
Pensive, she then leaned back, hands behind her head, elbows jutting out.

"Well?" Erva Mae coaxed in apparent confidence.

"First, what about summer? Either you or Lorna would have to sublet again in three or four months."

"I'm sure Lorna could find someone. The co-op always has an excess of women to accommodate."

"And Madison has sky-high apartment vacancies in summer. I don't think I want to go through two new housemates in the next six months."

"Roz." Erva Mae's tone implied pettiness.

"Another thing..." Roz shushed her with a hand gesture before she could protest further. "I don't intend to keep this a separatist household after you move out."

Erva Mae's eyes bugged out with the disbelief of one hearing heresy: Patriarchs are not pigs, God is not a woman. As her mouth remained agape, Roz took advantage of the silence: "You heard right. I need to broaden, not limit myself. I agreed to a separatist household only because of you. I'm not going to do the same for a short-term housemate."

"I'm sure you two could work something out." Erva Mae became conciliatory and slipped into her tinge of persuasive Southern belle: "Lorna's so easy to get along with. I was sure you wouldn't mind and I asked her to come over tomorrow evening to talk with you."

"I can't say you didn't think this out in advance." Roz looked away, devising strategy. She pushed down vigorously at her cuticles.

"What male friends do you have to bring over anyway?"

Could Erv know about Irv? Warding off panic, Roz quickly assured herself not and steadied her voice: "Juan Bellefleur, for example."

Erva Mae flew into high gear: "So you'd kick out a sister in time of need to consort with the patriarchy, to hobnob with the ruling class! I would've never expected this of you, Roz. Thank Goddess I'm getting out of here soon!"

"Don't give me that ruffled Southern belle routine. And, by the way, a partly employed, gay, Cuban-French Canadian male hardly qualifies as a member of the ruling class."

Eyes simmering with rage, Erva Mae strutted to the opposite end of the room, her backside to Roz. "I simply can't fathom this attitude of yours."

"It's my right to approve a new roommate, Erv. As you said earlier, I don't dictate to you who to live with and, I trust, you'll treat me the same."

Erva Mae whirled around, hands on her hips. "I just didn't think you'd be so unreasonable about Lorna." The Southern belle attempted to manufacture tears, without success.

"I have nothing against Lorna as long as she has nothing against men. And I might as well tell you now that I plan to banish the chem-free zone in all shared living space."

"You wouldn't."

"So you can consider any non-separatist, chemically impure people you know to take your place. And don't tell me you don't know any."

Erva Mae stood tongue-tied. Roz smiled to herself, evidently having stolen her comeback.

"All right." Erva Mae stomped out of the room and returned with paper and pencil. "Wanted: Boy-loving, substance-abusing lesbian, to share flat," she wrote, pronouncing each word. "I'll post it at Womynspace. I'm sure the calls will come pouring in."

Roz dropped her last bomb. "Who said anything about 'lesbian?' Or, 'woman,' for that matter?"

Erva Mae froze, as if waiting for Roz to tell her this was a joke. Roz met her eyes and held them.

"Goddess in heaven! I can't believe this!"

"Believe it."

"Then again, knowing you, I'd believe almost anything," Erva Mae hissed, not hiding her spite.

Roz was tempted to test her, but Erva Mae ran to her bedroom and slammed the door. Seconds later she heard Erva Mae's desk chair banging against the wall.

She made a mental note to warn the new roommate — whoever it ended up being — not to assume Erva Mae's half of the security deposit.

45

The telephone awakened Gil. He rolled over in bed, squashed a pillow over his head, then had a sudden flash — it might just be for him. He struggled out of bed, hurried naked into the living room and answered. For a second, he heard nothing.

"Is this Gil?" came a doubting voice.

"Yeah."

"This is Hunter." The voice, a nervous baritone, faltered. "You met me last week. Remember? At the, uh, bar."

"Yeah, at Happy Hour at the Bull Dyke. I mean, Bull Dog. I remember." He didn't remind him that he'd met him in the bathroom, where, copying down phone numbers, Hunter had claimed to be researching the graffiti.

"Are you alone?"

"Yeah, I think so. I just got out of bed. Lemme make sure." Gil stepped away, tapped on Irv's bedroom door and got no response. "Yeah, I'm alone."

"Do you want to get happy again?" Hunter's voice was chipper. "At your place?"

When Gil had seen him copying the number of someone willing to "service studs *only* with nine inches or more," he'd challenged him to measure up. And he had. "What time is it?"

"About 7:30."

Juan was gone until after ten; Irv, more unpredictable, would prob ably be away until midmorning.

"What do you say?"

Now fully awake and fantasizing about such a dangerous tryst, he felt a stirring in his loins. Then he looked down and saw the stirring. His response was automatic: "Sure."

"Great. Then why don't I come right over? Let's say by eight? That would give us at least an hour, wouldn't it?"

"Yeah. Come on over."

"What's the address?"

"1099 Willy St. Second floor."

The voice turned suspicious. "You mean 'Williamson?'"

"That's it."

Hunter hesitated. "OK. 8:00. I'll be there."

Two hours later, Gil lay in post-orgasmic lethargy on the bed. Beyond the wall, he could hear the bathroom pipes straining to produce a trickle of water. At length the plumbing gurgled triumphantly, spewing forth brownish water for Hunter's toilette, so that he could wash away the signs of sin. A minute later, the spigot went off.

Gil stumbled out of bed and pulled on a pair of bluejeans that wouldn't clear his hips. Evidently Juan's. He peeled them off and hopped into another pair. With a dirty T-shirt he wiped the dust from the soles of his feet before smothering them in red and grey thermal socks. He then crammed his left foot into a spiked-toed cowboy boot.

Having reassembled himself, Hunter appeared in the doorway, ready to pass for straight to the rest of the world. In his late thirties, he had sharply etched features and medium-short dark brown hair that threatened to recede. He seemed to grope for conversation: "Well, off to school for you and off to work for me."

Gil nodded agreement, felt awkward and wished he were gone. Hunter hung in the doorjamb, surveying the surroundings dubiously, as if awaiting something. Gil guessed that he was just as anxious to return to his professional, married life as Gil was for him to go.

Hunter cleared his throat. "Do you want to plan to get together again? That is, if you'd like to."

This was a new twist, plotting their adultery in advance. "Sure. My friend drives cab till ten Monday through Wednesday. So we could try for next Wednesday. But it'll still depend on Irv being gone. The other guy who lives here."

"Or," Hunter suggested, his eyes landing on a jockstrap on the floor, "we could aim for Tuesday. Then if Tuesday doesn't work out, there's always

Wednesday. If one of the other two guys answers, I'll just hang up and try the next day."

"Sure." He repressed a smile at Hunter's eagerness. He seemed to be the only or easiest outlet the guy had and he preferred to keep it that way. During their first stealthy encounter, Gil had pried loose from his hand the phone numbers he'd copied from the wall and flushed them down the toilet. Hunter now pulled out a small datebook and consulted it. Gil imagined him writing "Adultery: Tuesday, 8:00 a.m," or perhaps "Sodomy: Same time, same place."

"No meetings either day." Pleased, Hunter reinserted the book in his suit pocket.

"Great. We'll try for one of those two." Gil took the bottle of poppers from the nightstand and stuck it in his pocket. "But don't call before 7:30."

"Whatever you say."

Gil followed him to the door, hobbling in his lone boot. Hunter touched Gil's shoulder in a good-bye gesture then whisked down the stairs. It was understood that they wouldn't kiss.

Hunter obviously belonged to the closeted set, for whom genital hanky-panky meant getting your rocks off and was condonable, but mouth-to-mouth contact meant you were a genuine fruit, fag, queer. Gil didn't like kissing that much anyway.

He closed the door, limped into the kitchen and watched Hunter escape in his family-size car. He knew nothing about him but his name, had little doubt it was an alias and didn't care. The slightly seedy Willy Street house, he'd noticed, had seemed to rattle him a little. At least he'd graduated from public bathrooms to private homes.

He put on water for coffee and, back in the bedroom, pulled on his other boot and a T-shirt. An urge to return to bed overtook him, as did the desire for another orgasm.

At Juan's behest, he'd enrolled in a History of Science class the third week of the semester, having to get special permission and pay a staggering late fee to do so, the School of Pharmacy keeping him on hold. To go or not to go to class... It met at eleven, three days a week. He checked his watch. Juan would be home soon.

That decided it. He didn't want to risk encountering him so soon after the fact, as if his guilt might somehow show through. Back in the bedroom, he stashed the lubricant and towels away and arranged the sheets as if he'd just lazily gotten up.

A voice inside him said he ought to be ashamed. This was the first such rendezvous he'd ever had in the house, not to mention right in Juan's bed. He tried to tell it the voice to go away, but it came back, nagging.

He was younger than Juan, naturally had a higher sex drive and needed other outlets, he reasoned.

The kettle whistled from the kitchen. He rushed to turn it off and poured the water over coffee. It burned his tongue.

While the danger that someone might arrive heightened his excitement during sex, afterwards there remained nothing to heighten but guilt.

46

Cissy woke up with bleary eyes, a dull sense of anticipation filtering through her body, still numbed by sleep. Then her mind jolted awake: Today Sumner would observe her advanced class. She stared at the alarm clock: 6:20. Earlier than usual, she crawled out of bed, trying not to disturb Jeb, and went to shower. On her return, he sat in his robe on the edge of the bed. "Nineteen sunless days this month," he said.

"The sun doesn't rise outside this window." She raised the half-drawn blind, exposing the wall of the neighboring house, penciled over with the dead vines of last year's morning glories.

"I got up and looked out the kitchen window. Totally overcast to the east, babe."

Cissy walked to the closet and selected a sweater and a Mexican skirt. "In two days it's March and March means spring."

"And spring means rain, which means clouds."

Cissy knew the futility of cheering him up, but made a hopeful stab anyway: "Did you get a call to teach today?"

"No, I just got up to see it if was sunny."

"Oh, so you did get a call? Great. You don't have to be so sarcastic." She laid the skirt out on the rumpled bed covers.

"I'm not being sarcastic, babe. I just got up to see if the sun was out and now I'm deciding whether or not to go back to bed."

She'd tried and failed. "Sumner observes me today."

"I made a fire for you, babe. Why don't you apply for that job in Bakersfield? Three hundred or so days of sun a year and no woodstoves to stoke."

Cissy stepped into her skirt, pulled the sweater over her head. "Wrong specialty. Besides, I thought we agreed Bakersfield is not our idea of returning to California."

Jeb ambled off to the bathroom. Some days she lacked energy to deal with his depression. The snow was easy enough for him to take, but the temperatures worse and the clouds fatal. His depression worsened each day the past week that he hadn't been called to substitute, in spite of its being the height of cold and flu season. At least he'd applied to UW for grad school in Phys Ed next year. That is, if there was a next year for them in Madison. It might well depend on what happened today.

An hour later she had eaten breakfast and packed her lunch, as Jeb watched, adamantly glum.

She bundled up and grabbed her briefcase. "Wish me luck."

"I'll dream you lucky dreams. I'm going back to bed."

The outside temperature struck her as balmy. After the climatic horrors of the past month, she now understood what Wisconsinites meant when they called twenty degrees a heat wave.

After her Intro class, she had two hours to review her notes for the afternoon's observation. Taking a break to stretch, she wandered down the hall to her mailbox and found a letter from the University of Mississippi. She tore it open on the spot and read that the state legislature was not expected to fund the position. On the way back she passed Rickover's open door. By this time, he had usually finished his FAB duties and departed. She hurried on.

"Pankhurst, is that your hip I saw?"

Resigned, she stepped back into view.

"Come in." The voice was amiable; she balled the letter up in her fist and edged in. Rickover inclined in his swivel chair, hands locked behind his head. The posture revealed a tear in the armpit of his shirt, through which several hairs protruded. He hoisted one leg and draped it over the corner of his desk, littered by papers and journals. A stack of exams rested prominently on top of the mess. The first one displayed a large F+. "A question for you. You listed on your *vita* an article that was accepted by the *Southwest Review of Archaeology.*"

"Yes?" She moved in closer.

"When did they accept it for? 1999?"

Cissy's mouth fell open. Nothing came out.

"Didn't mean to shake you up there, Pankhurst." Rickover emitted a sinister laugh. "I thought I might get to read it in my winter issue that just arrived."

Fears swarmed through her mind. Had she lied on her dossier and said it would be out this winter? No. Did the Search Committee think she was falsifying publications? Reprimands followed the fears: She should subscribe to the review; She should have asked the probable publication date; She shouldn't have listed the article at all. She ransacked her mind for a response. "They have a terrible backlog of articles, as usual. I trust mine will come out within the year."

He tapped a red pen on the F+. "I always thought that journal accepted way too many questionable articles."

Cissy remembered his own she'd seen in the fall issue, dealing with exhibition of early Southwestern toilets, or some such nonsense.

"I had hoped to see something of yours in print."

"I have a manuscript copy," she offered quickly.

"Fine, Pankhurst, though I'll give you a hint: Its title doesn't resemble what we usually consider research in this department. But I'll give it a look-over, if you want, maybe offer a few pointers. Do you have it on you?"

Of course, right here under my pantyhose. "It's at home. I can bring a copy in tomorrow."

"Good." Rickover slid his leg off the desk, tumbling the F+ to the floor. "I'll let you go fight your other battles now. I hear you have a big one coming up at 1:20. Sorry I can't be there. Ten-four, Pankhurst."

Cissy headed away perplexed. If the department had already decided not to hire her, it seemed unlikely they'd have a burning interest in her scholarship. Then why did Rickover want to see the article? Maybe he only intended to pick it apart. She tried to interpret it all as some sign of interest in her candidacy. At least it meant he'd looked at her dossier.

After locking herself in her office, she stuck the letter in a drawer and pulled out her lunch. She poured pineapple mint tea and munched in desultory fashion, while rereading her lecture notes. The inevitable, interrupting knock came at the door. She swallowed and mustered up politeness. "It's open."

Evan entered, his bright eyes — today aquamarine — betraying seriousness. "Sorry to bother you, Cissy. I'll close the door."

"Sumner observes me in a hour."

"Oops." His eyes went a shade paler. "Maybe this isn't the time to tell you this then."

A carrot stick in her hand snapped in two. "Tell me what when?" A trace of panic tinged her voice. She averted her glance from the penetrating eyes.

"I figured you'd want to know before you found out accidentally."

She tensed, imagining an array of unpleasant scenarios.

Evan matted down an eyebrow with his finger. "A memo came out this morning. Ginger checked your mailbox and said you didn't get one. It could have been an oversight or maybe just was for tenure-track faculty."

"And..?" A lump stuck in her throat. The broken halves of the carrot stick wetted her palm.

"The department is flying in a candidate to interview for the tenure-track job. But I'm sure you're still under consideration."

She let the news sink in and tried to make a connection between this and Rickover's wanting her article. "Who's the lucky person?" Trying to keep bleakness out of her tone, she scribbled a reminder to bring in the article.

"Her name's Catherine Bellg, from New Mexico. She's coming to give a lecture in two weeks. Although the memo didn't say so, it's obviously in connection with the job."

Cissy's mind began to spin. She heard Evan's voice, but didn't concentrate on it for several seconds: "...just protocol to fly in another candidate, since it is tenure-track."

Evan lay a comforting hand on her shoulder, apologized for the bad timing and left.

She raised her tea to her lips; it had gone cold. Desire for the rest of her lunch deserted her. Beginning with her hands, she tried muscle relaxation exercises to unknot her body. She had little patience for the slow procedure and got up to head for the ladies' room. Inside she encountered Ginger with her hands under the automatic dryer. "I assume Evan broke the news to you already." she shrieked over the machine.

Cissy gave an exaggerated nod of her head.

"Don't worry," Ginger screeched. "I'm sure you're right up at the top of the list."

The dryer went off and Ginger made a horizontal move to the mirror. Compact in one hand, she touched up her blush with the other.

"Sumner's observing my class at 1:20."

"I know." Ginger stared at her through the mirror for several seconds and said nothing.

Cissy touched her hair. "Do I look funny or something?"

"No, no." Ginger laughed softly and faced her. "It's just that when Sumner observes you, it doesn't hurt to go that extra mile to look — how should I put it? — special. Not that you don't look fine, Cis."

Cissy looked at her own skirt and shoes. She caught a glimpse of her face in the corner of the mirror not blocked by Ginger.

"Don't look so dejected. You're fine." Ginger fluttered her eyelashes. "But I'll tell you this. When Sumner observed my class last year, his eyes rarely went above my neck and, judging from his report, which was of course positive, he hadn't heard two words I said."

The next thing Cissy knew she was at the mirror and Ginger applying blush to her. "If you won't make a pretty face, we'll just put one on you," Ginger purred. Cissy felt like a fool and prayed no one would walk in.

"There. We all need some color during this wretched winter. As for Sumner, just acknowledge his presence from time to time, smile nicely at him and you've got half the battle won. Good luck, Cis." Compact in fist, Ginger scooted out the double set of doors.

Cis, Cis, Cis. Why would almost no one call her Cissy? Perhaps she should start calling Ginger "Bro."

She walked back into the hall. Only minutes remained to review her notes. Rounding the corner quickly, she crashed into Davidine. "I'm so glad I found you. Something's happened."

Cissy couldn't bear to think what. Today's events had pushed her to the limit. Then she remembered the ridiculous makeup. She took a step back, wished she could make it evaporate.

"It's Sumner. He's taken ill and gone home. So he won't be able to observe your class today."

Cissy didn't know whether to laugh or cry.

"We can reschedule a time for him next week. Or, since I myself have no meetings until three, I'd be glad to come do the report myself today. I know that class observations make a person tense, during as well as beforehand. You shouldn't have to go through it again due to circumstances beyond your control."

"Well…" Cissy debated the politic answer.

"That is, if you'd like me to come. I'm by no means forcing myself on you. You have every right to say no."

Would she say no to this offer? Not in two trillion years. She hoped she could hide her bliss: "I'd be delighted. If you want, I'll give you a course syllabus so you'll know exactly what we're doing today."

"Oh, you needn't bother. I'm sure I'll catch on."

"It's no bother. The class is in Room 119."

"Don't worry. I'll see you there in fifteen minutes."

The dean scurried away. Elated, Cissy dashed back to the restroom and whitewashed her cheeks back to their Wisconsin winter pale.

47

About to leave the dorm for Verla's house, Lou looked longingly at the cafeteria line, where her fellow dorm residents queued. Tempted by the odor of food, she decided to walk down just far enough to read the menu. By then the wafting smells made a direct assault on her nostrils. If the line moved fast, she'd have just enough time to gobble down the ''pork surprise'' or pizzaburger offered as the entrées for the evening. She hadn't really intended to eat; it might make her late to Verla's dinner or somehow be a breach of decorum. She clenched her fists, closed her eyes and tried not to think of the empty pit in her stomach. After several seconds she managed to fight off the double-dinner urge.

She hiked up State Street, charged with energy. Outside temperatures had escalated to the comfortable thirties. Slowly she was weaning herself from Ladysmith, certain that Madison could make a happy home for the next two years. Rounding the corner off the square, she reached into her pocket to doublecheck the address, though she'd had it memorized for days.

She found Verla's house, its porch illuminated. Halting in front, she glanced upward and a droplet of precipitation grazed her forehead. She bounded up the steps, entered the foyer, knocked on the inside door and waited.

It opened to reveal a young man, blond and of ruddy complexion, in jeans and a red knit alligator shirt. "Um, th-this i-isn't where..?"

"You must be Lou. Come in." He beamed smiles at her. "I'm Bob."

Seconds later Verla whooshed into the living room, her hair bouncing. "I'm so glad you made it, Lou! You've already met Bob, I see. Let me show you around the house."

"Sure," Lou agreed, wondering how many housemates she had. She surveyed the livingroom: fireplace, comfortable old furniture reminiscent of her mother's, a chandelier hanging from a high ceiling. "It's a very nice place."

She turned, saw that Bob was gone and followed Verla down the hall. Voices emanated from rooms off of it. She caught up with Verla only when she stopped to tap on a door. The two of them went in.

"This is my room and my roommate Annie. This is Lou Lautermilk from my Autobiography class."

Annie hopped up, smiled widely, and shook Lou's hand with gusto. A Verla clone, she effused and gushed over Lou as if she were the most interesting person she'd ever met.

Verla interrupted: "Almost dinnertime." She led Lou back into the hall. "There are twenty-two of us here," she explained and oversaw endless introductions, as the housemates appeared at once. Lou shook hands like a politician at a rally.

"What kind of organization..?" Lou began, but Verla cut her off, hurrying with the others to the dining room. She was seated between Bob and Verla. Before eating, Bob led a prayer, a quaint, homey touch.

Here Lou had the proof for her parents that not all of Madison was a den of drug addicts and other undesirables. She had known that people with her down-home brand of friendliness had to exist here. Now she had found them.

They began to pass around food. Lou followed the others' example, taking only one spare rib. A ladle of corn and a scoop of whipped potatoes completed the main course. She looked doubtfully at the meager plate and forced herself to attack it slowly.

In between bites — which was most of the time - - she answered questions: "I'm a junior." "From Ladysmith." "Last semester was my first here." "I transferred from Eau Claire." "Majoring in psychology."

"I'm a junior too." Verla spoke — no, bubbled — as if this were an astonishing coincidence. "From Wisconsin Rapids. Majoring in music. I've been here three years, but Madison is always disconcerting when you're from small-town Wisconsin."

Lou nodded, letting a spoonful of potatoes slide down her throat.

"First years here are always so difficult," Verla went on dreamily, as if recalling the Middle Ages.

"I never thought I'd meet so many wonderful people so soon," Lou said, realizing she hadn't until tonight, but carried away by the congeniality. Smiles all around her widened.

"Where on campus do you live, Lou?" Annie asked, and Lou named her dormitory. Annie seemed to recall a long-lost fact: "I lived in a dorm once too. I'm so much happier now. Of course there are fraternities and sororities where you can live too, but that's another world..."

Lou spooned down her final bite of corn and saw two trays of desserts arrive. Her spirits rose, then plummeted as she glimpsed the slivers of chocolate pie with whipped cream, each easily edible in a mouthful. The desserts parceled out, Lou watched the others eat, prolonging their shards of pie into seven or eight bites, as if savoring their last morsels before a hunger strike. On her best Sunday manners, Lou painstakingly dissected hers into three. "What kind of house are you?"

"We're a group home. A Community," Verla answered quickly.

"United in purpose and goals," Bob added.

"One of which," Verla continued, right on cue, "is to provide a true *family* home."

"And to foster community spirit and a sane learning and study environment."

"Many students can't maintain too well on their own."

Lou thought of Beth: "It can be difficult."

The meal concluded, everyone carried dishes back to the kitchen. Lou followed Verla and Annie and thanked them for the hospitality. All around her she noticed the uniform smiles, differentiated only by the size and shape of the mouths. They certainly couldn't be smiling because of full stomachs. If tonight's meal served as an indication, perhaps they were all on a permanent spiritual high from hunger.

Everyone disappeared promptly and a muffled stillness took over. Verla glided back to her room. Lou followed, her sneakers squeaking.

"Annie's studying upstairs in the Quiet Room. That way you and I can work in here without interrupting anyone."

Lou sat on a desk chair and plucked text and notebook from her backpack. Verla leaned back on the bed, enshrining herself in Snoopy and Garfield pillows.

They worked earnestly, Verla's *joie de vivre* impelling them merrily past any gaps in their understanding of Violette Leduc or deconstructionism. Before Lou knew it, it was almost 10:00. Verla's animation wound itself down, indicating a completed task. Lou might have pursued the analysis of a particular line, but figured she could put on the finishing touches tomorrow.

They emerged from the room as other residents emptied into the hall, awhirl with vitality. Three hours of studying had produced none of the weary looks, complaints and demands for alcohol common to her dorm. Verla retrieved Lou's coat from the living room closet, while her housemates wished her well, hoped to see her again. Lou hoped so too and said so. More satisfied smiles. Verla wended her through the throng, now informally assembled in the living room, and whispered "house meeting" in her ear. Lou thanked her again and was off. In the foyer she realized she'd never penetrated the vagueness about exactly what type of house they were.

Hitting the first step from the porch to the sidewalk, she was flung forward and grabbed a railing just in time to avoid landing in a heap. A sheet of ice glazed everything. It was an ice storm, the plague of late winter's rising temperatures. Shaken but unhurt, she headed on. A steady, fine mixture of snow and rain fell, turning to ice by the time it touched the ground. She abandoned the ice-slick sidewalk for the snow, cracking its crusty top, her shoes sinking in.

A sheath of ice coated the tree branches, producing an almost magical, Christmas-card effect. Awed by it all, Lou felt a new contentment. Without realizing it, she was back on the sidewalk, sliding effortlessly over the ice. Everything seemed perfect, except her rumbling stomach.

The quickest route home went down State Street, with its myriad fast-food restaurants, ice cream shops and bakeries. Lou could almost smell them. She sped up her pace, letting the ice transport her.

48

Roz perched lotus-style on Irv's sofa. "You'd think there'd be one normal person to take over Erva Mae's half of the lease."

"Well, not *too* normal." Irv strained his voice above the music from Gil's room. "At least she's hardly ever around these days."

"But you never know when she might pop back in. If we stay there, there's absolutely no guarantee of privacy."

"Which this place can't offer either." Irv nodded toward the source of the music.

"I know it's stupid." Roz whispered; Irv gestured for her to speak up a few decibels. "It's just that I want the first time to be special. I know, it's not really the first time, but you know what I mean. I don't want to hear the guys' bathroom noises on the other side of the wall. I don't know, maybe I'm getting too old for communal living. And," she hollered, "noise."

She realized she'd just made an implication she might one day want to undo. In any case, it was probably all premature.

"I'll say something to him about the music. I don't want to rush you, Roz. That's the last thing I want."

"Well, I want to rush us." Although comfortable with Irv, she'd still felt her new identity tentative and had postponed sex. Two months ago would have been premature, but not now. She snuggled up to him. "I've made up my mind. I'm ready." A white tuft of hair protruded from his ear.

"When's the next weekend you don't have to work at the Co-op?" He turned toward her. Roz restrained an impulse to fondle his beard.

"Next weekend. Why?"

"What's your favorite city? Where have you always wanted to go?"

Roz had no quick answer. "Wounded Knee?" she joked. "Managua?"

"Let Juan do Nicaragua. We're not going anywhere as political observers. I was thinking... How about Cozumel?"

"Mexico?" Roz gasped. "But the money..."

"...is in the bank waiting to be spent. Do you think there's any way you could wrangle a three-day weekend?"

"I could ask Eric. He's always eager for extra hours."

"But there's Womynspace too, right?"

"I can always take one of my personal holidays. And if Erva Mae gives me a hard time, I can claim I'm celebrating International Women's Day or Rosa Luxemburg's birthday. They're both this month some time."

"Then it's settled."

"Maybe I'll find a renter in the meantime."

"Then you'll have a guarantee of no privacy."

"And no Erva Mae." The music ended. Roz kissed his ear and lowered her voice to a murmur: "Irv, I think I..."

Abruptly, The Pretenders came screaming over Gil's stereo. In any case, the last two words, "love you," had stuck in her throat.

"Think what?"

"Oh, nothing." She'd save them until she didn't have to qualify them.

She had composed a simple ad: "Nonsexist person to share flat with same. Smoking, pets OK." Although the lease had permitted pets, Erva Mae hadn't, claiming an allergy to cats and that dogs, regardless of their sex, were aggressive, "masculine" animals.

Inquiries had come, but never made it past the telephone interview stage: a member of a heavy metal band looking for a place to have jam sessions and sleep; a woman who held regular prayer meetings. Roz had managed to discourage them both. Begrudgingly, Erva Mae had handed over her half of the March rent.

A soft-spoken graduate student came to see the flat. Mystified, Roz watched as he measured the windows and stared out of them suspiciously from different angles. "How do you feel about house plants?" he asked.

"In spite of the evidence, I don't purposely torture them." She indicated a deceased philodendron in a sunless corner and a spindly Swedish ivy above the kitchen sink.

"You need a plant doctor," he said, not censoriously.

"Some cheery greenery and someone who knows how to take care of it is one thing this place could use." Roz felt optimistic. "How many plants do you have?"

"About 125, not counting the mosses and fungi I have to store in the refrigerator. I'm in Botany."

"You can have half the refrigerator, that's no problem. I could rent the room to the plants, but what about you?"

"Precisely the problem," he sighed. Sadly, Roz watched him depart, her own plants stuck with her black thumb.

Next came a tall, red-haired woman named Corinne, attractive, outgoing and smartly dressed. Too smartly, thought Roz, but ready to lower — or raise — her standards.

"I ought to tell you that I don't eat dead animals," Corinne warned as she finished the tour of the premises.

"I hope that doesn't mean you eat live ones." Roz swallowed a laugh at her failed humor; she, of all people, should know better than to joke about others' sacred causes. "I do keep meat in the refrigerator."

"Just so it's wrapped up and I don't have to look at it. I'm squeamish that way. Of course, we wouldn't want to eat together anyway. The room's available now?"

"Sure is. The few things in there we can move right out." Erva Mae only had one load to go.

"Then that's no problem. I'd need to move in by the weekend," Corinne explained, fidgety in her chair. "You see, I'm being, uh, evicted from my present apartment. Well, not exactly evicted, but I've been asked to leave."

Roz was ready to be reasonable. If Corinne had a kid, a boyfriend, a snake, whatever, she'd consider it.

"You said on the phone that pets were OK." Roz confirmed this with a nod. "You see, I'm very active in the Mobilization for Animal Rights."

Corinne paused, as though giving this time to sink in. It sank in none too slowly.

"I like animals," Roz said, neutral. The corners of Corinne's mouth curled into a slight smile. Anxious to get the bad news over, Roz leaned forward and narrowed her eyes. "How big's your menagerie?"

"So you guessed." Corinne's smile shriveled. "It all started when Matilda, my cat, escaped before I could get her spayed, and had kittens. I'm sitting another cat until the end of April and she's pregnant too. There's also my dog Boris. Then last month I rescued a terrier from the pound. And last week a member of MAR had to give up her dachshund, so I took him. They're all small dogs."

"So that makes three dogs and two cats, plus kittens. And the other cat pregnant."

"But only temporarily."

Roz shook her head, less in disbelief at the size of the zoo than in despair of ever renting the room. Which should have been Erva Mae's problem. Maybe she should have taken the first route, the chem-free separatist. On second thought, maybe not.

The following day, Erva Mae arrived with a borrowed truck to remove the last of her belongings. Roz told her tale of failed flatmates. Erva Mae looked on skeptically, implying exaggeration. "As long as you're being reasonable, Roz. I certainly hope you'll find someone soon so that I can be reimbursed for part of the $160 this month. You know what Womynspace pays."

Roz knew it paid Erva Mae more than her. "I'll be reasonable with anyone who doesn't come with a horde of live possessions, is quiet and will put up with smoke and men. If Lorna agrees to that, send her over."

Erva Mae shook her head. "She and Annette made up and are back sharing a bed at the co-op." Then she froze; a pained expression gnarled her face. "Roz, I hope I'm doing the right thing."

Roz tried to hide her surprise. What doubt was this?

"I guess this is it. The end." Erva Mae dabbed furtively at her eyes with a handkerchief.

"Don't say that, Erv." Roz hoped to avoid a teary-eyed scene. She could combat the ruffled Southern belle, but had less experience dealing with a crying adult. She put on a chipper smile. "I'll see you at work, won't I?"

"It's just that..." Erva Mae began, then stalled, as if about to make some horrible admission. "I guess I'm really afraid of change somewhere deep down inside."

Roz felt a sudden, but fleeting pity for her. "Just because it didn't work out between Roxanne and me doesn't mean..."

Erva Mae began to sniffle; tears made a brief appearance. Forcefully cheery all at once, she dried her eyes with a vengeance.

The phone rang right next to her. Her old self, she glared at it; Roz motioned her to answer. She snarled "Hello," then listened for several seconds. "It's for you. Someone calling about the flat."

Roz came over.

"Male," Erva Mae footnoted with disdain. She held the receiver at arm's length, as if diseased or contagious, and headed for the door, hoisting a crate.

49

Dejected, Beth left her Museums exam, had a yogurt and coffee lunch, then went to her history class. As the professor droned on, the exam still gnawed at her. Museums had been intended to raise her GPA, not entrench it. When Lou lent her her old exams to study from, she'd figured she'd have it made. But Pankhurst had prepared a new one, which touched on the same material, but was reworded and tricky. With luck she'd squeak by with a low C.

Her mind wandered back to History class: Manifest Destiny, gold rushes, railroads. A colossal bore. Mercifully, class ended soon; she had daydreamed most of the period away.

Listless, she dawdled on the way out and stopped to read a bulletin board of campus events. Before she knew it, the next class bell rang. All at once she heard an impassioned voice from a room around the corner and, curious, approached the open door of the class. The students, filling the seats and the aisles, seemed captivated. She stepped in farther. Behind the podium stood a thin, short man, who gestured animatedly. Apparently seeing her, he said, "Come in back there, if you want." She made a millisecond decision before every head in the room turned her way, scurrying in to sit on the floor behind the last row of seats.

Some fifty minutes later, she'd heard about class struggle, the bourgeoisie, the monopoly of capitalism, patterns of repression and working-class resistance movements in Europe. Never had she heard a professor lecture with such vigor, make so much sense and truly *feel* every word he said, enthralling his audience. The class had what hers lacked: relevance and revolutionary *chutzpah*. Wasn't this what a university was supposed to be about?

She returned to her dorm, still so wrapped up that she forgot about Amber's call until the phone rang. "How ya doin', Am? I was afraid I might miss ya this afternoon."

"You thought that I wouldn't call?" The diction was perfect, the tone wounded.

"No, not that," Beth reassured. "I ended up sittin' in on this wild class this afternoon and got back here late."

Beth carried the receiver across the room and tumbled languorously onto the unmade bottom bunk. She shut her eyes, let her mind transport her to an island of blue skies and beautiful women, a mythical Caribbean equivalent of ancient Lesbos.

Amber bemoaned her loneliness without Beth, who ate up every word of it, nourishment to her emaciated heart. When she opened her eyes, instead of an azure Caribbean sky, she met with a vision of Lou's mattress springs. Not to be outdone, she began a recitation of her own woes in lonely, icy Madison.

"I don't know how I'll endure until I see you on the twelfth," Amber interrupted.

"I can't get away until the sixteenth."

"The sixteenth! I thought you said spring vacation started on the twelfth."

"I was wrong." Beth conveyed the tiniest bit of exasperation over the wires.

"You don't love me too much or you'd come sooner."

Beth imagined her wearing her sexiest pout and experienced a stab of lust. "You know I'd come sooner, Am. Really. But I have a History exam the afternoon of the sixteenth."

"Exam, schmam."

"Am."

"After all, if you're going to drop out after this semester and live with me in New York, what can one little test possibly matter?"

Beth contemplated this reasoning, remembering the happily-ever-after fantasy they'd concocted. "Just listen, Am. After May we'll be able to be together all the time."

"May! And I was hoping you'd bring everything with you in March and not go back to Minnesota."

"Wisconsin."

"Whatever. The next thing I know, you'll have to get your mother's permission just to visit me."

She had come close to isolating the issue. Permission, *per se,* was not necessary. Her allowance from Nick, contingent on an improved GPA, was.

"I'd love to leave this place an' go live with you. You know that. Just be patient for a couple months." Beth felt a stubborn, reproachful silence from Amber's end. "What day are you flyin' back to New York?"

"Sunday. Come live with me."

Beth tried placate to her. "You know I would if I could but I can't. Not yet."

"Promises, promises. That's all I get. First it was the ninth, then the twelfth, now the sixteenth. I don't believe you'll ever come."

Beth exhaled into the receiver. "Please be patient. I'm doin' all I can. I love you, Am. If you love me..."

"*If* I love you?"

Beth rolled off the bed and planted her feet on the floor, hoping to dam the dangerous flow of the conversation. She heard noises at the door; Lou stumbled in and walked into the phone cord, stretched taut as a tightrope across the room. She ducked under it and Beth turned to face the wall. "You know I love you!" she said in an emphatic, but muffled voice.

"Speak up. The connection's bad."

Beth repeated her troth of love, slightly louder. Amber seemed not to hear nor pay her words heed. "This conversation is giving me a headache. Call me when you have better news."

Beth let out an urgent moan: "Am!" What else could she say with Lou in the room? Quickly, she revived her best bilingual skills, the sum total of six years of high school French: "*Je t'aime.*" After a second, the phone went dead.

She flopped face down on the bunk and let the receiver bang on the floor. She closed her eyes, heard Lou hang up the bruised receiver. She lay inert, her love metamorphosized into an ugly malignancy.

"Beth?" Lou coaxed. "Are you all right? Can I help?"

She didn't respond or move for several seconds. Lou must have heard the end of the conversation. And Beth needed to talk to someone. Could she actually tell Lou without switching pronoun gender?

"Lou, love sucks." She remained uncertain how much more to tell. Fear of revealing everything battled her need to. Embarrassed, but trapped by Lou's presence, she rolled away and faced the wall.

"Is there anything you want to talk about?" Lou sat on the edge of the bed. The mattress sagged, causing Beth to roll toward a depression in the middle, meeting her roommate.

"Reach me a Marlboro, kid?" Telling Lou would require at least a cigarette, if not a stiff drink. She'd have to spit it out quickly, before losing her nerve. Unless Lou was more naive than she thought — always a possibility — she probably knew anyway. Lou extended a cigarette and Beth fired it up and blew a smoke ring. "You heard the end of my conversation?"

"Sort of. Sorry I interrupted."

"That's OK, kiddo." She drew on her cigarette. Then an easy way to begin struck her. "You know that paper of mine you typed finals week?" An affirmative from Lou, a slight pause from Beth. "You know what it was about, don'tcha?"

"Yes."

Beth went on valiantly: "You know all these long-distance phone calls I've been gettin' lately? They're from a woman."

"I think I talked to her once."

"So now you know, kid." Beth hoped Lou knew the implication, but couldn't be sure. "I like women." She felt a sheepish smile ease onto her face. "Lou, can you handle that? You won't move out on me, will you?"

There. It was out. She was out. She breathed in deeply.

"Of course not."

"I probably shoulda told you earlier. But last semester... Now don't get weirded out, kid. Robin and I had... a little affair. I know she thought — now don't freak out — that I dumped her for you. She was so jealous, it never would've worked out anyway. Then in Jamaica I met Am. That was workin' out fine, by long distance, till today..."

"It'll be all right, Beth. Tell me whatever you want. You'll feel better."

"Really, kid?"

"Really. Tell me."

Beth relaxed a little and sat up on the bed. "Well, I was sittin' on the edge of the pool with Nick at the Windward Sloop in Kingston when I see this foxy beauty across the pool. The next thing I know she was smilin' and smilin' at us and I hoped to God it was at me and not at Nick..."

50

Before leaving FAB, Cissy detoured to the departmental office to check her mailbox. Wilhelmina was out, Sumner gone, and her box empty. As she closed it, the phone rang. She looked to the outer door, hoping Wilhelmina would rush — or at least, waddle — in to answer it. The second ring began and ended. The third came, persistent. Were someone to enter, she'd look foolish standing next to a ringing telephone. She went to Wilhelmina's desk and picked it up. "Department of Museum Studies." She feared the rumblings of a long-distance connection in the background.

"Collect call from Catherine Bellg. Will you accept charges?"

Catherine Bellg? The woman interviewing for her job? "Um..." She looked toward the door in desperation, praying someone would burst in. "There's no one here right now."

The operator was curt: "You're not accepting charges, then?"

"I'll talk to anyone," came the caller's brusque voice.

"I suppose I can take a message." Agitated, Cissy signaled at the closed door, as if casting a spell on it to open.

"You will accept charges then?"

"Yes, I suppose so."

"Go ahead."

"This is Catherine Bellg, from Albuquerque. I merely want to leave a message for Dr. Isaacson." The patronizing voice rattled off her flight information and arrival times.

Cissy scrambled for paper and pen. "I'm sorry. Could you repeat that, please?"

An exasperated sigh. "This is Catherine Bellg..."

The information reiterated verbatim, Cissy jotted it down. As she finished, Davidine swung the door open. Cissy motioned at her and blurted "Wait a second" into the phone, but heard a cool "thank you" and a click from the other end.

"I was the only one here, so I answered it. It was long distance, from Catherine Bellg. Collect," she explained, and handed over the flight information. "She asked for Sumner."

"I would have thought he'd be here." Davidine's face twitched in irritation. "Thank you for taking the message, Cissy." She paused and ran her hands down the sides of her suit, as though in thought. "So you've had an advance opportunity to talk with your competition."

Cissy tried to keep her feet anchored to the floor. Did this mean what it seemed to?

"You don't mean he hasn't even let you know?" Davidine's voice betrayed astonishment and annoyance, then turned apologetic. "The Executive Committee voted Monday to ask you to give a lecture as our other finalist. I can't believe he hasn't told you yet. All we need to do is pick a date in the next two weeks and have you give us the topic when you've decided on it."

Taking the bus home, Cissy fantasized a new future in Madison. As an Assistant Professor — if she were so lucky —she'd get a $2,000-to-$3,000 raise. Jeb could go to graduate school or maybe get a full-time teaching job.

At home her enthusiasm fused with his, which soon gave way to practicalities: "So can you give the same lecture you gave at the NMA in December?"

"No. Rickover and Davidine were there and heard it."

"What about a talk based on your article?"

Cissy shook her head. "Rickover just read it."

"Hmmm." Jeb toyed with his hair. "How about something out of your dissertation?"

She'd already debated and rejected this option. "I talked on that last year when I came for my interview. I've got to be versatile." Her forehead furrowed as the true extent of her quandary sank in.

"You've got two weeks, right?"

"Thank God for Spring Break between now and then."

"Oh, here's a piece of mail for you, babe." Long-armed, he held it out to her.

"George Washington University," she scoffed, knowing a rejection letter when she saw one.

The morning of her competitor's lecture, she dressed in her tan suit, low tan heels and a discreet gold necklace. She skinned her hair back and wore her glasses. In academic garb, she'd feel more self-esteem. She figured she'd need it when attending Catherine Bellg's talk.

No sooner had she arrived at FAB, hung her coat up and stepped out into the hall, she saw Rickover, flanked by a statuesque woman with black hair. Her dress most resembled an evening gown, turquoise and daringly low-cut, attire that almost made Ginger look dowdy in comparison. His hair greased back, Rickover beamed, the Ugly American escorting foreign royalty.

"Oh, Catherine. Let me introduce you to our newest member, Cicely Pankhurst. Pankhurst, this is Catherine Bellg."

Both women greeted each other as Cissy extended her hand. Catherine hesitated — as if perhaps Cissy should have curtsied — then reciprocated, her fingers long, slender icicles. She observed Cissy as though she were a lab specimen. "So you're the department's lecturer."

"Oh, but not this morning," Cissy retorted, putting on a wide, unassailable smile.

Catherine put her face on hold while Rickover broke into a wide grin. "Good one, Pankhurst." Cissy hoped he'd refrain from punching her in the shoulder. "Indeed, the lecturing honors today are Catherine's."

As if accepting her due, Catherine bowed her head demurely. "'The Impressionist Painting: Light, Lighting and Display.'"

"How interesting." Cissy touched her necklace. "I trust it will be..." Should she say it? Instead she said "illuminating."

"And enlightening, I'm sure," Rickover said it for her, and permitted himself a brief guffaw.

Cissy failed to repress a smile. Catherine shot a glance from one side to the other, uncertain whether to be miffed or to joke along. She looked down and preened her cleavage. "Cicely, what did Vance tell me that you do? Mayan boulders or some such specialty?"

Cissy's blood was reaching a slow boil. "Artifacts, I believe you mean."

"How quaint!" Catherine arched her penciled eyebrows and batted her lashes at Rickover. Even Ginger had better taste than that. "I've always found Mexican trinkets so cute!"

"Well, girls..." Rickover stepped between them, his grin awkward and adolescent. "We have to move on, Pankhurst. Catherine has an appointment with John."

Cissy followed suit and bandied with first names: "With John, did you say?"

"He's the only 'John' in the department, isn't he?" Catherine addressed Rickover.

"Right. Rutledge. Well, we're off, Pankhurst. Later." Rickover gave a modified salute.

"A pleasure, Cicely," Catherine uttered, unctuous, and let Rickover escort her on.

From her office, Cissy later glimpsed Catherine in the hall, unaccompanied. Her competitor half-smiled, hesitated, and to Cissy's relief, slinked on. Moments later Evan strolled in, closed the door and rolled his eyes. "I take it you've met her. I went out to dinner with her and the rest of them last night. I assume they didn't invite you as a matter of protocol. Be glad you didn't go."

Cissy restrained herself from brushing back a lock of hair from his forehead. "I expect the men in the department are all going fairly gaga over her."

"Except me." Evan smiled an irresistible smile. "As for the women, Ginger called her 'an outrage to good taste.' And Davidine's not easily taken in. From Bellg's dinner-table conversation last night, I could only conclude that her degree's in flirtation."

"And I thought it was Impressionism."

"Close. Impression-making. Shall we go hear what she has to say? It's almost time."

Glad to have an ally, Cissy got up to open the door, then turned back to get her glasses.

"I'm sure the men will all have their glasses on too," quipped Evan. "Right up in the front row. There's certainly a choice to make: the scholar or the overgrown debutante. May they choose well."

Cissy doubted the Executive Committee's collective wisdom, but tried to look hopeful.

51

The first run of the evening shift took Juan to the Battered Women's Shelter. He honked and the rider came out. She stood outside the cab and peered down at him. He lowered the window.

"I asked for a woman," came the annoyed voice.

"Just a second." Juan radioed his dispatcher. "We can't get a woman here for twenty or twenty-five minutes."

"Can't wait that long."

Juan had dealt with such cases before and followed his standard procedure, suggesting the Women's Transit Authority.

"Already tried. An hour wait there," she snapped, and inched nearer to him.

"Look, I can take you now or we can get a woman here, maybe even in fifteen minutes. If you'd rather not go with me..."

"How do I know you're safe?" she demanded, hunching up to the window, a female Goliath towering over a seat-belted David.

Juan gave his stock answer for the situation. "I'm gay."

She bent over, met his eyes in the semi-darkness and studied him. "How do I know you're telling the truth? You're not wearing an earring that I can see, I haven't seen you in bars, and you don't even look gay."

Juan's next answer wasn't stock, but he bet it might work: "I could perform fellatio if I had a willing subject."

The rider narrowed her eyes, cracked a smile and let out a belly laugh. Won over, she rounded the cab and hopped in the front seat. "You see, I barf if I sit in the back. So I gotta be careful who I sit next to."

Juan accepted the explanation and sped away, toward a neighborhood known among insiders as "Dyke Heights." Together they violated the city ordinance by lighting up cigarettes and joked all the way. Juan received a handsome tip and a promise to ask for him again when no woman was available.

The next call took him to a downtown hotel. Remnants of snowbanks still lined the streets, now free of the ice that had shut down the city two weeks ago. He opened the window to air out the cab; the cold wind chafed his face.

At the hotel, three portly conventioneers attempted to crowd into the backseat. Juan felt the cab almost tilt and turned around. The third rider pursed his thighs and did his best to pull the door closed.

"Listen, Eddie," said the middle one, "unless we're gonna play three fags in a pod, you better haul your ass into the front."

Juan bristled. "Yes, you'd better try the front."

"Yeah, Eddie, you think we're queer back here or what?"

Juan passed over the remark, which occasioned inordinate mirth on the part of the riders. Eddie laboriously hauled his ass out of the back, opened the front door and crash-landed next to Juan.

"Where to, gentlemen?"

"You're a regular guy, ain'tcha?"

Pondering this dubious "answer" and fearing its implications, Juan managed a customer-service smile. "I'm a regular working guy."

"I thought you was. Just hadda make sure, right Ronny?" Eddie said. "We wanna go see some flesh."

"Girls," seconded Ronny, as if they were an outlawed commodity where he hailed from.

"Burr-lesk. Strip shows," specified the third, lest there be doubt. "You must know where the action's at, a young stud like you."

Juan feigned regular-guy complicity. "Sure do." He lowered his window, his olfactory sense punished by a whiff of body odor from the front and an overdose of Brut from the back.

Hoots of lascivious anticipation went up as Juan turned on the meter and drove off. The last time he'd faced this situation, he'd driven to the sole spot that offered such entertainment. But a notion of what he'd always wanted to do lingered in his mind and tonight's trio provided the motivation. He'd deposit them at the Bull Dog.

"What's the name of this place?" asked Eddie.

Names raced through Juan's mind. The Bull Dog was hardly appropriate, the Bull Dyke even less. Other inappropriate canine takeoffs came to mind; he had to think fast. His passengers, as if unaccustomed to rapid-fire speech, seemed to think nothing of the delay. "Chez Fifi," he said, stressing the last syllable.

"Shay Fee-fee!" Ronny guffawed, stressing the first. "Ain't that a bust!"

"Sounds French to me," said Eddie.

"It's Ger-reek to me," added the third, called Deke.

Juan hit a pothole. Eddie's layers of flesh bounced like a sperm whale in heat.

"Think they got any French girls there?"

Juan decided to humor, to tempt them: "They've got all kinds of action, a little of everything. French, Greek, a few Southern belles."

"Ger-reek? Really?" Deke exclaimed, pleasantly flabbergasted.

"Yeah. Ger-reek, you asshole," Eddie retorted.

"Bet they rub olive oil on their pussy," opined Ronny, evidently the cosmopolite of the three.

As they went on discussing sexual practices of European women, Juan approached the Bull Dog. Could he actually pull this off? His heart thumped, his hands went clammy. He pulled into the parking lot.

"We're here, gentlemen." It looked believable enough. Men were streaming into the place. Juan flicked off the meter.

"I don't see no sign," Ronny said skeptically.

Juan had thought this out: "The city makes them keep a low profile. No signs allowed."

The three nodded. "So how do we get in?"

"You go up those stairs, where those guys are headed," Juan explained. His passengers listened as if receiving directions to discover El Dorado. He told them how to get right to the Bull Dog's main door, knowing that there were no signs inside or out. "That comes to $4.75."

The three extracted themselves from the interior of the cab. Among themselves they coughed up five ones. "Let's give him six, boys," said Eddie, panting like an orgasmic rhino.

Eddie handed over five ones and a pile of coins as the two others headed away. Juan saw a pair of effeminate blonds in matching jump suits and jackets coming down the stairway from the bar. He put the cab in gear, then noticed Eddie heading back toward him.

His foot hovered indecisively above the accelerator. He began to hyperventilate, but told himself to play it cool.

Eddie moved his jaw to speak. "So what's your name? We'll ask for you on the way back."

Relieved, he hesitated, then said, "Vito. V-I-T-O."

Eddie seemed confused by the foreign name and shook his head, puzzled. He nodded thanks, then turned away.

Juan was now ready to burn rubber, a regular hot rodder, an All-American guy. More or less...

Soon Eddie, Ronny and Deke were bounding down the stairs from the Bull Dog, exclaiming, "Queers! The place is full of queers!" Juan sat transfixed in his cab, watching the scene. The others following him, Eddie lunged from the bottom step to the parking lot and landed with hippopotamal force. The jump-suited blonds reappeared from nowhere. "Oooh! Fat, ugly straight men!" shrieked one. Eddie, Ronny and Deke jolted their corpulence into action and looked from left to right. Eddie glimpsed Juan in the cab and shouted, "There's Vito, that faggot ferr-ner! Let's get him, boys!" Juan pumped the accelerator. Nothing. He tried again, desperately. Silence from the engine. He slid across the seat and escaped via the passenger door, the outraged trio in hot pursuit. Unthinkably swift, they galloped after him. Juan ran out the parking lot and up the street toward the Capitol, which exuded phosphorescence high atop the distant Square. Behind him Eddie came within grabbing distance. Juan turned around, ran backward. "Get away from me, you... you..," he shouted, and launched into a stream of Spanish obscenities. He felt that someone had latched onto his wrist, was pulling him, jerking him...

"Juan! It's just a dream. You'll be all right."

He sat up, groggy but still shaken, and rubbed his eyes. "Roz... It's you."

"Yes, it's me. I'm not a nightmare. You're right here in your own living room."

"I must have fallen asleep." Juan blinked: Clad in Irv's bathrobe, Roz sported an uncanny tan. "What are you doing here? I didn't know you and Irv were..."

"Well, we are. We spent a three-day weekend in the Yucatan, last night at my place, and tonight we're here."

"It sounds serious." Juan rubbed more sleep from his eyes. "I drove until two, got home, and thought I'd lie down and read the paper. What time is it?"

Roz craned her neck toward the kitchen clock. "Almost four."

"What are you doing up at this hour?" He stood up, stretched and flopped back down.

"I could claim your raving in Spanish woke me, but the truth is I've gotten unused to sharing a bed. At least with a man who hogs all the blankets and sheets. Juan, you got a cigarette? Mine are in the bedroom and I don't want to wake Irv."

Juan handed her one. Roz ripped off the filter, lit the tobacco and inhaled. "You could chap your lips trying to suck taste out of these things! What're you smoking these days? Un-True, Disad-Vantage or De-Merits?" He held up a pack of the latter. "Hey, wanna smoke a joint? I'll need something to get back to sleep." He indicated a cigar box of marijuana and smoking paraphernalia. "So what was this Spanish nightmare of yours?"

Juan began to recount the cab ride as Roz rolled and lit the joint. She was soon howling with laughter.

"Roz, the dope is good, but not that good."

"I can't believe you took them to the Bull Dog!" She fell backward, hysterical.

He saw the bedroom door open and Irv appeared in boxer shorts. "Sorry we woke you."

Irv rubbed his eyes awake. "Our first night here, Roz, and you leave me for another man. I get up early, but not quite this early." He waved his arms in front of him. "It sure is smoky in here."

"Look!" Juan pointed, now fully awake. "Roz, your bathrobe's on fire!" The bathrobe, its hem spread out on the floor around her, smoldered. "You lost the end of the joint."

She grabbed a magazine and beat the fire out.

Gil came to the bedroom doorway, naked. "I smell pot."

"Put some clothes on, then join us if you want," Juan said, feeling an embarrassment Gil obviously didn't. He regarded the middle-of-the-night assemblage: Gil, naked; Irv in boxer shorts; and Roz in the bathrobe, which, besides the new hole, had collected a fringe of dust from the floor.

Gil walked naked into the bathroom, urinated loudly and emerged with a towel dangling in front of him. He sat down and threw the towel carelessly in his lap. "So what's the occasion? And where's the pot?"

Juan handed him the remainder of the roach to light.

"Cover yourself up, for God's sake," said Roz. "You're hanging out. You think this is a locker room or what?"

Juan yanked the towel down over Gil, who fiddled with the marijuana.

"So what is the occasion?" Irv asked, now at Roz's side.

"Well, Juan was having this nightmare about these three sexist, macho Hispanic creeps," Roz began.

"No, Roz. They weren't Hispanic. Or macho."

"You better tell then, if you're not too stoned."

Gil relit the joint. "No such thing as 'too stoned.'"

"You see, the whole night started when I went to the Battered Women's Shelter to pick up this lesbian person. And the next thing I know I'm offering to perform oral sex to prove to her that I'm gay so that she'll get into the goddamned cab."

"God, you people *are* stoned!" Gil exclaimed in between puffs. "*You,* Juan? Having sex with a woman??"

"No, I didn't have sex with a woman. Anyway, that's just the prelude. The main event was when I picked up these three guys who were in town for a 'Slobs of America' Convention or something."

Gil perked back up. "You picked up three dudes?"

"I picked them up in the *cab,* OK? Now, shut up and listen..."

52

Lou returned from Spring Break in snowbound Ladysmith to Madison, where spring, or some dreary likeness thereof, had materialized: forty-degree temperatures, clouds and drizzle. She spotted an occasional remnant of grey snow and arrived at her dorm sweating, suitcase in one hand and backpack flung over her shoulder. She opened her dorm room door and shoved the suitcase inside. "Beth! What are you doing here?"

"I live here too, remember. How was the vacation, kid?"

"The first day was dull and each day got duller." Lou moved into the middle of the room and stood sniffing a strangely familiar odor. She glanced over at Beth's reading material: *Social Change in Nineteenth-Century Europe.* "I know that book's not for any of your classes, but I take it you didn't decide to drop out and stay in New York."

"Sure didn't. I barely saw Am. She waitressed by day and starred by night in some triple-Off-Broadway lesbian production where they painted themselves wth menstrual blood. Don't even ask. Whether it was real or not, it was gross and Am got pissed off when I wouldn't go back to the show the second night. So while she worked, I spent the first two days roamin' the city, eatin' up atmosphere. By the third, she tells me this is gonna be her schedule for the rest of that week and why can't I stay another?"

"Another week?" Lou echoed, then ventured, "She doesn't sound too considerate."

"You got it, kid. Said if I really loved her, I'd skip classes for a week to prove it. I should've seen from the start how things'd balance out. So by the next day, I told her I was tired of gettin' dumped on and I left. She didn't even try to stop me."

Lou's eyes rounded. "Do you mean you've been back here for four days all by yourself?"

"No, kid. I went to stay with my aunt and uncle in Brooklyn. I think they were shocked, but glad to see me. They even called Nick and told her how nice it was to have a respectful niece like me who gives so much importance to family, etcetera, etcetera. Nick couldn't hardly believe they were talkin' about me."

"So you won't be dropping out after this semester?"

"Not unless this place drops me. Matter of fact, I think I'll stay here even if they do. Hey, if you're here too this summer, maybe we can share an apartment or somethin'."

"Yeah," Lou thought aloud. The idea sounded better than staying in Ladysmith. "Yeah, if I stay here. My parents still think I'll be spending the summer up there."

"Ed and Mildred? Oh, we'll soften 'em up."

Lou regarded her dubiously and dragged her suitcase across the tile to the closet. She opened it and her foot kicked a box of... She bent over to examine closer and heard Beth's voice: "I hope you don't mind, kiddo, but I thought havin' a kitten would make you feel right at home, you bein' from a farm and all."

She turned away from the litter box in time to see Beth lift a black kitten off the top bunk. Closer inspection revealed a white neck, paws and stomach. "It's certainly cute... and illegal."

"We've only got seven more weeks and it's small and easy to hide. You see, my aunt and uncle's cat had these kittens and this one slept with me. They said take it, so I did, named it Brooklyn and hid it in my coat pocket on the plane."

Hands on her hips, Lou stood, expressionless. A kitten, with a mind of its own, would prove harder to hide than appliances.

Before she knew it, Beth thrust the kitten's underside in her face. "Boy or girl, kiddo?" Lou grasped it gently and examined. "I'm only ninety-percent sure," she said, petting it. "But I think it's a girl."

"Good. I always liked girls better."

The next day in class Verla invited Lou to dinner that night. She'd already eaten there a second time, before Spring Break, when they'd studied for their midterm exam. That time she learned as much in the nutritional realm as in the academic: A miserly pea casserole had assured her that for any future invitations she'd go the double-dinner route, as she did tonight. Her only qualm was that she couldn't reciprocate. Though by summer, maybe she'd have an apartment and could.

After dinner, they chatted briefly about their vacations, then about the course, but Lou felt a tacit understanding that they wouldn't be concentrating on this week's text, *Memoirs of a Dutiful Daughter*. She had an intuition that tonight something would be foisted on her, requested in return for the interest and the meals. The two lapsed into silence, a rare commodity in Verla. But even when silent, Verla seemed to communicate with her irrepressible smile. Both the smile and the quiet held on. Lou had an inkling she knew what was coming. Better to ask than be asked. She bit her lip and began tentatively: "Verla, how can you always be so happy? I mean, your look of perpetual joy..."

Enthroned in her collection of pillows, Verla glanced up, amused or relieved, then spoke: "Lou, I'm so glad you finally asked. It's Jesus, of course."

"Oh," Lou muttered. So she had been right. "That's nice."

"It's more than nice," Verla said with meaning. Her eyes glowed, as if struck by divinity, before revisiting reality and Lou. "You really didn't know?"

"Not really. Not for sure."

"Jesus must not be very contagious in me these days," she chided herself. "I guess I'll have to strive harder."

"But you haven't talked at all about Jesus or religion around me," Lou said in her own, if not Verla's defense.

"We were waiting for you to come to us, Lou. We don't proselytize. We were hoping our joy would reach out to you," Verla explained, suddenly impassioned.

"I see."

Verla brimmed with expectation. "It would be wonderful if you were to join us. I could tell when I met you, Lou, that you'd fit in, want to become one of us."

"I've already got a religion," she stalled. "We're Lutheran. Just yesterday..." She was about to say that she'd gone to church, then remembered she'd taken the early morning bus back to Madison instead.

"For most of us here, our parents' religion just wore off. We've all been born again."

"Uh-huh." Lou remembered a joke she'd heard about born-agains and overflowing maternity wards.

"We've all been reinstructed in the Bible and how it really does apply to our lives and how to get by on a college campus in the eighties. As I've said, we're a community, Lou, a wonderful family. My whole life has turned around since I became a Truster." Lou nodded, taking in Verla's words. "But no one is going to pressure you. Do what you want, what your heart tells you to. But if you're interested, there's a Bible class that begins Wednesday night for those who are going to join and live here next year."

"I'll think about it, Verla." Lou realized this sounded like a brush-off. But she knew that her own churchgoing was little more than habit and wondered what revitalized religion would be like. "I mean, I'll really consider it."

As if she'd said yes, Verla lunged at her, giving her a precipitous hug for Jesus. "I hope I see you Wednesday. We all hope." A light blush — God's glory? — tinted her face.

Lou remained noncommittal, but supposed she could try it and, if she didn't like it, not continue. If she said no, would she ever see Verla again outside of class? Against her better judgment, she added, in a tiny, meek voice, "I hope so too."

"And if you do," Verla punctuated, "come at seven. After dinner."

53

Sumner shoved the seminar paper proposals aside, tilted back in his chair and stared at his reflection in the window, as if in the vague image he could discern the job strain lined into his face. He'd never wanted to work past age sixty-five and, with the recent push toward attractive retirement at sixty-two, had decided to cut three years off his career. But he wanted escape, distant and irresponsible, now, not in five years. A hidden Mexican coastal village, a houseboat roaming the Pacific shore, and, to complete the fantasy, a companion: young, attractive and female, but mature and intelligent. Someone like Catherine Bellg, he mused, or one of his seminar students. Or even a more friendly Cicely Pankhurst would do.

He got up and stared into the pane of glass and told himself he deserved better than this: a frigid wife, a gay son, no grandchildren and cantankerous colleagues.

He'd once had high hopes for the future, although a family to support came sooner than planned. Vonda was pregnant before their marriage and, after Pepper was born, put sex on hold until time for further procreation. Working on his dissertation at Penn, Sumner made little protest and less money.

Diploma in hand, and wife and son in tow, he first crossed the

Susquehanna in 1959, Wisconsin-bound. He fashioned himself a sort of pioneer, bringing Culture to an uncultured land, but soon saw that the university had little use for imported Eastern snobbery. So he adapted. He put down roots and busied himself with getting tenure. Jobs in the field were few, expenses many, and tenure anywhere not to be disdained.

While his academic endeavors paid off, parental duties didn't. Pepper proved to be his mother's child, ill-disposed to the fatherly fun he tried to dole out. The Isaacsons fervently wanted a daughter, Vonda became closer to forty than thirty, and they pursued their end with redoubled frequency. Vonda finally conceived, but miscarried, afterwards turning sexophobic. As if to emphasize the point, she had an elective hysterectomy.

Sumner sought solace in the arms of Davidine. Their three-year affair helped him weather the late sixties, even made him feel a part of the sexual revolution. Coping with other realms of the changing times was harder, but he read and discussed works on social change and weighed the arguments of Jews Against Zionism. He and Davidine demonstrated against the war, rubbed elbows with hippies and homosexuals and tried tofu.

But congeniality ceased to reign in the department. Though the older faculty had always considered themselves liberal, the younger faculty — long since denied tenure — called themselves radical and sided with the graduate students in the Teaching Assistants' strike. Chair Ned Raitt — member of the Abraham Lincoln Brigade, Communist Party member until 1969 and the only power capable of pulling the two sides together — died of a massive coronary the second day of the strike. Sumner and Davidine were called reactionaries and fascists and had to cross picket lines to go to work.

Davidine became chair, Sumner's relationship with her came to an end, and life seemed to normalize for a few years. Pepper went off to Stanford, earned his M.A. and Ph.D., then announced his homosexuality. End of normalcy.

Hobnobbing with antiwar homosexuals had been fine, but it didn't translate into acceptance when it came to his son. He'd lived with never having a daughter, but never to have grandchildren would be a devastating blow. He threw himself into his work; Davidine soon became an associate dean and he, chair. Vonda retreated into a world of fantasy, writing romance novels, which received almost as many rejections as they had pages.

Once convinced that he'd become at least an assistant or associate dean, Sumner saw this hope dashed when Davidine became head of the whole college and her replacement was from Art History. He tried to stem his jealousy, but frustration soon overcame him. His old colleagues retired, troublesome new ones replaced them. He lost interest in his job and, rote, went through the motions, occasionally forcing himself to care...

He backed away from the window and envisioned announcing his retirement, watching jaws drop, Davidine imploring him to stay on. The scenario was a cheap fantasy, but immensely pleasurable.

A knock on the door interrupted his reverie. Davidine got right down to business: "Since Cissy gives her lecture Thursday, when do you think the Search Committee might meet for a decision?"

Sumner stifled a laugh. As if there were a choice to make... Although he cared about the selection, he found it hard to be concerned with the details. "Friday, next week, whenever."

Cissy rummaged through her professional notes for a lecture topic: graduate courses, seminar papers, Master's thesis, Ph.D. exams, dissertation field work. Should she branch out, or, like so many, stick to her minuscule turf, fertilizing it, cultivating it and finally plundering its arability? Just before reaching desperation, she stumbled across the perfect topic, different from, but related to her other work: Mexican murals. After writing and polishing her talk, "Outside the Museum: Viewing the Mural in Mexico", she practiced it on Jeb, who sat across the room and coached her on voice projection.

The fateful hour arrived, 3:30 on Thursday. The entire faculty plus a handful of students showed up. Her heart thumped as Sumner introduced her. In the front row, Davidine winked at her.

She made opening statements on the artistic theory of murals and traced their Mexican highlights, from the Mayan depictions in Chiapas right up to Orozco, Rivera and Siqueiros. After touching on architectural considerations, she spent the bulk of her lecture on display and viewing.

Polite applause followed. Sumner stood up and invited the audience to question her. Her rigid smile hid incipient terror as the first hand shot up. She'd seem a fool if a student stumped her.

"You make a separate category for murals. But aren't some mosaics also murals? Does a geometric design automatically disqualify a mosaic from being a mural?"

Cissy hoped her relief wasn't too apparent. She elaborated on what she'd said and allowed that the definition could be expanded.

Beaming sweetness, Davidine unclasped her hands and raised one. "Why do you think that the tendency toward outdoor murals predominates so in Mexico and Central America?"

Either the dean was unthinking or, more likely, had purposely asked her an easy question. She started with the obvious climatic reasons, then offered intellectual considerations.

Sumner stood up at the side of the room. "Are there any more questions for Miss Pankhurst?"

Rickover's hand made the full climb upward. "We all know about the revolution-inspired Mexican mural movement. But why do you think the United States' mural movement — of course, I'm referring to the WPA — never caught on or thrived?"

Cissy tried not to panic. It was a sensible-sounding question, even a logical follow-up to Davidine's, though outside her area, Mexico. She knew little about U.S. murals, except that the WPA had commissioned unemployed artists to paint them in government buildings during the Depression.

"I suppose this question allows for some interesting conjecture," she began, having no idea how to proceed. Her mind froze; further speech curdled on her tongue. She grasped the lectern to avoid trembling. Silence prolonged itself uneasily.

"I'm ordering my thoughts," she said, having to say something. Davidine's reassuring smile began to waver. Ginger and Evan slid down in their chairs. Rickover and Sumner stood waiting, with impatience or hidden glee.

"I can only offer speculation," she began, slow and tentative. "Since in Mexico the outdoor mural lent itself to contemplation by the masses, as well as communicated a message they readily understood and to which they politically adhered, the mural thrived." She stopped, tried to think clearly and felt her knees wobble. Perspiration drenched her neck.

"In the United States, where the mural was neither generally outdoors —and less subject to wide popular view— nor usually carried such a direct political message, its popularity and impact were muted."

"Interesting, Pankhurst," Rickover said.

"And," Cissy went on in a burst of thought, "there was no muralistic tradition to fall back on in the United States, as opposed to Mexico, which inherited a dual tradition, from the pre-Columbian civilizations as well as from Spain, where the religious mural flourished at the time of the Conquest and primitive Iberian peoples had left some of the earliest extant murals, going all the way back to the caves at Altamira."

Astonished at her answer, she stepped back almost regally, though quivering inside. Sumner thanked her, then disappeared. Ginger and Evan occupied her with congratulatory chat and unkind remarks about Rickover.

Back upstairs, she collapsed in her office chair and unwound a bit more. She tried to banish second thoughts about her performance, but every-thing was now out of her hands: It would be she or Catherine Bellg. Then a distressing third possibility struck her: The department might not hire either one of them. Finally she got up, put on her coat, and hurried out of her of-fice. Head bowed, she rifled through her purse for keys, reached the elevator and pressed the "down" button.

"Homeward bound, I presume?" came a voice from behind her.

Cissy jumped almost a foot. It was Sumner. "Yes. I'm heading home," she answered, expecting him to congratulate her, or at least make some remark on her talk. He didn't.

The red light above the elevator beckoned, its doors opened. Sumner approached briskly and held the door for her. She went into the empty elevator and he followed.

Cissy stood to the left. She punched the first-floor button and saw that two things were wrong: Sumner had edged very close to her, and his breath gave off a stench of alcohol. She saw him reach out, middle finger extended arrow-like, to press the first-floor button.

"Oh, you pressed it." His tone struck her as a reprimand. "Yes," she said, stiffening. He stepped even closer. Their coats touched. His elbow grazed hers. She passed her briefcase from left hand to right, placing it between them. He stared at her, then broke into a leer. Her entire body tensed. She maintained composure, tried to think of an easy way to extricate herself from this invasion.

The elevator came to rest on the first floor. It seemed the doors would never open. Sumner held his ground at her side. Immobile, she felt her stomach churn. The doors began to pull themselves apart, Sumner's knee brushed hers.

She gave him a quick look of incomprehension and scurried out.

Juan left the Bull Dog without Eric and walked out into a blur of fog, the answer to another month of his "Wisconsin Weather Festival Calendar," which he hoped to market next year. March, originally intended as the "Wind Festival," would be the "Fog Festival," wind being appropriate for any month. He'd dubbed June the "Tornado Festival," July the "Humidity Festival," August the "Mosquito Festival," and named all the winter months, but was still toying with those of the less dramatic seasons.

He felt his way through the near-zero-visibility fog to catch a bus home from State Street. Within ten minutes lights framing the shape of a bus came plodding toward the Capitol. He got on and found some thirty totally silent passengers, the older ones reading, the younger with Walkmans or Walkmen? — wired to their heads. The bus rounded the Capitol and Cissy got on. He caught her eye and patted an empty seat next to him. "Hi. You look out of breath."

"I am. I just gave my job lecture and afterwards had the strangest experience, alone with the chair in the elevator. I'd swear he was drunk and trying to come on to me. It actually seemed more of an intimidation than a come-on. Anyway, I was so shaken, I ran out of the building and kept up a slow jog all the way up State Street. I guess that's one way to fit in my exercise."

Juan didn't know what to say, his mind occupied by the conversation he'd had with Eric.

The bus bumped its way down Jenifer Street. They got out at Ingersoll and headed to the house, the streetlights above them shrouded in fog.

"Be careful of that chair of yours."

"Don't worry, I will."

Upstairs Juan went to the refrigerator, took a handful of dilled Brussels sprouts from a Mason jar and popped a half-dozen in his mouth. He reached back into the jar and kept eating and eating. He realized he was having an AIDS anxiety attack. Having hit Madison, it was no longer some strange bicoastal disease. A friend of Eric's, also an acquaintance of his own, had been diagnosed.

Irv walked out of the bedroom and Juan spoke with his mouth full: "Howyadoin'?"

"I'd be fine if I could teach Roz to stop hogging the covers so I could sleep and wouldn't have to take these afternoon naps."

"Oh." The topic could hardly be exploited for further mileage. "How's Roz?"

"She finally found a flatmate. Some wilderness poet called Bear. Spends half his time in the wilds, the other half in his room, reading, writing, meditating, burning incense, God knows what..."

"Oh, yeah? Tell me more about him." He wanted to hear anything that didn't have anything to do with AIDS.

54

Davidine had suggested cocktails at the Mason Jar, a new bar/restaurant on the west side. Sumner didn't know the agenda, if any. They still got together at times for purely social purposes; other times Davidine saved administrative matters for a social setting. He only knew that Vance would not be joining them. Tomorrow the two of them would meet with him, convening the Search Committee for the final time.

His drive west did nothing to alleviate the day's tension. Students darted across University Avenue in blissful ignorance or blatant defiance of "No Pedestrian Crossing" signs. A bicycle swerved out of its designated lane to his right; a city bus cut him off.

Several stoplights later he reached the Mason Jar's parking lot and hefted himself out of the car. The building's heavy wooden door consented to open on the second pull. Fifteen minutes early, he sidled up to the polished wooden bar, with its brass rails and trim, checked to ascertain Davidine's absence, then ordered a martini, extra dry. The young bartender, as professional and sophisticated as the smartly coifed, dapper clientele he waited on, served it in a mini Mason Jar.

In a swift series of gulps Sumner downed it and ordered another. His watch crept toward 4:30. Stealthily, he emptied his second jar and fixed his eyes on the outer door. Still no Davidine, so he ordered a third. When she arrived, he could claim it was his first or second.

As he paid, he felt a tap on his shoulder. "Jar me up a brandy with a splash of seven, please," Davidine said to the bartender. She patted Sumner's ample bald area — no longer a spot. "Is it my imagination or has being chair taken a toll on your hair?"

"You should know." He made a point of peering down at her own ever-so-small bald spot.

Davidine's manner had always endeared her to him. She'd been the one constant in his career. With her he could relax, laugh and reminisce in ways not possible with other colleagues. They'd salvaged a playful camaraderie from their affair; Davidine was one of the "old boys" of his generation, a moribund species.

Jars in hand, they installed themselves opposite each other in a booth and chatted away their cocktail. Sumner sipped purposely slow. Only when the ice clinked in Davidine's empty jar, did he catch the waitress' attention, order another round and ask to run a tab.

"We need to talk about tomorrow's meeting, before Vance leaps into the ring." Davidine fit a cigarette into the corner of her smile as the drinks arrived.

Sumner tensed, felt displaced, his alcoholic buoyancy deserting him. This of all things. He should have known.

"We need to be a unanimous twosome, you know, otherwise poor Vance won't know whom to side with." Davidine smiled at Vance's expense and Sumner sensed imminent disagreement "We really need a theory person for this position. Curatorial experience is fine, but we need much more."

Davidine sounded reasonable, persuasive, and was all smiles. Sumner didn't like this beginning one bit. If he had a chance of besting her verbally, he'd have to remain cool, even-keeled. "Even though she's worked as a curator, Bellg seems very versatile."

"We're an academic department, not a museum. You and I not withstanding." She paused over her joke; a smile tugged at her lips, then dissolved. "The theoretical component of our faculty is essential. Bob and Evan are all the curators we need."

"Of course, but..."

"But what?"

Sumner steeled himself, felt perspiration circle his shirt collar. "You're not going to like hearing this, Davidine."

"I prithee, Oh Chair, elucidate me," she cajoled, good-humored. "At my age, I've heard everything." She clasped her hands primly on the table. "Well?" she said, when he didn't speak immediately. "Shoot. And preferably not from the hip."

"Your remark about Vance is well-taken," he began, the points of his argument swimming away in disparate directions. He reached for his jar and took a fortifying swig. "But it so happens that Vance and I already agree. We both have doubts about Pankhurst. So it's you I need to convince to spare Vance the quandary you mentioned."

Davidine gritted her teeth; the lines in her forehead grew menacing new creases. "So lay your cards on the table," she said in a tone perceptibly more formal. "And unless you know something I don't, you'd better have a royal flush." Her smile, still sweet in spite of her words, bore down on him as he spoke.

"Listen, Davy..." Logic that had seemed sound now teetered. The alcohol had emboldened him, but stunted his reasoning. He roped his thoughts in, tried to order them and hoped for coherence. "One: Pankhurst's student evaluations are quite weak in her Intro course. Two: Vance's faculty evaluation of her teaching is also shaky. Three: Look at her publications. Almost nonexistent. I admit that Bellg is a somewhat unknown quantity, but I think it makes more sense to hire someone like her than Pankhurst, a known quantity, whose knowns are negative."

"Is your *tour de force* of reasoning finished?"

Sumner glowered in affirmation.

"Good. Your reasons sound plausible. Now let's listen to a little true reason. Mine." She stole a quick drink and swatted at her hair, as if shooing away flies or pesky assistant professors. "One: You know how little importance almost everyone gives to student evaluations. And tightening up the grading, like you told Cissy to do, will never produce glowing ones. And you don't mention those from the advanced class, which are quite positive."

His first point effectively annihilated, Sumner sat in silence, not budging, his jar nearly empty.

"Two: I'd hardly give much credence to Vance's picayune criticisms of her teaching. And you ignore my observation of Cissy's class, the day you were too soused to do it."

Humiliated, he said nothing. But to show her he could handle his alcohol, he polished off his drink in a lengthy slurp.

"Three: What do you want her to publish in the six or seven months she's been here? She's gotten one article accepted, which is more than some do in a year or two. Her lecture last week could also be publishable with a little work and her answer to Vance's question showed that she can think on her feet and an ability to rein in pertinent encyclopedic information. And let's not forget her willingness in giving lectures at the departmental colloquium and the Archaeology Interest Group."

Sumner affected boredom. "The same one. No one can say she hasn't gotten mileage out of that little dissertation of hers. But you, Davidine, choose to ignore the most crucial reason." He replayed his last card, aiming for tact: "Vance and I constitute a majority of the Search Committee and we think Bellg should be recommended."

Davidine snorted. "So you two met without me and overruled me? Sumner, don't make me laugh."

Now he glared daggers, bared teeth and mustered all the nonverbal ammunition possible, his last bastion of defense. He could only hope that the Executive Committee not accept the Search Committee's recommendation. A rarity, but possible. So far Rutledge and Rothschild had declined to voice their sympathies.

"Really, Sumner. If it were John or Bob who agreed with you, it would be a different matter. But Vance! He'd teach standing on his head if you or I asked him to."

He realized the error of bolstering his argument with Vance's opinion, looked at his empty glass and searched for the waitress. "I feel a commitment to the department," he said impetuously, uncertain to what he was leading. "I'm afraid that if we hire her, we'll be sorry some day."

Davidine let out a controlled sigh. "It all comes down to the personal level. Can we work with her? I myself have always found Cissy cooperative, capable and pleasant. I'd like to hear what you think is lacking."

"Loyalty's lacking," he barked, using the first word that came to mind. "That's what's wrong with Pankhurst."

"Loyalty?" Davidine echoed with incredulity, fingering her cigarette case. "How has she been disloyal?" Before he could respond, she pushed on: "All you mean is that she doesn't bow down to you like Vance or Ginger."

Sumner stared into his empty jar, wishing it full.

"And, if you choose to remember, I believe last year we agreed informally to hire Cissy for the tenure-track position, provided she work out. Which she has. I consented when you wanted to fly in another candidate this year. I got us the money to do it and I was not impressed with her. Back to the point: Don't you feel any commitment to honor our word and hire Cissy?"

His fist clenched the empty jar. "Where's the waitress?"

"Screw the waitress and answer me." Davidine yanked out a cigarette, snapped the case shut.

"No, I don't feel a commitment to hire her," he snarled back, signaling the waitress.

"Well, I do."

"All right. We'll hire the bitch!"

"What??"

"We'll recommend her to the Executive Committee if that's what you want."

"What's gotten into you, Sumner? I've never heard you talk this way!" Vigorously, she shook her head to and fro. "How many drinks did you have before I got here?"

Befuddled, he miscounted and told the truth: "Two."

Efficiently, the waitress appeared and set down another round.

"Plus three more!" Davidine pointed accusingly at Sumner's full jar. "Maybe the drink is what addled your mind today, has addled it all too frequently lately."

"I assure you that I'm rational."

"Wanting to give Cissy Pankhurst her walking papers!" Davidine took a measured sip of her drink. "I can't believe you want to get rid of her."

"I said we'd recommend her, goddamnit."

"I still can't fathom your behavior in this matter."

"Isn't it normal to have a difference of opinion?"

"Of course. But I hope your manner is not the new norm. I fail to understand what's turned you so fiercely against Cissy. And that's what it is. Anyone who actually listened to Bellg's talk knows that she's all show and little substance." Davidine slid out of the booth and snatched her wrap off the brass coat-tree. "I think I'll be going. Can you drive home?"

"Of course I can."

"Good. Then do it before you drink another drop." Davidine tossed a five and two ones on the table. "Fire Cissy Pankhurst! I can't believe it!" she muttered, every word finely diced.

Sumner leaned back against the booth, swilled his martini and watched Davidine make her way to the exit. "Waitress!" Defiantly, he ordered one more.

If he and Davidine had never known intimacy, she wouldn't be able to treat him this way. For the first time he regretted their affair, regretted that he'd let her entrap him this afternoon and fumed that as long as she was around he didn't have one fucking ounce of real power.

55

When Lou approached the Truster House for the Wednesday night Bible study session, a swarm of familiar Truster faces greeted her. She was then led away with four other potential initiates to the Quiet Room. Sara, one of the advisers, began by filling them in on Truster history: The In God We

Trust House — its full name — had been in Madison since 1976 and formed part of a national network on college campuses. The Reverend Dwight McElroy, founder, directed national operations from his base in Texas. She went on to explain that the five of them —"neophytes," she called them— would be watching the Reverend Dwight's Biblical Interpretation videotapes. She asked for questions, then left the group alone to get acquainted before watching the first one.

A young man named Bruce began the introductions: "This is my second year in Madison. I'm from Hayward and was recruited to play hockey here, but quit. I've been discouraged by what I've seen here. Too much emphasis on success at any cost, materialism, even looks." To Lou, he didn't look bad at all. "After hockey, I ended up pledging a frat and that didn't work out. Now I'm here, knowing I'll fit in better."

"I'm Tinda," said a mousy young woman next to Bruce. "I guess you could say I've been like depressed ever since I arrived in Madison. I've had like zero social life here, I suppose you all know what it can be like. But since I've gotten to know the Trusters, I feel like for the first time in my life, everything, like, is on the upswing."

"I'm Susan Wallwright, a freshman from Waukesha," bubbled Tinda's neighbor, evidently a Truster clone. "I've been seeking the proper atmosphere in which to rediscover and celebrate the glory of Jesus, seven days a week. And here at the Trusters, I've found it."

Next came Felix, an effeminate boy with a hangdog expression, who barely appeared sixteen. He was a sophomore from Mineral Point and was "here to seek the strength to resist certain 'impulses.'"

No one snickered or winced; to the contrary, Lou could feel the unspoken support well up for him in the room. She could also swear she saw Tinda beginning to fix her sights on him.

Herself next, Lou felt a tiny tremble. She was fleeing nothing and felt uncomfortable talking about Jesus, whose glory was dormant for her. Unaccountably nervous, she opted for spitting out a mini-autobiography.

After several minutes of talk, Bruce turned on the VCR. The fluorescent light glaring above them, onto the screen came the Reverend Dwight: fortyish, but hip. His forehead was corrugated by a long serious wrinkle, balanced by an uplifting smile ironed into the lower half of his face. Lou recognized it immediately: Every one of the Trusters had mastered it. His eyes, with uncanny vivacity, leaped out to meet his audience.

He spoke about university life, changing times and difficult decisions; talked of home, wholeness and wholesomeness on campus, raising his voice as if an advocate against student abuse by an impersonal system and a depersonalized society in this era of weakened, decentralized families. He told them that they were chosen to escape the difficulties, the temptation, and, he emphasized, the decadence experienced by today's student masses.

As he paused to let this sink in, Lou took an uneasy inventory of her own alcoholic escapades and felt a tiny pang of shame.

The Reverend Dwight soon drew to a close and pulled out a spiral notebook, nothing other than... the Bible. This was a living, modernized Bible, free of the gobbledygook that baffled many. Before his image faded, he told them to look behind them, where they'd find their own Bible, their key to personal fulfillment, community and Jesus' love.

Lou looked behind her. Sure enough, there was a stack of five spiral notebooks on a table against the wall. She picked hers up; her name had been written on the front cover. Inside was a wish for spiritual peace from Verla.

The five talked briefly of what they'd just heard, Susan leading the chorus of praise for Reverend Dwight and the Trusters. The others chimed in. Caught up in the contagion, Lou contributed: "I came here open-minded, but ready to be skeptical. I have to admit I was impressed."

Friday night she returned for session two, trying to convince herself that a spiritual high was preferable to the alcoholic one Beth had proposed. The Reverend Dwight, however, seemed little concerned with the spirit. He dwelt relentlessly on practicalities in his bowdlerized Bible verses, in which even the most basic, "God setteth the solitary in families," became "Everyone needs a home." "Bear ye one another's burdens and so fulfill the law of Christ," became "Jesus wants you to help each other out." Lou wondered if this was a Bible for the illiterate or if the median Truster intellect was closer to man's average life span. Among the Reverend Dwight's litany of practicalities for student life, she wouldn't have been surprised to hear a pep talk on fasting as a builder of character. At least she was free of the Trusters' meals. Until Sara came in and announced a Sunday morning "devotional brunch" that she expected all would attend.

Lou contemplated the warm, sunny Sunday afternoon from the confines of a cubicle at Helen C. White. After six hours of prime study time spent at the Trusters last week, not to mention two more this morning —which left the body if not the spirit hungering— she was behind in her studies. Although the Trusters prided themselves on their academic support system, Lou had yet to reap any of its benefits. By three she'd finished the reading for one of her Psych courses and headed back to the dorm, having promised, on a whim, to accompany Beth to see an apartment to sublet for the summer. In any case, she was anxious to soak up what remained of the pleasant April day.

Entering her dorm room, she encountered Beth clad in a cobalt smock. Had the bulge underneath not moved, she could have sworn Beth had under gone breast enlargement.

"Ouch! Goddamn you, Brooklyn!" Beth opened her smock and Lou saw the kitten haltered in a bra, tiny claws extended. "Hope you don't mind, kid. Brooklyn needed some maternal comfort so I borrowed a bra of yours, me not havin' any."

"I hope you weren't breastfeeding her."

"Funny, Lou, very funny." Beth turned Brooklyn out, caressed her breast, then rebuttoned the smock. "Well, kid, wanna go check out this place to live in Dollyville this summer?"

Lou looked dumbfounded, then remembered this new nickname Beth had given the city, based on the unproven theory that it was named after Dolly, not James Madison. Although she had promised to see the apartment with Beth, she'd found out this morning that living at the Truster House was a summer possibility. It offered appealingly cheap room and board. What with the board, it should.

They left the dorm and crossed Library Mall. The mid-fifties temperature, combined with sun, had brought out students, who jammed the mall as thick as a rock concert. Frisbees flew, boom boxes blared, jugglers juggled, and street musicians strummed their guitars hoping for loose student change. Adolescents break-danced and skateboarded in and out of the crowd. Students in satin jogging shorts or brief halter tops attempted to sunbathe on the lawn and on Memorial Library's granite steps, ledges, and ample windowsills.

At the opposite end of State Street, groups of Cuban men — Lou now knew they were Marielitos — alternated with gangs of young teens sporting cigarettes, snippets of leather and tattoos. Around them streetpeople jockeyed for position on newly constructed benches. Madison police observed the motley crew from across the street.

"I'd let her arrest me any time," Beth said, her eyes on the female half of the pair.

"Beth!" To Lou, this was like saying the preacher's wife had a nice set of knockers.

Cutting diagonally through the Capitol, they inspected the immense dome, one of the largest in the world, Lou had heard. They emerged on the opposite corner and five blocks later found themselves at the base of Williamson Street.

Displaying her newfound knowledge — from the revolutionary history class where she squatted? — Beth told Lou that this was where Madison's radicals lived. She sensed that Beth was beginning to fancy herself among them. "I don't think we're on State Street anymore," Lou said in an eerie attempt at humor, knowing the wrong side of the tracks when she saw it.

"Thank God!"

Multi-hued hair highlighted the heads of the younger; berets, the older. Long beards and pony tails on men. Short hair on women and — in at least one case — chin hairs and a moustache.

"There's Cicely Pankhurst's house!" Beth pointed when they'd progressed a few blocks.

"Miss Pankhurst's house? How do you know? She's not in the phone book."

"So you looked too?" Beth snickered, then gave full rein to her laughter. "I've got my ways."

Lou observed the house. On the front porch rested a sofa, a washing machine and an old wicker chair. "Beth, are you sure this is her place? It looks like sort of a dump."

"Looks funky, I'd say. I'll go ring the bell if you don't believe me."

Lou skittered across the intersecting street, unsure to what length Beth might go. As Beth stood sizing up the house, Lou saw two men emerge from it.

Beth joined her a second later. "So much for the single-woman theory."

"You promised you wouldn't get a crush on her."

"I didn't. Yet."

They took a right turn off Williamson and two blocks down located the house to be sublet for the summer. Overgrown evergreens obscured its view. They went up to the second-floor flat and two women renters showed them the premises.

"Furniture go with?" Beth asked.

It did. What there was of it. The livingroom held orange crates and cushions on the floor, the walls were decorated with childlike art and an assortment of political posters. A kitchen, bathroom, two bedrooms — each with a mattress on the floor — and an enclosed front porch rounded out the space.

"Well, whaddya think?" Beth asked when they left.

"The rent can't be beat. Three hundred and fifty for the whole summer!"

"It's sure big and nice enough."

"It's just that the neighborhood is kind of… far." Lou omitted less flattering adjectives.

"Hell, we walked here, didn't we? We can always bike it or bus it."

Back on Williamson, they approached a house in front of which stood a half-dozen men and their motorcycles. Some wore leather, others had beer guts, and all clenched Budweisers in their fists. Behind them a child set off firecrackers. On the front porch sat two of the bikers' women, a naked tod dler at their side.

Lou sped up her pace and noticed Beth keeping up.

"You wanna see the real world or not?" Beth asked when they had safely passed. "That was it."

"Frankly, I don't know if I'm ready."

"You got used to State Street, you can get used to this."

"We'll see." What Lou didn't say was that it seemed much easier to get used to the Trusters — meals apart. Beth knew nothing about them and Lou sensed she should keep it that way.

56

Twelve days had passed since Cissy's lecture and she still had no word about the job. Ginger had eavesdropped on Rickover to learn that the Search Committee had met on Friday. Evan had read a memo over Wilhelmina's shoulder, informing that the Executive Committee would meet on Monday, its agenda one word: "personnel."

Cissy found nothing in her mailbox late Tuesday morning and felt depressed. She studied the tight-lipped faces of the Executive Committee: Rutledge and Rothschild passed her in the halls, formal and characteristically inscrutable. Even Ginger had been unable to penetrate the conspiracy of Executive Committee silence. The only possible sign came from Rickover: a slight upward curl of the lips. A restrained smile of congratulation or a simper of pity?

Cissy spent the day convinced the job had gone to Catherine Bellg.

After finishing her advanced class, she returned to her office, rummaged through folders for some old notes on Mexico's *Museo Nacional* and by 3:00 had filled her briefcase with the necessary papers for tomorrow's preparation. On her way out, she decided to check her mailbox once more.

There it lay: an ominous envelope, typewritten on departmental letterhead. She snatched it up, hastened back to her office and locked the door. Removing the letter from its sheath, she closed her eyes for a hopeful second, then remembered that what usually came by mail was rejections. Of course Sumner wouldn't call her in in person to tell her they'd hired Catherine Bellg. She stared at the envelope, then turned it over. She had no choice but to open it.

Dean Davidine Phipps of the College of Fine Arts has authorized me to offer you a tenure-track appointment as Assistant Professor, beginning in the Fall Semester, 1986... Her eyes zoomed on: an initial three-year contract, a salary of $22,900, which amounted to a $3,400 increase. As chair, Sumner had signed it.

Here it was: her oft-doubted admittance to the Ivory Tower, after seven years of graduate school, seminar papers, symposia, a thesis, dissertation, lectures, evaluations... She felt almost faint, then giddy. Her eyes wetted. She bounded out into the hall to tell someone, then remembered that Evan and Ginger had left for the day.

At home, Jeb showed little emotion at the news. He read and reread the letter, as though scouring it for loopholes. "I guess it's all there, babe. It looks legit."

"Of course it is," she replied, a bit miffed at him.

"But none too cordial. See?" He extended his arm, wrapped it around her waist and nudged her toward him. "No congratulations offered anywhere. No 'pleasure' in extending the offer. No one's even 'hoping' you'll accept. Hell, you're not even supposed to 'accept,' but rather 'reply' at your earliest convenience."

She skimmed the letter and turned up her nose at Jeb's findings. "In academia, you take what you can get. And I'll take this!" She burst into an unflinching smile; Jeb slowly broke into a satisfied grin.

"We'll go out for dinner. My treat."

"But I've got to prepare for tomorrow."

"You've worked years for this, babe, diligently, workaholically." He was firm. "Take the night off. Forget the preparation."

"Forget the preparation," she repeated, vaguely incredulous.

"Right," he insisted. "Yell a little, live it up, relieve your stress, make love."

"All right, we'll go to dinner."

"Today, whatever you want, babe."

"Maybe we can have a little celebration this weekend. Ginger, Evan, the neighbors..."

Roz finished her shift at the Co-op, detoured home, then headed to Irv's for dinner. As she reached the upstairs door, a pungent aroma enveloped her.

Clad in a white chef's apron, Irv greeted her with a kiss. "How about we eat at seven?"

"Fine with me, but is there a hurry?" She skipped behind him as he loped back into the kitchen.

"Oh, I didn't tell you? We're invited downstairs to Cissy and Jeb's for champagne at eight. The university hired her for the tenure-track job."

"You mean you're invited down."

"No, both of us. If you want, I'll go by myself and be back by nine. You don't have to go along."

Roz suppressed a grunt. "Maybe I'll go." Though Irv spoke fondly of his downstairs tenants, she harbored less fondness for them. She doubted she'd feel in place and examined her clothes — bluejeans and a flannel shirt. It was not so much true working-class as counterculture attire, which happened to coincide with the most common lesbian "uniform." All she lacked were work boots. Hardly smart cocktail attire for rubbing elbows with newly promoted faculty.

Irv stirred a pot of pasta. At its side, pesto simmered in a pan, its smell overtaking the whole upstairs. "Maybe I'll have downstairs tenants for another year."

"Don't count on it. She gets a promotion, they move up in the world, and those two will head straight to the west side."

Irv shot her a perplexed look, erased it, then said brightly, "We can't hide forever as a couple." He dipped a wooden spoon into the pesto. "Cissy and Jeb know we're a couple. It would be an easy place for you to 'come out.' You don't really know them, they don't really know you."

Roz considered this logic. Wanting to please Irv and goaded by his comment about "hiding," she decided to give it a try. For him. "OK, we'll make our heterosexual social debut. Or mine, rather."

At 8:15 they went down the stairs and encountered a well-dressed black couple sniffing suspiciously in the entryway.

"If you're looking for Cissy, you've got the right place," Irv greeted, friendly. They introduced themselves and entered the downstairs flat. The woman hugged Cissy and gushed with congratulations. Roz felt immediately alienated. She conjured up her best wishes, but kept her physical distance, not wanting to risk an allergic reaction to the rampant perfume. Of course, the fragrance could be dispelled by a little cigarette smoke, she thought with mischief, and caressed the pack of Camels in her pocket.

The four of them were the only guests. She heard Cissy lament to Ginger that "Evan and Anne couldn't get a babysitter." Juan — if not Gil — had been invited too, but he had to drive cab.

The six of them barely fit around the kitchen table. Champagne was uncorked and poured. Glasses held aloft clinked, tinkled musically to Irv's toast: "To Cissy!" The rest seconded it, then drank.

"To Cissy's new job!" toasted Melvin, Ginger's partner.

One toast segued into another. Jeb toasted to academia, with a cynicism Roz could appreciate. Ginger toasted prematurely to Cissy's tenure. Then they all looked expectantly at Roz. For a second she panicked, then offered, "To the east side!" As they raised their glasses, she bet that Ginger and Melvin were west-siders.

Toasts concluded, the champagne sippers chatted around the table. Roz took a slug and eyed her festive companions: two straight couples, plus Irv and herself. Three straight couples. Did everyone perceive her as half of a

heterosexual unit? Undoubtedly Ginger and Melvin did. After her initial encounter with Cissy at the Terrace last fall, she doubted she thought highly of
her, heterosexual or not. At least it was mutual.

If only Juan were here, people wouldn't be so neatly defined. When
she'd lived in the commune, she'd been straight, but no one there was ever
defined by heterosexuality or partnership. Of course, these were the eighties
and this was not a commune. She shuddered at the thought of being an ap-
pendage to a man, as she felt tonight. Women, when together, didn't define
themselves by partnership to others, did they? Not the ones she knew.

"Roz, a refill?"

She realized that Cissy's tiny flute-like voice had asked the question
twice. "Uh, sure." She plastered a decorous smile on her face as Cissy tilted
the green bottleneck in front of her. Her glass bubbled full. She saw that the
long-stemmed glasses were especially for champagne. She thanked Cissy,
brought the glass to her mouth and set it back down. Craving a cigarette, she
saw no visible ashtrays. Seated next to her, Irv smiled. She acknowledged his,
mechanically. His hung on a second longer. He began to speak to her, was
tapped on the shoulder and excused himself. She picked her glass back up to
drink. Under the table a foot collided with hers. She recoiled in her sneakers.

Cissy sported a pink pantsuit. Where was the gold waist chain? Ginger wore a necklace and navy blue sleeveless dress. She raised her glass and
her arm, met Roz's eyes. No underarm hair, no surprise. Probably about to
ask sweetly, "And what do you do, Roz?"

She took a swift interest in contemplating the differing patterns of her
and Irv's flannel shirts, coughed and drank a gulp of champagne. Across the
table Melvin caught her eyes as Jeb moved his jaw animatedly, detailing Cissy's
new contract. Ginger nodded knowingly. Jeb himself had applied to graduate
school in Phys Ed, but hadn't been accepted yet. Ginger nodded politely.

Roz snitched an olive off a tray. Her bluejeans pulled taut at her legs,
white anklets growing out of her sneakers. She ate a second olive. Ginger rose,
her shaven legs encased in pantyhose, and went to the john. Melvin beamed
after her, turned back to Irv. Probably a lawyer too, but of a different ilk. She
heard him say "building up equity."

Roz saw that her shirt hung awkwardly. Ginger returned from the
john. Lover beams. Or husband? Heterosexuals in love. Am I one of them?
No. These are advanced, west-side yuppies. Irv squeezes my hand under the
table. Why not above? Of course, my nails aren't painted, like Ginger's. But
I'm here, Irv, palpable. Squeeze my hand again. I need counterculture heterosexuality, that's all. Hold me. Please.

Oops, my drink's gotten freshened again. By the perfect hostess. Pink
Pankhurst, pink pantsuit. Pink, for girls. Drink up, Roz, that's why you're

here. To celebrate, to drink. Where's the pot? I bet Jeb gets high. Smile, Roz, this is a special occasion. A momentous event for Cissy. Who has a mole on her cheek. No, a dimple. Better yet, a love mark. Whose hand's on my leg now? Irv's, of course. That Jeb has long arms, though. Ginger eyes me again. Melvin distracts her, takes possession of her shoulder with his arm. Proudly. Now caresses her ringed hand. Above the table. How sweet. Irv's still got mine, underneath. Champagne in my other one. Occupied hands, no need to smoke, right? Watch out for me, Irv. Eat an olive, Roz, drink up, do something. Cigarette, cigarette. Is it nine yet? Irv, you promised this'd be quick. If only Juan were here. That's right, drink up, Jeb. Feed your face, Cissy, today's your day. What are you doing here, Roz? Champagne, unlit candles, tenure-track Pankhurst. Emmeline Pankhurst! Feminist crosswords. Eat up Melvin, drink down Ginger with your round cheeks and ruby lipsticked lips, Cissy you're no feminist, Irv are you there, squeeze my reality now, right now Irv, I can't...

Roz got up slowly, glued on a semblance of smiling cordiality, hoping not to embarrass Irv. "I've got to go. Thank you all. Irv, see you upstairs. Good-bye everyone."

She headed evenly toward the living room door. Outside, she restrained an impulse to gallop up the stairs, but remained immobile, hearing shushed conversation inside. "Champagne must've gone to her head," opined Melvin.

Jeb: "Maybe she had to puke."

Yes, but not for the reasons they think.

"I'll be all right. I am all right." Roz puffed avidly on her Camel upstairs.

Irv sat next to her on the sofa, its surface pitted by sundry exposed springs. "I should have taken better care of you down there."

"It's not you, it's not them, it's me."

Irv kissed her, held her tightly. With her free hand, she flicked ashes over his shoulder.

"I just let the champagne and the atmosphere weird me out. I wasn't freaked out or anything. I just got a little phobic and had to leave before I displayed antisocial behavior. Nor did I have to puke, you can tell Jeb-boy."

Irv comforted her with an arm around her neck. She put out her cigarette, the better to cuddle. After several minutes, he got up to switch the TV on, a tiny black-and-white portable on the floor. A documentary on cranes was airing on the public TV station.

They settled back and watched, Roz giving half-attention to the program while reliving her near-fiasco. She perked up when the narrator mentioned the Crane Foundation in Baraboo.

"What do you say I do my own documentary?" she said, determined to be cheerful. "I could call it 'Going Straight in the Eighties.'"

Irv gave her an abstracted look. Roz winced at her own joke. The evening truly hadn't been that bad. Or shouldn't have been. She now remembered why she'd left academia.

Academic community, lesbian community, straight community. Hippie, drug, commie communities. Neighborhoods and politics. All communities. Like everyone, she'd forged her own niches, but would now have to alter some of them. Or at least one of them. It shouldn't be that hard, should it?

She rested her head on Irv's shoulder and refused to let herself answer "yes."

57

A light morning rain shellacked the windowpane. It was May 1, International Workers' Day and Juan's thirty-third birthday. He did his monthly balancing of his checkbook and totaled it at $559.95. His net worth sounded like the price of a trash compactor. He took out his avocational checkbook: the Wiscaragua fund, the YUDs and SPELL had a combined total of $35.02 in assets, down six dollars from a year ago.

He yawned and a wave of exhaustion infiltrated his limbs. He had read that after age twenty-five, the body annually lost one percent of its efficiency. This meant that he was still ninety-two percent physically efficient, a bright prospect, which served to counter unflattering notions about aging and energy. In any case, he opted for a nap, shucking his Levi's and his socks. As he walked toward the bed, he realized that something had stuck to his foot. He bent down and removed a business card from the heel. It read "Winnebago Baptist Church. Edward Hunter, Pastor." Address and telephone followed.

Where could this have come from? No passengers had given him a business card. It could have been dropped in the cab, but this couldn't account for its ending up in the house. He placed it on the nightstand and climbed into bed.

An insistent rapping at the door woke him.

"Coming!" he barked. He stepped into his bluejeans, then snagged a T-shirt off the floor. The rapping recommenced.

"Coming, goddamnit..." The rapper went silent. Muttering under his breath and disoriented from sleep, he reached the door and flung it open.

"Happy birthday!" Roz thrust a small brown paper bag at him and Juan envisioned an ounce of marijuana inside. "Sorry, it's only a book. You gonna ask me in?"

"In, Roz." He let her pass and opened the bag. *"Exercising on Drugs!* Thanks."* For her birthday he'd given her another of the series, *Health for Hedonists*. He kissed her on both cheeks.

"And with the book goes this little number I brought." She winked and produced a cigarette case. Out of it she pulled a rotund joint.

He saw that the rain had ceased while he'd slept. "Shall we do it?"

"What? Exercise or drugs?"

"Why not both?"

"Mmmm." Roz mulled over the proposition. "I suppose doing both is healthier than calling 'Athletes Anonymous.'"

Juan sent her a befuddled look.

"Whenever you get the urge to exercise, you just call a fellow AA member who rushes over to ply you with whatever substance you're in the mood to abuse and then you forget about exercising."

"Are you a member? Can I join?"

"It's a joke, Juan. But now, if you ever do feel like exercising stoned, you have this trusty little manual to tell you how."

"How about we pass on the manual for the moment, get high and jog to the lake?"

"How about two out of three?"

He craned his neck toward the kitchen clock. "It's ten till twelve. You have time to get high and come down in time to work at two, right?"

"We don't have to worry about getting too high. It's Wisconsin Green. And what I meant was I'd pass on the jogging, not the dope."

"Come on. We can handle a four-block jog to the lake, stoned or not. Look how it's cleared up outside. Sun for my natal day." He lowered himself onto the sofa, lit the joint and passed it to Roz. They inhaled it down to the last toke, securing the roach between fingernails.

"Ready to jog now?" He jumped up; Roz regarded him bizarrely. "Are we going to be healthy hedonists or just plain hedonists?" He went to the bedroom, exchanged his jeans for cutoffs and put on socks. He returned with tennis shoes in one hand and a pair of shorts for Roz in the other.

Roz eyed him with a tinge of exasperation. "All right. You win. But only because it's your birthday."

Moments later he charged down the stairs, Roz behind him. They passed the recently roto-tilled patches of dirt that would soon be the garden. This year, all his, unless Cissy stayed on and wanted to negotiate the space.

They began their pace slowly and after two blocks reached Orton Park, crossing it in a long diagonal. Puffing for air, they reached the park's end and came to a slow stop at the foot of Few Street, where its final block dead-ended into Lake Monona. A small municipally maintained green space filled the strip between street and lake. Winded and panting, they flopped themselves down on a bench.

"Cigarette?" Juan gasped, reaching inside a sock for his ultra-lights.
"No."

As they recovered their breath, a launch sped by on Monona, sending ripples to the shore. A light breeze sailed off the lake, the sun hid behind a cloud. A lone duck swam by, rocking in the water from the wake of the boat.

Juan inhaled deeply on his cigarette. When it reached the filter, he stubbed it out and deposited it in his sock. "Did you get off? I did."

"I don't know. I suppose a little." She frowned and faced him. "My body's been playing tricks on me lately."

"Menopause already?" he joked.

She scowled, unappreciative. "Maybe it's the Pill."

"What are you taking?"

"*The* Pill." Juan looked dumbfounded. "'Pill' with a capital P."

"You don't mean..?"

"What?"

"Uh-oh," Juan said to himself. What fib could he invent? He lit another ultra-light to stall for time. Out of one eye, he saw a duck family pass by near the shore. "I mean, are women still using the Pill? I thought it went out with the seventies." Seeing Roz observe him doubtfully, he went on: "I was just surprised to hear you were taking the Pill. I don't follow birth control trends much."

Roz pounced on this: "That I believe. And I also think birth control trends don't interest you, that you weren't going to ask me about the popularity of the Pill in the eighties, and that you're hiding something from me."

Trapped, he inhaled deeply, looked from the ground to the duck family, and said nothing.

"Juan, what aren't you telling me?"

A nonverbal standoff followed. As soon as he dared to meet her eyes, he knew he'd lost. "Roz, first you'd better have that cigarette I offered."

After ripping the filter off, she lit it and made an expression of distaste. "OK. Tell me, damn it."

He turned to her. She sat on the opposite end of the bench, sucking with apparent urgency on the ultra-light. A head of black hair, shorn short enough to decimate the frizz, capped her thin, almost frail body. She suddenly appeared fragile and vulnerable. He dreaded having to tell her what Irv should have and hadn't.

"Roz, Irv's sterile. And put your cigarette out before it becomes part of your hand."

She let the cigarette fall to the ground and leaned forward, arms and head dangling.

"I'm sorry, Roz."

"Why didn't he tell me?" she erupted after several seconds, facing the lake, as if addressing it rhetorically. "The first time we made love this year, I told him not to bother about condoms and he didn't say a single word." She completed a slow turn toward him and let out a coarse, bitter laugh.

Before he formulated a rejoinder, she went on: "Sterile! I suppose poor Roz Goldmann was the only one in town who didn't know!"

"Goldwomyn."

"Did he think I wouldn't want him if I knew?" She marched back and forth in front of the bench. "Now I remember why I became a separatist. Because men are a bunch of self-centered shmucks! The less women have to do with them, the better! How could he not tell me?"

Juan felt obliged to say something to defend his comrades in gender. "I'm sure he was getting around to it. It's not something you usually go around announcing. Plus, I mean, being sterile has its advantages, doesn't it?"

She let out a shrill laugh which ended up sounding like a sob. He patted her on the shoulder. At least she didn't forcibly remove his arm as in her early separatist days when men would innocently touch her. "It'll be all right."

She sniffled, as though battling tears. "I don't suppose it would be a vasectomy."

"I don't know that they're always reversible anyway. He only mentioned it to me once. Some childhood disease." He racked his brain for the name. "Orchitis, I think. Something to do with your balls."

She gave a derisive snort. "Evidently he has none."

"Look at the bright side. You can go off the Pill." Roz's glower put dimmers on the brightness of his observation. "OK. So you want to have a baby, right? There are alternatives, you know. You can have a baby without Irv's sperm. There's a regular lesbian baby boom in San Francisco... Once the two of you talk about it, you'll feel better."

Roz cast him a disparaging glance. He hiked up his drooping sock, adjusting the pack of cigarettes that had slid down to his ankle. "Come on. Let's jog back."

"I'm not high any more and I don't feel like jogging."

"Then we'll walk. I came down too. We can smoke another one at home."

She sat back down, shoulders slouching. Motionless, she stared right past him, her gaze fixed on some distant point. Monona's duck family had swum away.

"You go," she said finally. "Just let me stay here a minute. I'll catch back up to you in the park."

He nodded, then bolted up the one-block hill and into the park, where he plunked himself down by a burr oak. As he felt the breeze on his forearms and legs, the minister's business card came back to mind.

Moments later Roz appeared, wearing a strained smile. Without conversing they walked back to the Willy Street house and found it still empty. Juan pulled out a pre-rolled joint of his own and offered it to her. "This one's weak too. You still have an hour before work." They sat on the sofa and smoked it, silent except for their inhalations and exhalations.

He set the roach on the edge of an ashtray. "Cheer up, Roz."

"Why should I?"

He tried to make her laugh: "Because you're about as much fun as a Mormon at an orgy."

Her bleak expression hung on. She reached for her Camels.

"Speaking of bigamy..," Juan began, and saw her face turn grave upon hearing the word. "Don't worry. I'm not talking about Irv. I need your opinion on something."

Roz loosened back up, drew on the tobacco.

"Let's say, for example, that you're in the bedroom you and your lover share and you find a man's business card that you're ninty-nine-percent certain no one gave to you. Suspicion, naturally, gravitates toward your lover, who, to your knowledge, has once been unfaithful, but gave you a solemn promise of fidelity forever after. Well, more or less. The business on the card, by the way, is religion. Question: Do you think your lover is committing adultery with said man of the cloth?"

"I take it this case is not exactly hypothetical."

Juan bowed his head grimly. "You take it."

"Do you want me to answer as if under truth serum?"

He gave an affirmative jerk of the head.

"I'd say it's ten-to-one in favor of adultery."

"Remember, we're in an AIDS crisis, Roz."

"OK, nine-to-one."

"Gee, thanks."

"Well, you said to give you my truthful opinion," she protested, propping her feet up on the trunk that served as coffee table.

"Yeah, but you don't have to sound so goddamned certain of your truthful opinion." He placed his feet next to hers. "But with a Baptist preacher??"

"Clergy gotta have sex too, I suppose. Take Brigham Young, for example... Maybe Gil's converting."

"From what to what?" he demanded, jutting his lip into a pout. "From monogamy to bigamy? Trigamy? Quadrigamy?"

"I believe the word's 'polygamy.'"

Juan ignored her comment and stood up. "He probably figures that as long as he's fucking a man of the cloth, it's somehow condoned from above!" He paced, stopped to stick an unlit cigarette in his mouth, and flung his arms as he spoke. "On my own fucking birthday he chooses to fuck some preacher right in our own fucking bed! Well, he can fucking fuck him until it fucking falls off!" Punctuating this, he kicked a pile of newspapers, scattering them. His eyes fell on a Village Voice headline: "Gays and Monogamy: Can They Coexist?" He turned to Roz. "Sorry. I needed to have a tantrum."

"You certainly succeeded. Now, are you a little calmer?"

"I guess so." He let out a brittle laugh as his eyes again fell on the headline.

"Sit down. Look, you don't have any concrete evidence, right? So there's no need to get so riled up. Let's sit here and think of a logical explanation for the card."

No one said anything for ten seconds.

"See!" he declared in triumph. "There is no other logical explanation!"

"No fair! You weren't even trying."

Juan scowled at her as he heard a door open on the first floor. "Someone's coming."

"It sounds like two sets of footsteps."

"It is. But it could be Cissy and Jeb bringing up the rent check."

"Juan." Roz lowered her voice: "Today's your birthday. Don't ruin it by accusing Gil tonight. Promise? Good. Observe him. Look for little signs. Put the card right back where you found it and see if it disappears."

The footsteps reached the top of the stairs. "Don't you make a scene with Irv either," he whispered before darting into the bedroom to put the card back.

"Hello, there!" Irv's voice boomed in surprise at seeing Roz. He stepped inside, followed by Gil.

"Oh, hi," Gil said, as if taken aback at seeing Juan.

"Hello, Irv, Gil," Juan greeted crisply.

Irv's nostrils perked up. "Smells like you two have been celebrating the birthday."

"Sure have." Roz's face blossomed into a smile.

"Indeed," Juan said. "And having an edifying little discussion while we were at it." To this, no one replied. His glance scanned the room and Roz sent him a discreet facial warning. Defiantly, he went on, with false jollity: "I trust the two of you have had a pleasant morning." Roz's eyes sent him another warning signal, sterner.

"Smells like you two had a pleasanter one," Gil observed, sniffing the air like a bloodhound. "Can we join you?" He removed a joint from behind his right ear.

"Smoke away," Juan said. "As for me, I've had enough right now." He forced himself to walk calmly into the bedroom and closed the door. The card lay on the floor by a pair of socks. He made a deal with himself: If Gil moved the card and said nothing about it, it would prove his guilt and give him the right to confront him. If not, he'd have to wait for more clues. He returned to the living room, where the three of them sat, Gil smoking a joint alone.

"On second thought I will have a toke," he said, feigning sociability.

58

I t's not easy being a Truster.

The words repeated so often rang in Lou's mind, but took on new meaning: Being a Truster meant spending every waking moment she was not involved with them having to catch up on her studies. The end of the their Bible study sessions was nearing, but so was the end of the semester. She'd considered dropping out, but not a quitter, had vowed to finish the Trusters' course and then decide.

The announced topic of tonight's videotape was sex. Jovial, the Reverend Dwight jumped right in. "Sex is in the forefront of today's students' minds. And do you know what? The word 'sex' hardly even appears in the Bible. Many references to it do appear and some of them seem contradictory. That's why, in today's permissive age, which bombards you with all kinds of information about sex, I want to talk to you about this very important topic." The Reverend Dwight then proceeded to read various verses from his low-IQ Bible. Lou found herself daydreaming until she heard his tone turn ominous when he translated Timothy 6:9 into "When you're not mature enough and don't have the blessing of the Lord, sex can ruin your life and put an end to your university career."

This didn't sound like the Reverend Dwight she'd heard before, when everything was love, support and trust. She saw disquieting or perhaps repentant looks on the others' faces. Felix had long ago opened the topic with a confession of his own misdirected drives. One night Bruce had poured out a chilling cautionary tale of his girlfriend's pregnancy and her abortion against his wishes. Not to be outdone, Susan Wallwright had volunteered that she'd lost her virginity "many times." Tinda's glances at Felix had progressed to unconcealed, unabated lust. Only Lou seemed free of past or pending sins and tonight felt out of place. She became impatient spending prime study time to hear this and repressed a glare at Susan, whose glance seemed to imply secret sexual sins on Lou's part.

After a longer than usual rhetorical pause, the Reverend Dwight plunged back in. "One of the secret forms that sexual experimentation takes is homosexuality." Lou fixated on Beth, thinking of her unhappy affairs of the past year. When she tuned the Reverend Dwight back in, he seemed more carried away than usual, translating Romans 1: 26-27 into language that left no doubt: "Men of any age do not have sex with other men and women not with other women." A brief pause, then a new blast: "On this point, the Bible never contradicts itself. The guilt caused by homosexual acts guilt leads to despair, their practice to disease, and perpetuation of such acts to nothing short of the end of the human race." The Reverend Dwight let this sink in, then picked up with renewed tempo. "But let's think about your future. Although one isolated homosexual act may seem harmless now, one leads to two, and you could be trapped in a vicious cycle of sin. Where do you want to be ten years from now? Living alone in an apartment or with a roommate? Twenty years from now? Alone and childless? The Trusters are here to provide you with a supportive community so that you're never lonely and never give in to the temptation of this particularly vile practice."

Lou's thoughts strayed back to Beth. What would happen if she moved in with her this summer? So far, it was her only concrete possibility for housing, and she'd managed to fend off Beth's pressure for a decision. She pictured the two of them living together, not by chance, but now by choice. Indeed, Beth seemed to fit the pattern of loneliness and lovelessness that the Reverend Dwight was describing. If Lou aimed to be a real Truster, maybe she should help Beth out. How she'd find time or energy for such a project, she didn't know. But it wasn't easy being a Truster...

After the tape finished, Felix waxed on thankfully about his "salvation." Tinda, as always, glowed at his side. Bruce and Susan contributed tidbits of homosexual horror stories of acquaintances. Lou had absolutely no intention of bringing up Beth. The farther she could keep Beth and the Trusters from each other, the better.

After the session, she encountered Verla downstairs. "There's definitely going to be room here for you this summer!"

"That's great." Lou's tone failed to rival Verla's enthusiasm. She saw no reason to get excited. Before it had been "almost definite." Big deal. She hadn't absolutely made up her mind "to go the Truster way," as they put it. But it was an alternative to living with Beth. And she didn't have money to live alone.

"You haven't made other summer plans, now have you?" Verla teased.

"Oh, no," Lou said lightly, then repeated what Verla already knew: "It's just that my parents don't know yet that I plan to stay in Madison." Having put it off too long, she made a mental note to inform them this week.

"Oh, and one other thing, Lou. I met your roommate, Beth, this afternoon."

Lou went hollow in the stomach.

"I didn't get the assignment in Autobiography class, so I stopped by
your dorm about 4:30. You weren't there, but I found Beth instead."

"I was probably in the cafeteria already." Lou tried to mask her uneasiness over their meeting. "Do you still need the assignment? It's the next
seventy-five pages."

Verla nodded absent-mindedly. "Beth seems quite a wonderful person." Lou doubted that Verla had ever met anyone who wasn't "wonderful."
"She's also quite her own person."

"I'm glad you liked her. It's nice when your friends like your friends,"
Lou responded, wondering what on earth did Verla mean by "quite her own
person?"

Probably nothing in particular, she concluded, walking home. Maybe
she needn't be so leery of the Trusters' meeting Beth. After all, she didn't
have the word "lesbian" stamped on her forehead or anything.

In their room, Lou found Beth with a cigarette in one hand, a wine
glass in the other, dancing to music from the stereo. Although Beth appeared
happy, Lou reflected that this was probably how she combated her "condition."

"How ya doin', kiddo?" Beth screamed over the wail of the music.
"Heavy night with Helen, huh? Me, I did time with Museums till about nine,
then said 'Screw it,' time to get loose. By the way, some friend of yours
stopped in this afternoon. Viva or Velva or somebody."

"Verla. Why don't you turn the music down a little?"

Beth stopped gyrating and complied. "Yeah, Verla, that's it."

Lou focused on her T-shirt and let out a tiny gasp. "Beth! What does
your shirt say?"

Oh, this?" Beth extended the piece of fabric above her breast where a
word was monogrammed in rectangular black letters, each one fitting inside
the other. "It says 'DYKE'. Neat, don'tcha think?" She sashayed over to the
window and lowered the volume, then set down her wine and stroked Brooklyn, who peered out as if scouring the world for other signs of feline life. "Got
it mail order from California. Came today. Whaddya think, kid?"

Lou hoped she hadn't gone too pale, tried to keep her composure.
"This might sound strange, but... Have you had that T-shirt on all day?"

"Ever since it came at noon. Why?"

Lou's stomach did somersaults. "Just curiosity."

59

Nine a.m. Juan stood by the kitchen window. Tentative, the morning sun poked through a cloud. He had the day off from driving cab, but almost wished he were working. Gil had gotten up extraordinarily early and left, as had Irv. Juan could tell by the closed door that Roz was asleep in Irv's bedroom.

The sun burst the rest of the way through. Juan averted his glance. Its appearance made him hark back to happier, sunnier times, to his boyhood, to the innocence that childhood endowed. A childhood oblivious to the pursuit of pesos or dollars, an age when one was unscathed by the wily ways of the world, relationships and lovers.

He roused himself from his lethargy and went outside. From the porch he observed the roto-tilled garden plot. Fidgety in his need to do something manual, he walked to the shed that squatted behind the house, entered and located last year's seed packets. He told himself that the seeds would probably germinate, but his need to do something overrode his concern about their usability. If they didn't germinate, he'd replant with newly purchased ones.

Leaving the shed, he made a visor with his hand to shield his eyes. He knelt down in the front yard. Packets of carrot, lettuce, pea, Brussels sprout and broccoli seeds rested in his hand. He decided to begin with the lettuce, which he should have planted weeks ago, and with a trowel made a furrow for the Red Sails. His mind wandered to last night's birthday dinner. Soil adhered to his hands and he rubbed them together, dislodging the dirt. He cupped the lettuce seeds, too tiny to separate adequately, in his palm. They stuck to his hand. He attempted to drop them one by one into the shallow furrow and in his mind relived last night's scenario.

"You found your business card, I presume?" he'd said when unable to contain himself longer. "I saw it on the floor this morning, but by afternoon it was gone." He was aiming for a cool and detached tone — amicability, even — and prided himself on this. "So tell me about Edward Hunter."

"I don't know what card you're talking about or who is Hunter Edwards or whoever you just mentioned." Gil appeared totally unflustered and continued to eat his salad at the French restaurant.

"Then I'll tell you who he is." Juan paused over his own salad. "He's a Baptist minister."

"I may have joined a frat once, but I never went in for religious cults," Gil joked, his mouth full of lettuce. Oil from the dressing coated his lips. "Where would I know a Baptist minister from?"

"That's what I was wondering," Juan let himself say. "Maybe I can help you remember. It's the Winnebago Baptist Church on the north side of town."

Juan knew he shouldn't have added that that was what he was wondering, knew he could not discuss matters of the heart, especially fidelity, tranquilly. The remark didn't get Gil's dander up, but probably did pave the way for it, he realized upon later reflection.

"Some passenger of yours probably thought you looked godless and left it for you," Gil went on joking. "Or you drifted off at the wheel and started spouting atheism in your sleep." Gil seemed amused by his own words, laughed a little too loudly.

In silence, both returned to their salads. He'd sensed that a storm cloud had settled over his birthday dinner.

He smoothed a thin layer of soil over the seeds, picked up the packet of pea seeds and stood up, telling himself not to dwell on negativity. The peas needed to be planted along the fence at the corner of the property, where the ground hadn't been roto-tilled. He returned to the shed and brought back a long-handled shovel to attack the small, intractable patch of dirt.

"That's strange about the card," he'd mumbled upon finishing his salad. Gil shook his head in apparent perplexity, urged Juan to forget it and enjoy his birthday. Evidently, Juan figured, Gil had good reason for wanting to terminate the discussion. As things stood, he could neither enjoy his dinner nor abide Gil's hypocrisy. He'd put out one more feeler, then let the issue rest for the night: "Things just don't appear out of nowhere like that."

"Maybe it's Irv's." Gil was emphatic.

Such an improbable suggestion gave him a green light to continue his pursuit of the truth. "That's unlikely."

"If you're gonna imply something, say it."

A tuxedoed waiter brought the entrées. Juan waited until the plates were served, then said, "If it's not mine and it's not Irv's and it's not yours, then whose is it?"

"Do you wanna hear it's mine? Wanna hear that this guy and I fuck like wild beasts every chance we get? Will that make you happy?"

"Happy, no. Satisfied to hear the truth, yes." Juan tried to calm himself. On the off-chance that Gil was telling the truth, he didn't want to be unfair to him. He brought a forkful of asparagus swathed in hollandaise to his mouth.

"Well, you got the truth." Gil mangled the words as he swallowed. Juan observed him for a few seconds as he tried to corner a tip of beef in béarnaise sauce. After stabbing it and seeing Juan's eyes on him, he said, "What a time for accusations."

"In the past, you've..."

Gil cut him off with an unmodulated slam of the fist on the table. Diners gawked, turned away discreetly. "I do something once and you never let me forget it. What do you want for satisfaction? Blood? My right ball?"

"People can hear you."

"You started this." Gil lowered his voice only slightly. "I'm sick of being accused every time you find a new wrinkle in the bed sheets."

Juan began to protest, but Gil got up and stomped away.

Eric's presence jolted him back to reality. "So you like peas," Eric said, seeing the packet in Juan's hand. Juan took several seconds to react, both to Eric and to the comment, wanting to address the specific question about the peas. He was about to say that he froze them and used them in stew, when Eric patted him on the shoulder and said, "I gotta be at the Co-op in two minutes. Take care, old man! Don't look so shaken up. It's only peas!"

Eric, like Gil last night, laughed at his own comment, then rounded the corner onto Willy Street. The pea packet still in hand, Juan absent-mindedly tried to reapply himself to the task of pea-planting. He thought, not for the first time, that was too analytical or sensitive for normal social relations. He wished the garden were in the backyard, and less public. He trained his eyes on the peas he was depositing in a row next to the wire fence.

Roz appeared on the porch, a mug of coffee in her fist. "Hey, Juan-Boy! Coffee?"

He gestured affirmatively, needing a touchstone with reality. While Roz returned inside to fetch him some, he went to wash his hands at an outside spigot.

On the porch, she handed him a steaming cup. "Great day, huh?"

"Your demeanor's certainly jubilant for someone who's just gotten up. I take it you and Irv discussed your dilemma."

"Nope," she said, glowing incongruously. "I told myself to wait till tonight. Bet you didn't."

Juan wrinkled up his nose and sipped, then made a face at her as he lowered the mug.

"Out with it, Juan."

He ordered his thoughts and began an arduous recounting of the incident, his narrative lurching forward, backtracking. Incapable of excising detail, he got as far as Gil's marching off, then stopped. He reflected and drank more coffee.

"Don't leave me hanging."

"So he stomped away. I didn't know where he'd gone. He could have grabbed his jacket, which was checked by the door, and left, for all I knew. After about five minutes, he came back, apparently from the john, sat down, and glared for the rest of the meal. Which was by then cold. And I'd already eaten mine." He punctuated this, sullenly, with the word "alone." He moved off the porch and into the sun, which drenched his back.

"By this time, he'd made me feel guilty, so I offered to pay for my own dinner, but he insisted on paying for both." Out of his own guilt, Juan thought, but didn't tell Roz this. "It was supposed to be his treat, dinner and drinks. Still feeling guilty and not really caring about the drinks, I let him decide where we'd go." He took a breather, continued: "So where do you think he wanted to go? To the goddamned Bull Dog, obviously his idea of a romantic setting."

"So you didn't find out anything about the card?"

Juan drained his coffee mug. He felt a rush from the caffeine and an queasiness in his stomach. He knew he'd drunk too much coffee and consumed too little food this morning. "No. So I'll try to forget about the damned card and see what happens. Nothing to be gained by dwelling on it, is there?"

"So you married a slut. Worse things have happened."

Juan tempered his ire at this remark and tried to face Roz without flinching. "So I did. But I'm not only pissed off, but hurt, which is worse."

"Anger can be a healthier mode than hurt."

"What about you and Irv? Are you more angry or hurt?" Juan believed she was more hurt, but wouldn't answer truthfully.

"Don't know."

"I'll expect to hear all the dirt tomorrow morning," he said, grinning thinly.

Roz left shortly afterwards to go home before putting in her eight-hour shift at the Co-op. Juan returned to planting, feeling less burdened than before. He idly envisioned founding a support group for partners of unfaithful spouses and lovers, and had little doubt such a group would lack for membership. Finished with the peas, he took to depositing carrot seeds individually, painstakingly, into the soil and his thoughts turned to Irv's sterility.

His back to the street, a few minutes later he saw Irv rattle behind the house on his bicycle. He came around to the front and let out a hoot of approval upon seeing Juan's garden work. "What brings all this on?"

"Early spring and nervous energy." He stared down at the pack of carrot seeds, trusting that Irv understood "nervous energy" for the euphemism that it was.

"Anything you want to rap about?"

Juan looked up at Irv, dressed in tennis shoes, black Levi's and a T-shirt imprinted with a tuxedo and tie. "No, but you need to talk to Roz."

"Oh?"

"Yeah." He turned back to the row of carrot seeds. If he told Irv, wouldn't he somehow be betraying Roz? But if he said nothing to him...

Irv stood in the middle of the sidewalk, waiting. Juan got up, shook the flecks of dirt from his hands, and ambled up to the porch. Irv followed. Juan lowered himself onto the sofa, which sagged threateningly under him.

"I guess I should tell you I let a certain cat out of the bag yesterday." Irv faced him, transfixed. "It was a neutered cat, if you get my drift."

Irv blinked, plunged fingers into his beard. "I'm not sure I do."

"Let's say it was a sterile cat, its sterility deriving from a kittenhood disease."

"Your drift is clearer now, I'm afraid."

"I take it from the would-be mother cat that she'd been planning on having kittens, or at least kitten, though it seems that she and her tomcat haven't discussed this yet. I thought I'd give you advance warning."

"Ho-boy!" Irv exclaimed, and let out a laugh of the type that feebly masked concern.

"Sorry if I..."

"Don't worry," Irv put in quickly, still facing him. "She had to know. I shouldn't have put off telling her. Thanks for the advance warning." Irv disappeared inside, his battered briefcase dangling from one hand.

Juan directed him an envious glance, in wonderment of how calmly he handled such matters. Ten-to-one, Roz wouldn't be so calm. OK, nine-to-one. He let a smile flower full on his face, plodded back to the garden and wondered how long Gil would postpone his return home.

60

Sumner regarded the faculty, seated in a semicircle around the seventh-floor FAB meeting room. It was the next-to-the-last week of classes and the last departmental meeting of the year. He faced a large picture window, to which the faculty had their backs. It was a warm May day, which he'd earlier contemplated from his office, observing the spring mating rituals of students lying on the lawn below. So much exposed skin and so many intertwined body parts had served to take his mind off things academic. He now felt fairly fresh, despite the late afternoon hour.

To his left sat the younger faculty: Schultz, Carter, and Pankhurst. To his right Rothschild and Rutledge conversed *sotto voce*. Almost defiantly, alone and in the middle of the room, Davidine had perched herself, keeping her cigarette smoke at bay. Immediately to Sumner's right, Rickover sat poised over an electric typewriter. After receiving tenure, Rickover, like so many before him, had gotten uppity: He would only agree to continue as departmental meting secretary provided he could do it time-efficiently, which meant typing the minutes up as the action happened.

Staring straight ahead, Sumner met Davidine's gaze. A complacent smile was visible through the shield of smoke around her. The two had been personally incommunicado since their disagreement over Cicely Pankhurst's hiring. His signature had crossed her desk and vice versa, campus mail and secretaries acting as couriers.

But he had planned his revenge on all of them, to take place at the end of today's meeting: He was going to announce his *untimely* retirement, slated for the end of the next academic year. He'd made a point of not discussing it with Davidine first, as would have been protocol. Already he'd begun to savor what would doubtless be her look of low-grade horror at the thought of the department functioning without him.

"Can we begin?" He had to raise his voice above the junior faculty, who were chattering away loudly. The room went quiet, except for the hum of the typewriter. "As you can see, today's agenda is quite short," he continued in a more amiable vein, relishing his momentous pronouncement. "Do you all have a copy of last month's minutes? Are there any questions or corrections?"

Ginger's hand waved; Sumner recognized her. "What do the asterisks after our names mean? Evan, Cissy and I were all at the last meeting." He looked to Vance, who elucidated: "Asterisks indicate tardiness."

Sumner looked on impatiently as Ginger made a snort of disgust and heaved her round, firm breasts, only partially eclipsed by her plunging neckline.

"They strike me as unnecessary," Evan piped up. "This isn't a junior high detention period, after all."

"Other comments?" Sumner asked, anxious to stifle this upstart uprising. A dependable ally, Vance regarded the junior side of the room with a mixture of disgust and hauteur.

Evan's hand shot up and he spoke, unrecognized: "I'd like to move that in the future there be no such asterisks or other marks used to indicate tardiness to departmental meetings. And that those appearing on last month's minutes be stricken."

"Second," said Ginger, beating out Cicely.

"Very well." Exasperation oozed into his voice; his cheeks puffed out, then deflated. "All in favor?"

He counted three hands, to his left. A second later, Davidine's followed. It was now academic. "All opposed?"

Rothschild, Rutledge, and Rickover raised theirs.

"Motion passes, four to three. So strike the damn asterisks, Vance."

Rickover produced a bottle of correction fluid. "Now we'll get on to the real business. Item Two is the approval of the fall course offerings. You've all brought your copies, I trust. Questions, comments, a motion for approval?"

Rutledge and Rothschild made and seconded a motion to approve. A hand went up to Sumner's left. "Yes, Cis'ly?"

"Unless things have changed from this year, whoever teaches the Intro course never teaches three courses in that semester. And I'm scheduled here for three, including the Intro." She held up the sheet of course listings as evidence.

Sumner's face betrayed his annoyance. Now that she was going to be on a tenure-track, she'd probably go from aloof to impossible. "Is it true, Vance, that she's down for three, including the Intro course?" Rickover nodded that it was. "It would have been helpful if I'd known about this beforehand." He directed a look of reprimand at the overscheduled party.

"I just found the course list in my mailbox fifteen minutes ago," she said.

Sumner refrained from a crack about coming in regularly and checking one's mailbox, since the senior faculty, the worst culprits at avoiding the place, might take offense. "The course lists were supposed to go out two days ago."

"Well, they didn't, Sumner." Davidine was matter-of-fact, verging on accusatory. "At least they didn't make it to my box."

Rickover offered the clue to the mystery: "Wilhelmina."

"It couldn't have taken her two days!"

No one contradicted him.

"Very well. We'll just, we'll simply have to..," he stammered, then stopped, distracted by what seemed a whiff of whiskey in the air. His glance, interested yet stern, took in the room: Both Davidine and Evan held coffee mugs and one of the two... Not that he minded; what irked him most was his own lack of drink. And now he'd forgotten what he was saying.

"...frankly, I don't think the Intro course is being given sufficient publicity," he heard Vance comment.

"Don't we distribute a thousand leaflets advertising it during Registration Week?" asked Cicely.

"What do you want, Vance? For us to etch it on the restroom walls?" shouted Evan, a longtime troublemaker, even before he'd become an Instructor with *de facto* tenure.

Subdued chuckles came from both sides of the room. Vance backed off, reddened and looked to Sumner for help.

"Let's have some decorum here," Sumner scolded the chucklers, directing his glance at Evan in particular.

Davidine spoke up, restoring order. "Let's get back to the original point. One of Cissy's advanced courses has to go. Unless, that is, someone else wishes to teach the Intro class." She smiled, letting it be known her last remark was facetious. "Which do you prefer to give up, Cissy? Artifacts or Inorganic Materials?"

Sumner started to sputter something about this interference with parliamentary procedure.

"I'd give up Inorganic Materials," came her voice, achingly soprano to his ears, whenever she bothered to speak up.

"You'll probably have to give up Artifacts, since Inorganic Materials is too many hours to cram into anyone else's schedule," he replied, largely to counter them both. "So strike her name, Vance, and we'll have to come up with someone else to teach it." His gaze swept the room, contemplating possible candidates. Some avoided his eyes, but most met his glance head-on, daring him to tamper with their schedules. Pleased that he could make them all cower at the thought, he went on: "Can we finally vote on the amended course schedule for fall?"

"It doesn't have to be amended," said Vance, the resident expert on minutiae. "We're only voting on the offerings, not who's teaching what."

Sumner sighed and called for the vote before anyone could add anything. The offerings approved unanimously, Vance typed it in.

Item Three, a request for joint sponsorship of a lecture with the Art History Department, passed without argument. Item Four, an identical proposal, except that it required co-funding, failed. Item Five dealt with the fall Welcoming Picnic.

"Waste of money," opined Rutledge, stroking a scraggly goatee he'd sprouted for god knew what purpose. "There are only usually two or three new grad students to welcome anyway."

"Invite the undergrads, then," said Evan.

"I don't plan to attend no matter what you all end up doing," growled Rutledge. "And, I might add, I resent the money I have to contribute to the departmental Social Fund being spent on such frivolity."

"Indeed, we're not the local Welcome Wagon," Rickover put in, as Sumner sat back, detached from the proceedings, content to let them argue for the moment. "We should at least save our money for receptions for the more distinguished names who come to lecture here."

"Agreed," said Rutledge.

"If you all feel obliged to have some damned reception or picnic," began Rothschild, as if about to endow his colleagues with the thoughts of a superior mind, "you could cut out the beer and wine and have a healthy savings that way."

At the mention of eliminating alcohol, Sumner perked up, as did Davidine. "Really," she said. "I fail to see the problem of this expense. We've done it for years and we do little else socially for the graduate students. If we're not going to have anything to drink, we might as well line them up in the seminar room and get to know them by an oral exam."

"At least that would give them a taste of what's coming!" chortled Rickover, who broke off abruptly when no one joined in.

As no one contradicted Davidine, they promptly agreed on a "welcoming function," its exact nature to be determined later by the Social Committee. As the newest faculty member, Cicely Pankhurst was bestowed with the unwanted role of next year's committee chair.

The official agenda over, Sumner's moment approached. He asked for announcements, the last of which would be his. Vance mentioned an early fall conference at Michigan, as if anyone gave a damn. Sumner readied himself to speak, then saw Davidine stand, hands clasped in front of her. "I do think that congratulations are in order..."

Annoyed by another postponement, Sumner wondered who the hell had won what award now.

"...to Cissy. As we all know, she's accepted the tenure-track position next year, but I haven't seen or heard any official mention of it."

Ginger and Evan began to applaud, Davidine followed, and others joined in less heartily.

"Anything else?" Sumner asked, angered by Davidine's intrusion, probably meant to get his goat. He saw that she was still standing, waiting for recognition to go on.

"One more item, then I'll sit down and we can all go home," she said brightly. She seemed dressed up today, wearing a family brooch or some such gewgaw above her breast and even having put a slight curl into her hair. "This seems as appropriate a place as any to tell all of you the news, which may come as a surprise. I haven't discussed it with anyone except the Chancellor."

Sumner tensed, not liking the sound of this.

After pausing once more, she said, "I've decided to retire after next year..."

Sumner heard no more, began to simmer, staved off an explosion. How dare she steal his moment? How could she not have told him in advance? And how could they both retire at the same time? He sat dazed by the news, until realizing that his mouth was agape and the faculty were looking at him expectantly. He closed it, then opened it for motions and a vote to adjourn. He remained immobile next to Vance, as the junior faculty surrounded Davidine.

"Vance, let's go have a drink," he barked, more of a command than an invitation. Seeing Rickover, cheapskate that he was, hesitate, he added, "On me. Come on!" Almost numb, he hustled out of the room, knowing it would take Vance time to unplug his typewriter and carry it back down. Meanwhile, he'd have time to take a few needed slugs from the bottle in his desk drawer downstairs.

61

Irv called Roz immediately and suggested they meet for dinner as soon as she got off work. He had to contain an urge to try to explain why he'd hidden the fact of his sterility — not a subject to be treated lightly, or telephonically. He'd simply have to wait until dinner at Ho Chi Minh's. For Irv, such public places often lent themselves better to intimacy and diminished the chances of a scene.

By 9:15 they were drinking Mad City Suds, brought by a pink-haired waitperson wearing a "Question Authority" button. They ordered Reubens, Irv's the vegetarian variety. Roz lit a cigarette and Irv bummed one. Having given them up five years ago, he now used them as a manual crutch.

He couldn't stall for long by pretending to be occupied with the filterless Camel, nor did he want to. Roz's cigarette smoke gravitated toward him. She mumbled that the restaurant's ventilation system didn't seem to be working well. Irv sniffed the air, agreed. Indeed the restaurant was safely noisy for private conversation. The time had come and he didn't want her to beat him to it. "Roz, I'm sorry I didn't tell you about my, uh... defect."

"Ah, so you know I know." She scattered ashes with a vengeance toward the tarnished metal ashtray, spraying the table with them. "I thought Juan might tell you," she said, clearly displeased.

"After he told you, he simply balanced the equation by telling me."

Roz stubbed her cigarette out and aligned her elbows on the blue-and-white tablecloth. "Two things: Don't think of it as a defect. And don't light that cigarette if you can help it."

He handed it back to her, eager to get back the conversation back on track, but she jumped in first: "I had started to take the Pill, you know." The tone verged on confrontive.

"I didn't know, I'm sorry. I know you told me not to worry about using condoms."

"You remember well."

"But I didn't take that to mean you were necessarily on the Pill," Irv said in his defense.

"You must have known it meant something. IUD, diaphragm, whatever."

Irv studied her; her expression seemed to lose some of its sternness.

"Let's start this conversation again." He grasped his beer bottle, which sweated, and took a swig. He looked for some sign from Roz.

She shook her head enigmatically. "What's happened to us since the sixties?" Irv didn't know if she meant the question rhetorically or not. "I've been taking the Pill without your knowing, you're sterile without my knowing. We've been intimate, but haven't even talked about the consequences of our intimacy."

"Or lack thereof."

"Yes, rather." She looked away, eyes following the pink-haired waitperson. "I suppose I could have mentioned I was going on the Pill. It's as much my responsibility for not communicating as yours. And let me add that the Pill has been no picnic. It's done strange things to my body."

"I'm really sorry, Roz. But let me take the responsibility for not communicating. If I'd told you in the very beginning that I'm distressingly safe from paternity suits, this never would have happened."

"No. As a feminist woman, I insist on my right to share equally in the blame. Though if I'd talked to you yesterday about this, I dare say I would have portioned out the blame differently. Fortunately I took a day to calm down, as opposed to Juan, but that's another story. Just tell me one thing: You didn't know about your sterility fifteen years ago, did you? I remember the pains we took... Correction: the pains I took to avoid pregnancy back then. Don't tell me that all of that was for nothing too."

Irv held up his hands as if to say "whoa." "I assure you I was in the dark back then. I found out only after marrying Harriet. We wanted children. When we weren't able to, she had tests done and told me the problem wasn't hers. Later I had tests and found out it was me. It stemmed from some disease I had when I was a kid..."

"Orchitis," she said, and Irv regarded her, astonished. "Juan," she added.

"Of course." He nodded, recalling Juan's phenomenal memory. "But seriously, it seemed to me presumptuous to tell you at the time. Presumptuous to imply that we might want to have a child together. By the way, do we someday?"

"Let's take one thing at a time. I think I know what you mean about presumption. But you might have construed it just as a matter of birth control, not as a commitment to raise kids with me."

Relieved by the turn of the conversation, Irv reminisced about their relationship fifteen years ago, flashed forward to the present, saw Roz again watching the waitperson. "The first night in Cozumel, it seemed so right." His eyes went starry; he was moving unashamedly into the dangerous realm of romance, where objectivity deserted his legalistic mind. "It seemed that maybe fifteen days had passed since we'd last been together, not fifteen years."

"It did to me too." Irv watched as an aura of radiance graced her. "If it hadn't, you can be sure I wouldn't so much as have stuck my toe into your bed."

"I remember your talking of adopting a Vietnamese child back then."

Roz smiled, then frowned at the recollection. "If I'd known then that I was truly straight, I probably would have pursued it. Oh, was I mixed-up then. But to be a lesbian feminist was quite enough then. Lesbian motherhood was unthinkable."

"Don't take offense," Irv said, and took the last gulp of his beer. "But I always suspected that there was a part of you that was ever-so-slightly traditional. Even when you said you couldn't ball me any longer because of your politics."

"I wish someone would've told me then that I had a traditional bone or two hiding out in my feet somewhere. Maybe I needed the eighties to tell me that."

"Nonsense. The eighties won't change you or me. It's maturity, not the decade."

The waitperson arrived, dumped their sandwiches on the table and took their order for coffee. Large doses of alfalfa sprouts lurked around the sandwiches.

"I know her from Womynspace," Roz said, indicating the waitperson. "Her hair used to be green. The pink threw me off. I think she recognizes me. She's not straight and thinks I'm not either."

"It's hardly as though you're violating some separatist pact by having dinner with me."

"You really would have had a child with me back then, wouldn't you?" Roz shoved her sprouts onto Irv's plate.

"I would have tried." Irv took a ravenous bite into his sandwich.

"Of course I wasn't ready then." Roz held her sandwich, inspecting what remained after the removal of the sprouts. "But I could be now, or soon. At my age..." She trailed off, seemed to rethink her words. "I just hope you understand that it wasn't easy seeing my maternal desires dealt another blow yesterday."

"I do. But there are ways, Roz, if we really want to. I've handled cases, had clients..."

"Let's not talk law at the table, OK? I'm just glad all the cards are on it. They are, aren't they?"

"Believe me, they are. And so is the food. Let's eat."

"But one thing first." She leaned over the table, her lips puckered. Irv bent over his Reuben, met hers and held them.

The waitperson slopped the coffees down between them. "Breeders in love. Jeez," Irv heard her mutter as she marched off.

Roz broke off the kiss. "Good," she said, following the pink hair. "Now she knows. And who the hell cares? Maybe I'll tell the whole restaurant! Announce it in *Isthmus!* You know, we'd make a great success story for the *Isthmus* personals. That is, if we've both gotten over today's little hurdle."

"I have if you have," Irv said, restraining an impulse to lean over and kiss her again.

Instead he walked around the table to do it.

62

There was only One Way and that was the Truster Way.

It was another message that Lou heard again and again. The Truster Way — which at first had seemed to encompass only love, community and success — now became more and more narrow, each successive tape specifying what it most definitely did not encompass: homosexuality, masturbation, premarital sex, abortion, laziness, drugs, alcohol and acceptance of non-Christian religions. For starters.

Lou still held doubts about the alcohol prohibition. But reflecting on her own forays into drink, not to mention Beth's, she began to reconsider. Beth herself became a source of preoccupation, since, according to the Trusters, she was clearly headed down the Wrong Way. She tried to put Beth's unsaved status out of her mind.

Indeed, she had little time to worry about the state of her roommate's soul, as more tangible concerns preoccupied her: successful completion of the spring semester and housing for the summer. Although space was available, the Trusters wouldn't guarantee her a place until she became a full-fledged member. Finally, uncertain and undecided, she'd told Beth to feel free to look for another roommate, without exactly ruling herself out.

After the last videotape, only a final interview awaited her, scheduled for the last week of classes. She returned directly to her dorm, planning to go to bed early in preparation for her usual Saturday study marathon.

She found Beth asleep at her desk, surrounded by stacks of texts, notebooks and papers. Lou's entrance woke her. She looked up, eyes bleary, and scooted her chair backward. Brooklyn whined and jumped off her lap. "Hey, kid. Must've dozed off. What time is it?"

"Just a little before ten."

"Still early." Beth stretched and grunted herself into wakefulness. "Oh, Verla called for you."

"She must have just missed me. When did she call?"

"A couple hours ago."

"That's strange. She knew I was at the Hou…" Lou caught herself in time only to swallow the final S.

"Yeah, kiddo, the How-ssss. She said you could call her there, but it wasn't important."

"That's weird, anyway." Lou paced in front of the window. "She should have known I was right there."

Beth scooped up Brooklyn, who was growing perceptibly. "Verla and I had a nice little chat. She said I might want to go with you and visit her at the House some day."

Lou cringed. She had noticed that Verla took an increasing interest in Beth. How were her classes going? Did she have many friends? Any particular problems? Lou was especially concerned since the day Verla must have decoded Beth's "DYKE" T-shirt.

"Lou, what's this 'House' business?" Beth swept the kitten away and decapitated her pack of Marlboro Lights to extract the last one.

"Oh, that's where Verla lives," Lou said offhandedly, and observed Brooklyn dining on a spider plant on the windowsill.

"Kiddo, you can do better than that." Beth went over and blew smoke in Brooklyn's face, an apparent disciplinary measure, and the cat jumped down. "That's the kinda answer I give Nick when I don't wanna talk."

Seeing that nonchalant evasion was not going to work, Lou turned to the window to concentrate. High up in the Fine Arts Building, lights glowed from scattered offices, signs of professors and graduate students laboring late into the night. Which she herself would have to be doing soon.

"Lou, I don't wanna pry. We all got our private lives. And if you got somethin' goin' with Verla, far be it from me…"

Lou spun around, brushing the spider plant with her backside. The pot tumbled to the floor and cracked. "I have nothing 'going' with Verla, as you put it."

"OK, OK, I believe ya, kid. But you don't have to break plants to make your point." Lou went to the closet for a broom and dustpan as Beth went on: "But this 'house' is the place you might be livin' this summer, right?"

Lou agreed meekly, swept up the plant remains and dumped them in the waste basket. "Did you find a roommate yet?"

"Not since you asked me this afternoon." Beth extinguished her cigarette. "So even though you got nothin' goin' with Verla, you're still not talkin' about the House, huh?"

"Really, Beth, you wouldn't like it, wouldn't understand and don't want to know. Let alone go visit."

"Lou, you're not gettin' into somethin' weird, are ya?"

"Nothing you have to worry about," Lou said, impatient, angry about the plant and trying to think of a way to blame it on Brooklyn.

"If you say so." Beth's tone implied doubt; she threw herself on her lower bunk. "I thought we were friends."

"What ever gave you the idea we weren't?"

Brooklyn now walked across Beth's stomach, ensnaring her claws in her T-shirt. Petting Brooklyn and muttering sweetnesses into the kitten's ear, Beth seemed to console herself of Lou's "desertion" and pointedly ignored her. Lou stood in the middle of the room, adrift.

Finally, Beth spoke: "When I first met you, kid, I took one look and thought, 'God, she's a weird one.'" Lou winced at the remark. "Why do you think I practically hid from you for two months? Then I woke up one day and realized, 'Hell, she's OK,' and you and I had a lotta good times, end of last semester. I felt close enough to you that I even let you know I liked women. You didn't even seem to mind. I was impressed. I considered you my best friend here, the only one I could count on. I still want to consider you my best buddy, Lou. And best buddies don't keep big, deep dark secrets from each other."

Lou dragged her desk chair over to Beth's bunk. She had to placate, if not soothe her, but remained firm in her resolve not to tell her about the Trusters. She put her hand out, grazing Beth's bent knee. "Beth. First, I'm not involved in anything weird, so you don't have to worry. If I needed help, you can be sure I'd come to you." Lou stopped to think if she'd really do so in a pinch and decided that, under duress, she might. "Of course, I consider us friends. Good friends." Lou mustered her best persuasive powers, implored with her eyes. "Damn good friends."

After several seconds, Beth's impassive face cracked and she let out a low whistle. "OK, I believe you, kiddo." She stretched her arm out to Lou.

"That's good." Lou wrung Beth's hand in hers. "I really haven't meant to be mysterious about anything or spend less time with you. I just have so many things on my mind right now. I've just written my parents about my summer plans and expect an unpleasant call from Ladysmith."

"I can lie for you, if you want. Tell 'em you got kidnapped by a sorority, went to cruise Chicago for the weekend..."

"Please, Beth, I'll handle it myself. Now back to housing. I'll know by next week if I'll be living with Verla this summer. When I know, I'll tell you everything about the House. All there is to tell. A deal?"

Beth hesitated, suspicious. "Deal," she finally said, and squeezed Lou's hand, still clasped to hers. "Meantime, don't do anything funny, kid. And if I don't have a roommate in a week, the offer's still there."

"Thanks." Their hands separated. "Thanks a lot."

Wednesday night Lou positioned herself on a cushion in the Truster living room. The entire membership had shown up to witness her final interview. Most spread themselves out on the floor, others inhabited the furniture. Lou glanced up at the chandelier high above and felt a pang of nerves. After all, this was not unlike an oral exam, with an audience of more than twenty or, worse yet, with all of them as potential examiners.

But she knew her material well. Verla had quizzed her Monday night on community, spirituality and carnality — the Trusters' polite word for sex. But then Verla turned the conversation to Beth. When Lou came to live in the House, would she invite Beth over? Could Lou live as a Truster with Beth on her conscience and just let her go the Wrong Way? Lou strained not to show her impatience with the incessant prying. Verla left her with the admonition to think about all this. She now was sure that Verla had seen and understood Beth's T-shirt, though she hadn't commented on it. She had, however, remarked on Beth's well-stocked liquor supply, apparently in use at the time of her visit.

Last night Felix and Tinda had sailed through their interviews; tonight Bruce would follow Lou. She imagined Tinda spitting out all the right answers on carnality, all the while secretly lusting after Felix, and passing with an A+. They had all been shocked to hear that Susan — the preeminent Truster clone — had dropped out at the last minute. Lou's guess was that she had done more than lust secretly after Bruce and quit when she was rebuffed. Lou herself felt quite pure, compared to the rest of them.

House advisers Lee and Sara led the questioning. Lou talked about her university experience before and after meeting the Trusters. Next she spouted responses to the expected questions; Verla's coaching had served her well.

Around the living room the Trusters bounced smiles off each other. Lou saw them nodding in reassurance as she reeled off the Reverend Dwight's teachings. In the back of the room, Verla stood glowing next to Bob. All of them seemed to ooze an elemental goodness. Lou felt herself enveloped by all the good vibrations.

The floor was opened for questions from the members. Lee and Sara scanned the room. Seeing none, Lee spoke: "Lou, I think we'd all say you seem to be an excellent Truster candidate." He paused for the group to give its approval. "But just one more question." He hesitated, then proceeded slowly: "It seems you have an attachment to someone who is clearly headed down the Wrong Way. A roommate, isn't it?"

"Yes." So Verla's questions hadn't been prying, but further coaching. But that she'd told the others about Beth's lesbianism or drinking irritated and surprised her.

"Is it true she's headed down the Wrong Way?" Lee asked, grave but gentle.

Lou heaved a sigh before answering, smelling trouble. But once asked, she couldn't help but tell the truth. "Well, she drinks. And smokes. Plus she's Jewish. And I think she's a lesbian. But I don't think she practices."

Lee's eyebrows jerked up an inch. "You don't think she practices which one? Judaism or lesbianism?"

"Judaism, I meant."

"So she does practice lesbianism?" The earnest gazes of the Trusters converged on her.

"Well, she told me she was a lesbian, but I've never seen her practicing it or anything."

"It's usually a very secretive and guilt-ridden practice." Both Lee's words and tone duplicated the Reverend Dwight's. "Actually, it's surprising she told you. She must have been consumed by self-hate and needed support. And you gave her the support she needed?"

Lou nodded yes.

"We all know that you're prime Truster material," Lee continued. "But you know, Lou, that it's wrong to give someone support to continue down such a path?"

"I suppose so," she said, meaning to agree.

As if sensing doubt, Sara broke in: "Lou, you do know that your roommate's homosexuality is wrong, don't you?"

Her Germanic stubbornness setting in, she gave an answer she knew was not the best: "That's what I've learned here."

"But you agree that it's wrong?" Sara persisted sweetly.

Lou weighed this, wanting to be honest, yet not to offend. "I think it's wrong for some people, maybe most."

"But it's a path to damnation," Sara said, less sweet. "And under the influence of alcohol, a person is more likely to engage in carnality. Do you feel a need to help her get off this path?"

"Not if it has to be done by coercion."

"Have you told her about us or invited her here?"

Verla broke in from the back of the room. "Lou, not yet being a regular member herself, could hardly invite her. Though I've talked to her."

"I never thought I could invite her because she's Jewish," Lou added, entering the realm of white lies.

"So was I," piped up a boy named Howard. "That's not an obstacle. Trusters don't discriminate against lesbians, Jews or alcoholics, as long as they give it up."

Lou flinched at the use of "alcoholic." "But she was born that way," she blurted out in frustration. "Jewish, I mean. If you're born that way, it can't be wrong. Maybe she was born a lesbian too. Maybe that's why it's OK for her."

Grave murmurings went up everywhere. For several seconds no one addressed her. Lou's stomach began to descend a roller coaster; she felt as if she were about to be accused of Nazi war crimes.

Verla's roommate Annie broke the silence. "Lou, you say that if you're born Jewish, that can't be wrong. I know these are not easy issues and we're all here to help you understand. If you were born to parents who practiced Satanism, that wouldn't make it right for you to do the same when you're old enough to decide. Sometimes we need to correct the ways of our parents."

Lou nodded, seeing this logic, but another doubt stymied her. "But if you're born a lesbian, then what?"

"No one's born that way," two Trusters answered at once. One went on: "It's a path you fall into, like alcohol. But you have to renounce it and be healed."

Heads bobbed up and down in agreement. Although the last remark made sense, Lou had never thought of it that way. She said nothing, awaiting further enlightenment or an end to the interview.

"Lou." It was Sara who spoke. "You do renounce all non-marital carnality and non-Christian religion, don't you? I'm sorry to have to be so blunt, but I think hearing your answer would make everyone here feel better."

"For myself, of course," she responded, grateful that Sara had omitted "alcohol." "But not necessarily for others."

Lee's eyes glued themselves to Lou's. "We see," he said heavily. "We'll have to talk more about this," he went on, his tone reverting to typical Truster brightness. "That's all for tonight, Lou. Trusters, take ten."

Anxious to escape, she stood up. Verla faced away and whispered to Bob. Lou felt guilty for having embarrassed her and headed toward the door. She collected her backpack and coat and stole a last glance around the room. The Trusters stretched and talked among themselves, not meeting her eyes.

63

Cissy taught her last Intro class and held her last office hour of the semester. Beckoned by warm temperatures and impending freedom from teaching, she, Ginger and Evan decided on a lunchtime escape from the sterile confines of FAB. They walked outside to Library Mall, where the sun filtered down on the various foodcarts offering exotic lunch fare. Cissy choose a soybean burger with a side of avocado and bean sprout salad, Ginger went to the falafel cart, and Evan brought back a small pile of Vietnamese eggrolls. They ate in the shade as an evangelist preacher harangued some fifty feet away, stirring Cissy to reminiscence: Here was where she'd first encountered the same preacher as well as Irv. The conversation at her side distracted her from her musings.

"Of course, they'll go for the worst possible candidate: Sumner," said Evan, as he unwrapped an eggroll, then attempted to pop it, whole, into his mouth.

Davidine's announcement had left the department abuzz with speculation over who would be the new dean. Although they had talked the topic to death, they always seemed to revert to it in spite of themselves.

Ginger waved away Evan's idea with her hand, her lacquered fingernails smudged with sauce from the falafel. "They'll want someone younger and more vibrant."

Cissy jumped into the debate: "Does the department even have a good candidate? And if they chose Sumner, wouldn't that mean he'd have less to do with us in the department?"

Evan shook his head, his blond hair mussed by the wind. "He'd have even more power over us then."

Cissy and Ginger agreed glumly and Ginger proceeded to the logical follow-up, equally unpleasant: Who would become chair if Sumner became dean? They all deemed the worst possible candidate the most likely: Rickover.

The lake breeze was chilling Cissy's exposed arms. "Let's change the subject."

"OK. You *did* hear about this morning, didn't you, Cis?" Ginger's tone implied that anyone who hadn't must be mentally impaired.

She hadn't heard, but didn't have to admit it, as Ginger went right on: "Sumner arrived this morning reeking of alcohol. Rickover said his breath could have knocked a person across the room. Now when Rickover, with his own body odor, says that..."

"Sumner's had a drinking problem for some time," Evan put in, between eggrolls.

"Someone was drinking alcohol at last Wednesday's meeting," Cissy said with disapproval. "I smelled it."

"That was me," Evan said, and Cissy reddened. "My Valium presciption ran out. You have to do something to get through those meetings."

"Sumner's wife is rather shrewish," said Ginger, wiping her fingers daintily with a paper napkin.

If made in Sumner's defense, the comment was an odd one, thought Cissy. "Let's be charitable. I admit Sumner is no favorite of mine, nor am I of his, I'm afraid. But maybe the pressure of being chair is getting to him. It mustn't be an easy job." She saw Evan and Ginger roll their eyes. "All right. You two know better than I do."

They strolled through the sun before returning to FAB. Ginger had to teach at 1:20, Evan was ready to head home, and Cissy only had to await the arrival of the papers from her advanced class, due by 1:30. She'd canceled today's session. Since the course work had been completed, there was no final exam, and, therefore, no need for a review session. Only six of twelve papers had been delivered by noon.

Two more had been shoved under her office door when she returned. She sat down and began to peruse them, then decided to make a cup of tea. Having gone first to the restroom to wash out her cup, she espied Wilhelmina's black pumps behind the closest stall door. The secretary was an inveterate shoe-watcher and would start up conversations from inside the stall when she recognized someone else's, a circumstance which rendered Cissy prudish. She moved to the farthest sink, washed the cup and scurried out before Wilhelmina could identify hers.

She went to the service room, where hot water and coffee were dispensed, filled her cup and dropped in an herbal teabag. As she'd used up the heated water, she began to refill the pot. Standing at the utility sink, she heard a shuffling of feet behind her and took it to be Wilhelmina's. She glanced over her shoulder, but saw no one. While she faced the sink a few seconds later, a hand fell on the nape of her neck, then let go.

She flicked the spigot off, imagined Evan about to sweep her into a playful good-bye embrace — a fantasy becoming reality? — and turned around.

There stood Sumner. His breath badgered her face, an unsettling smile hung on his lips.

"Trying to make yourself useful, Cis'ly?" The smile evaporated, replaced by a strange sheen in his eyes, which she chalked up to alcohol.

"I'm just refilling the hot-water pot," she said firmly, the carafe still clenched in her hand, and went to place it on the hot plate.

"That's not necessary!" Sumner's words came out with near-ferocity. A drop of saliva landed on her upper arm.

She jerked away from the sink and met his gaze. A brazen stare of appraisal confronted her. She decided to scoot out and moved forward. Sumner stepped in front of her, blocking her path. More angered than scared, she backed up to the sink.

Sumner stepped up to her, swaying slightly. "This," he said with gritted teeth, "is Mrs. Wiggins' job!" He pointed to the hot plates, then inched even closer to her. As she looked for an escape, his hand fell squarely on her white chiffon blouse, grabbing her left breast with force. "I mean what I say!"

Too stunned to react, Cissy did nothing for a second. When she moved, his hand moved with her, squeezing tighter. Over his shoulder, she saw Wilhelmina appear in the doorway.

"What are you doing, Sumner!? Leave her alone!"

His hand disengaged itself. The panicky look of a quarried animal crossed his face. He tried without success to skirt out the door, barricaded by Wilhelmina's bulk.

"You... You... You brute!" Wilhelmina stammered, then moved aside. Sumner zoomed by. The secretary raised her hand as he passed, either to swat at him or to protect herself. Dazed, Cissy stumbled to the door in time to see him lurching down the hall toward the elevators. Wilhelmina stood immobile, one fist clenched in the air, one hand on her hip. She motioned Cissy back inside and shut the door behind them.

Wilhelmina quivered with rage. "Are you all right, dear? I saw what he did. Who does he think he is..? I don't think I can say the words to describe him! Let's see, honey. Did he hurt you?" She put her arm around Cissy, who remained expressionless, and repeated the question.

"He grabbed me here," she said in a dull whisper, and pointed. "He grabbed me, tight."

"I'll say he was tight!" cracked the secretary, setting her chin firmly. "Can you show me where he grabbed you?" Then gently, as if in apology: "That is, if you don't mind? We, or at least you, should see if he injured you."

Cissy complied, reaching behind to unbutton her blouse and loosen her bra, and felt the residual pain. On the counter she saw her cup of tea.

"He left marks on you! I always thought he might drink himself off the deep end one day. But I never expected this! Come to think of it, I should have sent him home this morning."

"Wilhelmina, please don't think it's your fault."

"Let's dress you back up and go back to your office." Wilhelmina opened the door, shook her head as if in disbelief. "Sometimes I think they ought to close down this whole damn department!"

Down the hall, someone applauded.

Inside her own office Cissy scuffed two recently arrived papers.

"You gather yourself together, honey," Wilhelmina instructed. "You must want to get out of here, don't you? Is there someone you can call to come pick you up?"

"If he's home yet." She moved toward the telephone.

The telephone was ringing as Jeb bounded in the door, an uninspected clump of mail in his hand. He tossed it down, picked up the receiver just in time to hear a dial tone and muttered an obscenity. He thought it might have been Cissy, then looked at his watch. No, she would be in class now.

He had returned from a day of teaching in time to watch *General Hospital*. He flicked on the TV, stretched out on the floor and undid his Velcro tennis shoes. At the first commercial break, he remembered the mail and got up.

Under several pieces of junk, he found an envelope from the UW Phys Ed Department. He tore open the envelope and read, "We are pleased to inform you…"

"Hot damn!" He let the letter fly across the dining room.

Cissy would be delighted. Their Madisonian future was sealed, for at least a few years. Now all he had to do was to convince the university that he had been a legal resident of Wisconsin since fall, so he could avoid out-of-state tuition.

He fetched the letter and read the details, debating whether to call Cissy with the news — she'd be out of class by now — or to wait until her arrival home. As the next segment of *General Hospital* came on the air, the phone rang again. "Persistent son of a bitch."

"Jeb." The voice was Cissy's, a near-whisper that he found sexy.

"Cissy! Guess what?"

"What, Jeb?"

"You don't sound too interested. This is big news! The Phys Ed department accepted me. I got accepted, babe!"

"I got assaulted, Jeb."

He'd evidently heard wrong. "You got what?"

"Assaulted. Don't worry, I'm all right, but I want to get out of here. Just come pick me up."

"Assaulted??" He imagined blood, the thought of which made him squeamish, the sight of which made him faint away. "What happened? How? Where?"

"I'm not hurt." Cissy's voice was calm. "I'll tell you the rest when you get here."

He hopped into his tennis shoes and left without turning off the TV. He darted in and out of traffic, took narrow corners and honked the Fiat's muted horn with the urgency of an expectant father. He arrived at FAB in a record six minutes.

By the time they returned home, he'd pried the details out of her. "You'll file suit, press charges with the DA and take the bastard to court! We'll go to a doctor this afternoon and get the medical evidence to use against him. How dare that son of a bitch..!"

"Hold me, Jeb."

He hugged her, steadying her as she began to tremble. They broke the embrace, *General Hospital* signed off the air, and he saw that she was starting to sob. He took her in his arms again, stroking her back. "You'll see a doctor, won't you, babe?"

"I don't know if I can handle it now."

"You should before the bruises go away. If we wait till Monday..." He let go of her, stepped back and observed her, ascertaining once more that she was in one piece, at least physically.

"You're probably right." She fell onto the sofa. "But who? I've never even used my health plan and I'm certainly not a case for an emergency room. All I feel like doing now is forgetting the whole thing."

The television still blared in the background. Jeb paced down the floor's slope, turned it off, then headed back up. "I've got it! We'll ask Roz. She works at that Women's Place Space. She'll know what to do."

"I thought you couldn't stand Roz," Cissy said feebly.

"I thought you were the one who didn't like her. But this is an emergency, babe. I'll go upstairs. If she's not there, they'll know where she is."

Cissy didn't protest and Jeb headed out the door, leaving it open. As he took the first four stairs in one step, he heard her raised voice: "Oh, congratulations on your acceptance."

64

Lou pondered the statements made during her interview, but contemplated another question even more: Where would she live, if not with the Trusters? With Beth, who could be either fun and outgoing or secretive and moody? Then the matter of the "Wrong Way" raised its head. Did she really want to live in a place where lesbianism might be practiced on the premises? The idea left her uneasy. She had no other options. Heidi and Amy had their own two-bedroom apartment and probably wouldn't want to move to a new one to accommodate her.

As expected, Sara called the following morning, asking if she didn't want to come over and clear up some of her statements before Sunday night's initiation. This was not a casual request; she knew that if she wanted to be initiated, she had to go.

Friday night Lee and Sara greeted her warmly and led her to a windowless office, furnished with a large metal desk, two plastic-covered green chairs and a couch. Invited to sit, Lou took the couch. On the opposite wall a photo of the Reverend Dwight smiled benignly at her. Below him hung a red pennant, which read, "Do It the Truster Way."

"Do what?" Lou wondered, as everything seemed to be prohibited.

"We thought maybe some of our questions confused you the other night," Sara said in such a tone that no one could disagree with her. Lou doubted that they guessed how prepared to recant she was.

"It's easy to back yourself into a corner and say things you don't mean, with everyone talking at you at once," Lee said with a lighthearted chuckle, and fixed his eyes hopefully on her.

Lou picked up her first cue. "I'm not even sure exactly what I said, but I didn't mean to condone my roommate's activities. I know it's not a good path and I hope some day soon she'll see the light. The Truster Way, that is."

"You're an open-minded person, Lou, and that's good. Up to a point," Lee said. "You can always show compassion, but when you're too open-minded, you can become susceptible to the evils that are out there seeking acceptance. University towns are good breeding grounds for the devil's works and, believe us, he meets with notorious success in Madison."

Sara nodded in agreement; Lou followed suit and said she hadn't meant what she'd said.

"We knew you didn't," Sara affirmed, and Lou saw the two resident advisers flash looks of satisfaction at each other. They'd done their job by retrieving the wayward neophyte.

"Glad we cleared this up," said Lee.

"So we'll see you for initiation Sunday night. It'll be a short ceremony that won't cut into study time for finals. Lee, do you think we have a robe that'll fit Lou?"

Lou flinched at the indirect reference to her size as Sara stuck her head into a tall metal locker. As she rummaged through the robes, Lou felt a sudden unburdening. She had finally found her university home, was ready to be initiated. It was now only a formality.

"Here's one that should fit. Let's try it on."

Lou stepped into the robe, which fit perfectly.

Beth got up from a long Sunday afternoon nap and took out and filled her coffeemaker. She curled up with her Museums notebook to begin studying for her 7:45 final in the morning. She hoped to cram in a half hour before meeting Lou for dinner. Her notebook was in near-mint condition, not tattered from a semester's diligent use.

She flipped through it and began trying to memorize the names of nineteenth-century museum benefactors, but her thoughts strayed. Her lack of a summer roommate plagued her, as did the necessity of earning a 2.25 this semester. The coffeemaker finished dripping and she got up to pour a cup. She picked up the Museums notes that Lou had left her from last semester and, back on the bed, coffee at her side, opened Lou's notebook. The handwriting was neat and the notes organized in outline form, complete with Roman numerals and the works. Brooklyn hopped agilely onto the bed, demanding affection. Beth stroked her twice, then shooed her away. She managed to concentrate on Lou's notes for a few minutes, realized the inferiority of her own and began to feel depressed.

Lou showed up just before 5:30 and they went down to the dining hall. Sunday evening dinner featured goulash and "tuna surprise" for entrées, as well as a third, selected from favorite recipes submitted by students who missed Mom's home cooking.

"Let's hope for porkchops," said Lou, smacking her lips. Beth seconded Lou's porkophilia.

Tonight's recipe from Mom's kitchen was lima bean casserole. Beth and Lou reluctantly accepted plates of goulash.

While Beth picked at her meal, Lou ate heartily, revealing what she remembered of the Museums final in between bites.

"You mean it includes slide identifications?"

Lou nodded soberly, finished her goulash and attacked a piece of apple pie. "Pretty tasty for cafeteria food."

Beth left the last half of her goulash untouched, took a few drops of Lou's milk for her coffee and lit a cigarette.

"We're at a no-smoking table," Lou whispered urgently.

"I'll fix that." Beth took the no-smoking sign from their table and deposited it on an adjacent unoccupied one.

"One more thing about the exam. Be sure to review your notes from the Elvehjem Museum exhibits. She sneaks in a lot of questions about them."

"Shit." Without an ashtray, she began to coat her goulash with ashes.

"You did take notes on them, didn't you?"

"Hell, I didn't even go see most of 'em," she admitted, angry at herself.

"And they're not the same ones as last semester. So my notes on them won't do you any good."

"Maybe I can find someone who went," Beth said without hope, and smothered her cigarette.

Lou gave several other tips on the exam. Already disheartened, Beth paid scant attention until Lou announced her departure.

"So soon, kiddo?" She tried to sound casual: "Are you gonna see Verla tonight?"

Lou hesitated, which Beth took as a sign of equivocation. "Just briefly. Then I've got to study late."

Beth's sixth sense went to work. Lou was up to something odd with Verla. They weren't studying for their Autobiography final; Lou was wasting what she called her "precious" study time the night before finals. "Are you sure everything's all right, kid?"

The question seemed to exasperate her. "I promised," she said with emphasis, "that I'd tell you all about it soon."

"Tomorrow. After we both finish our exams. Deal?"

Lou agreed without enthusiasm, and only managed a crooked smile.

More evidence that she was up to no good.

Alone again in her room, Beth cursed herself for skipping the Elvehjem exhibits and sleeping through the slides she'd have to identify tomorrow. Why even bother to study? She'd flunked the exam before she'd started it.

But she couldn't concentrate, at least not right now. Well-honed from years of eluding her mother's vigilance, her detective instinct got the better of her. She had to find out what Lou was up to. Then she'd study.

Lou hadn't been gone three minutes and Beth knew which direction she was heading. She grabbed her Museums notebook for pretense and bolted out the door.

Seconds later she was making a brisk trot up North Park Street. She reached Library Mall and caught sight of the neon-orange backpack up ahead of her. She sped up and followed Lou at a discreet distance as she proceeded up State Street among the many pedestrians. Fortunately, Lou wasn't a fast walker. Praying that she wouldn't turn around, Beth would pause to feign inspection of a store window, then dart forward to another.

After several blocks, Lou turned suddenly to the left, on West Johnson Street. Beth hung behind before turning the corner, then, rounding it, espied the bobbing backpack. Now the going would be rougher, as the sidewalk was deserted, with nothing to shield her from view. She let Lou advance a block, then lurched forward with a jackrabbit's loping strides.

Lou was evidently headed to a location just north of the Capitol. Beth hurried to the corner, shaking off a dog in pursuit, and saw Lou cross another street. None too close, Beth ran to keep up. Lou crossed Wisconsin Avenue. Beth crouched behind a parked car across from a church and saw Lou go up the steps of an unassuming two-story house on the next block of Wisconsin Avenue. She opened the front door without knocking and disappeared from sight.

What to do now? Until nightfall she couldn't get much closer without risk of being seen. She felt suddenly silly. She was behaving as if Lou had been snatched up by a blood-drinking cult. Beth's academic conscience intruded: She should be tracking down the notes she lacked, not her roommate.

But her qualms quickly disappeared. She hadn't come this far for nothing. She remained crouched behind the car, at the base of a parking meter. Sunday evening churchgoers crossed the street to their cars and eyed her suspiciously, as if she were stealing hubcaps or about to uproot the meter. Aware of how ridiculous she looked, she crossed the street, counted the houses, then scampered over to the next block, where the backyards bordered Verla's. She found the house with the adjoining yard and crept down its driveway. A wire fence separated the properties, but didn't go all the way. It was an obvious shortcut from one block to the other and she took it.

Notebook still in hand, she reached the side of the house Lou had entered. She wasn't tall enough to see into the first-floor windows, which were, in any case, drawn with shades. More secrecy, just as she expected.

She knelt down and let out a frustrated sigh. She'd tried; there was nothing else she could reasonably do, short of faking an emergency and boldly knocking on the door. She might as well return to the dorm.

Then she noticed a series of basement windows along the ground by the driveway. She stuck her head down and tried to peer into the back one. Seeing nothing, she crawled to the middle window, equally black. One more window remained; she inched up to it on her haunches and lowered her head to the ground. She pressed her nose to the window. All was dark inside too.

Then she saw a flicker of light. She pulled away and told herself she was imagining things. She looked again. Another flicker, then two, then a whole line of flickers. Candles.

"What the fuck!?"

Another glance verified that the candles were moving. That meant that someone had to be moving them. She glued her body horizontally to the foundation of the house, notebook under her stomach. Adrenalin coursed from her head to toes at full speed. Involuntarily, she quaked.

She focused her gaze on the parading candles, trying to see more. All at once, the movement came to a halt. The candles began slowly, faintly, to illuminate their surroundings.

"*Oy veh!*" Could she really be seeing what she was seeing? Almost instinctively, she placed her notebook between her face and the glass. Then, slowly, she pulled it back to steal another glance.

"*Oy!*" She was.

Each person holding a candle was dressed in a white robe.

Had Lou gone *meshugge* or what?? Her very own roommate and best friend was being inducted into the Ku Klux Klan!

Having grown up in Skokie, she knew well about such scum as the Klan and the neo-Nazis. But here in Madison? And they'd ensnared Lou! No wonder she'd been so secretive.

Trembling, Beth dared to look in the window once more. The room had brightened, ever so slightly. No one was wearing a hood, but the white robes were there. The hoods were probably only put on in public to protect identities. She couldn't quite make out faces, but, sure enough, she saw a large cross on the wall. It was the Klan, all right. And they'd gotten poor, naive Lou into their clutches.

Contradictory impulses — concern for Lou versus self-preservation — immobilized her. On one hand, she felt like heaving a stone through the window, imparting a few select curses and rescuing Lou. On the other, she thought she'd better skedaddle, and get her little Jewish self the hell out of there.

She opted for the latter. She'd deal with Lou later.

65

I t was hard for her to concentrate after the spectacle she'd witnessed. In the dorm she tried to absorb Lou's notes, then stalked the halls, aching to tell someone. But who would ever believe her? Finally she took the notes to bed, waiting for Lou to come in and explain it all. Midnight arrived and the notebook fell from her hand.

She awoke in the middle of the night, there was no trace of Lou, and she turned out the light. Concern for her roommate battled sleepiness. A fitful sleep won out, racked by dreams. She was being pursued by a headless horseman — or horsewoman — clad in a white sheet. Later, she stumbled into a dark forest: There was Lou performing spooky incantations, naked except for a hood, a candle protruding from her vagina. She'd dreamed of naked women before, but this was no erotic dream.

At 7:00 the alarm clock sounded. Both she and Lou had finals in less than an hour. Lou had probably pulled an all-nighter and would bound in the door at any moment. Beth let herself lounge in bed, almost counting on Lou to come in and rouse her. She awoke again twenty minutes later, threw on her clothes and ran to the dining hall for a quick pre-exam coffee.

She had to leave almost all of the slide identifications blank and simply marked C for the multiple-choice questions on the exhibits she'd missed. Then came 150 questions on trivia from the lectures. She bet that Cicely Pankhurst would have a hard time getting an A on her own exam.

When she left the large lecture hall, some half-dozen students remained, either working feverishly or staring numbly at the walls. Through the narrow slit of window in the door, she cast a wistful glance at Cicely Pankhurst, her nose in a gradebook, oblivious to the woe her exam had caused.

Still, hers was the only official class that had stimulated Beth to anything — even if lust — this semester. Of course there was the invigorating history class she'd unofficially attended as often as some of her regular classes. That history prof, unlike her own, was cool: He didn't even give a final. Continuing to observe her Museums professor, Beth blew her a theatrical kiss, then hurried off.

Returning to her room, she expected to find Lou snoozing peacefully in the upper bunk, probably having aced her final. When she found it empty, she panicked. Had the Klan drugged her or maybe kidnapped her?

The time to do something had come. She didn't know Verla's last name, couldn't call the "House" and doubted the Klan was listed in the phone book. Nor was she about to go there in person. The dorm's House Fellow was the proper person to contact in such a case, but Beth knew better than that. The Fellow did things like consult rule books for the most minor questions or infractions. If Beth confided in her, she'd probably end up at the police station repeating her statements to a lie detector.

She needed to talk to someone older, responsible and level-headed. She thought of the dean who had guided her into Cicely Pankhurst's class this semester. Then she thought of Cicely Pankhurst herself. She'd give Lou a half-hour to return.

Cissy had gone through the morning's mail and was preparing to leave the office. She felt weary from lack of sleep, leery of encounters with the faculty and disgusted with academia. Overwhelmed, she scowled at the exams that stuffed her briefcase. At least the grader would correct a portion of them and Cissy would only need to return to FAB once more, to drop off final grades.

Roz had arranged for her to see a doctor Friday afternoon. On Saturday Davidine had phoned to apologize in the name of the department and to ask about her well-being. On Sunday she contacted her again and informed her that she and Rickover would perform the end-of-semester chair's duties and that Cissy needn't worry about running into Sumner.

Cissy came back to reality as someone rapped on her door. For a moment she didn't move. Then thinking it might be Evan or Ginger, she got up to open it. In front of her stood a small, thin girl with mauve eyes and short, curly, dark brown hair.

"Yes?" Cissy snapped, imagining the inquiry, for which she had ready-made answers: No, she didn't know when she'd have the exams graded. Yes, she'd post the grades on the door when she did.

"Hi, uh, I'm Beth Yarmolinsky from your Intro class."

"What can I do for you?"

"I need some advice from somewhere. I don't know where to turn."

Cissy recognized the student as one of those who had agonized over the exam to the bitter end. She had probably come to her now with a teary tale of failure. The student stared into her eyes, communicating urgency.

"Come in, then."

The student didn't wait for a cue to begin: "You see, it's like this. My roommate, you might remember her, Lou Lautermilk, she was in your Intro class last semester, she's disappeared, and I don't know whether to call the cops or what. She's been associatin' with some mysterious group of people and last night I followed her and watched through a window. It was the Ku Klux Klan and she never came back to the dorm. She had an exam this morning and she's still not back and I'm startin' to get really worried."

Beth Yarmolinsky stopped, as if waiting for a reaction. "Why me?" was all Cissy could think. In the catacombs of her mind she remembered memos from deans telling where to refer troubled students. It might not be a bad idea to have referrals for stressed-out professors too. Cissy had her repeat the story, slower.

"I know from experience that during finals week students often find themselves unprepared and pull an all-nighter. Don't you think that could be it?" she suggested.

The student gave a timid smile and rolled her eyes. Cissy thought she understood an allusion to her own exam, a notion Beth confirmed: "By the way, that was a hell of a final you gave us."

Cissy directed the conversation back to the missing person, passing over the reference to the Ku Klux Klan, and got the student to calm down. "Why don't you wait until noon, then tell your House Fellow? If she thinks it appropriate, then she can call Campus Security for you."

The student shook her head in agreement, then got up slowly. "Oh, I also wanted to tell you I really enjoyed your course and learned a lot, even if my grades don't show it." She let out a tiny, mirthless laugh.

"Thank you, I'm glad. That you liked the course, that is."

"Do you know what you'll be teachin' next semester?"

Cissy repressed an urge to say she didn't know if she'd be back — exactly what she felt — and instead replied, "Probably Inorganic Materials, and the Intro class again."

"I hope I don't have to repeat that one, but maybe I'll see you in the other." She seemed nervous but sincere, the compliment not the bogus flattery heard from grade-hungry students.

"That would be a pleasure."

"Well, I hope I see you again. And thanks for the advice." The student backed out of the office and went her way.

Cissy would take whatever praise she could get. Teaching, she supposed, did have some rewards. At times. Grateful for the compliment, she snatched up her briefcase and let the door slam shut behind her before anyone else accosted her.

Lou stood placidly wrapped in her green bathrobe when Beth returned. She froze in her tracks. "You oughta thank God for my cool-headedness or the FBI could be poundin' on the door this very minute!"

"Can you close the door, Beth? I'm dressing."

Beth gave the door a robust kick. "'I'm dressing,' she says! You been out the whole night, I'm tearin' my hair out, and that's all you got to say?"

"I'm sorry, Beth. I would've called if I could."

She nudged Brooklyn away and began to circle the room. "Well? What the hell happened to ya?"

"I fell asleep studying at the Truster House." Lou's back to her, she slipped on pants without removing her bathrobe. "I overslept this morning. I had to take a two-hour final in forty-five minutes. I just got back and showered."

Beth focused on the key word. "The what house?"

"The Truster House, where Verla lives," Lou replied, unperturbed. She slipped out of her bathrobe, deftly fastened her bra and pulled on a T-shirt.

Beth stopped circling the room. "So it's got nothin' to do with the Klan?"

"The clan?" Lou gnarled up her nose and regarded Beth oddly. "What clan?"

"*The* Klan," she explained, exasperated, and saw Lou's incomprehension. "As In Ku Klux, kiddo."

"Ku Klux Klan," Lou repeated in a baffled monotone and contorted her face into a question mark. "What on earth ever gave you that idea?"

"Well, kiddo, uh... It's a long story." Beth felt herself flush from embarrassment. Following and spying on Lou, imagining all sorts of villainy, running to Cicely Pankhurst with a wild tale...

"Beth, what's wrong?" Lou pulled on her socks. "You've turned absolutely red!"

"Burgundy," Beth said, then tried to justify herself: "I may have a lot to tell you, but you got more to tell me. Why don't we go down to the Brathaus? We can have beers and brats and you can give me the lowdown on Verla and the Trustees."

"Trus-*ters*." Lou looked at her watch.

"Lou, you promised. You do too have time. Neither of us have any finals till tomorrow night. We'll get back here by noon or so and start hittin' the books. Now you're gonna tell me everything, right?"

"OK. All I remember."

It took Lou her first beer and brat to tell how she met Verla. The second round got her up through the mean-portioned dinners served up at the Trusters. The third round led her into the Reverend Dwight's videotapes.

"You can cut the theology crap," Beth got in edgewise as Lou repeated "family, community and the Truster Way" for the third time. "Hurry up and get to the good stuff."

Lou looked up peremptorily, questioning Beth's judgment. "All right. Now you come into the story, more or less. The night of my interview I said

I thought Judaism and lesbianism were fine, since a person's born that way. That didn't go over too well and I had to go back and 'clarify' my statements, if I wanted to become a member. So I did. Well, last night was our initiation. A nice little ceremony in the basement, with white robes..."

"And candles."

"Did I tell you that? No, I'm sure I didn't!" She fixed a suspicious gaze on Beth.

"All right. I peeked, kid. I was afraid you were gonna get into trouble. So I followed you and I watched through a basement window. That's how I got the idea that, with the robes an' the cross an' all that, it was the Klan."

Lou was amused, but went on with less gusto, now that Beth had intruded on the story, spoiled her rhythm and diminished the suspense. "So I went through the ceremony and afterwards they brought out a little cake to celebrate our becoming members, then there was a big, supportive study session, where everyone begins by praying, and I decided to study there."

"Yeah, yeah, yeah. You already told me."

Peeved, Lou cut down on narrative detail: "OK. So I read my Psych until about 2:30 in the morning, when Bob, Verla's friend, was the only other one left in the Quiet Room and we started to talk." She paused to catch her breath and finished off her beer. "Bob started chatting about Verla and how good I am for her and how she likes being around me. I asked him again where she was, since she hadn't even been at the initiation or study session. Bob said, 'Now that you're a member and the two of us are alone, I suppose I can tell you. Verla's a recovering alcoholic. That's why her parents, who once had her confined, put her here with us, with strict orders to keep watch on her. Then Saturday night she went out and got so drunk, when she came back we had to lock her in her room, strap her to the bed because she'd escaped before, and hold prayer vigils around her. Of course we're letting her go take her final tomorrow afternoon.'

"By then my blood was starting to boil. How dare they lock up anyone and strap them to a bed! So right there, on the spur of the moment, I pulled out my residence contracts, one for summer and one for fall, and tore them to pieces right in front of him. His look went blank, he didn't even try to persuade me to reconsider, and he left. Then reading my last few pages, I fell asleep. Well, they call it the 'Quiet Room' for a good reason. I didn't hear a thing until 8:45 this morning. I ran to the Psych Building, then remembered the final was in Van Vleck and got there at nine."

"Yeah, yeah, you told me the rest." Beth tipped her glass to her mouth. "If you think of more details, save 'em for later."

"All right," Lou agreed, beginning to feel hoarse.

"Just one more thing, kiddo. Am I still too evil to room with? Since you tore up your contract with the Jesus freak born-agains, you'll be needin' a place for summer, won't ya?"

"Oh, that," Lou said casually, almost having forgotten. "Yes, I will."

"You will?" Beth seemed stunned by the answer. "You mean you'll live with me? That's great, kiddo!" She got up and planted a big kiss on Lou's cheek, attracting the attention of patrons at the bar. Defying their gazes and slightly drunk, Lou grabbed Beth's neck and gave her a sloppy kiss on the lips. In unison the onlookers rapidly turned away.

"I'm a little drunk, but I love ya, Lou."

"I love you too," Lou whispered loudly, as Beth zigzagged back to her seat.

66

Stressed-out, overworked and still shaken, Cissy made a unilateral decision to fly to Los Angeles, with or without Jeb, for a much needed escape. Although substituting daily at a county school, he readily agreed to give up babysitting pimply adolescents in games of dodge ball. He cited a "family emergency," told the school district his last day would be Tuesday and took Wednesday off to help Cissy. The two would fly out Thursday morning.

She gave her grading assistant an ultimatum: Finish the exams by Wednesday noon. The grader consented to have 100 exams done by the deadline, leaving Cissy with over 200 to correct. By late morning she finished her own portion; at 12:30 the grader delivered the remaining hundred. Calculating final grades, she saw that at least half of them hung on borderlines. She looked hopelessly at Jeb. "I'll never have time to size up each case individually. I'll just have to give them all the higher of the two grades."

She wore jeans and a UCI T-shirt emblazoned with the school's ant-eater mascot; her hair was piled wildly on her head, knotted with a red kerchief. She focused on the grade sheets on the dining room table. "In the fall, they told me to clamp down, so I clamped. Then Sumner told me I'd clamped too hard and implied it was my fault for the low enrollment. So I'll just unclamp."

She studied the averages for several more minutes and began to think aloud: "Sumner is gone for the rest of the semester. No one would dare challenge my grades." But then a new twist of thought took over: "But how can I be fair to them all? After I push up those grades on the borderline, then there are those one-tenth of a point below who get the lower grade."

"So you just give them all an A."

Cissy's eyes bugged. "Not after all this work, I'm not. Besides, the department would fire me for that."

"Fire you? They just hired you! And you just said that no one would question them."

She scanned the hopeless averages again, then faced him. "True, it wouldn't look good for them to fire someone who's just been sexually harassed."

"That's the spirit, babe."

"A's for 324 of them?" she said with doubt, then began to contemplate the possibility. "Grade inflation is rampant, so maybe I can catch up with the trend." She looked at Jeb for agreement. "But what about the four who didn't even bother to take the exam? Then there are those who got under 30% on the final and a few who skipped class from February to early May. I have to maintain some standards."

A half hour later, Jeb had finished filling in the final grade sheets with 297 A's, while Cissy isolated the flagrant cases, assigning C's to fifteen, D's to eight and F's to four. "There! No one can say we passed out blanket A's!"

"That *you* passed out blanket A's, babe."

Cissy made a mock-sneer and signed the sheets. "We're done. I'm free!" On a whim she grabbed an exam, shaped it into an airplane and sailed it into the living room. Her eyes lit up with glee and she folded another. "There! Take that, department!"

"What are you doing, babe?"

She ignored him and folded happily away, sending one airplane-exam into one room, the next into another. She raised the screen of the kitchen window and sent one flying into the backyard.

"Don't you have to keep those exams on file somewhere?"

"Probably," she answered, distracted. "Wait, I've got a better idea!" She grabbed a stack of exams, hefted them under her arm and ran upstairs, where she knocked on the door. After a brief wait, Juan answered, wearing only a towel.

"Oh, sorry if I woke you, Juan. Uh, I know this sounds strange, but could I borrow one of your windows?"

"Sure, Cissy," he answered, as if this were a routine request.

"Great!" she exclaimed, energized. "Which window can you spare?"

"Well, it's Roz's day off and she and Irv are napping." A long passionate moan came from their room. "Well, it sounds like their nap's over. Gil's in our room, sleeping off his exam. That leaves the kitchen and the living room. Which one do you want?"

"Oh, if everyone's sleeping, never mind."

Juan insisted and Cissy ended up accepting.

The four upstairs neighbors eventually joined her in the kitchen. Jeb, having seen the evidence of her spree, appeared soon after. She had opened the front window, facing Willy Street, and the side one, outing on Ingersoll.

Everyone but Gil folded exams for her as she scurried back and forth between the two, sailing exam sheets to the wind.

"Take that, Isaacson, you sleazebag, you slimy..." As she ran out of epithets, Roz completed it for her: "Shithead." Cissy smiled and flung three exams at once. She changed windows and dedicated the next batch to Rickover.

Taking advantage of the favorable wind, she continued heaving exams frenetically and landed one in the middle of Ingersoll Street. Another rode the current all the way to Willy Street, then fluttered to the pavement in the middle of the intersection.

"Great therapy," said Irv. "Almost as good as primal."

"This is what academia does to you," commented Juan, now in shorts and sandals.

"Cissy passed out 297 A's in her Intro class," Jeb informed them. Cissy turned around and sent him a cautionary glance, remembering the BC she'd given Gil in the fall.

Up until now sitting groggy in a corner, Gil belched and came to life. "If she was gonna go bonkers passin' out the A's, why couldn't she have done it last semester?"

"I've seen many assault-related traumas before," Roz observed, "but never anything quite like this." Then, lowering her voice to Jeb: "She wouldn't jump, would she?"

Cissy turned around and cast Roz a playful, reassuring glance. "Come on, gang! How about a little help?"

Jeb shook his head in amazement. "I've never seen her like this before."

"Academia," Juan said soberly. "I've seen it ."

The five joined her, quickly helping her dispatch with the pile of exams, and Irv opened the back window too. Cissy hollered and whooped, continuing her verbal abuse of the department. The others picked up on the names and invented their own slurs. Caught up in the moment, she felt a strange elation, similar to the night she'd found herself joining in Sandinista chants at Ho Chi Minh's. She belonged in Madison, belonged in this neighborhood, belonged with these friends.

"Stop, everybody!" Irv's voice dampened the merriment. He pointed at a police cruiser halted at the traffic light.

"Oops!" Cissy hiccuped. Two exams had landed on the hood of the police car, one lodging itself under a windshield wiper in imitation of a parking ticket. "I'll clean up inside and out!"

"We'd better do the outside first." Irv ran his fingers through his beard, as if fingering rosary beads.

"Uh-oh." Cissy's giddiness evaporated. "I suppose I should go explain."

"We'll all go confront them," said Jeb.

"Are you sure Cissy's up to it?" asked Roz. "Another confrontation with the system is just what she doesn't need.

"I'll be all right, Roz. Oh, Jeb, somebody has to take the grades to FAB by 4:30. I was thinking of you."

"Oh, I'll go for you, Cissy," Roz piped up, eager.

"And you'll give them a piece of your mind while you're at it," Irv said. "If we're going to avoid more conflicts with the system, let's let someone else go."

Two sharp knocks at the door rendered them all silent.

"I'll get it," Roz barged through the living room, brushing by Jeb, and pulled it open, as the others circled her.

Two policewomen faced them. "Roz!" they greeted together.

"Hi, Hank! How ya doin', Bomber?" she greeted back. "Group, this is Henrietta and…" She paused, as if forgetting the other's real name.

"Evelyn," Bomber supplied.

"Just a little end-of-semester party," Roz explained. "Which the wind helped us with, a little too much, I'm afraid. You two know what the trauma of finals week can do to a body, don't you?" Turning to the others, she instructed, "You all go pick up the litter and I'll answer any questions Hank and Bomber have."

Glad to have an excuse to hurry down the stairs, Cissy felt a wave of after-the-fact panic. She led the way outside.

"Cissy's a survivor!" Jeb said loudly, as they reached the exam-strewn yard and garden. Irv raised his voice in agreement and Juan gave her a tender pat on the back. Stifling an overt display of emotion, Cissy began to gather up exams.

"We'll flatten them back out, I'll get the grade sheets from inside. And you'll run the grades down to FAB, Jeb?" He didn't protest. "We've got twenty minutes before they close. And considering the grades, I'd better not post them on the door."

As Juan instructed him to avoid stepping on seedlings, Gil sauntered between the rows of the garden and sidled up to Cissy. "I could drop 'em off for you, too."

She looked up, startled at the offer.

"There couldn't be a chance of a retroactive grade change for last semester, could there?"

Summer 1986

67

It was, essentially, the first day of summer for Gil. He had finished his only final exam the day before. Sunlight trickled in the bedroom window and he awoke, alone in bed. He hadn't even heard Juan leave.

The clock-radio read 7:30. Gil flailed at the sheets, tugged them out from under the mattress and mummified himself. When sleep didn't come, he jolted the radio into functioning with a deft swipe of the arm, content to lie inert and listen to music.

He had no plans for the day nor any particular desire to make them. This summer he would have only a month of vacation, during which he planned to do as little as possible, to indulge in whatever fell his way. Then he'd enroll in summer school, with his father's blessing and money. The Academic Progress Committee of the School of Pharmacy had yet to let him continue the program, nor had they terminally banished him. So he'd decided to take two professionally related courses in the summer, present evidence of improved grades to the committee and hope for the best.

Shortly after eight, he stumbled out of bed and slung a robe over his shoulder. He stopped in the doorway and, seeing and hearing no one, proceeded naked into the living room. Irv's bedroom door was open, the bed made. He picked up the morning newspaper, which someone had retrieved, sank into a chair and spread it over himself like a gigantic napkin. He scooted back, met with an exposed spring and decided to sit on his robe. Flipping lazily through the paper, he came across a short item titled "Finals get to profs too." He sat up, alert, and read:

> *An incident witnessed by Madison police*
> *proves students aren't the only ones who*
> *suffer during Finals Week, but that faculty*
> *get frustrated too.*
>
> *Madison police were driving yesterday*
> *afternoon on the east side of the city when their*
> *cruiser, stopped at a traffic light, was suddenly*
> *pelted by papers.*
>
> *Stopping to investigate, police found*
> *computerized exam sheets that had been folded to*
> *resemble airplanes, hurled from the second-floor*
> *windows of a nearby house. Wind gusts of 20-25*
> *miles per hour had carried the exams into the*
> *intersection.*
>
> *Police reported that a University of*
> *Wisconsin faculty member explained that she had*
> *just finished correcting over 300 exams,*
> *was "frustrated, burned-out and letting off a*
> *little steam."*
>
> *The faculty member apologized to officers and*
> *cleared the exams from the street and sidewalks.*
> *No citation was issued.*

Gil wondered why they'd protected Cissy's identity, skimmed the rest of the paper and laid it on the floor. Leaving his bathrobe behind, he got up to head to the bathroom when the telephone rang.

"Is Gil there?" came the familiar voice, nervous and distrustful.

"Hi, Hunter."

After a moment's relief, the caller spat out the expected question. Gil stalled; these morning encounters were getting dangerous. Although Juan's presence was predictable, Irv's, and now Roz's, weren't. About to muster up the forces to say "no," he said, "Yeah, come on over now. But it's gotta be quick."

Juan had one more hour to drive when he was dispatched to pick up a passenger on Willy Street. He'd been sniffling all morning and now saw the opportunity to stop, run upstairs and pick up his nasal spray.

He loped up the stairs, quickly but noiselessly, and let himself in. He tiptoed to the bedroom door so as not to wake Gil and opened it.

Gil knelt on the floor, his face nuzzled into the crotch of a tall man.

The name came right back to him: Edward Hunter, pastor of the Winnebago Baptist Church.

Juan froze first. Then the minister caught sight of him, eyes registering horror, and pulled the fastly deflating reason for Gil's interest in him out of his mouth. Sensing an interruption in his pleasure, Gil caught Juan with his peripheral vision and froze.

"Get out of here!" Juan said with calm intensity, teeth bared.

The minister dove for his clothes, thinking the words meant for him, and pulled on pants, not bothering with his underwear. He began to mumble apologies and excuses at large, berating Gil for "not telling me about your friend."

"On second thought, don't hurry, boys. I work for another hour so you've got time to finish. Pardon the interruption."

Juan pierced Gil with his eyes in a brief staring duel. Gil stood as if dazed, not bothering to cover himself. Juan turned around and hurried out, leaving both the bedroom and the apartment doors wide open.

He had forgotten the nasal spray. Numb, he finished his last hour of driving. At the end of the shift he parked the cab in the company lot. Common sense told him that Gil had probably left, but he put the house off-limits to himself, refusing even to walk past it. He crossed Willy Street and headed toward Morrison, where Lake Monona loomed behind the houses to his right. The sun had risen high and bright in a sky dotted with scant cumulus.

He came to a lakeside clearing — dubbed "Suicide Park," Irv had once told him — and sat down against the rough bark of a tree trunk and burst into convulsive tears. He saw two youngsters approach, stop and observe him with curiosity. Evidently trained to avoid funny-acting adults, they skittered away.

The destruction of his romantic ideal, to which he'd long tried to cling, sank in with renewed force. A second swell of tears flooded his eyes, streamed down to his chin. It was not that infidelity was unfathomable to him; it merely spelled the definitive end of the relationship.

He dried his eyes and, after what seemed an hour, walked back to Willy Street. Purposely avoiding even a glance at the house, he jumped into Irv's little-used pickup and drove to Picnic Point on Lake Mendota. He made the fifteen-minute hike to the end of the point and perched on the rocks, staring at the lake bottom, focusing on occasional sailboats and studying the leaf patterns around him.

By afternoon he doubled back slowly along the north side of the point, off the path. Two skinny-dippers frolicked offshore, but he paid them no heed. He ached at the thought of what he would find — or more precisely, not find

— upon arriving home.

He first encountered Irv and Roz in the living room and greeted them curtly. In the bedroom, Gil's clothing, records, clock-radio and drug paraphernalia were gone. He walked back into the living room and announced, "I found Gil in bed with a preacher this morning and told him to leave and he has."

"Maybe he just left in a huff," said Irv.

"Juan just said he told him to get out," Roz snapped.

"He moved out his most important possessions. So you were right, Roz, when you said it was nine-to-one in favor of adultery."

"I'm sorry." She looked at him almost as if blame lay with her or she had willed adultery by her odds.

"You don't have to feel sorry for me. And whatever both of you do, don't ever say, 'It'll be all right.'" Juan crossed his arms and glared at them both to make sure they got the message.

68

Beth paid little attention to the countryside as the Greyhound rambled over hour after hour of interstate. It could have been anywhere in the Midwest: Flat land and small bleak towns marked the way.

She dozed restlessly, alone in the smoking section, since Lou had deserted the back of the bus for cleaner air. She thought intermittently of joining Lou in the front, but sleep would overtake her before she could move.

A long rest was in order; the bus ride was an adequate beginning. She had received her final grades, but at least there was one bright spot: Intro to Museums, where Cicely Pankhurst had flabbergasted her with an A. Lou, who'd only gotten an AB in the course, had received the information coolly. Beth had talked to others in the course and withheld the fact from Lou that either there had been a gross computer error or the prof had gone wacko.

When Lou suggested she accompany her to Ladysmith, she jumped at the chance. Lou said she would provide a buffer zone between her and her parents, unhappy over her decision to stay in Madison for the summer. In two quick trips in Heidi's station wagon, they'd dumped their possessions in their near-east-side flat and Brooklyn at Heidi and Amy's.

After a bus transfer at Eau Claire for the final leg of the journey, they sat together. Beth noticed that the houses and hamlets became sparser and suppressed a comment about being in the middle of nowhere. "So what are we gonna do this week, kiddo?"

The question seemed to take Lou by surprise. "Not much. That's the point, isn't it? See the farm, relax..."

"What's Ladysmith known for?"

"Well... We've got the largest cottonwood log in the state of Wisconsin."

"What's there to do? Any hot spots?"

"Ladysmith doesn't have 'hot spots.' It has five or so taverns downtown, and a popular supper club out in the country. That's about it."

Within an hour, the bus rolled into Lou's hometown. On the gas station on the main street, a small plaque marked the Greyhound drop-off and pickup point. To Beth's right she saw only a sign indicating the mileage to the next town and an expanse of fields. To her left stood two long rows of commercial buildings. Where was the rest?

"This is it," Lou said without apology. "The center of Ladysmith."

Beth resigned herself to the worst, which for her had always been boredom. She tried to tell herself that boredom — or rather, absolute and total relaxation — was what she'd come here for. She steeled herself, ready to sail intrepidly into Lou's alien culture: rural, Protestant and German.

Ed and Mildred Lautermilk pulled in a minute later, greeted them laconically and hauled their bags into the back of a station wagon. They backtracked down the main highway, past Mount Scenario College and a hospital. The town ended abruptly; they were surrounded by fields.

"Oats and corn," Ed explained, answering Beth's unasked question.

"What a pity you girls missed church this morning," Mildred said as they drove down the drive to a large, white farmhouse surrounded by hydrangea bushes. Inside she launched into the ministerial difficulties their church had been having, directing her remarks to Lou. Then she asked Beth, "What church does your family go to?"

"We don't," Beth blurted out at the same time Lou said, "They're Jewish, Mom." Lou had warned her that her parents had never met a Jew or, if they had, they hadn't known it.

Ed ambled in from the other room. "Had some of those a few years back, passin' out pamphlets around town. Even made it all the way out here to the farm, didn't they, Milly?"

"Those were Jehovah's Witnesses, Dad," Lou said, and sent Beth an I-told-you-so glance.

"Are you the ones who don't eat meat?" asked Mildred.

"Oh, I eat meat," Beth put in quickly. "Pork's my favorite."

"Oh, good. That's what's left over from dinner."

Sunday afternoon and the following day Beth toured the farm, which made its living off a combination of corn, oats and a barnful of dairy cows. She visited the cows' quarters, scaled the silo and peeked into a deserted chicken coop. She snoozed in the hayloft, swung on an old rubber tire hanging from a tree and, evenings, rocked on the porch swing and listened to the

crickets chirping. Contentment came easily, almost naturally. Ed seemed grati-
fied by her interest in the farm and remarked on her "tomboy" ways, which
he said Lou used to have. She detected a condemnatory note behind the amused
smile when Milly — as she'd taken to calling her — remarked on her ability
to sleep "until half the day was gone." For Beth, it was just starting at eleven.

That evening Ed drawled, "S'pose you're both old enough to have a
beer before supper if you want one." Beth barely contained her gusto when
he went to the refrigerator and took out three.

"You know they raised the age, Ed," Mildred cautioned from the pantry. "Maybe Beth's not old enough."

Ed waved away his wife's objection and handed out the Leinenkugels.

Recently sensitized to oppression by patriarchal authority, Beth was
glad for it at the Lautermilks.

After her parents retired, Lou allowed that they could probably sneak
two more beers. After they drank them, Beth began to scour the pantry cup-
boards in search of further drink.

"Not there," Lou said, obviously guessing the object of the search. Beth
followed her into the dining room, where, in the sideboard behind the good
china, she produced a dusty bottle of Old Crow.

"How about we do Ladysmith's saloons tomorrow night?"

Lou looked as if she'd just suggested they do a striptease for the locals. She answered, imitating Ed's voice: "Nice girls don't go to them places.
'Specially not alone."

"No problem. I'm not 'nice.' And if I take you, we won't be alone."

"No way, Beth. He won't have it. And don't say he won't find out.
Ladysmith's a small town."

"Got that right. Oh well, so much for patriarchal authority."

The last morning Milly roused them early for the bus back to Eau
Claire. Over breakfast Lou had the necessary talk with her parents about summer plans. In spite of her groggy state, Beth conjured up verve about the likelihood of their finding jobs in Madison. Lou shot her furtive, skeptical glances.
Beth hoped that her own enthusiasm had some correspondence to reality.

"Don't you gals waste all your money. Big city'll eat it right up," Ed
admonished, friendly. Milly threw them her own stern cautionary glance.

On their way to the Greyhound, Beth thanked them effusively for their
hospitality. Once there, she befuddled Ed with her outstretched hand and disconcerted Milly by hugging her. She watched Lou give her mother a quick
peck on the cheek, then they boarded the bus.

The second-floor flat at 541 Ingersoll came with the minimum necessities. To
Lou's thinking, a missing one was curtains. Unknown to Beth, Lou's mother

had given her two pairs of frilly white ones, plus longer ones for the living room.

"Forget it, kid!" Beth shook her head as Lou unpacked the frilly pairs she intended for the kitchen and bathroom. "These look like a tutu!" She took half of one pair, wrapped it around her waist and executed an ungainly pirouette.

"Maybe you'll like the other pair better." Lou produced the long ones, a deep purple.

"Those look like they belong in a mortuary!"

Lou took umbrage. The "mortuary" curtains had hung in her living room until she was fifteen, but she kept this detail to herself. "But we have to have curtains in the bathroom." She knew Beth would be hard-pressed to argue with her on this.

A compromise was effected: The frilly curtains were hung in the bathroom and, provisionally, the kitchen; Lou took the "mortuary" curtains for her bedroom. That decision made, she next sought to rid the living room of the wooden orange crates and plastic milk-carton crates that supported the TV and stereo.

"Lou! Crates are ecologically correct."

Lou weighed this term, coming from someone who had hauled a microwave and a wall of appliances to their dorm room fall semester.

"Think about the practicalities of multi-use furniture, kid. Why should we kill off a tree to make a table when an orange crate does the trick? Somebody's gotta save the environment."

Lou considered that Beth's Spring-Semester History class had warped, if not damaged her mind. Frankly, she didn't know which she preferred: the old, irresponsible Beth, or the new one, purporting to be politically aware and "correct."

She'd grown up being instilled that there was a proper and an improper way to do things. Then there had been the "Truster Way" versus the "Wrong Way." Now, in near-east-side Madison there was a "correct" and an "incorrect" way, mixed up somehow with sixties politics. Having won the battle of the curtains, she was disposed to relent on this one. "OK. We'll keep the crates."

"Glad to see ya comin' around, kid. I knew ya wouldn't want our friends to think we were ecologically incorrect."

"What friends, Beth? The few we have all have left town for the summer."

Later in the day, Lou finished unpacking her books and came across the spiral-ring notebook Bible from the Trusters. She thought fleetingly of returning it, then squelched the idea, and repacked it with the year's academic lore. Afterwards she walked to a nearby supermarket.

"Lou, where'd you buy those?" Beth interrogated as she unpacked the small expensive sack, back in the kitchen.

"The place down on the corner. Why?"

"We gotta shop at the Co-op. Every place else exploits the people! The people are you and me. We'll go down and get a membership tomorrow. Fifteen bucks for the whole year."

"Fifteen's a lot of money, Beth. We're not going to live here a whole year. And we don't even have jobs."

"Don't worry, we'll get 'em." Beth plunked herself on a kitchen chair and Brooklyn sharpened her claws crawling up her bluejeans.

That week they scoured the campus, answered ads and dialed their index fingers raw. Beth soon exhausted all the progressive and feminist establishments where she'd fancied she'd like to work. Funds dwindled. Beth proudly notarized her A, which raised her GPA to an acceptable height, sent it off to her mother and waited for her monthly check.

Their job expectations lowered, by Friday they went to Temporary Secretarial Services and took the required typing test. Beth failed — to no one's surprise — and Lou scored a medium-high pass. On Monday she was sent on her first job assignment. They decided to celebrate by dining at the nearest neighborhood restaurant, Ho Chi Minh's.

While ordering drinks, they overheard a woman, who spoke with an owner's authority, bemoaning the lack of reliable buspersons. Beth's eyes followed her back to the bar.

"'Scuse me, Lou. This could turn into somethin'."

Beth deserted her and Lou sat alone at their table, vaguely uncomfortable. Five minutes later Beth returned wearing an apron. "We'll have to celebrate later, kid! And we'll be celebratin' two jobs."

69

T he Willy Street house was almost silent. Gil had never returned; Jeb and Cissy had gone to California; and Juan, when not driving, was barely to be seen, let alone conversed with. Roz's flatmate returned from the wilderness only to leave again soon after. Irv and Roz spent the last week in May left alone to their own devices, with scarcely a peep from the outside world. In between work and bed, they decided that Roz shouldn't renew her own lease in August, but rather move in.

By Memorial Day weekend they were ready to escape the quiet of the city for the noise of the country. They'd planned to go to the Wisconsin River, with its sunbathers, motorboaters, water-skiers and canoeists. Saturday they would canoe a portion of the river and spend the night camping, then return home Sunday. Irv hauled his canoe out of the shed and his tent out of the attic.

"You think we might invite Juan?" Roz contemplated the musty tent. "After all, we've had a whole week alone. I wouldn't mind the company."

"I don't know if he's working, but it is a holiday weekend and he gets depressed on holidays." Irv stood facing the downstairs flat.

"But we've got to find him before we can invite him."

Irv shielded his eyes from the sun. "He should be home soon. I'll leave him a note."

The note written, he and Roz proceeded to go off and do errands. An hour later, they found Juan's one-word response: "Negative."

By early afternoon they were paddling on the Wisconsin River, she in front, he in back, and their gear in the middle. Within a half-hour they glimpsed topless women and bottomless men on the shore. "Bare-Bottom Beach" was a stretch that the media had discovered, popularized and rendered notorious.

"Let's stop," Roz suggested. "My arms ache."

"Stop and do what?" Irv said, mildly aghast. "Gawk?"

"It seems we're already doing that. Let's join in and follow suit. Or rather, unsuit. Don't tell me you're too modest."

"Meee? Modest?" Irv gulped. To prove himself, he steered the canoe past the sandbars to the shore. They shed their clothes at one end of the beach, where scores of sun-worshipers — most totally unclothed and many sporting dark total tans — basked or walked around socializing. A group played volleyball across a net placed at the edge of the river. On its opposite side loomed bluffs. To their backs grew scrawny willows marking the edge of a wood.

"I don't think I would have done this in the past around men." Roz lit a Camel, surveyed the beach, and said, "Nudity, I think I like it."

"Oh?" Irv said with interest. "I remember some naked encounter sessions we had at the commune."

"Those don't count. What I mean is, I now know that most of these single men around here are ogling each other and not me." She smiled smugly.

Irv shot tentative glances around the beach. Everyone seemed comfortable, at ease with nudity. So why shouldn't he? He snapped out of his musing and saw cigarette ashes fall between Roz's breasts. "Don't burn yourself."

"You're the one with the more sensitive parts," she said, missing or ignoring his meaning.

She lay on her backside, propped up on her elbows, and tossed him a bottle of sun screen. "I'd lather up good if I were you."

"'Maximal protection,'" Irv read from the bottle, and applied the cream to his body, giving an extra dose to his white stripe.

"'Maximal protection' or not, I'd turn over before long." She ground her cigarette butt into the sand.

They both turned over, ten minutes on one side, ten on the other. After repeating the cycle, they put their clothes back on, retrieved Roz's cigarette butts and launched the canoe. Irv backpaddled, heading them downriver.

By 5:30 they stopped for the day, without having glimpsed the "canudists" rumored to be on the river this weekend. They set up camp where Roz had spotted a protected site on an undeveloped piece of land without a "No Trespassing" sign. On an ancient Coleman stove they cooked lentil soup and home-canned beets. At dusk Roz went off in search of wood.

The fire crackling, they settled in and smoked a joint, to a view of the river and its opposite bank. A sole canoe passed by, paddling swiftly to its destination before nightfall. As daylight ebbed away, their campfire shrank proportionately. Flashlight in hand, Irv made a hike for more wood.

"I missed you," Roz said when he returned with an armful of branches.

"I missed you too." Irv rekindled the dying embers. He sat on the ground, hands on his knees. Roz cuddled at his side. He let himself fall back, prone; she reclined next to him. Both turned on their sides to face each other. Their mouths met and their hands explored. Within minutes, their shirts and bluejeans were open.

"Yuck!" Irv said during a pause from licking. "That's the worst tasting sun screen you've got on!"

"That's mosquito repellent. But there are places I didn't put any."

They removed each other's remaining clothing. Irv's tennis shoe ended up scorched by the fire and their backsides scratched from rolling in the brush. Irv examined an injury, Roz ran to get a sleeping bag, and they lay down on it, this time making love more gently.

"Let's never separate," Roz moaned, as their movements ground to a slow halt.

"I'm afraid that's a physiological impossibility, love."

"Then let's just never leave each other."

"Let's not," Irv agreed. "Oops."

They were silent for some time, hands still caressing each other's scratches. In the sky, clouds shifted and a slice of moonlight faintly illuminated them. The campfire at their side had reduced to coals.

"I could be happy like this forever," Roz said. "And I can't believe I'm being so goddamned romantic."

"Me, too." Irv remembered the night long ago on the shores of Mendota and let similar words tumble out: "We should make ourselves a baby, as soon as we're both ready."

"Is there a new medical discovery I don't know about?"

"I've been thinking," he began, engrossed in thought, still lying on his side, unclothed. "We only need a surrogate father, which is, fortunately, much easier to get than a surrogate mother."

"I know the process."

"Now, who would we both want to be the biological father of our child?"

"Juan?" she said, as though startling herself.

"Juan," he said, glad that they agreed.

"The kid would sure be melting pot. French Canadian, Cuban, Jewish, and Armenian, all rolled into the three parents." After a pause, she asked in a low, tender voice, "Would it ruin things if we legalized it?"

"I didn't think we were talking about the baby-buying market."

"No, I mean us. As..." she hesitated, then spoke swiftly, "in marriage. I've got my philosophical objections to it. But if we're going to have a child and both of us aren't the natural parents, a legal union would help, wouldn't it?"

"Right. And apart from that, if I just heard a proposal, I accept." He stretched his neck and kissed her.

"Let's sleep under the stars."

Irv looked upward. "I think you mean under the clouds."

"Under the clouds, then."

"I'll get the other bag out of the tent."

"Let's not use the second bag, huh? I don't want to be that far from you."

"Then we'd better suck in our diaphragms. Or at least I should," he said, and scooted in.

"Our first stumbling block, you know, could be Juan." Roz hobbled barefoot and gathered up their clothes in the darkness. "I can hear him now, self-righteously insisting on his right to be the last of his line."

"I think our first stumbling block may be getting both of us into this bag," Irv said, comfortably occupying the whole space.

"Anything's possible tonight."

Roz slid into the bag and nestled her way down inside. Irv could feel their knees, loins and stomachs meet. Her chin came up to his collarbone. She kissed his neck.

"I love you, Roz."

"Ditto, Irv."

70

S eated on the front porch of the COB House, a can of Miller clenched in his fist, Gil felt more relaxed than he had in days. The afternoon was bright, his responsibilities few, and his personal worries on the wane.

Two weeks ago he'd dragged his scant possessions to the frat house, having nowhere else to go and figuring that, as an unofficial brother emeritus, the fraternity should at least take him in for a few days. Beds became available as brothers finished their finals, began alcoholic blitzes and vacated the House. Each celebration gave him a reason to forget his own troubles, and he kept up with the best of them. Only the spotting of a PC Cab would momentarily jolt him out of his alcohol and marijuana high.

The House had closed down officially on Saturday, the last day of finals, when room and board contracts expired. Arnesen and Blair were to stay on as caretakers for the month until Summer Session. Gil easily convinced them to let him share the duties, which consisted of occupying the House, not destroying it and making sure no one else did. The workload, for which they received free room, suited him perfectly. Arnesen and Blair promptly decided to leave town from Sunday to Wednesday, since Gil would be safeguarding the House.

Whenever he was alone, his mind strayed to Juan. Though Juan had demanded monogamy, Gil had never exactly consented to it. The issue had hovered over them uneasily, unresolved, finally proving the relationship's undoing. It had to happen and, he realized, he had rather courted it. The dissolution was inevitable, ordained from the beginning, he told himself.

But something had happened along the way. A dull ache pervaded his body; a sense of loss staunchly lodged itself in his emotions. He had accustomed himself to the Willy Street house, its occupants and his relationship. Not only had he become acclimated; he had, in spite of himself, fallen into some sort of love. To blunt the pain, he would routinely drink and drug himself until paralytically plastered.

By Saturday night only the three caretakers remained at the House. Their girlfriends having left town, Blair and Arnesen proposed they cruise the State Street bars to get laid. Gil accompanied them.

Since the overwhelming bulk of the student populace had cleared out, the selection was slim, at least numerically. Gil noticed Blair and Arnesen ogling a pair of buxom redheads, who barely appeared of legal age.

"So Kreuzer, what's your story again?" Arnesen was just loud and aggressive enough for Gil to tell he was tipsy.

"I already told you guys. The cops stopped by the house on Willy Street. They thought big-time drug dealing was goin' on there. So I decided to get out, lay low for a while. You want me to get arrested or what?"

"I don't know, Kreuzer," said Blair. "Maybe the cops got you under surveillance. We probably shouldn't even be seen with you."

"Yeah," Arnesen agreed drunkenly. "Maybe now they'll put our house under surveillance. That's all we need is a drug bust."

"Damn right," said Blair. "Bein' on academic probation and all, they'd probably kick us off campus."

"Fuck off, you guys." Gil drained the last of their second pitcher of beer.

"I wanna get laid," Arnesen whined.

"There's the beef." Gil pointed to the portly duo. "Go get it."

Arnesen blinked, belched then focused. He stood up, swayed, then, as if setting his sights on the goal, made a beeline for the pair. Blair went for a pitcher refill, leaving Gil alone at the table.

As his eyes scanned the bar, he saw Arnesen making inroads with the redheads, apparently an easy feat. He could join him, leaving Blair as odd man out. After all, he was horny and these two seemed to be easy prey. Then, once Arnesen and Blair left town tomorrow, he could find sexual paradise at the Bull Dog.

Blair returned with a full pitcher, slopping beer on the table. "Looks like Arnesen's puttin' the moves on."

"Well, there's two of them and three of us," Gil commented neutrally. "How horny are you, Blair?"

"You wanna flip to see who goes over?"

Gil debated the proposal. It would leave him a fifty-fifty chance of an easy lay. But then again, why shouldn't he just let Blair go over, since he himself could find satisfaction elsewhere? "You go ahead," he offered. "I'll do better on my own."

"You sure?" asked Blair, as if suspecting some trick were involved.

Gil gave a firm downward shake of the head. "I'll take off, you take the pitcher and the broad."

"You're all right, Kreuzer," Blair said, as he made to join Arnesen, grasping the pitcher handle with his fist.

In ten minutes Gil was at the Bull Dog. Within forty-five, he left, accompanied. They went to the other guy's house downtown, finished by two-thirty, dozed, then went at it again. He stumbled back to the COB House around five.

He awoke with an erection at noon and went off to the Bull Dog's beer bust. As Arnesen and Blair had left now, he took his two latest conquests back to the House. The three satisfied themselves and one of them left. Gil and his remaining partner slept in separate bunk beds and did it again in the morning.

Monday afternoon he read a gay community newspaper one of the two had left behind. AIDS news abounded. Reflecting on his recent behavior, he read about safe-sex guidelines, reflected again. His tally of unsafe activities indulged in far exceeded the safe. He hid the newspaper away among his clothes.

By Tuesday heterosexuality began to look good. He stayed at home, uneasy but less frantic about AIDS, and smoked himself to sleep.

Late Wednesday afternoon, Arnesen and Blair returned. After alluding to his own Saturday night experience — pronouns changed, of course — Gil pressed them for details of their night. The obese teens had indeed accompanied them back to the House, helped them consume a twelve-pack, then mustered up enough energy to barrel out of the house together, their virtue still intact. So much for heterosexuality.

By Thursday a relationship with Juan, even a monogamous one, began to seem enviable.

On Friday he explored new masturbatory techniques and let himself fantasize about Arnesen and Blair.

By the weekend Arnesen dared them to accompany him to the nude beach near Mazomanie. Gil perked up at the idea. Voyeurism could be a new sexual realm to explore. He egged them on, daring them to back out, and off they went.

After several wrong turns, they located the beach. Voyeurism inflamed his desire, necessitating that he lie on his stomach. Blair and Arnesen did likewise, either out of modesty or arousal. They spent an hour and a half before Arnesen, as driver, tired of the novelty. Finally limp himself, Gil wandered off into the woods with the excuse of taking a leak before they left. Ensconced among low willows, he stared brazenly. His gaze landed on a hunky man with dark, curly hair, who flipped onto his back to reveal… Gil's heart almost skipped a beat. It was none other than Irv, Roz at his side. He ducked down and found another path out to avoid their spotting him.

He now sat on the COB front porch, beer in hand. Two days without drugs at his parents' house had revitalized him. Sex seemed less imperative. The atmosphere was relaxed, Blair and Arnesen good buddies to hang out with. His classes would begin soon.

He took the final swig of his Miller, decided to wait until evening to have another. As he got up to head inside, a horn sounded next door. He looked over and saw a PC Cab honking for a passenger. A second glance disclosed Juan at the wheel. His heart fluttered. Juan was looking in the opposite direc tion. Gil stepped away, still watching the cab. Suddenly Juan turned his head to the fraternity house porch. Gil met his eyes for a fraction of a second, then stole into the House. Bounding up the stairs, he heard the cab roar out of the driveway. He flew into his room and felt an unexpected urge to fall apart.

71

Juan wrangled increased cab shifts, though became wary of further sightings of Gil. Even when exhausted from driving, he couldn't sleep. When not trying to sleep, it was hard to avoid Irv and Roz, both more than eager to offer unwanted consolation.

He found a remedy to both problems. First he took to sleeping in his sleeping bag, placed in the corner of his room, where he found it easier to sleep alone. Preferring not even to think of his bed and what had transpired in it, he advertised and sold it. Then, to escape from Irv and Roz, he began to frequent Ho Chi Minh's after finishing his night shift. He would take the first volume of *Remembrance of Things Past* and order a pitcher of Point, Mad City Suds not being on tap. Seated on a bar stool, he'd drink directly from the pitcher with a straw, Proust positioned carefully under a light. In the original French he would lazily savor the cadence and rhythms of Proust until midnight, by which time he would be floating, the prose swimming away from him, and Irv and Roz safely tucked in bed.

Even when they slept at Roz's, they always drifted back to the Willy Street house. Fortunately they left for Memorial Day weekend and Juan took the opportunity to finish planting his garden. Occupying himself incessantly, he redoubled his efforts with SPELL and sent out a spate of infractions right on Willy Street. Ho Chi Minh's had a new menu that offered "Soup of du Jour," minor compared to errors such as "marital arts" for "martial arts." Then again, maybe the two were inextricably linked.

Roz stayed on Cloud Nine after returning from the camping trip. Even when her hours were cut at the Co-op, her bliss remained unmarred. As if fate had set out to help her, she discovered the next day that the other part-timer at the Womynspace reception desk had quit and a replacement was needed. It was about time they gave her full-time hours. The process should be a shoo-in.

After a week's more discussion, she and Irv made tentative wedding plans for early July, giving themselves a month in which to change their minds, just in case. A judge who was a personal friend of Irv's would marry them. In order to avoid unnecessary fanfare, Roz's mother -- with whom her communication was by choice infrequent -- would not be informed of the wedding until the *fait* was *accompli.*

As Roz had predicted, the immediate hurdle to overcome was Juan, whose studied avoidance prevented them from informing him of their plans. They finally decided that his silent suffering was too much for them to bear. In the three weeks since Gil's departure, he'd shown no signs of change. If anything, he'd gotten worse, having taken to hiding behind a tome of Proust, discouraging any uninvited conversation.

They made plans to wait up for him, discussed their strategy in advance and barricaded his bedroom door with the sofa. Under no condition would they express sympathy for him, something which was becoming easier by the day. They'd inform him of their wedding and, unless he seemed overtly hostile, ask him to be a witness. Only if this much went well, would they sound him out on their childbearing plan.

They began their vigil at ten, when he got off work. Not unexpectedly, he failed to come straight home.

Irv gulped air in a gigantic yawn. "He'll have to be home by one, when the bars close."

"Unless he meets someone and doesn't come home."

"Think again, love."

"Right. I've got the joint all rolled and ready for when he gets here."

"That's the last thing I need." Irv moved into a reclining position.

"Remember, this is all for Juan's sake." Irv's eyebrows rose at a sharp angle, resembling diacritical marks. "OK, for ours too."

"Wake me up when he gets here." He placed his head on a pillow.

Roz gave a playful tug on his beard and blew him a kiss. Within moments, he began the deep breathing of one sleeping. She nuzzled herself into his lap and fell into a light doze, lulled by his low snores.

She awoke to the turning of the key in the door, nudged Irv and sat up. Her watch read 12:10. Irv grunted and rolled over as the door fell open.

A second later, Juan stepped into view. "Camping out again? When I saw light under the door, I figured you might be up to something."

"Call it an ambush." Roz doubted their task would prove easy.

"Does this mean I sleep in your room tonight in view of the fact that you've rendered mine impregnable?" he demanded, Proust adangle from one hand.

"In our room, at least you'd have a bed." Roz furtively elbowed Irv.

He took the cue, rolled back over and said "Juan, we want to talk to you."

"Isn't it past your bedtime?" Juan marched off to the kitchen and returned with a glass of water and a saucerful of Brussels sprouts. "All right. I see I'm cornered. You've successfully ambushed me. So when do the torture and maiming begin?"

Roz worked up enthusiasm: "Why don't you sit down and smoke a joint with us?"

He popped a Brussels sprout into his mouth. "You kids smoke it."

She lit the joint and looked hopefully at her companions; she was getting no takers. After two tokes, she shoved it at Irv's face. He hesitated, then took it. Juan sat down on the floor in front of them, drank water from his glass.

"This powwow is going nowhere fast." He inhaled another Brussels sprout. "I take it you're not detaining me just so I can watch you get stoned."

"You could join in," Roz said. "Juan, we're worried about you."

"Well, don't be."

She took the joint back from Irv. "We want things to go back to normal."

"This is the new norm."

She choked on a mouthful of smoke, cleared her throat and grabbed Juan's water glass. "Are you purposely exiling us from your life?"

Juan turned his palms upward. "OK. You win. Give me the damned joint. It can only help me sleep."

Irv sat upright on the sofa. "So what's this new norm of yours?"

"I'm living the life of the ascetic."

"So we've seen."

"It's the new me."

"Well, I'm glad ascetics still get high." Roz let out a laugh that turned hollow and took the joint back from Juan as she returned the water glass to him.

"You've always done your own thing..," Irv began.

"And we're doing ours," Roz broke in, anxious to move the conversation along. "We're getting married, Juan."

"How wonderful." His voice betrayed no happiness.

"Obviously you're thrilled," she said.

"Thrilled to the hilt. No problem. I'll move out."

Irv's voice came out quick and firm: "You'll do no such thing. That's the last thing we want."

"Oh, are we converting to a commune again? I thought those went out with the seventies."

No one commented. Juan's face locked like a safe. Wary, Roz eyed Irv and saw him shrug. The major burden had evidently fallen to her. She toked quickly on the roach, scorched her finger and shoved it back at Juan, as if this were the remedy for everything. He refused it, so she pinched it out.

"I suppose congratulations are in order. A nice little legal union bonding you together. How sweet. I should have expected it. I forgot that marriage has come back into style. Now, do I trust our little powwow has been sufficiently fruitful to satisfy you two? May I go to bed now?"

Roz overcame an urge to tell him to "cut the crap," leaned forward and blurted out, "Juan, we want to have a baby." Out of the corner of her eye, she saw Irv throw her a reprimand. She had hardly gotten a favorable response to the marriage announcement, had forgotten to ask him about witnessing and had plunged on ahead. It was too late to retreat now.

"Ah, yes. The heterosexual desire to procreate."

"No more anti-straight remarks, please," she retorted.

"I'm euphoric for the two of you," he went on. "Am I to be the little tyke's godfather, the beatnik gay uncle or the black sheep of the extended family?"

"Try biological father," Roz said, purposely avoiding Irv's face.

"Now I've heard everything." He raised his voice and threw his head back. "I did wonder how you two were going to multiply without help. But just because you've gone straight, Roz, doesn't mean the rest of us want to. And besides, I'm celibate now."

"Will you lay off, please, and listen?"

"If he doesn't want to hear about it, he doesn't," Irv said.

"But he doesn't even know the details yet."

"Spare me the details, please," Juan replied, shielding his face with his hands. "Heterosexual Copulation 101. Sorry, kids. I'd never pass the entrance exam."

"You know how some lesbians do it. When I'm at the right moment, you merely masturbate into a turkey baster or a widemouthed syringe, which someone then puts inside me. It's simple. What do you think?"

"I think it sounds nauseating. Malodorous."

"Let's let Juan go to bed." Irv crossed his arms over his chest and made as if to stand up.

"I couldn't do it anyway," Juan said, matter-of-fact. "I could have AIDS."

"What!?" Roz choked. "What do you mean, Juan?"

"I didn't say I had it," he elaborated, changing his position on the hardwood floor. "It's just that I could have been exposed to it. Though I've been monogamous, my ex-partner probably screwed half the city and could have passed the virus on to me."

"Don't scare us like that" she said, realizing this could account for his stange behavior, and weighing this unexpected complication. "Maybe having an antibody test would help."

"If you must know, I already have. I've rather been on pins and needles waiting for the results."

"You could have talked to us. We could have offered you some support," Irv said.

"In any case, if I were you two, I would certainly not count on my participation in this little venture." He stood up and stretched.

"You should have let us know the stress you're going through," Roz said. "We're here to help you. You'll probably test negative, anyway," she added, hoping to inject an upbeat note.

"You're the one who said 'nine-to-one in favor of adultery' and you were right."

"Will you please drop that?" Roz said, anger getting the better of her. "You asked me a question once and I innocently answered it."

Juan went right on: "If you're prepared to wager nine-to-one odds on a negative antibody test, I'd suggest you save your money, since you could lose it. Now, am I going to move this sofa with or without you two on it?"

Irv stood up, revealing boxer shorts hanging out below bluejean cutoffs. "I'm sorry, Juan." Then turning to Roz, "Let's move this sofa and get the hell to bed."

"No need to get snippy." She anticipated an apologetic kiss from Irv, but got none. This was the first note of discord between them in months. Evidently she'd pushed a little too much with Juan, who was now helping Irv move the sofa back to its place.

"Excuse me, Juan, if I said anything wrong." Roz tried to get him to meet her eyes. "I didn't mean to push or pry. We just wanted to talk. We're your family."

He acknowledged her words, as if accepting the apology. "Good night, lovebirds," he said, and pulled the bedroom door shut behind him.

72

When Cissy was a sophomore in high school, her biology lab partner pressed his groin against her. She reported the incident to a guidance counselor, who informed the Assistant Principal, who told her that as a developing young woman she should dress more conservatively and perhaps these things wouldn't happen. When at eighteen, she admitted her virginity to her twenty-year-old sister, the response was, "Get with it. No wonder you're not popular." Three years later she had finally "gotten with it," suffered a pregnancy scare and, in a weak moment, confided in her mother. Result: She was interrogated, lectured and compared unfavorably to her trouble-free sister.

On the current visit home, Cissy wasn't telling anyone anything.

In the last two weeks she'd developed the nervous reflex of jerking her head to look whenever she sensed anyone approaching from behind. Jeb pinpointed the assault as the cause. In California, her parents noticed it too.

"What's gotten into her?" Ruth Pankhurst said to her husband, as if Cissy weren't present. She and Jeb accompanied her parents, the four of them strolling down a sidewalk between the Italian restaurant where they had dined and their car. "You'd think the Night Stalker was lurking around every corner."

"That's nothing to laugh about," Cissy said.

"The next thing you know, she'll develop a nervous tic," her mother went on, as if Cissy were endlessly troublesome. "Is she still so jittery, Jeb?"

"It's that job that does it to her," said Donald Pankhurst. "Working with all those university kooks could make anyone neurotic. I told her years ago she should have studied dental hygiene."

"At least she's finally earning money, Donald."

Her father changed the subject: "Women who don't get married develop odd quirks. Reminds me of an old gal I had for Advanced Calculus…"

Cissy broke in: "Please, Dad. That story's insulting to women."

"She goes to Wisconsin, of all places, and now she's a women's libber!"

"There! She did it again!" Ruth Pankhurst wailed as Cissy threw her head over her shoulder.

"So when are you going to marry Cicely, Jeb?" her father joked.

"Don't start. Please, Donald. If they don't want to get married, that's their business."

Her older sister had overcompensated for her in the marriage realm: She had divorced husband number three, given birth to child number four and was now living with a vasectomized hardware dealer in Montebello. "When we start earning more money, we'll probably get married, Mom."

"Better marry her soon, Jeb," said Cissy's father. "Before you know it, she'll be over the hill and no one else will have her. Ruth, how old is Cicely now?"

They cut their stay with her parents three days short.

Back in Madison, Cissy found a note at home from Davidine, asking her to contact her as soon as possible. She set up an appointment for the following afternoon.

The seventh-floor view from the Dean's office revealed sailboats on Lake Mendota, visible between the Union and the Red Gym. Cissy hadn't sailed in years. She looked at Mendota again —not the Pacific, but navigable — while the dean finished a telephone call.

After hanging up, Davidine brimmed over with amenities, motherliness and the extra ounce of special attention she'd always shown her, then switched to a more serious vein: "Let me update you on what's happened. Sumner has decided to take early retirement at the end of next Spring

Semeseter and has resigned as chair. Vance is serving as acting chair until a new one can be elected next spring. And Sumner's getting counseling as well as attending Alcoholics Anonymous.

"I know what a trial the last month has been for you. I want to let you know the deep personal regret this incident has caused me. I'm truly sorry for the pain you've had to go through."

Cissy shook her head in acknowledgement. It grieved her to think that Davidine too had suffered over this. She wondered if new strands of iron grey in the dean's hair were the visual proof of her stress.

"I hope that you won't need to take any official action in this matter, Cissy." The comment caught her off guard. We're doing what we can to insure such a thing won't happen again. But if you feel you do need to..."

Cissy summoned up a smile, as if obliged to indicate that all was well, that of course she wouldn't file a complaint, that the account of Sumner's rehabilitative endeavors had placated her.

"Let me know if you decide anything, Cissy. I'd rather not have to learn about it through other channels."

"Of course." At least Davidine hadn't asked her about her final grades.

News of her return spread like a Wisconsin winter cold. Ginger called first. She had a grant to go to Europe for the summer, was leaving for Rome in a week and expected to get two or three articles out of her trip. Now that her job was secure for three years, Cissy knew that she herself had no excuse not to be publishing. The conversation began to depress her. Ginger then turned it to Sumner and asked, point-blank, "What are you going to do?"

She recounted her meeting with Davidine. "Since he's getting counseling and will be retiring, I don't know what's to gain by pursuing a complaint."

"Counseling!" Ginger said with scorn. "What the hell is that supposed to accomplish? Don't fool yourself, Cis. He feels you up, or worse, and, as rehabilitation he goes off to see some old fart and the two agree as to how men have these lapses, Sumner says he won't do it again, and they pronounce him cured."

"Hmmm." Cissy could have sworn she was talking to Roz.

"Look, Cis. I know that the men in the department, except Evan, think of me as a sex object. And I'm not saying that this doesn't have its little advantages at times. But the day one of them lays a hand on me..."

"Though Sumner will be retiring in a year, the rest of them will still be around. If I file a complaint, they're not going to like it and not going to forget."

"Precisely why you should file it," Ginger answered breezily. "If a little counseling is all Sumner's got to go through, every other male professor in the university will think he can get away with it too, and then it will happen to another one of us."

"You've got a point," Cissy said, lacking particular conviction.

"You do what you think is right. I'll shower you with postcards and look forward to seeing you when I'm back. Hang in there, hon."

The next morning a call from Vonda Isaacson floored her. Both Vonda and Sumner were very sorry for what had happened. Vonda too had suffered trauma in her day and knew what it was like. No woman deserved to be treated like Cissy had; she inferred that Vonda knew firsthand. Then her tone turned strangely thankful: If what had happened, hadn't, Sumner wouldn't have gotten the treatment he needed. Vonda offered to do anything she could to help. Cissy thought of answering, "Buy him a one-way ticket to Mongolia."

"I do hope you won't find it necessary to file a complaint or press charges," Vonda said in a postscript.

Cissy hung up, a little dumbfounded, and tried to analyze the call. Why should she file a sexual harassment complaint if Sumner was actually getting better? Vonda must have had a hard enough life with him and it sounded as though it was starting to improve.

But, then again, she understood Ginger's point, as well as Davidine's position. And both the negative and positive implications regarding her work environment.

After dinner, Roz called and asked if she could stop down to chat. Jeb unplugged the television, carted it to the bedroom and shut himself in to watch a baseball game. Cissy put on water to make a fresh pot of spearmint tea.

She offered her best wishes on Roz's upcoming marriage, but Roz hadn't come for small talk. She pointedly asked what she planned to do in the "aftermath." Cissy related her recent conversations. Willing to hear another informed opinion, she asked Roz for hers.

Roz warmed promptly to the topic, mincing no words: "It sounds almost as if you're already falling prey to the 'victim syndrome.' 'It was my fault this happened.' Bullshit. You deserve punitive damages for the physical and emotional pain he's caused you. They should lock him up or at least put him to work like they do with the teenage vandals cleaning up litter along the highways."

Cissy chuckled, conjuring up a picture of Sumner: "I can just see him in the Museum Studies office, wearing a little blue apron, watering plants and making coffee."

"Hardly what I had in mind." Roz's tone went icy: "I'd have him chained to Abe Lincoln's lap in front of Bascom Hall, flog him, hog-tie him and roll him down the hill. Then let him spend the first three years of his retirement cleaning the university's toilets.

"Retirement isn't the issue or the solution here. And so what if it was only fourth-degree sexual assault? If he'd cut you, it wouldn't matter whether you needed two stitches or twenty, you'd press charges, right?"

"Right."

"There you have it. And don't worry about Vonda. The more he's humiliated, the more he'll shape up and treat her better. She just wants to avoid publicity, but knows he's got it coming. And don't think he didn't put her up to that call. Hell, he was probably right there dangling his weaponry in her face as some sort of sick threat!"

Cissy made a feeble protest: "He's supposed to be getting better."

"Wait until you hear that from an unbiased source, then believe it. Look, filing a sexual harassment complaint isn't that complicated. I'll go along and help you. It'll be a snap."

"Thanks for helping me sort this out, Roz. I just have to think a little more on my own. I'll let you know."

"Just don't wimp out, Cissy, if you can help it. I know it's not easy." Roz stood up and offered her parting words: "We sisters have to be strong."

"So what are you going to do, babe?" Jeb asked before they went to bed.

"I'm not sure yet."

"Well, just don't be a wimp about it. Do something."

Jeb's tone struck her as flippant. Suddenly she had to hold back tears. Was she really a wimp? If two people thought so, maybe she was.

"I'm a Libra," she said in her defense. "I have to weigh all sides before I make up my mind."

"If you do that, it'll be Christmas first."

Cissy's hurt turned to anger. Anger at Jeb's incomprehension, at his lighthearted treatment of it all.

"Just decide!" He stretched out on the bed with a *Sports Illustrated.* "Whatever you do, I'll support you." His nose remained in the magazine as he spoke.

"I see this isn't even important enough to command your full attention. Roz is giving me more support in this than you are!" She challenged him with her stare.

"I can't believe this conversation!" He slid under the sheet and covered his head with it.

Cissy climbed into bed. The assault, she realized, was beginning to have an impact on her relationship. The next thing she knew, Jeb would be holding her responsible.

Did she believe this, even remotely? Was she maybe the one who needed counseling?

She turned out the bedside light, snuggled up to Jeb. He remained wooden, apparently dozing and without cares. She gave a snort at his peaceful sleep.

She'd always known that women were disadvantaged, but had never fully felt it until now. She could learn a lot from her assault and from Roz. She rolled away from Jeb and tried to fall asleep without depending on the security of his body.

73

Erva Mae scowled at the walls of Roxanne's office at Womynspace. Framed portraits of feminists adorned them. She recognized Susan B. Anthony, Belva Lockwood, Lucretia Mott, Simone de Beauvoir and Kate Millett. Although she went in and out of Roxanne's office all day long, she rarely remained there long enough to give it her full scrutiny. It was rather larger and plusher than her own, she again noticed with envy.

Roxanne breezed back in and sat down next to her. The two of them had the task of tallying the points of the seventeen applicants who had solicited the half-time Information Desk position. Points were awarded in three areas: job experience, involvement in the women's community and Affirmative Action. After the points were added up, the Board of Directors would vote on the highest three.

Womynspace had its own Affirmative Action point scale. All women received one point for their gender. Heterosexual mothers got two. Lesbians started with two, while lesbian mothers got three. Women of color started with three, then could earn points for lesbianism and motherhood. Differently abled women started with four and garnered bonuses for lesbianism, motherhood and color. And so on.

Erva Mae counted up Affirmative Action points, which Roxanne then added to the other categories and came up with grand totals. "Hayes, three," Erva Mae began.

"Hayes. Total: ten," Roxanne spat out efficiently.

Erva Mae looked back down at her own list and jotted down the total for verification. "Hankins, one."

"Hankins. Total: eleven."

"Rainmaker, four."

"Rainmaker. Total: fifteen."

"Yarmolinsky, two."

"Yarmolinsky. Total: two."

"Goldwomyn, one."

"Goldwomyn. Total: fifteen." Roxanne raised her glasses from their chain and slid them onto her nose. "Wait a minute!" She peered close up at the totals and took the Affirmative Action sheet from Erva Mae. "There's got to be a mistake here."

"Let me see." Erva Mae stole both parts of Roz's application back away from her. "One plus seven plus seven is fifteen. Your math is fine, Rox."

"I know my math is fine. I'm talking about the AA points. Roz forgot to mark 'lesbian.' So we'll give her a point. Sixteen for Goldwomyn."

"I don't know, Rox." Erva Mae's tone was doubting. "She didn't mark it. I think we need to go by the book."

Roxanne grabbed Roz's application out from under Erva Mae's nose and leaned back in her own chair. "You're right. She didn't mark it."

"You could have believed me," Erva Mae snipped, stroking her hair and stuffing it behind her ears.

"I assume it's an oversight. The least we can do is call her to make sure she's still one of us."

"You call, then." Erva Mae thrust the telephone at her lover and re-cited the East Wilson Street phone number.

Unexpectedly, Roxanne took her up on it and dialed. Erva Mae heard the rings: two, three, four. Part of her hoped Roz wouldn't be home; the other part wanted to hear her have to answer the question. She had no doubt that Roz had made an error. But it was her error, after all.

"No answer."

Erva Mae found the telephone shoved in front of her and set it down with an intentional clatter. "No point then."

Roxanne leaned away, observing her at greater distance. "I don't know what gets into you sometimes."

"Into me?" Erva Mae feigned incomprehension. "I'm just trying to insure that the selection process is fair."

"Yes. To everyone but Roz, it seems."

"How can you say that?"

"You know as well as I that I could have given Roz the expanded hours without even announcing the job. It was only because of you and the board members you stirred up that I even advertised it."

Roxanne's use of the first-person singular rankled her, reminding her who wielded more power. She fingered her hair and untangled a knot, as she thought up a response. "I thought we owed it to women of color to open the search. After all, Roz is a mere two-point minority at best. That's nothing when you line her up against women of color and others. Womynspace needs these women if we're going to achieve an equitable feminist society." She donned a complacent smile.

"Don't forget that your own affirmative action quotient is a mere two and one-eighth."

"I'm more of a lesbian than Roz ever was." Erva Mae's voice came out petulant.

"Having known you both intimately, I won't dispute that. So calm down, and let's stop digressing. I dare say Roz will figure among the top three, so the disputed point won't make any difference. OK?"

Erva Mae wrinkled up her nose and bit her tongue, finding no response. Roxanne had verbally bested her once again. "By the way, Rox..." She took in the office with a sweeping glance. "Don't you think it's about time you put some women of color up on your walls?" Erva Mae herself was an octoroon, and before coming to Madison, had been part of the Black Students Association at the University of Cincinnati until a newcomer had denounced her as "whitey." She'd felt the sting of racism firsthand.

"Let's see..." Roxanne rifled through her wallet and pulled out a photo of Erva Mae in a bathing suit. She rolled a piece of scotch tape onto the back and slapped it on the wall above her desk. "There. That should do nicely."

"Rox! You know what I mean! How'd you get that anyway?"

"You don't remember? When I went on vacation in May, you gave it to me so I could..."

"I remember, damn it! I meant a real woman of color."

"Don't forget that that eighth of a point got you the job as Assistant Director."

"Thank Goddess. I certainly wouldn't have stooped to kissing your white, racist ass to get it."

"Fuck off, darling. And, if it makes you feel better, my 'white, racist ass' has just ordered Rosa Parks, Sojourner Truth and Lolita Lebrón to fill up the space in here. Now read me the next score."

Irv had gone to a fundraiser for "Men Stopping Rape" at Ho Chi Minh's, leaving Roz alone at the Willy Street house. She'd been moving in her possessions little by little, beginning with clothes, books and magazines. Stretched out on the sofa, a blanket protecting her from the exposed springs, she sifted through a stack of periodicals, some hers, others Juan's or Irv's. She came up with *Mother Jones, The Progressive* and *off our backs* and was skimming the latter when the telephone rang.

"Roz? Hi. This is Marijo Pisciotta. This number you're at is none too easy to find."

"Marijo?" Roz echoed. Why on earth was Marijo Pisciotta calling? Certainly not to tell her that she was hard to reach. And she'd evidently gone to a lot of trouble — if not downright sleuthing — to find her.

"How've you been, Roz?"

"Fine, Marijo." The two were acquaintances who lived in the same neighborhood and had been involved in some of the same women's groups. Beyond a hello, they hadn't talked in two or three years.

"Roz, you know I'm the single mother representative on the Womynspace Executive Committee. The board met tonight and I'm calling unofficially to tell you what went on."

She had remained hopeful even when they'd announced an official search for the part-time position. But from her intuition about this call, she was fast becoming cynical about what had happened.

"Your application caused a little stir, Roz. Roxanne and Erva Mae were supposed to bring the three top applications to the full committee. Personally, I would have just given you the expanded shift and been done with it. But I happen to know that Erva Mae called all the women of color on the committee and promised each of them that if they opened a search, at least a three-point minority would get the job."

"So did I get it?"

"Then tonight," she recommenced, pausing to blow a series of nervous, short breaths over the wires, "the top two turned out to be an African-American and a Latina. Right behind them, you were tied with a Native American and a Hmong."

"'Among?'"

"A Hmong woman. And right in front of the full board Erva Mae and Roxanne got into an argument as to whether or not you were a lesbian, since you needed another affirmative action point to make the top three. In short, they voted on the top two and the Latina won."

"I see."

"I'm sorry, Roz. It sounds like Erva Mae's got it in for you."

"We'd been going together and broke up. And she's the vengeful type."

"Was your not marking the box for the extra minority point on purpose?" Suddenly apologetic, Marijo added, "I'm sorry. That's none of my business."

Roz decided to make another leap out of her closet door. In three weeks, there'd be no keeping the secret. "It wasn't an accident."

"To tell you the truth, I sort of did wonder. I'd seen you around the neighborhood with Irv with the funny last name."

"I shouldn't have expected to get the hours."

"Don't let it get you down, Roz. Everyone at Womynspace appreciates your work. It must have taken ovaries to come out, if that's what it was, on a job application."

"Thanks for letting me know. And, by the way, I'm marrying Irv with the funny last name in three weeks."

"Really, Roz? That's... great. And, by the way, I never had this conversation with you."

A few weeks ago, she hadn't even been fazed by the cutting back of her hours at the Co-op. But as the ecstasy of premarital bliss had begun to ebb ever so slightly, she'd decided not to let herself turn into a love-dulled zombie. She needed to remain an independent woman and for that she needed money.

She heard steps on the stairs, likely Irv's. Instead Juan bounded into the living room. Astonishingly, he was bright-eyed, not carrying Proust and didn't rush into his bedroom.

"Roz!" he greeted expansively and hugged her.

"What's gotten into you?" She stepped away and scratched her elbow. "Either you've taken mood-altering drugs, just had your best lay in a decade or somehow got a new lease on life."

"The latter, Roz."

"You gonna explain?"

"My antibody test came back negative today. So now you and Irv and I can have a baby!"

Roz took a second to process the information. "That's wonderful, Juan! I mean about your antibody test. Not to mention the baby." She went up to him, embraced him and put a quick kiss on his lips. "I just had a call from Womynspace and found out I didn't get the extra hours. I was trying not to get too bummed out."

"Forget them, Roz. We'll be one big, happy family right here, raising little Barmejian-Goldpersons..."

"Singular, Juan."

"We'll be our own little, happy commune, just like in the sixties, except for the riots."

Roz's mood did an about-face. She felt her spirits rise, her future about to fall into place. "Sounds super, Juan-Boy." Tempted to get up and hug him again, she refrained, deciding to save it for Irv.

As if right on schedule, a knock came at the door. She jumped up. "Irv probably forgot his keys."

She pulled the door open. A person with a partially shaved head topped off with a shock of turquoise stood in front of her, smiling uncertainly. Just as the identity dawned on her, Juan exclaimed from behind: "Pep! What are you doing back? Uh, come in. Now, let me see. Roz," he went on unsteadily, "This is Dyspepsia. Or Pep. Pep, this is Roz."

The visitor offered her hand and said, "Pep." Roz took her hand, which felt warm and sweaty.

"Well, Pep, why don't you have a seat? You too, Roz," he added meaningfully. "Irv's out for a little while, but should be back any minute. This will be a surprise, to say the least. How about a drink, everyone? Oh, that's right, you don't drink, Pep. So we won't have a drink, then. We could share a joint. Or we can just chat. Can't we, Roz?"

"Juan, pour me a double."

"A double what?"

"A double anything."

As Juan went into the kitchen, Roz remained alone with Dyspepsia, wondering how Irv could have fallen in love with such a creature. Then again, tastes were unaccountable; she herself had once fallen in love with Erva Mae. Pep smiled alternately, stared blankly. Someone had to break the ice. Roz had little idea what to say; she doubted that Pep's famed monosyllables would do the trick.

She grabbed at filaments of opening lines. "So, Pep. You've come back to visit Madison?"

Pep shook her head no. "Irv," she said with a broad smile.

74

Lou stepped out of the air-conditioned office building on the Capitol Square and the heavy Wisconsin humidity enveloped her. A string of buses approached and she quickened her pace, hoping to avoid the "bus drought" before the next wave came. She sped up more, seeing herself in reach, and began to scurry around a huddle of young women who stood talking, blocking the pedestrian crossing. One of them turned around blithely and walked into her.

"Excuse me," Lou said, recognizing the sandal-dropper of Intro to Museums, who neither recognized Lou nor excused herself.

Lou saw the light change to red, and all three buses passed by.

When the light turned green, she began to plod across the street. Already awash in perspiration, she looked straight ahead and saw... Verla.

"Lou! How great to see you!" Verla lunged at her with a hug, melting away any doubts Lou had about hard feelings from last month.

"Let's move out of the street before the light changes."

"I was afraid I'd never see you again. Just because you won't be living at the Trusters is no reason for us to lose touch." They stepped onto the wheelchair-accessible curb and sidewalk.

"Of course not."

Verla asked about her living situation, summer job and fall plans, and kept repeating that they should get together. Lou remembered her meals and devotional brunches at the Truster House, hospitality never returned. Tomorrow was Friday, the night the Trusters had to eat out on their own. "Verla, would you like to come over for dinner tomorrow night?" One of her dinners would equal at least three of the Trusters'.

"Why, thanks. That'd be marvelous, Lou!"

Her last job had ended and no new call came for Friday. Early that morning Lou made purchases equaling five hours of hard-earned salary. She had grown up skilled in pinching pennies, but now had to master the art of spending them.

As she separated and washed lettuce leaves in the late afternoon, Beth arrived home. Of all nights, Beth didn't have to work tonight. She could hardly make dinner for Verla and not Beth. Last night she'd lectured her on endangering Verla's sobriety and had mandated an alcohol-free evening.

Beth pulled a bottle of wine out of a sack and uncorked it. "Hey, kid, don't worry. Just my afternoon cocktail hour. By the way, do born-agains take communion?"

"What?"

"Just thinkin', kid. If Verla can't drink, how does she take communion? God-eaters, I'll never understand 'em.

Lou whirled around, a half-peeled carrot in her hand. "What on earth..?"

"God-eaters. People who eat their deity. You know. Wafer and wine. Communion. You eat Jesus' body and drink his blood, don'tcha? I know a thing or two about religion."

Lou had never considered communion in such earthy terms. "In my church, we drank grape juice."

Beth swilled her wine and took a second bottle of Burgundy out of its sack. She held it aloft, then pointed the bottleneck toward her mouth. "Verla!" she commanded in a baritone. "This is Jesus speakin'. This bottle is fulla my blood. So drink thee up! Swish this wine down thy gullet!" She touched the cork to her lips and made glug-glug noises.

Lou's reproachful stare dissolved in the face of Beth's antics. "Don't drop it," she said, trusting Beth would get the mischief out of her system now.

Beth put down the bottle. "I'll be on good behavior tonight."

"You promised." Lou returned to chopping celery at the cutting board and hoped Beth's word was good.

Verla arrived promptly at six, in a light blue pantsuit color-coordinated with a handbag. Lou immediately noticed something different and after a minute put her finger on it: Verla was wearing not only lipstick, but purplish eye shadow. She reintroduced her to Beth.

"Verla," Beth gushed, "could we interest you in some grape juice? Or iced tea, perhaps?"

"Either would be fine. Oh, what a cute kitchen! And pretty little curtains!"

"Thank you, Verla," Beth effused while pouring three glasses of iced tea. "Why don't we retire to the living room until dinner's ready?"

Lou wondered if Beth was enacting a parody of Verla's social graces. Or was this her idea of how one treated the pious? Beth escorted Verla into the living room. Lou stuck her head into the oven for a peek at the pot roast and followed on their heels.

Verla had lowered herself into a beanbag chair. Beth sat on the edge of the sofa they'd bought at a garage sale. Lou took a folding chair that read "Skramm Funeral Home" on the back.

"Cheers!" Verla lifted her glass.

"L'chaim !"

Lou held her glass and said nothing.

"Such a nice place you two have. Are you staying here in the fall? What are you doing this summer, Beth?"

"I'm a busperson and activist at a neighborhood restaurant with close ties to Nicaragua."

Lou coughed loudly as Verla leaned forward, all curiosity. "What's it called?"

"Ho Chi Minh's. You see, it was founded as a result of the antiwar protests..." Beth launched into a mini-lecture on capitalism, socialism and Third-World oppression.

"Lou, do you by chance have any wine?" Verla asked. "I know it's improper for a guest to be asking, but..."

"Sure, we got wine," Beth volunteered. "And vodka, gin, tequila..."

"Beth!" Lou shot her a murderous glare. "Verla, I thought..."

"I know what you're thinking, Lou," Verla said, showering persuasion. "Trusters aren't supposed to drink. Especially me. But tonight won't hurt. They'll never know."

Lou was debating this, when Beth raised her voice: "Lou, Verla would like some wine. Are you going to get it or should I?"

Seething underneath, Lou put on a charming-hostess face, got up and returned to the kitchen. "Hey kid, pour a glass for me too!" came Beth's voice from the living room. Distrustful, Lou half-filled two glasses, then added ice and water. The pot roast required a few more minutes. She'd serve it quickly before the wine could take effect.

"...and I'm taking an advanced course in organ," Verla was saying as Lou delivered the wine. "And private lessons in beginning oboe. Thank you, Lou."

Beth regarded the ice cubes scornfully, got up and left with her glass. Lou took the opportunity to ask about the Trusters.

"Oh, them," Verla said, as if dredging up ancient artifacts. "Let's see… Felix and Tinda have both moved into the House and are happy as can be. Bruce will be living with us in the fall. Bob will be graduating at the end of summer school."

Beth popped back into the room, the wine bottle in one hand, a new glass for herself in the other. To Lou's shock, she saw that Verla's was empty and she stuck it out for Beth to refill it.

"So how are the Trusters? Funny, how I thought you guys were the Klan," Beth said as she poured.

In a swallow Verla chugged down half the glass. "Oh, the poor, old, loving Trusters," she mused in an uncharacteristic tone, not getting or passing over the Klan remark. "The Trusters are fine. Fine for some people. But Lou, you may have made the right choice." She polished off the rest of her wine.

What dark side of Verla was this? The effect of alcohol on her Pollyanna personality? The wine had certainly gone to her head. Lou excused herself and hurried off to the kitchen. She removed the pot roast, with its carrots and potatoes, and set everything on the table, hoping dinner would soak up some of the wine.

At dinner Verla showed an appetite she never could have indulged at the Trusters. Lou pushed the food and sent Beth visual scoldings when she poured out more wine. For dessert Lou forced pie and ice cream on them. Over coffee they sized up courses, departments, professors and teaching assistants. Lou felt in control, her dinner party back on course.

She was about to suggest they sit on the screened front porch, when Beth said, "Why don't we adjourn to the parlor for after-dinner drinks?"

What parlor and what after-dinner drinks? Lou smelled trouble again.

"What perfect hostesses you are! After-dinner liqueurs!" cooed Verla.

As if this were common practice at the Trusters, thought Lou, mildly incensed at both of them. "Do you really think..?" she began, but Beth had already pulled out a tall bottle of Galliano from a floor-level cupboard and was filling three large glasses of it.

"Don't worry about me. I'll be fine, Lou."

Lou had the distinct feeling that the two were in some sort of conspiracy against her.

In the living room, Verla retook the beanbag chair and Lou quickly occupied the closest seat, as though better to control her consumption. Beth moved the Skramm Funeral Home chair up next to them.

Verla raised her glass in another toast. "To freedom!" Before Lou and Beth could echo the toast, she continued, "You two make such a pretty picture!"

"But we're not..." Lou protested upon catching Verla's implication, but didn't know quite how to phrase it. To her shock, she saw that Verla had nearly polished off the generous dose of Galliano. "Well, summer's here officially," she said.

"What a serendipitous evening!" Verla slapped her thighs.

"Let's hope it doesn't rain this weekend," Lou went on, dogged, and saw that Beth was freshening Verla's Galliano. "Verla, are you sure you're going to be all right?"

"You can relax, Lou. I'm fine. I'm having a fantastic evening!"

"I just wanted to make sure you'll be able to get home safely," she said, envisioning them depositing a drunken Verla in a cab, address pinned to her.

"Verla can take care of herself," Beth said, lighting a cigarette. When Lou heard Verla ask Beth for one, she feared that Verla's sobriety was a lost cause.

Lou took her first sip of Galliano; it burned her throat. She excused herself to go to the bathroom. Inside its small confines, she paced. The evening was getting beyond her control. She flushed the toilet for pretense and washed her hands. As she passed through the kitchen, she refilled Verla's coffee cup.

As she brought it in, Verla announced, "Do you know what? I think I'm having a relapse!"

Lou shoved the coffee at her. Verla now lay back in the beanbag chair, her empurpled eyes roving from the ceiling to Beth. The situation was stranger than she thought. Lou rushed back to the kitchen and returned with coffee for Beth, who ignored it.

"I think I'm soused!" Verla proclaimed without noticeable repentance. "It does happen, you know, even to Trusters. This is just the kind of evening I needed."

"But you don't want to get sick, Verla," Lou said, then added firmly, "And neither do you, Beth."

Verla faced both of them, glassy-eyed. "I got bombed once last fall, staggered into the House and vomited. Lee and Sara slapped social probation on me for forty fucking days!"

Lou gasped, startled at Verla's language.

"Forty fuckin' days!?" Beth gasped, startled, apparently, at the punishment.

"Forty fucking days!" Verla affirmed, and let out a soprano belch, at which Beth giggled.

"I suppose I deserved it." Verla's cigarette burned, unsmoked, in an ashtray. She reached for her glass of Galliano and nearly missed it. Huffily,

Lou moved away her coffee cup before she could topple it too.

Depositing the coffee back in the kitchen, she began to count to 100 in German to calm down. She tried to convince herself she had no responsibility for Verla's or Beth's behavior. By the time she got to *dreissig,* she decided to return to the living room to monitor the situation. She saw that Verla's shoes had been removed. Her feet now rested on Beth's... crotch. Was this what it seemed to be? She'd never imagined this.

"Oooh, that feels good!" Verla moaned, then looked up, as if not expecting to see Lou.

"Verla has sore feet and wants a massage," Beth stated, then turned her attention back to Verla's feet.

"I think I'm going to have another kind of relapse too." Verla seemed resigned to an inexorable sequence of events.

As Lou dashed out of the room, she heard Verla hee-haw: "Even Trusters have fun, Lou!"

In the kitchen, she marshalled her remaining wits. The evidence of the dinner party that lay on the table certainly didn't bespeak the evening's conclusion. She had to escape, relinquish all control.

She tiptoed stealthily through the livingroom and saw that Beth's feet were now nuzzling Verla's... crotch. She averted her glance; thought of commenting on how a nice basin of cold water might be just what their feet needed.

Instead she stole down the stairs and out into the warm June night.

75

C issy had followed Roz's advice, filed a sexual harassment complaint and, hesitantly, informed Davidine. After two weeks she had no news.

"Look, babe." Jeb turned over a shovelful of dirt to plant a clump of spearmint they'd bought at the Farmers Market on the Square. "No news is probably good news. Should mean there's no problem."

Cissy sat on a back porch step. "I should've followed my own instincts and taken Davidine's advice."

Jeb looked up at her as she watched him work. "Sounds like a contradiction to me."

"Or at least followed my own instincts then."

"Which were..?"

The mint secured in the soil, he reached for a six-pack of parsley. He again directed his glance to Cissy, pressing the point. She was open-mouthed.

"Face it, Cissy. As we both know, you see so many sides of an issue and understand so many points of view, that it screws up your ability to make a decision. In this case, everyone had a bias but you. The strongest of them was bound to sway you and that was Roz, right?" Jeb palmed the dirt flat around a small parsley plant. His back ached from bending over. He straightened his spine and looked down. Grass stains streaked his knees.

"I've gone and stirred up a hornet's nest."

Jeb hadn't expected to hear this again, nor the tone of distress in her voice. "Isaacson's the one who poked his pecker into the nest. And it deserved to be stung." He stretched, tilting his head skyward. Low clouds hemmed in the day.

"But if I hadn't filed the complaint, that would mean I tolerated his behavior, which would only make things worse for others." Cissy faced Jeb, her jaw firm, and clasped her hands. "So I have to stand up for myself and fight."

"That's better." Jeb looked down at his exposed legs, bony and white.

"*If* I stay here," she added.

"Please, not that again."

"Oh, no."

"Don't get upset, babe," Jeb said, abandoning the parsley for Cissy.

"I'm premenstrual right now," she sniffled. "When I have PMS, anything can make me cry."

"Let's forget about all of this. We should get out of town, lie on a beach somewhere and get ourselves a good precancerous tan."

"I have to finish writing my article."

Jeb sat down next to her, compared their equally white legs. "I thought you hadn't started it."

"That's the point: I haven't. And I have to begin class preparations for fall."

"It's only July first. There's lots of time. We'll take off for a three-day weekend and explore Wisconsin, Chicago, wherever you want."

Cissy broke into a feeble smile. A ray of sun slanted down on them between the clouds. Jeb shielded his eyes and put his hand on her knee.

They opted for Wisconsin, going first to Milwaukee, where he persuaded her to go to a Brewers game in exchange for accompanying her to museums. From there they traveled north, then zigzagged across the center of the state, driving via back roads through towns and villages with odd names. Cissy studied a Wisconsin map, highlighted their trajectory with a yellow marker and categorized the state's quirky place names.

Beginning with the "cute" category, she read the names to him: "Chili, Lily, Phlox, Waldo, Avalanche, Hustler and Embarrass."

Then came the "sauk" series, which combined and led to confusion with the "prairie" names: "Sauk City, Saukville, Pensaukee, Sauk Prairie, Prairie du Sac, Prairie du Chien and Sun Prairie." She followed with the "wauk" se ries: "Oconomowoc, Manitowoc, Packwaukee, Pewaukee, Waukesha and Milwaukee."

"'M'waukee' is how they say it there," Jeb corrected. "Two syllables."

"Tackle these then, if you're so smart: Weyauwega, Wyocena, Necedah, Mukwonago, Mondovi and Minocqua."

Back in Madison, Jeb helped her design a routine to minimize anxiety and maximize productivity. Mornings were to relax, meditate and exercise. Afternoons she would spend writing her article and, commencing in mid-July, begin fall class preparations. Evenings were for mutual relaxation and exploration of Madison.

The first three nights they took in a Madison Muskies baseball game, an outdoor movie on the Union Terrace and a Concert on the Square, where concertgoers picnicked and drank beer on the Capitol lawn while listening to music ranging from Beethoven to The Beatles.

Jeb saw no outward manifestation of her anxiety, but often sensed she was merely going through the motions of relaxation. Smiling at his side, she seemed distant, encased in her own worry. Her period came and her sexual desire went. He attributed her state to the assault and became as anxious as she that the complaint be resolved.

He lay on the front porch sofa, reading a popular paperback of baseball anecdotes. The night before Cissy had tossed, turned and talked in her sleep a large part of the night, keeping him awake. This morning they'd argued when he complained of his poor sleep. She'd called him "unsympathetic" and the argument ended up dwelling on their dwindling checking account balance. Fed up, he'd taken off on a five-mile run. When he returned, he found a matter-of-fact note from her: "Jogged to art library."

The temperature soared to ninety-five; the humidity was its nasty high self. Although usually less hot than southern California, Wisconsin's weather exceeded it in discomfort.

Lack of sleep and the morning's exertion left him pleasantly exhausted and he felt punch-drunk in the heat. Ready to slip into oblivion, losing his place on the page, he'd sometimes jolt himself awake, other times not.

"Hi."

Jeb heard the voice, opened his eyes. Luscious lips, black eyes and turquoise hair appeared above him. Reality or a dream? He forced his eyes open, craned his neck backward and saw very tangible cleavage.

"Pep," he said, blinking his eyes.

"Jeb." Her mouth traced a serpentine smile above him. "M'back."

"So I've heard." He'd also heard that her untimely arrival had flustered Juan, shaken Roz and panicked Irv. Then they'd hit on the ingenious solution of shunting her to Roz's apartment, where she was peacefully installed, at least for the moment. She was also taking a course at Womynspace in, of all things, midwifery.

"Good to see you." He was now fully awake. "So you're passing through or staying a while in Madison?"

"Stay," she said, immobile, still offering him the same tantalizing view.

"I heard you're taking a course in midwifery. Never would've guessed. What for?"

"Kids."

"So what happened in San Francisco? What about your band?"

"Failed," she said, glum.

"Too bad." Jeb warmed up with concern. "What are you going to do here?"

"Band."

"What kind?"

Rolling eyes told him that he'd asked the obvious. "Punk."

"Dumb question." He began to undress her mentally, what little there was to undress above the waist. "How many are in it?"

"Four."

"Sounds good, Pep," His utterances were mechanical, his senses dominated by the sight of her. He let his gaze rove down her face, over her breasts and down her stomach. He had to quell an urge to reach out and cup his hands behind her. "What's its name?"

"Groins."

"The Groins?"

"Yep."

"Interesting." Jeb focused on his own and broke out in a nervous sweat. Transported by the temperature and his physiological reaction to her, he felt himself elevate to an oddly carefree state. "Let's see... You could also call yourselves 'The Crotches.' Or 'Loose Genitals.' What do you think?"

Pep giggled, then said, "Long."

"Name's too long, huh?"

Pep nodded. Jeb saw the familiar intertwined safety pins dangling from one of her earlobes. Her lips, still appealing, had been whitened. Chainlink bracelets jangled on her wrists. A gold cross pointed to her cleavage. As if it needed emphasis.

He spread his legs slightly, the better for his crotch to breathe. Unconsciously he licked his lips. Above him Pep's smile held on. If he grabbed her and pulled her down to him, would she refuse? He needed a cool shower to combat the heat or a cold one to smother his urges. But he was content to lie on the sofa, take in her sensuality and fantasize.

He fixed his glance on her eyes, which met his. Her lips curled into a smile, slight but inviting. He stared harder, let his eyes roam to her breasts and kept them there. Involuntarily, his mouth fell open. "Pep, you shouldn't do this to me."

Her eyes locked his again. Jeb melted, content to flow with his sensual high. Suddenly, her eyes riveted with alarm. "Something wrong, Pep?"

"Yep." She cast her glance toward the street.

Cissy marched up the sidewalk and onto the porch. Her glance went from Jeb's face to Pep's, from his body to hers. She turned on her heels and hurried into the house, slamming the door.

"Uh," Pep emitted, in what could have been a tiny belch or clearing of the throat, then added, "Oh."

"You said it," Jeb sat up, no longer needing a cold shower. "Excuse me."

He loped into the house. Rounding the corner into the kitchen, he found Cissy whimpering, her head over the sink. "Babe, it wasn't what it looked like. Whatever it did look like."

She paid him no heed, cried even louder.

"Really, it wasn't," he pleaded, now in a cold sweat.

Cissy pulled her head out of the sink and straightened her hair, elbowing a dish rack on the counter. "I saw what I saw! If I hadn't shown up, she would have been on top of you in another minute. And you certainly weren't fending her off."

"Babe, I'm sorry."

"Don't try to fool me!"

Jeb saw her face cracked with pain, tears silently streaming down her cheeks. "It wasn't my fault. I swear. I was lying there asleep when Pep came up and we started talking. That was all, babe."

"I don't know which of the two of you revolts me more!"

"We didn't do anything. Really. I was lying there innocently. Call it sexual harassment."

"Sexual harassment!" Cissy shrieked. "Don't make fun of me, Jeb! And don't tell me you're not interested in her!"

He knew he'd said the wrong thing, fumbled through his mind for a response.

"And now you'll probably tell me that if we made love more often, she wouldn't tempt you."

Jeb deemed it prudent not to agree with her under the circumstances. He went over and put his hand on her shoulder.

"Don't touch me!" she wailed. Breaking into loud tears, she ran to the bedroom and closed the door.

Jeb turned the knob, realized she'd pulled the door chain. Inside she continued to cry audibly. He knelt down, spoke through the keyhole. "I said I'm sorry. I didn't mean the 'sexual harassment' remark, babe."

"Don't 'babe' me. Your 'babe' is on the front porch."

76

The skin on Davidine Phipps' forearms bristled with gooseflesh as the air conditioner pumped arctic air into her office. "Swelter outside or freeze inside," she muttered, gazing out the window at Library Mall. She got up and reached for a sweater that served her year-round, sat back down and cuddled into it.

She squinted at the clock. The short hand pointed at two; she had hoped for three. When she relaxed her eyes, the clockface blurred. Behind the clock, the wall held a map of Wisconsin, its counties shaded in various colors. She blinked and the pastels blended. She strained her eyes to verify that Dane County was still pink, lit a cigarette and smoked idly. She watched the smoke rise, amorphous, and float toward the ceiling. Her sister had urged her not to come in today, maintaining that she worked too hard.

A secretary knocked on the door and brought in the campus mail. An envelope from the UW Office of Affirmative Action and Compliance topped the pile. She summarily ripped it open: "After conducting its investigation, our office has determined that sexual harassment did occur in the workplace..."

She dialed the office of the Vice Chancellor, doubting the likelihood of finding him in on a ninety-degree Friday afternoon in July. More likely he'd be at the Blackhawk Country Club. After going through an administrative assistant, and being put on hold, she was greeted by the voice of the Vice Chancellor himself.

"Affirmative Action sent the findings of the sexual harassment complaint today."

"Positive or negative?" The Vice Chancellor yawned into the phone.

"That depends on how you look at it." Davidine chuckled into the receiver; the Vice Chancellor did not chuckle back. Quickly, she went on: "Sexual harassment did occur in the workplace, as alleged, by Sumner Isaacson..."

"Damn. Now we'll have to do something."

"Indeed."

He adopted a sudden tone of severity. "You know how serious this is."

"I certainly do."

"Refresh my memory, if you will. What did Isaacson go and do?" The tone was cranky. "And who was the girl involved?"

"The so-called 'girl,' Cicely Pankhurst, was a Lecturer and in the fall will be on a tenure-track."

"Oh, little by little, it's coming back to me. Yes, it's becoming clearer." She imagined him looking into a crystal ball. "Pinched her tit, I mean breast, didn't he?"

Davidine cleared her throat lengthily. "Yes, that's right. There's a medical report too. She sustained bruises."

"I see. Has anything been done with Isaacson so far?"

"As I believe you know, he's opted for retirement at the end of next Spring Semester." She refrained from calling it a "public service," considering his behavior the past year. "He'll be on leave in the fall and..."

"Is she done filing charges and complaints over this?" he snapped.

"To tell you the truth, I don't know. But my hunch is that she'll stop here."

"Let's hope she does." The Vice Chancellor's irritation was almost palpable. "We can't have these problems being aired on the evening news. But we'll have to release this to the press before they accuse us of trying to cover it up. We've got to stamp out this sexual harassment business! Send Isaacson an official letter of reprimand!"

"Yes."

"And have it placed in all the appropriate files!"

"Of course."

His tone turned worrisome. "Do you think we're doing enough?"

"With his upcoming retirement and in the meantime voluntary counseling — though the university might want to mandate that now — I'd say we're adequately managing."

"That's what I like to hear. By the way, who is Museum Studies' S-H-O?"

"S-H-O?"

"Sexual Harassment Officer."

"Sexual harassment officer?" The question caught her off guard. "Why, I don't know that we have one."

"Well, get one! And see that this sort of thing doesn't happen again! Good day, Davidine."

She let the receiver fall into its cradle. "Bastard." Maybe Ralphetta was right; she should have stayed home.

She inserted a sheet of stationery into the typewriter, wrote "Dear Professor Isaacson" and paused. She had standard form letters for hirings, firings and raises, but none for the case in point. She finished the letter — awkward at best — and would take it home with her and touch it up over the weekend.

She felt tired, longed for a drink. Kept in her cabinet for entertaining occasional visitors, a bottle of Johnny Walker Black beckoned. She dialed the outer office. "Michael, could you bring me in a glass of ice water? I've got a slew of pills to take." It was true. She had her blood pressure pills, among others. "No, never mind. I'll get it myself. Yes, I'm sure. Thank you."

She stood up, sank back into the chair and redialed. "On second thought, Michael, if you could bring it in... I'm not feeling too spunky this afternoon. It must be the heat."

"Or the cold. It's like an igloo in here today."

Under her sweater she felt the gooseflesh raise up again. She wheeled in her chair to the cabinet. The bottle of Scotch was there, as was a small air-line blanket. She abandoned the idea of Scotch for the blanket.

Davidine worked all day Saturday. Sunday morning she got up at seven. By nine she had finished her breakfast and the newspaper and had rewritten the letter of reprimand for the third time.

She felt a wave of sudden pity for Sumner and harked back to happier times. Fleetingly, she recreated the scene where she'd first seduced him. A crooked smile came to her lips, then faded. The reminiscence grieved her. She took a final glance at the letter and showered it with a puff of cigarette smoke. Facing the window, she felt the day's heat and thought of the sundry tasks that awaited her.

Outside she pruned last year's dead growth from the backyard rose bushes. Shortly, she went inside for a glass of ice water.

"Eighty-four and climbing," announced Ralphetta, puttering on the screened-in back porch. A large fan whirred behind her sister, buffeting plastic plant pots.

Sun flooded the rose garden and, soon after, the back porch. Ralphetta retired inside to prepare lunch. Outside Davidine turned to weeding and worked another half hour.

"Eighty-nine in the shade," Ralphetta clucked reproachfully as she set down lunch in the dining nook, then indicated the thermometer outside the window.

"I should be the one telling you."

"Here, have some iced tea."

Davidine drank the tea, then bit into a hard-boiled egg and choked. Ralphetta refilled the tumbler.

They discussed whether or not to go to the Art Fair on the Square. Ralphetta shook her head scoldingly as she eyed the thermometer. "And it's going to get worse."

In the kitchen Davidine rinsed dishes and handed them to Ralphetta, who set them in their proper niches inside the dishwasher. By the time it was filled, the sky was clouding over. "What do you think, Phetta?" she said, nudging her, and pointed at the clouds.

Ralphetta glanced outside. "We could go and hope that the clouds hold, though there's no avoiding the humidity. It's up to you, Davie. Or we can wait and go next year."

"What the hell. Let's go today."

Downtown Ralphetta began to storm the crowd counterclockwise until Davidine turned her around. The sun reemerged promptly. Always prepared, Ralphetta opened up her parasol, snagging passersby.

After two hours, they'd seen almost everything. Ralphetta had bought a painted wooden owl for a cousin's collection. Davidine had admired a piece of stained glass. Under the parasol, Ralphetta's curls drooped from the humidity. Davidine felt drowned in perspiration.

"What about the stained glass?"

"There'll be another fair somewhere, sometime." What with the sun's microwave rays and the saturating humidity, she wasn't about to trudge back to buy it now.

"You never end up buying anything."

"I'll survive without buying it. Let's head home."

Davidine raced the car westward. She pressed hard on the accelerator, trying to make the stoplight at Breese Terrace and University Avenue. Seeing this impossible, she slowed down and a sharp pain rended her chest.

Ralphetta shrieked as a tiny, stertorous moan escaped from her sister. Davidine slumped over the steering wheel.

Ralphetta shrieked again, slid over next to her and aimed her foot hopefully for the brake. The front wheels hit a curb and the engine died. Belatedly determining that the car was stationary, she scrambled out and waved her hands furiously in the middle of the street. As she was blocking traffic, the first car had little choice but to stop.

"Can you take us to University Hospital, sir?" she panted, her curls flattened. "It's an emergency." She pointed with one hand toward the hospital, with the other at Davidine, inert, and, for all she knew, quite dead.

77

T hree things struck Cissy about the wedding reception upstairs: As bride and groom, Irv and Roz wore their normal working-day attire; Pepper Isaacson seemed an exact physical replica of Sumner, a generation younger; and Pep — in revenge? — stole the show with hot pants and a bodice that risked arrest for indecent exposure.

When Pep departed suddenly, her face in tears, Cissy felt a wave of pity. When Jeb departed a minute later, Cissy began to fume in silence while graciously chatting with other guests. When neither one returned, Cissy went to investigate. She found Jeb alone in the downstairs living room.

"Pep and I talked." He brought up the subject before she could. "On the front porch."

"Your walking porno fantasy strikes again."

"She had to talk to someone," he whispered. "She and Juan have never gotten along. Irv was hardly an appropriate candidate for a heart-to-heart. Gil wasn't invited. And you've never taken the time to know her."

Cissy considered this reproach. "What did she need to talk about?"

"How many guesses do you want? She thought she could handle Irv's getting married and coming to the reception, but she couldn't handle it as well as she thought." Jeb's voice dropped a register lower: "She thinks she's unlovable or ugly, so she dresses the way she does to call attention to herself."

"She certainly did that tonight. And now that she's lost Irv, she needs to prove to herself that she can attract a man and she's chosen you?"

"Not so loud, babe. She knows I'm not available. I'm just the only one who'll talk to her."

After Jeb's last brush with Pep, Cissy had slept alone that night and didn't speak to him for a whole day. "How do I know you'll never give in?"

"Because I'm telling you. Anyway, she's been in the bathroom and I think I hear her coming."

Cissy tensed; her throat, coated with mineral water and lime, dried on the spot. Seconds later Pep appeared, tears having erased her mascara, her hand-sequined bodice now approaching decency. Cissy smiled automatically.

Pep flashed her a contrite look and stopped in front of them. "Thanks," she murmured to Jeb, then turned to Cissy and said the same. She walked out the door and up the stairs.

"C'mon, babe. Let's go back up and be civil. No hard feelings?"

Cissy stalled, not wanting to give in too easily, nor to seem unreasonable. "All right. No hard feelings."

"We'll just stick together and avoid Isaacson's kid."

"Pepper? It's not a case of 'Like father, like son.' He's charming. He used to live in the commune with Irv and Roz. And, unless I'm blind, he and Juan have been flirting all night."

Jeb seemed to mull this over, moved next to her and embraced her. Cissy let herself fall into his arms.

After an outing to Spring Green Sunday and Monday, they returned home late and Cissy collapsed into bed, worn-out. Tuesday morning she was vaguely aware of Jeb's getting up and leaving. She half-opened her eyes, murmured good-bye and rolled over.

Dropping back into a light morning sleep, she began to dream. She was enrolled in a university course titled "Beer Drinking 101." "Miss Pankhurst, do you know you're failing?" the instructor, Sumner Isaacson, told her. "You need remedial work. And, it's been discovered that you plagiarized your dissertation." Terror-stricken, Cissy fled, running endlessly toward home. As she headed down the middle of Williamson Street, she met Jeb coming from the opposite direction. "Wrong way, babe," he said. "We're bunking in the campus brewery." "I know. It's part of my remedial work. But I don't want to sleep in a brewery!" Now she jogged with Jeb toward campus. "I'll fight it and I'll win!"

"Cissy, are you there? Cissy?"

With a start she sat up in bed.

"You won, you won!"

Won what? She tried to shake off the nightmare, and realized someone was pounding at the back door. She put on her robe and stumbled toward it. She fumbled with the lock and let Roz in. Roz was displaying the front page of the Metro section of the *Wisconsin State Journal.* She pointed to a story in the lower right corner and shoved it up to Cissy's face. "UW prof guilty of sex assault," it read.

"You won, Cissy! They found your complaint justified!"

"I won," she repeated, processing the information.

"Why didn't you tell me?"

"I didn't know."

"You didn't know?" Roz's tone turned disbelieving. Without her glasses, Cissy blinked, tried to force Roz into focus. "Nothing like learning about your case in the newspaper," Roz said.

"I'd think Davidine or someone would've let me know."

"Academia. Bureaucracy. Piss on 'em both." Roz pulled her beret down to her eyebrow, resembling a thug in Cissy's dim vision. "But the important thing is you socked it to Isaacson. So does this mean you're staying in Madison?"

"Staying?" Cissy shot her a puzzled frown.

"Jeb told Irv that the two of you might not be here next year. That you didn't want to have to go back and teach in your department, that you were upset by Pep being here. And that even if you did stay in the city, it might be better to move."

Now Cissy was disbelieving. "Jeb said all that?"

"That's what Irv told me. Glad to hear it sounds like you're staying.

Here, Cissy, keep the paper. Gotta go."

"Thanks, Roz." Roz let herself out and Cissy sat at the kitchen table with the newspaper. She peered close up at the story: "The investigation concluded that Isaacson was guilty of fourth-degree sexual assault of a female employee in an incident that occurred in May."

She got up, put the teakettle on and went to dress. Back in the kitchen, now wearing her reading glasses, she poured the steaming water into a mug and lowered a tea strainer into it. She sat down and reread the article, then casually flipped the page. Out of the corner of her eye, she caught the boldface heading to a short item, "UW dean stable after heart attack."

A terrible premonition came to her, and zeroed in on the story: "Professor Davidine Phipps, Dean of the UW-Madison College of Fine Arts, was in stable condition Monday at University Hospital and Clinics after suffering a heart attack while driving her car on University Avenue Sunday afternoon. Police said..."

No wonder Davidine hadn't informed her.

She had to find out more. Ginger was in Rome, Evan holed up in the northern Wisconsin woods. Then it came to her: Once again, Wilhelmina to the rescue.

78

The Isaacsons' move from their rambling Shorewood Hills home to a smaller one on the far-west side of Madison constituted a painful admission: They would never have grandchildren to fill it for visits.

Where they now lived, Sumner didn't even know his neighbors. He wondered if they knew who he was, as he scanned the newspaper story headed "UW prof guilty of sex assault." Mercifully, his home address had been omitted.

It was late afternoon. He lay on the sofa, his head propped up on a stack of velvet pillows. He wore casual light pants and shirt, short sleeves acknowledging summer. Across the room, Vonda sat in a modern rocker, her feet tucked under her. Sumner glanced at her to see if she was paying him attention.

She sat reading impassively, her face hidden by some new romance novel. She turned a page; the movement rattled a gold bracelet.

"I can't believe the bitch went and filed a complaint!" Sumner said, knowing he'd get her attention.

"You will not call the victim a 'bitch,'" Vonda said coolly, without looking up.

He went on, determined to distract her: "Davidine said Pankhurst wasn't going to file a complaint."

"She said she *hoped* Cicely wouldn't, but if she did, they'd almost certainly find in her favor. Consider yourself lucky she hasn't pressed charges with the DA."

"Bitch," he whispered.

Vonda lowered her novel. "Whether you're referring to Cicely or to me, that makes two 'bitches' in one minute. Are you going to write them down or am I?"

"I was referring to her." Sumner grabbed a notebook from the end table. His therapist had him keep a journal of his derogatory words and thoughts about women. Vonda too kept her own count of the former, and presented it to him weekly. So far her list had always exceeded his. Sumner jotted down the words, then went back to the newspaper story. "Will you listen to this!?"

"I'm trying to read, if you please, Sumner." She lowered her book, exposing eyes like bayonets. "At least I occupy my time productively. You'd do well to do the same and to treat this summer as a trial retirement." She raised the novel back up.

"Do you want me to work like Davidine and end up like her?"

"Of course not. Just busy yourself with something."

Vonda had written three unpublished romance novels, but had allowed him to read only her first one. An idea clicked in his mind; he hadn't voiced it since last summer: "You know, I'll be glad to read your last two novels for you."

She looked up, not amused. "Your only comment on the first one was to include more sex scenes."

"That's what sells books. I was just trying to help."

"One of them will get picked up soon." Her tone was confident.

It's not easy to get things published these days."

"You should know," she quipped, and went back to devour the romance.

Mitzi, their French poodle, trotted into the living room and let out a sickly howl.

"Here, Mitzi!" called Sumner. "Nice girl. Let's play!" He clappped his palms together. Mitzi went up to her master. "You'll talk to me, won't you girl?" He picked up the dog. "I can legitimately call you a 'bitch,' can't I, Mitzi? You lovable bitch!"

Sumner regarded Vonda out of the corner of his eye. Still reading, she had lowered the novel to breast level. Her glasses had slid down her nose, which pointed like an eagle's beak. Should he record "eagle's beak" as derogatory to a woman's nose? As he grabbed his notebook and recorded it with a question mark, Mitzi jumped down. Having been incited to play, she now yapped and danced in a circle on the floor.

"OK, girl." He wadded up the page that contained his story and tossed it toward the fireplace at the end of the room. "Fetch, Mitzi!"

"Sumner! I haven't read that!"

"Sorry." Mitzi returned and he extracted the tooth-dented page from her mouth. "I suppose you're saving it for the family scrapbook."

Vonda paid his comment no attention. He unwrinkled the damp page and placed it on the end table. He patted his stomach, flat for his age, as a cue for Mitzi to come back and boosted her up.

Last night he'd gone to an Alcoholics Anonymous meeting, one of several a week. Tuesday and Thursday mornings he had "rehabilitative" therapy. Thursdays Vonda accompanied him, thus, in his mind, spreading out the stigma between the two of them. Friday afternoons they discussed their sex life, or absence thereof, with a thirtyish husband-wife team of sex therapists. The multiple therapies at least gave some sense of structure to his life.

"Rehabilitative" therapy was the most trying experience. He had undertaken counseling on his own, was advised to select from a list of therapists specializing in gender attitudes and had chosen the only male on the list: Scott Hanover, MSW, ACSW.

The first session had dealt with cozy preliminaries. Sumner thought it might even be fun to spout off about how he felt about women, then let Hanover discover why.

"Why did you hire Cicely?" he was asked at the second session.

"I was told to by Dean Phipps. We had to hire a woman to please the Affirmative Action people. Never mind that we'd just hired a black one the year before."

"In your opinion, was Cicely well-qualified?"

"She was probably the best qualified of the female applicants," he admitted. "Which wasn't saying much." Seeing the therapist raise his eyebrows, he added, "Strike that. I didn't mean it."

Scott Hanover seemed pleased and went on: "Did you resent being told by a woman to hire a woman? After all, you were the chair, the one who supposedly had power."

"I was indifferent to hiring her."

Hanover pursued his point: "When Cicely arrived here, do you think you expected something from her? A favor, some sort of thanks?"

Sumner made a face and begrudgingly confessed it was possible.

"And did she appear appreciative?"

"No. She struck me, and the other senior faculty, as standoffish."

"We're not talking about others. Was the victim sexually attractive to you?"

"Victim? Yes, I suppose the so-called 'victim' qualifies as moderately attractive," he scoffed. "What is this, an interrogation?"

"Not 'so-called,' and not meant to be an interrogation. But as our first session was not what I'd call too productive, I thought I'd get us moving along today. Objections?"

"No, move along."

"Now, if Cicely had been plain, might you have reacted differently to her?"

Sumner didn't know offhand. "Perhaps I would've been more indifferent to her."

The therapist placed his forefinger on his pencil-thin moustache. "Did the fact that she didn't acknowledge you, except as professionally necessary, anger you at some level?"

"I suppose so."

"What about the Christmas party? You said that was one of the few times you were together socially."

Sumner realized he preferred the type of questions when Hanover put the words in his mouth and he had only to agree. "I saw the young man she was with. It surprised me. But it was a colleague, Vance Rickover, who made a pass at her."

"But we're not talking about him. That evening you realized that she was romantically attached to a young man, correct?" Sumner nodded yes. "Afterwards, did you bear her a more active grudge?"

He steamed and admitted the possibility, feeling as if he were on a witness stand.

"And what about leering at her on the elevator one day in April, which was also mentioned in her complaint?"

"According to her, I probably leered at her every time she saw me."

"Did you want to communicate, perhaps subliminally, your anger to her that day? Or make her feel uncomfortable or even scare her?"

Sumner made the slow, painful admission.

"Aha!" Hanover showed his customary delight, as Sumner cleared another hurdle. "And why was that?"

He became somber and gave the answer he expected Hanover wanted to hear: "To show her who was the boss, who had the power." Having said this, he hoped to be off the hook and suggested that his therapist ought to have been a District Attorney. But, he learned subsequently, Hanover had only skimmed the surface.

"There!" Vonda exclaimed, startling Sumner and Mitzi out of their reveries. "One hour and fifty-two minutes!" Mitzi jumped down.

"What?"

"I finished reading the novel in less than two hours. And took notes.

Did you want to talk to me?"

"I already said what was on my mind."

"Fine. It's almost five. Mocktail Hour. I'll go make them." Vonda got up and left the room. She too had gone on the wagon.

After several minutes, he ambled back to the screened-in porch. Surrounded by trees, it resembled an outdoor environment, but was mosquito-free. Vonda appeared holding a tray with a dish of cashews and two drinks, her own juicy and frothy.

For a minute they drank in silence, which Sumner broke: "I've been thinking about Hanover. The guy's got to be a fag."

Vonda threw him a warning glance, almost choked on her rum-free strawberry daiquiri.

"I don't have to write that down. I'm not talking about women. I don't hear Hanover talking about his own dealings with the female sex. Because I bet he doesn't have any."

"Although I doubt your perception, I'm glad you brought this up," Vonda said in between sips. "This hardly bodes well for tomorrow's dinner with Pepper. I should tell you that I met alone with Scott last week and brought Pepper up. Scott thinks it's a good idea we both deal with the issue now. Don't you find it embarrassing that when he comes to Madison, he stays with Amelia instead of us?"

Sumner didn't answer. First AA, then gender attitudes, and now this. It was too much to take in one summer. He fished the maraschino cherry from his whiskey-less sour, tilted his head back and dropped it into his mouth.

79

It happened again: Lou prepared a three-course dinner for herself and Beth; Beth worked late and forgot to call. Lou kept the main course warm and the gazpacho chilled, while, forgotten on the counter, the watercress wilted.

The church pew swing on the front porch groaned as they lowered themselves and their dinner trays onto it. It was 9:20.

On one side of the house two dogs yelped. From the other, neighbors' jazz floated through the sultry night air. A pair of dueling flies buzzed around Lou's head. Brooklyn trotted in, tail straight up in the air.

"I am sorry, kiddo." Beth slurped down a spoonful of gazpacho.

"It's OK." Lou's voice came out staccato.

"It is not. Something's wrong." Beth paused to swallow. "By the way, I'm not gonna be able to eat too much, kiddo. I grabbed a bite at Ho Chi's."

"That's OK too." Lou tackled her watercress salad. Beth had become a vegetarian and, although Lou still liked her meat and potatoes, she'd consented to prepare and eat occasional vegetarian dinners. Maybe it would help her lose a few pounds.

"Lou, this is a really great meal!"

"Thanks," she mumbled, her mouth half-full.

"It's the lease you're upset about, isn't it?"

Lou chewed on stuffed zucchini — the main course. The previous tenants had decided not to reoccupy the premises, so the two of them had the chance to rent them for next year and needed to make up their minds. The time to reserve a room in a university dorm had long passed. "Yes," she answered. "Though I'd say 'concerned,' not 'upset.'"

"Whichever." Beth set her tray on the floor, her zucchini untouched. Brooklyn came over to sniff. She picked up the tray upon seeing Lou's severe glance. "I know. You didn't spend hours in the kitchen for a cat to have a gourmet meal."

Lou dug into the zucchini stuffing and went on chewing, a defense mechanism from having to talk.

"Look, Lou..." Beth began. Suddenly she stopped, closed her eyes, put her fingers to her temples and breathed deeply.

The first time she'd seen her do this, Lou had panicked. To be "politically correct," Beth had stopped smoking a week ago. Right now, she was trying to control her craving. She had equally strong cravings for pork.

"There." Beth shook her head and blinked her eyes as if emerging from a trance.

Lou winced after-the-fact. "I'm happy you quit, but just don't stop breathing or anything, OK?"

"Yeah, but don't let's change the subject, kid." Beth gnawed briefly on her finger and went on: "Now don't tell me you really wanna live in that place you found on Mifflin Street. The bedrooms are like closets and the bathroom's a postage stamp."

"It's cheaper."

"By forty bucks. Twenty apiece. And for our money, we get a place half the size of this one."

"But when classes start, I won't have time to keep working. I don't know how I'll afford it. What my parents send doesn't quite cover everything."

"So Ed and Millie are backin' out on the deal, huh? I thought they'd agreed to pay for your two years here."

"They pay what they can," Lou defended. "You know how farm prices are."

Brooklyn leaped up onto the swing, purring between them. Beth protected her tray. "Why don't you apply for the job at the bakery on Willy Street? You're a super cook."

"I won't have time for one job, let alone two." Lou brushed Brooklyn away. "But there's another thing. I don't fit into this neighborhood."

"Nonsense. This is a multicultural neighborhood. Everybody fits in."

Lou observed her roommate, the light from the livingroom dimly illuminating her. Beth seemed to have an inordinate capacity to adapt to everything: the university, at least in her own off-beat way; lesbianism, about which Lou didn't yet care to know more details, especially after the episode with Verla; and this neighborhood, to which Lou thought she'd over-adapted. If the History class she'd visited had politicized her in the abstract, Ho Chi Minh's had done it in practice. Beth now donned a beret and plastered herself and the apartment with political buttons, posters and decals. Lou had finally protested when she brought home a large banner from the restaurant that read "US Out Of Nicaragua or Wisconsin Out Of US." When she'd wanted to hang it outside from the porch, Lou suggested that what it advocated was illegal. So they'd compromised and hung it in the living room.

"You're not gonna back out on me now, are you, kiddo? We have to sign the lease by tomorrow if we're gonna."

"I don't know what to do."

Beth got up from the swing. "Let me know when you know." She walked into the house with her tray. Lou reached out to pet Brooklyn, but the cat followed Beth.

It seemed to Lou that things always happened *to* her in Madison. She had engineered her own arduous path here, but once she'd arrived, she'd floundered and swum wherever the current took her. Now she was in a neighborhood of crazy people, where she lived with a lesbian who worked in a communist restaurant. If Lou's parents knew what her "tomboy" roommate was really like, they'd send the county sheriff to rescue their daughter.

Which would be downright disgusting, she thought with a trickle of clarity.

Beth had come here to be herself, just like Lou had come to escape her parents and small towns. Who else did she have in Madison who would put up with her? Certainly not Verla, who couldn't even put up with herself. You had to have someone who'd tolerate you wherever you were. In Madison, for Lou that person was, unquestionably, Beth.

She got up and headed into the kitchen with her empty dishes. Beth sat at the kitchen table, composing a letter. Brooklyn lay on the table, peacefully asleep.

Lou knew that Beth had given Brooklyn her leftovers. She could almost see it in the cat's fat belly, which expanded and contracted as she breathed. Not that she'd ever known cats to prefer vegetarian diets. She'd grown up with cats and dogs, never allowed in the house. To allow them on the kitchen table was unthinkable.

"Beth, I'll sign the lease."

She looked up, as if to register that she'd heard right. "Super, kiddo! But, sit down, I gotta tell you somethin' else."

Lou sat, wary but prepared.

"See, I'm writin' to Nick to tell her I'm gonna go full-time at Ho Chi's. I shoulda told you before, but I'm also gonna drop outta school this fall. It's really elitist to go straight from high school to college all on your parents' bucks, like I did and you didn't. You can read all the lit, poly sci, and history you want, but unless you give up your privilege, you can never *feel* what it's like to be part of the proletariat. So I'm gonna stop takin' Nick and Steve's money. I won't have to notarize my grades. Hell, I won't even have any to notarize! To finally be out of school, be part of the real world for once! Whaddya think, kiddo?"

Lou contemplated before answering. None of this should have surprised her; she determined to let nothing show. "Well, one: I don't know if you should consider Madison the 'real world.' Two: Sometimes I think you're cuckoo and this is one of them. But as long as you have money to pay the rent…"

"Oh. Sure." Beth seemed almost disappointed by Lou's even reaction.

"I said I'd sign the lease."

"Right!" She whipped it out from under her letter and handed it to Lou. "Super! I always knew you'd come through, kid!"

"I didn't."

80

Roz knew that conception had to be easier than dealing with her mother.

"Hello. This is Rhoda Goldmann," came the metallic, nasal voice over the crackling wires when she'd called.

"Shit, the answering machine."

"Who's this!?" squawked the familiar voice.

"Mom?"

"Rosamond!? Do I sound like a machine? It's about time you called. Your Aunt Myra asked about you yesterday. What do you want I should tell her when I don't know a thing? So how are you, darling?"

"I'm fine, Mom. And I've got news for you."

"You got yourself arrested again. You're calling from jail. *Vey is mir.*"

"No, Mother! But you might want to sit down for this." Pause. "I got married." The other end of the line went dead. "Mother? Are you there? Did you hear?"

"I'm not deaf yet, you know. So explain yourself, Rosamond. I suppose that gay rights law you have in Wisconsin lets women marry each other."

"No, Mom. I married a man."

"A man!? Not just some woman in men's clothing?"

"Yes, Mom. A real man."

"This isn't just another phase or a joke?"

"No."

"So then the other was a phase, just like I always said. My only daughter marries and doesn't even let me know. So tell me about him."

Roz gave a nutshell biography of Irv.

"So you married a *shegetz*. That's fine. I never expected you to marry a Jew."

"Mom, there's more."

"Remember my weak heart. I'm not going to need my nitroglycerin, am I?"

"No, mother. It's just that Irv and I are going to have a child."

"Conceived out of wedlock? Is that why you married?"

"Mother, I haven't even conceived yet."

"Then how do you know..?"

Roz explained what very little she could: "We're planning it this month." She'd be at the peak of her fertility this Friday evening, for when the event was scheduled. If the child ended up looking more Hispanic than anything else, she'd deal with that later.

"So you're wasting no time, at your age."

"I'm only thirty-six, Mom."

"Thirty-seven by the time it's born. You're not going to pass on that silly Goldwomyn name, especially if it's a boy, are you?"

"We haven't dealt with surnames yet."

"I'll come for the birth."

Roz passed over this remark. "Mother, Irv and I would like to come visit you early next month, as part of our honeymoon. How does that sound?"

"Your father and I went to Coney Island and a Dodgers game for ours. So when are you arriving? I'll need the exact date so we can plan the reception. We'll have Myra and her family, Howard and his, cousins you haven't seen in years. Then on your father's side..."

Roz had read the book *Lesbian Motherhood,* devoured articles on conception without intercourse and called her old friend Baronet Stapleton. Baronet had progressed from their Lake Mendota commune to a separatist one in northern California and dealt regularly in sperm donations.

"An orgasm a day keeps a boy away!" Roz joked to Juan. "According to Baronet."

"I thought you wanted me to stockpile it all."

Roz knew that he was taking his duty very seriously. Almost too seriously. "Just kidding, Juan-Boy! Either sex is fine. Don't worry. If it doesn't work out this month, we'll try again next." She slapped him on the back, hoping as much for his sake as hers that it would work this time. She didn't want him to think that he had failed and fall back into a depression.

"In which case, you can do drugs for another month, right?"

"There's a good side to everything, no?"

She had decided she needed a woman to assist her in the process; men still seemed inept in certain practical matters. Her situation being what it was, she had ruled out her lesbian friends. When Pep had come by peddling "Support Legalized Midwifery" bumper stickers, Roz had an idea. Why not let her participate? Pep agreed.

The planned hour arrived Friday evening with a solemnity akin to a funeral. Roz lay in the bedroom, where Pep had enveloped her in a sheet. Irv was to take the ejaculate from Juan and bring it in. Pep would insert the widemouthed syringe into her. She hoped the process wouldn't somehow be botched.

Outside the door she heard Juan say to Irv, "Give me ten minutes."

Pep squeezed her hand, imparting strength. "Calm," she said.

A smile crept onto Roz's lips, a sweet security seemed to flow through her. When she thought of sisterhood, she'd never imagined this.

At the last minute Juan decided to take the syringe into his bedroom instead of the bathroom. He undid his pants and began to concentrate. This was no ordinary event. His romantic side wished there were someone there to hold him. But for the moment, what he needed was a fantasy. He concentrated on Pepper.

Irv tapped at the door. "Any luck yet?"

"Don't distract me!"

"Sorry."

He put his mind back on Pepper, let himself imagine a titillating seduction scene, which would probably never be repeated after the fifteen-year hiatus.

"Ready!" he yelled a few minutes later.

Irv barged in, grabbed the syringe and ran out. Juan pulled up his pants. Thinking of what he'd just done, if the procedure proved successful, he dabbed at an imaginary tear. Too squeamish to take up the invitation to Roz and Irv's bedroom, he went outside.

It was still light. In the garden he crouched down, examined the buds that would turn into Brussels sprouts and marveled at the idea of sprouting seeds. At length, it darkened. He saw Pep stroll out of the house, metal clank-

ing as if to some secret inner rhythm. Moments later he saw the light in Irv
and Roz's bedroom go off. He looked at the crescent moon, tried to un-
scramble constellations and wondered why astrology didn't reflect the position of stars at the moment of conception as well as at birth.

He went back into the house, cavernously quiet. After tiptoeing into
the kitchen, he drew a glass of water from the faucet and gobbled down dilled
Brussels sprouts. In the living room, he turned on the television — a rare act
— and the local nightly news came on.

"A coalition of local ministers and conservatives," began the lead story,
"have joined forces under the banner of 'Madisonians for Morality' and today
announced their goal of getting rid of homosexuals in local government and
fighting to abolish the city's gay rights law..." Such reactions from the Right
popped up from time to time in Madison, though usually faded fast. "Speaking for the group, at the coalition's press conference this afternoon, was the
Reverend Edward Hunter, of the Winnebago Baptist Church."

Juan gulped, glued to the image on the TV screen. Although clothed,
it was the same person, he could tell.

The telephone rang. He wanted to hear the end of the news item,
but pounced on the phone before it could wake Irv and Roz.

"Juan!" the voice blurted. "Turn on Channel 15 quick!"

Startled, he realized that the caller was Gil. "I have it on."

Gil seemed deflated: "Just thought you'd want to know, maybe."

"Thanks. I think you or I could supply a piece of information that could
nip this little coalition in the bud."

Gil's voice brightened. "I think so. But you're the one with the political connections."

"We'll have to see if anything comes of it."

"Right. Well, just thought I'd let you know. I'm at the COB House,
I suppose you know."

"Sure thing." Juan said, already knowing more about Gil than he cared
to. If he was right, Gil was reaching out to do more than simply report a piece
of news. And he was certainly not ready to reach back now, if ever.

He yawned, flicked the TV off and went into his room. The sleeping
bag curled in a fetal position in a corner on the floor. It had served its purpose. It was time to buy another bed.

81

C issy checked in regularly with Wilhelmina about Davidine's condition.
Several days after the heart attack, she was removed from the Intensive
Care Unit to a regular ward and allowed visitors. Her condition was now
"good" and she'd be released soon.

"I should go visit her," Cissy said to Jeb. He was stretched out in front of the television, where the Yankees were playing the Brewers. "She's one of the few people here who have been really supportive of me."

"Better go soon, before she's released," he advised without looking up.

"We could go tonight."

"We?"

"Come on, Jeb. Go with me. Please."

He consented and, after the Brewers went down in defeat, off they went.

"By the way," he began, as he drove the Fiat past campus. "You've never thought that your assault contributed to the stress that caused Davidine's heart attack, have you?"

"Well..." Cissy ruminated. "In May I was so upset and confused that I might have, but not now."

"Thank God!" Jeb sent her a broad smile.

Cissy found herself laughing for no particular reason. She flashed back to May (traumatic), June (uneasy), surprised that now, in July, she could actually be laughing. "By filing the charges, I did do the right thing," she affirmed again.

Jeb parked the car in front of University Hospital. They went in and wandered in circles, stalking the labyrinthine halls in search of Davidine's room.

"At this rate, she could be released before we find her," Jeb said.

The correct wing, ward, hall and room finally located, they hesitated outside the partly open door. Cissy recognized Davidine's sister from the Christmas party. As Ralphetta noticed her, Cissy saw her go pale and look disconcertedly around the room. From behind, Jeb nudged her inside.

Just past the door Cissy stopped in her tracks. Straight in front of her lay Davidine. To the patient's left stood Ralphetta, hovering protectively over her. To her right, the Isaacsons.

The six pairs of eyes darted anxiously around the room, looking for others with which it was safe to connect.

Cissy's knees knocked; Jeb steadied her. She saw mouths struck dumb, fingers tapping out drum rolls and feet doing involuntary dances. After a chorus of ahems and swallowed greetings, Vonda broke the ice: "How nice to see you, Cicely. It's been so long and you're looking so well."

Cissy acknowledged her words with a brief nod. The silence broken, the room swarmed with niceties. Only Cissy and Sumner directed no words to each other. Under her blouse, her sweat glands overworked. Her legs trembled; she repented having exposed them by wearing a dress.

The pleasantries soon fizzled out. Cissy was about to announce that she and Jeb had just passed by to say hello, but Vonda broke in: "We need to be leaving."

Sumner seconded her with a mumble and proffered a farewell over Davidine. Vonda flung good-byes at the two sisters and Cissy watched her edge Sumner toward the door, toward Jeb and herself. There was nowhere for her to go, unless she ran down the hall. The idea struck her favorably.

As the Isaacsons inched nearer, Cissy moved backward, but Jeb blocked further movement. In front of her, Ralphetta cooed over Davidine, who gazed supportively at Cissy.

The Isaacsons approached and Sumner bobbed his head and puffed his cheeks, his version of a smile. Vonda fingered her hairdo.

Sumner made his way up to Jeb. "Good to see you again, young man," he said with an air of fatherly dignity.

"I don't know that the two of us have formally met," Vonda chimed in, giving everyone a chance to cut the tension with apologies for not making the introduction.

Sumner now faced Cissy. She stepped back to allow for wider passage. Her fingernails dug trenches into Jeb's forearm.

He cleared his throat. "Cis'ly." All eyes fell on her. She glued her lips into a frozen, lopsided formation.

"I, uh..." Breathing in the room seemed suspended as he faltered. Cissy bit into her lower lip.

"I... I hope that your second year here is kinder than your first," he managed, and everyone breathed again. "I sincerely wish you the best. I regret the turn your first year here took."

She nodded in response and forced her lips to unfreeze.

Behind him, Vonda elbowed her husband then grasped his arm, keeping him in place. "And, uh..," he continued, "I'm personally sorry for all the distress and pain I caused you in the last year. In the future, that is, the one year we have left together, I hope we can can be, uh, congenial colleagues. That is, if you can forgive me."

Before Cissy had to respond, Vonda nodded in triumph at her husband's words and scooted the two of them out the door. When they were safely around the corner, everyone let out perceptible sighs of relief.

"It was probably good to face him sooner rather than later," Jeb said. "Now you can put it all behind you." Everyone murmured agreement. "You can stop shaking now, babe." He wrapped her in his arms.

As he loosened his hold on her, Cissy saw Davidine and Ralphetta regarding them warmly. Davidine raised herself up on her pillow. "If the potential of that confrontation didn't revive my heart, nothing will!"

Ralphetta seemed unamused by her sister's remark. "We're all very sorry about what happened to you, Cicely."

Cissy moved closer to the two sisters. Ralphetta, who looked older, seemed to be the archetype of the old-fashioned schoolmarm and wore low black heels with laces. Cissy guessed that her seemingly soft manner could quickly turn severe.

"Davidine is going to avoid confrontations from now on," Ralphetta stated.

Davidine smiled weakly, as if unable to defy her sister's authority, then said, "I'm much improved."

"Just because she's not dead, she thinks she can be working in the rose garden by next weekend and be back at her office the following Monday!"

Cissy saw Davidine again smile helplessly. Head protruding from under the sheet, she gave off an impression of fragility.

"Davidine will be retiring at the end of the coming year, if not sooner," Ralphetta went on.

"It will be hard on the department to lose you," Cissy said.

"The department's changing," Davidine said.

"I dare say for the better, with Sumner gone." Ralphetta looked toward the hall, as though casting blame.

"And I hope you'll be part of the change, Cissy." Davidine propped herself up higher on the pillows.

"You've accomplished enough change, Davie. It's time to let others take over the reins."

"Yes, Phetta," Davidine said patronizingly, feigning childlike obedience. Facing away from her sister, Davidine beheld Cissy and Jeb, her face alive with mischief. Cissy looked over to see Jeb wink at Davidine, who winked back.

"Maybe we'd better let you rest," Cissy suggested.

She and Jeb wished her a speedy recovery, shook Ralphetta's outstretched hand and said good-bye.

Outside Cissy squeezed Jeb's hand. The warm summer air nuzzled her face.

"Do you think Isaacson really meant it?" he asked after he'd crammed himself into the Fiat.

She snickered as she put on her seatbelt. "You could see that he was petrified."

"Isaacson? What about you? You both earned a niche in the Petrified Forest!"

She slapped his arm and screwed up her face. "It's hard to tell, but I do think that at some level he *is* sorry."

"Never believe an academic."

"The ones like Davidine make up for the bad ones," she countered. "Besides, I'm one and you too are going to be this fall. Teaching Assistant Jeb Holloday. Beginning Swimming."

He grunted at her as he steered them onto Bassett Street.

"I really do think I detected a trace of sincerity in his expression."

"Don't be so gullible, Cissy."

"Don't be so cynical, Jeb."

"'Yes, Ralphie.'"

"She goes by 'Phetta.'"

"Sorry. I forgot we're in Wisconsin. Land of cheese. And milk, if not honey."

Cissy laughed in spite of herself. Then, turning censorious, "That's right, Jeb. Make fun of everything."

"It's a way to cope."

"Remember our trip. We saw fresh honey for sale in the country."

They rounded the corner onto John Nolen Drive. To their left, towering over the city, the Capitol topped the Isthmus. Joggers, bicyclists and hand-holding couples peopled the narrow strip of landfill to the right, between the road and Lake Monona. Behind the panorama, the moon hung low in the eastern sky. They passed a Volkswagen with a bumper sticker reading "Eat Cheese or Die!"

Cissy smiled as she saw it. "I've coped somehow."

"Next year you'll do more than cope, babe. You might even learn to joke, or at least have fun without being written up in the newspaper. And I'm not talking about your assault."

"Madison. Home, sweet home," she observed. It would now be home, at least for the length of her new contract.

"Madison? Home, maybe, but sweet?" Jeb snorted. "Hippies, Ho Chi Minh's, homosexuals. They ought to call the place 'Madlands.'"

"Madlands," Cissy repeated, liking its ring. "But what do you have against hippies, Ho Chi Minh's or homosexuals? You've certainly had your share of dealings — pleasant ones, I thought — with all three this year."

"You're right, babe." Jeb stopped the car at a traffic light. "But don't you miss LA?"

Cissy let a beat pass before answering. "Only the smog."

The light changed and the Fiat sputtered onto Willy Street, leaving a trail of exhaust fumes as they headed home.